Tom Fleck

a novel of Cleveland and Flodden

by

Harry Nicholson

Published by YouWriteOn.com, 2011

Here are Tudor kings and their nobles - their documented lives are rich material for writers - but now they play a minor part. This is the story of Tom Fleck, a penniless farm labourer, who shares his dwelling with cattle. He is fictional only because he leaves no record - his people live before the keeping of parish registers, so they make no marks on parchment and are lost to history.

We find his rare surname in the register of St. Hilda's church at Hartlepool:

Baptisms 1596, September 19th: Christofer ye child of Willm. Fleck.

Perhaps William heard tales of how his great grandfather, Thomas, loved a strange woman and stood with the army on the terrible battlefield of Flodden. This story brings him to life.

For Beryl - with love

Acknowledgements

Many have encouraged Tom Fleck on his journey.

Vivienne Blake travelled with affection through two revisions; her faith in the story has maintained me. I was rarely confident of my grammar until Linda Cosgriff had cast an eagle-eye over a chapter. Peter Bullen never failed to nourish with his confidence in 'a good tale'. Other fellow Open University students, who reviewed the first draft, were: Livia Bluecher, Rachael Talibart, Susanne Lockie, Martha Rose and Michael D Robinson.

Ann Bowes of Fryup Press not only formatted the text but, with her farming experience, helped me avoid some errors of fact.

My wife, Beryl, has lived with the odyssey of this first novel for five years. She has been a sounding board for my enthusiasms and has gamely wandered Flodden Field in the sun and in the rain.

I thank you all.

Sleights, Whitby

December
2010

Contents

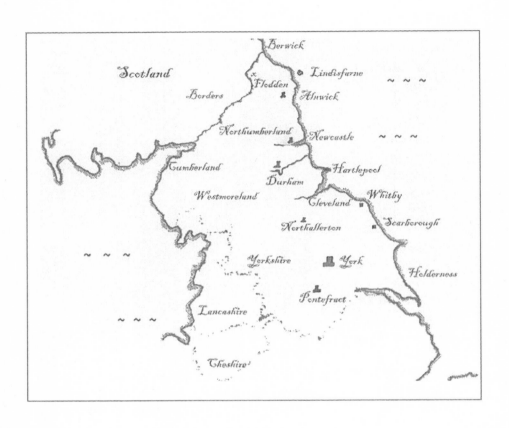

1

Green and White

29th June 1513

Wings clattered through branches. Tom Fleck stayed his axe in mid-swing as two wood pigeons flung themselves into the mist. He looked down at the dog as her throat rumbled. She raised a paw, shot him a glance, then - ears cocked - faced along the track. Metal clinked somewhere.

He whispered, 'Whisht now. Come away.'

Soft-footed, they crept off the path and into a thicket. They huddled close together, among ferns and willow stems, as the cracking of twigs grew louder and voices filtered through the dripping trees.

'It's thinning - a wind's sprung up.' The helmeted man seemed a giant as he squelched past Tom's hiding place. Two other burly men followed; all three wore green and white tunics. One of them groaned as his leg plunged into the mire. He wrested it free.

'Shite! My boot's full o' clarts! How much more o' this, Sarge?'

'The river's close I reckon.' The giant paused. 'Though it's a few years since I was this way.'

Five more tunic-clad men pushed out of the mist; all had round shields on their backs and swords at their belts. They trudged alongside a pair of black horses. Each horse carried a gentleman cloaked in red. Three brown-smocked labourers, holding the ropes of pack-ponies, took up the rear. The column wound through the dripping alders until a fallen tree blocked the way.

Tom tried to work out who they were, he'd seen that green and white before - at the manor house. It meant power that cared naught for the likes of him - power that could seize a man and take him away. In these times it made sense to hug the ground and just watch.

The giant raised an arm. 'A dead wind-throw. She's hacked about like someone's been at her for kindling - I did hear an axe.' Tom shrank lower as the seamed face looked around. 'But we need to get on. We'll work our way around it. Dobson, you see nobody tumbles

7

into that root-pit.'

Tom squinted through the sodden ferns. The shattered roots of the ancient alder reared above the strangers' heads like the antlers of stags entangled in combat. The mass groaned as the trunk settled deeper into the mire. A horse snorted and shied away; the rider cursing as he heaved on the reins. Tom flinched as the mount staggered sideways off the track and sank onto its forelegs in the ooze. With gasps and snorts it pulled free, pitching the rider from the saddle. A pair of over-fleshed buttocks thudded into the mud.

'God damn!' The man clambered to his feet. He glowered at his stained breeches then punched the horse on the neck. 'Blast you, nag! You and this bloody bog!' The reedy voice choked into a squeak.

His lean companion looked down from the saddle. 'Hold yoursen together, York. After the ford we'll be on ground more to your comfort - and only two hours from the soft bed you crave.'

Tom wrapped a hand around the dog's muzzle and stroked her neck with the other. He saw two bearded men grin at each other as they splashed forward to grab the horse's bridle. One shoved a biscuit under its nose while the other calmed the shivering beast and held it for the rider to remount. Back in the saddle the man, face as red as his cloak, wiped his brow then yelped, 'My ring! It's gone from my hand! It'll be in the mud. Find it! I'll give a reward.'

The dog's muffled snort went unheard as men laughed while they grubbed among the rushes. Tom glanced at the pack-ponies stood in a line, heads drooping. Their drivers squatted, chewing crusts, indifferent to the pony-dung that thudded around them. As the mist condensed into drizzle the two gentlemen pulled down their hats and moved to the shelter of a tree on drier ground. With their backs against the trunk they drew out corks and sipped from flasks. Tom caught the searchers' low banter:

'Yon will have a sore arse. He hit the deck like a sack of cabbages.'

'More like that feather-bed wench at the inn last night, when she skidded in your slopped ale.'

'Hast' seen his cacky bum?'

'Get on with it, Jones.' The giant spat, then growled, 'Have a care - if York hears thee mock him, he'll not forget.'

'It should fetch some coin, eh, Sarge? What's the reward do ye reckon?'

'Knowing him - a piss-pot of sour ale,' someone cackled.

'We'll have to see. Now clam up, Bentley! Get cracking or we'll be

8

camping out in this muck.'

Taking a final sip before pushing the stopper back into his flask, the lean gentleman called out, 'Sergeant! It's late. If we don't make Norton by dark, we sleep rough. In an hour the tide runs up river, and we've yet to ford the Tees. Two men will return at dawn to search again.'

'Aye, sir.' The giant snapped a branch off the fallen tree, broke it twice across his knee and pushed the pieces upright into the mud. He rubbed his big palms together. 'That's marked the spot - now let's get shifted.'

Through the tracery of twigs, Tom Fleck's keen eyes had also marked the spot. A shower of heavy drops, from the leaf canopy overhead, began to drum against his leather skullcap and the shoulders of his battered jerkin, but he did not move. Midges were becoming lost in his young beard; he scratched at the itches but stayed crouched. When the last pony had faded into the gloom, he listened on. After a few minutes the agitated tew-tew . . . pity me . . . pity me . . . cries of the pair of sandpipers that nested on the riverbank told him the travellers had reached the ford.

At a snort from the dog he took his hand from around her jaws. 'They're away now, Meg - whoever they were. Stay hushed while we see what might be sniffed out yonder. Come on.'

He rapidly scanned the flattened bog plants mangled by boots and hooves, then the bruised earth, until he became aware of a hollow. Shaped by a beefy backside, he thought - so one stride away is where the rider's hands would grab the ground to crawl back onto the track.

Stretching out an arm, he snapped his fingers. 'Seek!'

The little black mongrel rushed to the spot, tail wagging in a blur. She circled a few times, nostrils sweeping the ground. She stopped, lifted a paw, stiffened her tail, pointed her nose close to the earth and let out a whine.

'Shift,' he whispered and pushed her snout away to rake his fingers among the roots. They closed on a hard, round shape. He wiped the lump on his sleeve, held it up and saw a golden gleam. Trembling, he looked around, but the vague shape of a night screecher, perched on a high branch, made the sole witness. The owl bobbed its head a few times then launched on silent wings deeper into the trees.

He dropped the object into his skin bag, safe among the moss that wrapped a clutch of mallard eggs. The dog's ears got a quick rub before he slipped the axe into his belt, picked up a bundle of firewood and heaved it across his shoulders.

'Right, let's away for our supper.'

The ground lifted in a gentle rise as the wetland faded. He pushed out of the sodden alder carrs and stopped in the meadow to breathe in air that was not loaded with rot. Through fading drizzle loomed a yellow glow that brightened in a shaft of weak sunlight. The glow sprang from the mass of gorse blossom on the slopes of Whinny Bank and gave the bearing for home.

He halted his stride through the buttercups to kick down a fresh molehill. He scattered the moist earth with one sweep of his clog. It did no good to let them harden; let them set and next thing there's hummocks sprouting with thistles that cows wouldn't put their noses near. Besides which, it was always worth seeing what black mouldy-warp had tossed out. Stooping, he flicked aside a few scraps of the usual red pot to pick out a round bit of metal. He gave it a rub with his thumb and saw the familiar faint outline of a horse. He would keep it with the other horse coins the little tunneller had shovelled up.

A line of five cows now straggled around him as they made their way home for milking. Tails swishing at flies, they sauntered along carefully, nursing the weight of full udders. The cattle gazed with soft eyes - they knew him well. One or two paused to spatter the track with cow-clap in a companionable manner. Meg trotted behind at a safe distance, herding the heels. He strode between the kine, happy to pull into his nostrils the warm belches of fermented grass.

He grimaced as he neared the cow byre, it looked like a broken-backed ship. Could he manage on his own? While he was fit, Dad had done his best with running repairs - but now . . . A lump came to his throat. Those walls were bulging - the wattle-and-daub giving way. The thatch should have had new reeds last year. That eastern end, leaning where the ground had gone soft with ages of cattle piss . . . It needed a good fettling. Only the thick back wall held the building together. Those long forgotten men had sense, building onto the wall of the ruined chapel. He stopped by the lean-to. Just this morning he'd patched it where the bull had smashed his head through. The auld lad got restless when he caught the scent of his cows ambling past twice a day.

Tom reached the middle of the byre's front and pushed against the planks of the only door. The cracked leather hinges groaned. He

10

stooped beneath the lintel with his load of firewood and ducked as a cluster of fledgling swallows flew to the opening. They fluttered around his head, then darted into the open air. Their parents swooped chortling from the byre's sagging ridge in greeting. Once inside he turned to the right and set down his burden. The cattle followed, but turned to the left.

His clogs rustled through a layer of straw as he squeezed between a stack of buckets and a churn. On a barrel stood tinderbox and candles; his fingers worked fast with the flint and soon the wick's flame melted a pit into the tallow lump. Tom carried the light behind a partition of woven hazel stems and knelt on the floor beside a pallet of hay. He drew back the corner of a sheepskin.

'I'm home, sister. How are you feeling?'

In the candlelight, Hilda's forehead gleamed like oyster shell.

'Ah, Thomas. You've been out a long time. I'm not good. I've not been on my feet much today. Just rested here in a sort of dream, seeing Mam and Dad's faces coming and going in them cobwebs fluttering under the thatch, and sometimes listening to the squabbles of the mice.'

Tom looked into the drawn features, framed by red hair studded with hayseeds. Beneath green eyes lay crescents of dark skin. His stomach tightened. She's not combed through her locks today - them tangles are not like her.

'Your belly still hurts?'

'Aye, today it's lower down. It nags at me all the time. Will you put your hands on me again, please?'

'I'll warm them first. Tell me when you're ready.' He cupped his hands around the candle flame and faced away from her so that she could roll back the bed-covers and pull up her shift.

'I'm ready.'

She had draped her private places with the sheepskin. He saw only the rise and fall of the shallow dome of her stomach. Except for the pink of two flea bites, it had the colour of milk. She followed his movements as he clenched and unclenched his fingers before placing them on either side of her navel. She closed her eyes and he closed his own.

Murmuring, 'Breathe easy and think good thoughts and I'll do the same,' he moved his hardened palms over her soft skin. 'Is this where it hurts?'

He felt her become tense. 'No, it's further down.' His hands slipped

11

beneath the covering. She uttered a gasp, 'Aye,' she whispered, 'just there . . . ah . . . ah . . .'

He concentrated on his palms and, holding them still, thought of how much he loved his sister. She breathed out a sigh and he felt the hardness leave her stomach. The warmth of her flesh mingled with the coolness of his hands. He took his mind to the region around his heart. The comings and goings of their breath came together as though they were one.

Minutes later he murmured, 'Is there summat you've not said?'

'When the time comes,' she whispered. 'That's helped. You can ease off.'

He covered her with the sheepskin. 'You'll be famished. I found a mallard's nest; do you fancy a couple of duck eggs?'

'Oh, I don't know whether I could hold them down.'

He considered for a moment. 'I'll boil them, then mash them in a drop of hot milk and mix in some chopped sorrel-dock. You can shift them with a bit of bread and butter - how's that sound?'

'My mouth waters - by rights I should cook for you.'

'Don't fret on that. I'll make supper once I've seen to the beasts. Meg will stay by you.'

The milking would take an hour. He washed and dried the udder of the first cow. Seated on a stool he rested his forehead against her warm flank and wrapped his fingers around just two of the four teats; the other two quarters were for her calf. He drew down the milk with a steady rhythm, first on one teat and then on the other. Squirt, splash, squirt, splash - the milk spurted into the wooden bucket. The smell of cow hair, mixed with the vapour of foaming milk, drifted around his face. After humming for a while, he sang in a lilting voice:

'I cannot get to me lass
her freckles to see,
for the flood o' the Tees
gans between her and me.

I maun wait on the moon
when the heron gans yem,
and the shiv'ring salmon
has done her last run.

When the watter o' the wath
drains down to the sea,
then I'll sharp gan across
and she'll sit on me knee.

We'll sing the words fluted
since Adam was born,
like the coo o' the cushat
from yonder blackthorn.'

He sang to help the cows let down their milk and because his sister
enjoyed his made-up songs. As the buckets filled, his mind wandered,
sometimes back to the marsh, sometimes to imaginings of the future.

The cows waited meekly, in a row of stalls, with their heads swung
towards the end of the byre where a group of tiny calves bawled. The
calves spent their days confined when their mothers roamed the
pasture. They now gathered, shoulder to shoulder, peeping with
hungry eyes through the slats of their stall. After the milking, Tom
unhooked a gate and they tottered out, each one to find and nuzzle its
own mother's teats.

Outside in the dusk, among softly fluttering moths, he fed and
watered the bull in the lean-to. The beast snorted and nodded his
great head.

'Never mind, auld lad.' He patted the hard brow. 'Tha'll be on grass
tomorrow, for some of the girls are wanting thee.'

Back in the byre, he built up the fire in the chimney alcove.

'Not much longer. I'm about to boil watter.' He filled a blackened
iron pot and hung it on a hook above the blaze. With the eggs
unwrapped from their layers of moss he paused, took out his find and
gave it a rub. Rotating the ring in the firelight to admire its gleam, he
saw the engraving of a rose surmounted by a crown. Staring at the
symbol he became lost in thought.

A creak came from the bed-place. 'What's happening in there,
brother? Have the fairies got you? Apart from that cow with a bad
cough it's all gone quiet.'

'Nowt's happening. I'm just sat here, thinking.'

'You take after Dad, he was always doing nowt - just thinking.
What are you thinking on?'

'Pictures keep coming into me head of a farm on dry ground; one
that has a hollow spot with a patch of mere where snipe and plovers

13

nest. It has good black kine, grass that talks in the breeze, and it's all our own.'

'Ah, if only the fairies could weave us a magic spell -' She broke off to cough. 'You've made that fire smoke and it's getting on my chest.' She coughed again, spat, then wheezed, 'Tonight's milking song was bonny - about crossing the wath to see a freckled lass - is it another one you've made up?'

'It came today when I was chopping at the dropped alder. The words floated up in me mind, like bubbles in the duck pond. I'll get the wise-woman to make a potion for that chest if it gets no better.'

The water simmered. Tom lowered five clay-coloured eggs into the pot and watched them sink. Rising from his squat he tiptoed to the centre of the back wall - the old chapel wall, double skinned and built of chiselled sandstone. He located the unmortared joint just above head height. The stone squeaked as he drew it out. His fingers groped inside the void until they closed around a skin bag. He opened it and dropped in the ring. It made a faint clink as it fell against another object. After pulling the drawstring tight, he replaced the bag and eased the stone back into position.

Tom knelt once more to watch the eggs, remembering his mother's words: 'Boil them hard. You've to go canny with duck eggs - ducks are mucky feeders.'

After shelling two eggs he mashed them in milk and stirred in the chopped sorrel; the tang of it pricked at his nose. He arranged the food on a trencher board, into what he considered a pretty mound, then from a bucket, ladled ale into a wooden bowl.

'Food's ready. Stay put, I'll bring it through.'

He set the meal beside her and propped her up against a linen bag of feathers.

'I can manage, brother!' Her voice sharpened. 'And that pillow needs burning - it's alive and feeding off me.'

'I'll change the feathers tomorrow.' He squatted on the floor to peel himself an egg.

'Why did you go raking about behind the loose stone?' she snapped.

'Raking about?' She's hurting inside, he thought.

'Yes, you rummaged in Dad's secret place.'

'There's nowt wrong with your lugs today. It's just summat I found that's worth keeping hold of.'

She picked at the food, and sniffed. 'So - what is it then? Aren't

14

you going to tell me?'

The words formed slow at first, then flooded out. As Hilda listened, she leaned back and frowned. Seeing her reaction, Tom faltered until the words dried up. Hilda straightened, narrowed her eyes and looked hard at him.

'Brother - you're daft! Think for a bit. If we try to sell it there'd be questions and we've no answers.'

'It's gold and might buy a cow or two. We could set up on our own instead of slaving at the beck and call of those hard buggers at the manor.'

'I don't like you using words like that, our Tom - Mother would never stand for it. You can't sell that ring either - it's a special one; we'd be found out and then what? That dreamy, duck-pond of a mind will get us hanged.' Her green eyes flashed.

Tom's mouth spread into a grin. 'That's better, it's good to see a bit of spark and spit; you're not bad looking with your freckles aquiver.'

She flicked egg at him from her spoon. 'Now don't you try to butter me up. I mean what I say. I'm older than you - you're nowt but eighteen remember, and I'm not having you getting us into trouble.'

They ate in silence. From the corner of an eye Tom saw her hands tremble. She looked up from her trencher and glanced at him. 'Tom . . . When will you wed?'

'That's a queer question. I've never given it a scrap o' thought and I've no mind to. Why ask?'

'It struck me today that I never want yoking to a man, though I can't bide alone. If you do wed, maybe we could still shelter under the same roof.'

'A dripping, crook-backed roof like this one, you mean? Scraping along beside the beasts, among the cow-clap and black-beetles?'

She fixed him with a desperate stare and struggled to speak. 'Where else can we live? We can't just wander the tracks from parish to parish. But I don't want to stay here, not now Mam and Dad are gone.' She let out a sobbing cough.

Tom stopped eating and moved to her side. He put his arms around his sister and felt the trembling of her thin shoulders. 'Now, don't fret. We will have our own spot. There'll be apple and damson trees, with hens of all colours scratching about underneath. Mind - thou will have to tend them. Meg can have some pups and they'll have white stars on their foreheads like her own. I see a milking nanny goat to build you up and you'll have a cosy bedchamber - with a mirror of polished brass so you can see to comb through your bonny locks.' He stooped to kiss the crown of her head.

She straightened up and hugged him. Then, pushing him away, she wiped her eyes with the back of her hands and giggled. 'Have a care! I might hold you to that! Now eat your supper.'

After bolting the rest of his food he pulled on a tattered cape. 'I'm off out for an hour. I've one or two things to see to. Meg - you stay here.'

He ducked out into the drizzle and hurried downhill towards a cottage a half-mile distant.

2

Agnes

The morning sun warmed Tom's back as he bent to fill a bucket at the spring. From wet hollows, the mewing cries of peewits reached him and stilled his chattering thoughts. He straightened to watch the pair of plovers display over the pasture. As they swooped, tumbled, and rose again in the sun their plumage flashed green and bronze around their white breasts. His mother's words came to mind: *the peewit comes to bring us joy.*

Beneath the birds moved two women; they paused for a few moments to gaze upwards before continuing. Tom shielded his eyes against the glare and watched them approach. Agnes Humble ambled up the slope on the arm of her fair-haired granddaughter. Though Agnes's body was thin and bent, it moved well enough for an old woman. Her healer's eyes scanned the ground, forever on the lookout for herbs. After a few minutes they stood beside him at the spring where Agnes, catching her breath, leaned on her stick.

'Good morning to thee, Tom, I see you've let the bull out. We got a bit worried about getting past him and then the great black beggar followed us for a space. By! That's a rare crop of watercress in that spring! I'll take a bit if you don't mind.' Agnes's blue eyes twinkled at him out of her lined face.

'Grand to see you, Agnes, and good of you to come. Take whatever you need; here, I'll get it for you . . . Hello, Mary.'

Dimples pitted the girl's cheeks as she replied in a sweet, laughing voice, 'Mornin', Tom. We're all up wi' the lark today.'

He met her gaze, felt his cheeks flush and looked instead at the knitted tan shawl where it draped her curves. He fumbled for the knife at his belt, then bent to sever a bunch of cress, shook off the water and dropped the glistening bunch into Agnes's basket.

'I'm glad you've come to see Hilda so quick. As I said last night, I'm troubled for her, she's nursed a bad belly for a week and it gets no better. Her chest is crackling, as well.'

Agnes sighed. 'I worry about you both. It grieves me to see you

17

two alone - it's bad losing your mam and dad so close together. I brought them both into the world, you know.' She stared into the pool, her eyes growing distant. 'Your gran and me played by this spring as bairns, a lifetime gone, though sometimes it seems like last week.'

Tom took her basket and offered his arm. As they walked to the byre, Mary kept close to his other side. They peeped at each other out of the corners of their eyes and Tom knew that he trembled.

He pushed open the door as a pale-faced Hilda stopped dressing her locks and laid aside her comb. A shaft of sunlight fell onto the mass of waves. They glinted as if spun from copper.

'Hello, neighbours,' she said. 'It's lovely to see you both. I got up when I heard you talking; let me get ready and I'll make you some hot milk.'

Agnes pushed inside and put a hand on Hilda's shoulder. 'No, you won't, you'll get back to bed so I can look at your trouble in the proper way. And thee, Tom Fleck, can get busy outside with summat useful and let Hilda and I talk. You an' all, Mary. Find me some tormentil, it wanders among the stones of the auld chapel - it's the roots I want.'

Mary tucked a wheat-pale curl behind her ear. 'Is there summat to dig with, Tom? You could help.'

Behind the byre lay hummocked ground, overgrown by dark nettles. Beyond ran a sheep-shaved turf studded with half-sunken stones and crumbled mortar.

'Mind the stingers, Mary - they're a terror this month.'

'Oh, I'm used to nettles, I've to gather them for making ale. See - there's the tormentil, isn't it pretty?' She pointed to a sprawl of tiny yellow flowers where they clambered over the rubble.

Tom loosened the ground with a mattock. Kneeling together, they peeled back the turf to begin pulling up lengths of brown root.

'Gran will boil these up and make a red dye,' Mary said, seeking his eyes. 'My! Listen to those chaffinches in the whins. Hear what they sing? *Sweet . . . will thee . . . will thee kiss . . . me . . . dear . . .?*' She gave a tinkling laugh.

He focussed on her tanned cheeks. The down shimmered where it caught the sun, as though dusted with gold. Her breath told of her breakfast of bread and honey and her blue eyes shone like the sky after rain. They inhaled each other and tried a kiss, and then another.

Sighing, she reached for his hand and moved it up her body to cup the toughened palm to her breast.

On their return to the byre, Tom saw tears on Hilda's face and the old woman holding her hand. Agnes, without turning round, said in firm tones, 'Mary, get that fire built up, we need some hot water. Tom, you check on them heifers up on Whinny Bank; we'll shout if you're needed.'

'What's the matter with her?'

'Never you mind, lad. It's women's business.'

He shambled to the fire and made the logs spark with a kick of his clog, then squatted to clear the ashes.

Agnes snapped at him, 'Mary can do all that, now gan away wi' thee.'

Tom sensed the blood rush to his cheeks. He lowered his head and muttered, 'Right. I'll look to the stock.' With that, he stamped out into the sunlight with Meg at his heels. He took three strides, then stood motionless, glowering into the distance.

The byre door creaked open and Mary's head poked out. She frowned and waved him away. Tom slouched towards the empty bullpen. He picked up a muck fork and, with violent force, stabbed it into the compacted dung. Lump by lump he flung the old bedding through the opening onto a dunghill outside. Each time he ejected a fork-full, a cluster of scratching hens scattered. Meg watched, looking bored, until she wandered off in search of rabbits.

With the floor scraped down to its cobbles, he straightened up to ease his back. As he wiped his sweating palms, the women's muffled voices reached his ears. A few quiet paces led to where a ventilation slit pierced the byre wall. He held his breath and listened.

'You're bleeding a bit. Now I see what the trouble is, I reckon you'll get over it. How's that water doing, Mary?'

'Needs a bit longer.'

'Now, Hilda, when did it happen? I need to know.'

There were sobs. 'Three months ago. I couldn't stop him. He was like a bull. I tried to push him off me . . . I tried hard.'

'He forced you, did he? Who did such a thing to you, honey?'

'Mark Warren at the manor. But I don't want trouble - it'll go bad for us.'

'Ah, so that's why you gave up your work at the manor all of a sudden. Aye, aye - it's a bad world. For now though, I'm sure we can cope with losing it at three months. You'll bleed for a bit and we'll need to make sure you're clean inside afterwards. We'll soon have you right as rain.'

Tom strained to hear, with his back stiffened and teeth clenched.

'I want that water hot, Mary; put it in a clean pot then boil some more. Get extra from the spring if you're running short.'

Moments later Mary appeared with a bucket. She came to his side and stroked his trembling shoulders. She chewed on her lip.

'I've to get water. Come with me.'

They knelt at the spring. She parted the cress and dipped the leather bucket. As the water flowed, each watched the other's image swirling in the surface. She whispered, 'You've guessed what's happened, haven't you?'

He got up. 'I know what he's done to her, if that's what you mean. But truth is there's nowt I can do about it - except break his head.'

She flinched as though his eyes were cold iron. 'You mustn't! They'll hunt you like a buck - with dogs, and when you're caught Hilda will have no one.'

'I know! I know!' He passed a hand across his brow. 'You'd best take your gran that water.'

She hugged him and stroked his neck until his body relaxed, then picked up the bucket and lugged it away, slopping, to the byre.

Mallet in hand, Tom gave the pool of the spring a black stare. The fence posts are rotten, he thought. If I don't fix them soon the beasts will burst through and foul our drinking water. I'll get on with it.

He heaved the old posts out of the soft ground and rammed the points of new stakes downward into the same holes. He pulled his crazed leather jerkin over his head, peeled off his dead father's shirt, and swung the post driver. The head of the wooden mallet, big and blunt like the head of the bull, fell onto the post. The post responded with a dull thud. The earth threw up a sucking noise as it took the first thrust of the stake. After three blows, the point was through the subsoil and met stiff clay. Its progress slowed and the sound of mallet on ash became a series of ringing thwacks. He eyed the top of the post until it showed signs of spreading under the punishment, then stopped and checked it for a tight grip.

He worked fast in the hope that the effort would shift the mass of violence in his heart. After driving in six posts, sweat gathered in beads on his hairless chest; rivulets trickled through the fine hair of his forearms and ran down to his fingers. He stopped to wipe his palms before tightening the belt buckle across his flat stomach.

The next post hit a buried rock and the mallet rebounded. He spat on his hands, rubbed them together, grasped the mallet and gave the stake another blow. His bunched muscles shuddered as the impact reverberated up his arms.

'You bastard!'

The top of the post had taken the form of Mark Warren's head. Filled with hate he struck again. The stake shivered and half of the sawn top broke away. He struck harder. The tortured length of ash shattered. Wiping tears of frustration from his eyes, he flung the mallet aside and reached for another timber.

Two hours passed. Tom sat on a rock and stared southwards at the manor house a mile away. His dog gazed up at him, whined and wagged her tail. She had dropped a fresh-killed rabbit at his feet, but today she got no fondles.

Agnes Humble limped, stiff jointed, from the byre towards him. Leaning on her stick she wiped a drip from her nose.

'It's all over now, honey, it wasn't much after all. Though the lass is weak, a few days' rest should put her right.'

Tom sprang to his feet and shouted, 'It wasn't much? I'm not daft! I know what's happened - I heard enough of it.'

'Oh you did, did you? Well you can take hold of tha sen! I'll not stand a young'un yelling at me.' She fixed him with her pale eyes. 'Just know this - I didn't take it away. She lost it her sen. And it's as well - the poor lamb were not properly made.'

He felt his limbs grow weak as his anger drained. 'I'm sorry, Agnes, I lost my temper there. You're always so kind to us. I don't know how we'd manage without you. How much do I owe for the healing? I've got five-pence saved up.'

'I don't take money from Oswald Fleck's grandson. Him and me might have wed; it's my loss that he favoured your gran in the end. I could use a spot of butter though and perhaps that rabbit yon dog's guarding. If tha's passing sometime you can drop off some straw for the hen house.'

'You're a good neighbour, Agnes. If there's any heavy jobs you want doing . . .'

She sighed. 'I'm bothered about all this. You might have thoughts to settle scores with Mark Warren - just bear in mind his father is master and he'll hoy you out. Your dad learned to live with the Warren ways. A canny, proud man with roots in this land, he learned to hold his tongue for the sake of his wife and bairns. You still have to find that patience. You take after your grandfather - you vex easy, and that's no good.'

He listened to the old woman with respect before blurting out, 'I want to get out of here - set up on me own somewhere. I've got a few things to sell that could get me and Hilda out of this muck-hole.'

'Are you on about the auld bits your dad dug up? I thought they went after the bad summer.'

'Summat like them, but the thing I've found is better. I need a buyer.'

Agnes grunted in sympathy and pursed her whiskery lips. 'Hmm - I suppose you do. Now might be the time. I hear the wapentakes are to be roused, the Scotchmen are at their burning and thieving again. They've raided this far in the past - though well before my time.'

'Raiders are nowt to do with me, I'm never a yeoman. They want landed men for the militia; they don't trust my kind with weapons.'

'That's as maybe. But there's not enough yeoman in a fit state, these days. They're giving out bills and iron hats to day labourers now. You'll have no choice in the matter -'

'How do I trade a small thing that's worth good coin?' he interrupted.

Agnes narrowed her eyes. 'When the landlords need money in a rush they seek out that stray Jew. They sell him their silver pots and the like and the Jew sells them on for a profit. I hear he's in Northallerton again and is buying.'

Mary called from the byre, 'Hilda says she's hungry, Gran; what should she have?'

Tom whispered to the old woman, 'I'm going to Northallerton straight away. It's a bare twenty-five mile, I'll be back tomorrow. Can you and Mary look after things till I get home?'

'I suppose so, lad, I suppose so.' She sighed. 'You take care. Trust nobody in Northallerton, some queer folk bide there these days - and mind you keep out of the Swan.'

3

Northallerton

Tom set out within the hour leaving his sister worried; now a woman of twenty, Hilda thought her young brother headstrong. Mary stayed at his side for the first half-mile and he grew impatient, she fussed too much about the belt of low cloud in the west. Once away from the women he hoped to think through his troubles - his anger, his frustration.

After a final wave to Mary, he set up a fast stride. The bag on his back rode well; it carried food and his dad's leather hat. He wore his father's best long stockings for the journey to town. From the moist feel of the breeze in his face, he knew rain was coming. Meanwhile the sun began to cook him; inside his leather jerkin and knee-length breeches, sweat beaded and trickled. Meg trotted a few paces in front, with her tail up.

On either side whole families, children and the old, were bent in the fields. The track meandered southwest for seven miles then joined a straight route from the north. The drove road made a broad hollow-way between hedges. The going was usually hard, dusty and fast in summer, but now, in this wet year, it was broken, slippery and slow. He mused on how wheels could cause such sump holes - holes that cried out to be filled up with fieldstone. His clogs gathered mud and his stockings picked up splashes of reeking cow-clap as he caught up with long herds that ambled southwards.

Self-assured men followed each cluster of black cattle. Tom wondered at the drovers' straight-backed pride, he had never seen such confidence among labourers. They were men big in build and big in voice. They sounded their words from somewhere deep in the chest. Yet their speech rang with musical lilts, the voices lifting at the end of a sentence, making all they uttered seem like a question.

'Now then, bonny lad? What does ye knaa today? Tha's in a rush, man? Tha's got a canny bit sweat on? Where's tha' from and where's tha' gannin?' The drovers bantered with him, plying good-hearted questions, doing their best to slow his pace to their own at the rear of each sauntering herd.

He needed to stride faster and so broke into a trot for half a mile, threading his way through the beasts until he joined the vanguard. Here, he measured his pace to that of a youth of his own age. The lanky boy wore the same wool and leather as his fellows. He marched in tall boots, slung a quarterstaff over his shoulder and kept a large, workmanlike knife at his belt. Whenever a beast slowed to pull at herbage, the quarterstaff swung out to give the dawdler a poke to its hindquarters. A fair, amiable face glowed beneath a leather hat with a brim that covered the back of the neck.

'Where do you belong?' Tom asked.

'By Hexham,' sang out the youth. He grinned at Tom's blank expression. 'That's on the Tyne, man. Ya knaa that big beck?'

'I've heard of it. Isn't it up by Scotchland?'

The youth hawked and spat. 'Not too close - but now and again too bloody close. Ya must ford Tees and Wear to reach Tyne - and Skerne and Derwent an' all - mind, those two are naught but ditches. Though it all adds up to a lot of watter to swim bullocks across.'

Tom fell silent - then: 'Do you think I could get drover work? I've grown up with kine.'

A quick glance assessed Tom's body shape. 'Ya look a useful sort and, if ya have legs sound enough for the long trod, ya might get a start. There's always plenty wanting the job, mind, 'cos the wages are good and men are not knocked about like serfs. But it's easy for me, these are in my dad's keeping - he's up at the head wi' me brother, on them hosses.'

'Where's the market?' Tom asked.

'York, this time. There's plenty of hungry bellies in yon town, and many a man with a tooth for beef and coin to pay for it. We always take it steady, no point in running the fat off the beasts. We get paid when they're sold, then we swill some ale and sing a bit.'

'Did your dad breed this herd?'

'Why no, man! We've not that much grass. Some we bred, some we bought in and grew on. Then there's stock belonging to those that pay us for droving them. Some of these black devils are Scotch, sold on by Tynedale reivers who lifted them - we divn't ask questions. There'll be beef here that's as tough as bull's lugs - though it'll stew well enough.'

He kept the drovers company for a few miles, listening to their stories and jokes. Meg enjoyed herself zigzagging with the big cattle dogs as they kept the beasts moving. He thought to travel the whole way in their company, but they halted wherever they found water and grass. Worried about the slant of the shadows, he pressed on alone.

The next few miles became a sticky trudge; rain bursts lashed down heavy enough to trickle inside his clothes. Water seeped into his clogs and raised a sore spot. He limped, feeling miserable, until he overtook a swaying oxcart. Offered a lift, he climbed up gratefully beside the driver. Meg jumped into the rear to curl up on sacks that covered a load of coal. The cart moved at a trundle; he relaxed, thankful to ease his feet and watch muscles work on the glistening backs of six oxen. He gazed at the stooped women in the passing field strips, listened to the groans of the swaying waggon and to the droning words of Jack Swales, the barrel-chested driver.

'So you're a Cleveland Fleck, you say.' Jack Swales's coal-impregnated, leather jerkin creaked as he twisted round to speak. 'There's one or two in Northallerton now - they could be your kin. They're decent folk. Plenty of work for them - real canny with stone, coming from the hills.' He scratched at his short brown beard before speaking again. 'Now, I seem to remember a Fleck, on and off, over the years, from up your way. He used to come to town about once a year - it's likely I met him in the Swan. Let's see now . . . Aye, that's him - Francis Fleck.'

'He was my dad,' murmured Tom.

'Is that right? Now I think on it, you've got his chisel jaw and them shoulders have the same rake. You say he was your dad, has he gone?'

'Last freeze. He went to find wages in the lead mines up Swaledale - but the workings caved in. He lay alongside others for a week afore they dug them out. They found Dad among the living, but he never stood straight after that - summat inside was crushed.'

'Ah! I'm sorry to hear that, truly sorry. And your mam, have you still got her?'

'She went in the winter, not long after Dad. The wise woman said she'd a lump.' Tom wiped some moisture from his eyes.

'That's sad. There's ower much of it about among the womenfolk. I've lost a lass to it, and her that never fed a bairn. The handywomen can't seem to fettle it, though they do take some of the hurt away. Ours gave my daughter liquor made from fairy stools, the sort that make rings on sheep ground; she slept a lot.'

They both brooded, listening to the creak of cart wheels and the plod of oxen feet. Tom frowned as he thought about where the women's lumps might have grown. He thought of Mary; this morning she had held his hand to her breast, it was smooth and warm like a new-laid goose egg. He flushed a little and coughed, peered over his shoulder to check that Meg lay safe on top of the coal, then opened his bag.

'Do you fancy summat to eat, Mister Swales?'

'Aye, I do. What've you got?'

'There's a bit of rabbit, some oatcakes, and a couple of hard-boiled duck eggs.'

'I'll have an egg, wi' an oatcake if you can spare it. But first I have to stop and stuff some waggon fat into those gudgeons, yon axles are squealing too much for my liking - they're running on the dry side.'

He jumped off the cart and, holding the goad in front of the leading ox, called out, 'Whoa! Whoa!' The oxen slowly came to a halt.

'This won't take long.' Clutching a skin bag of tallow, he crawled beneath the cart. With a piece of hide, he smeared the axle bearings with the animal fat, forcing it into gaps between moving parts and the gudgeon pins. Attracted by the riot of vegetation along the hedge-bottom, the oxen drifted onto the edge of the drove-way. They wrapped long tongues around lank herbage and ripped it away in mouthfuls. The coalman took the opportunity of the cart's motion to ram more fat into the waggon's vital parts.

Satisfied, he rolled out from under the cart and climbed back into his seat. He slapped the oxen's broad backs with the goad, shouted 'cush!', and the team lumbered forward again. The carter's face glowed beneath its film of coal-dust.

'That grease should see us home. Now where's that duck egg?'

Tom cracked the egg against the side of the waggon, peeled off the shell and, after wiping off a thumbprint, handed the egg to Jack Swales.

'Grand! This'll fill a gap. I've been feeling hollow since Yarm. Mind you, I'd a good feed off the colliers' wives at Ferryhill where I picked up this load. By! They have it rough, those men; them bell-pits can be killers. Yon women feed their men-folk like fighting-cocks. If I'd my time over again I'd take one of them Durham lasses for a wife, for certain - not that there's owt wrong with my own good woman. So, what takes thee to Northallerton?'

26

Tom grew nervous. 'To sell a few things.'

'Ah, like your dad. I do remember that's why he came to town - to sell a few things.' The driver's eyes narrowed. 'Auld things off the moor, I dare say. By gum! You Cleveland folk know how to keep going in a thin year. What have you fetched this time? Is it pretty?'

'Only a few beads and such like.'

After a few more yards, Jack Swales grunted. 'A long trail for the sake of a few auld beads - unless, under the muck, they're yeller 'uns.'

Tom sank a little more into his jerkin.

'You'll be seeking out the secret Jew. Let's hope he's about. It's his time of year. Be sure to keep quiet about what you're in town for, Northallerton's got more than its fair share of bad buggers - they keep moving in. The auld spot isn't the same. I'm right glad I work for me-sen. If you take my advice, Francis Fleck's lad, you'll do likewise and be your own master. It's done well for me. Another thing, while I think on it, you go canny with that dealer; his sort are not liked in Yorkshire - there's all sorts of tales about them. Anyway, folk have sayings around here; one is: whenever the Jewman's in town, a Clevelander is first through the gate. Aye, aye, take no mind of me, son - I'm given to blather.'

Tom did not interrupt as Jack Swales rambled on. He relaxed, answered the odd question and listened to the rich tones as the carter boasted of the long roads he had travelled and the things he had seen.

Under the rain clouds, the sky darkened before its time. In dull light, they reached a straggling line of buildings that marked the outskirts of Northallerton. The oxcart stopped by a timber-framed cottage and barn. A round-faced, homely sort of woman appeared in the doorway with a thin girl holding onto her arm.

'This is my spot. I'll be roving no more for a fortnight. Now look yonder - see the church tower? That's the High Street. If you want, you can stay here tonight. We've plenty of room since the sons moved out. There's only the wife and daughter. Help me stow the cart away and get these beasts onto grass. After that, we can sit by the fire.' He lowered his voice. 'The lass was touched by the fairies - even so, she's still a sweet child.'

Under the low beams of her kitchen, Ellen, the carter's plump wife, fussed around her visitor with food. The daughter sat beside the fireplace, with a cat on her knee, darning stockings and watching bread dough rise. The girl kept peeping at him, but each time he returned her gaze she would look away.

'You'll know Agnes Humble - she lives your way,' Ellen Swales watched him eat as she probed. 'Is that pie enough? There's more if you've space for it.'

'She's our neighbour. She rents a cottage, grows bits for the pot and keeps goats. Her granddaughter Mary lives with her. Canny pastry, mistress - as good as my mam's.' Meg watched from her prone position before the fire, saliva dangling from her jaws.

Ellen beamed and folded her broad forearms across her middle. 'That crust is how my own mother made it. She used to call it her granny's secret mix. She passed it on to her daughters and now I've passed it on to young Janet, here. She'll soon fettle up a man's dinner better than me.'

He met the eyes of the girl by the fireplace and gave a wink. 'That will set you in good store, Janet.' The girl blushed.

The women watched in silence as Tom wiped his trencher with a lump of bread.

'I think the goose has got our lass's tongue today.' Ellen Swales gave a sigh.

The girl flinched and chewed her lip. Tom watched her blue-veined hands go back to her darning. 'I can feel a hole in my stocking foot,' he murmured.

She brightened. 'Oh! I can mend it for you - if you like.'

He kicked off a clog; a black nail had burst through one of his mother's last darns. He rolled off the splashed stocking and blushed to see dirt-encrusted toes. 'I've lost all shame, Janet.'

She giggled. 'So, go and have a plodge in the beck - after you've whittled a bit off them nails.'

Her father stamped in through the back entrance. 'I've had a word with a neighbour. He reckons your man stays at the Swan; but you watch out in there, it's market day tomorrow - the town's crowded with all sorts of queer folk.'

'Thanks, Mister Swales. I'll go as soon as Janet mends that hole. I'll be straight back once I've seen the dealer.'

4

The Swan

Spreading clouds, edged with moonlight, filled the sky. Drawn by dim lamps and the sounds of livestock, Tom found his way along High Street. In front of the church, the cobbled road widened; sheep pens full of wether-lambs waiting for next day's auction, lined both sides. He passed men and women who worked together putting up stalls, and others making ready for sleep beneath the planks of their booths.

A cracked voice yelled, 'What are you doing in these parts, Fleck? Who's looking after the cows now you're here? Does the master know?'

He saw the shadowed face of a shepherd from the Warren estate and went up to him. The whiskered man squatted with a blanket around his shoulders, at the side of pen of sheep. Tom caught a whiff of sour beer. His stomach muscles hardened.

'What's it got to do with you?'

'Oh, hark to the raggy-arsed cowman. Crawls out of his byre and comes to town full of airs. Has the stink of cow-clap forced you out into the open for once? And what sort of a dog do you call that little waster?'

Tom glared at the bleary-eyed shepherd for a moment, trying to think of a response, but decided not to waste effort on a drunk.

The Swan jutted into the street an arrow-shot distant. Yellow light showed in every twisted window of the lopsided building. He tried to gather his thoughts on what he needed to do. The shepherd's taunts had made his heart pound and stiffened his resolve to break free of Thornaby Manor.

Sounds of raucous singing, backed up by a fiddler, poured through the entrance. He took a deep breath and strode inside, straight up to a row of barrels that lay between chocks on a long table. A stout man, resting his apron-wrapped belly against the table, nodded to him. Meg squeezed among drinkers' legs, sniffing for scraps of food, until she got into a fight with a lurcher. A jug of beer crashed against the

29

stone-flagged floor and a voice cried out in dismay. Tom cleared his throat and asked for ale. A tankard and a slopping wooden jug thudded onto the table.

'There you are, young man, a quart of the town's best, passed by Northallerton's properly elected ale taster.' The innkeeper laughed at his own joke and a group of men at a nearby table groaned aloud. 'You lot can shut up! How long will you cuddle that ale? You spend a farthing and clutter up my inn for the rest of the night! And that's a farthing to you, me brave boy. Have you come far?'

Tom took a drink. 'From Thornaby way, to see the market.' He lowered his voice. 'I'm told you've a dealer lodging here, I want to talk to him.'

'Can you keep that dog in hand? I've a few dealers here - the Swan's full tonight.' The men at the table set down their tankards and stared. 'What are you lot gawping at?' the innkeeper shouted - then beamed at Tom. 'Take no mind of that lot - they're inbred half-wits from top o' Swaledale, where they all sleep in one bed.'

'He's a travelling Jew,' Tom muttered.

Meg, having come off worst, slunk across the alehouse floor and settled at her master's feet.

'Oh, him?' He leaned over and whispered, 'And what bright things have you fetched from the hills today?'

'Nowt, I've come to speak with him, that's all,' Tom whispered back.

'Oh, aye? Nowt, eh? Well, young'un - me and him have a business arrangement. He likes me to check things out afore I send folk upstairs to his chamber. Bonny stuff, is it?'

'Only bits of auld bronze.' Tom took a pace back and glanced at the door to the street.

'All right, all right, never fret. He's up in his room having his supper.' He called to a plump girl ladling out broth, 'Izzy! When you've served that lot, go and tell Master Coronel there's someone asking for him.' He winked at Tom. 'And what name are you known by today?'

'Fleck.'

The landlord shouted above the fiddle music, 'Izzy! Tell him it's Fleck, fresh in from Thornaby.'

Tom eased himself onto a stool at one end of a crowded table. He kept his gaze lowered, sensing the weight of scrutiny. Even the fiddler watched him, still stamping a foot and working the bow.

A broken-nosed man drew up a stool close alongside; he winked, then looked Tom up and down. A soft breast brushed the back of Tom's head - Izzy had returned.

'He says he can see you now.' Her plump, round face, with its turned blue eye, gave him a bold grin. 'I'll show you the way if you'd like to mount the stairs wi' me.'

The instant Tom left the table, an old man reached across, grabbed the unguarded ale and quaffed it down. Holding his breath Tom followed Izzy's buttocks up the narrow stairs. She needed a bath.

'This is the gentleman's room; I'll leave you to it. See you later?' She rolled her eyes.

Tom waited until the girl had gone. He told Meg to 'stay', then knocked on the door.

There was rustling on the other side. A light voice called, 'Who is this?'

'I'm Fleck, come to see the merchant.' He took a pace back.

A bolt slid and the door creaked open. A tall, dark-eyed young woman stood with firelight behind her.

'You are Fleck of Thornaby?' Her eyebrows arched.

'Yes.'

She stared at him for a few moments until her eyes widened as though in recognition. 'My father will see you. Come in.'

She gestured for him to enter. He tingled as he passed her and took a few uncertain steps into an atmosphere of perfumed warmth. Burning logs crackled in the fire-grate and shadows danced across the whitewashed walls. A slender man, dressed in black velvet, rose from a chair by the fire. Despite the thin, hawk-like nose and arched nostrils, Tom discerned a mild expression as a hand was extended in greeting.

But the tall man stiffened, then stroked his grizzled beard before saying, in a disappointed tone, 'You are not the man I expected. Who are you?'

'I'm Thomas Fleck, sir. From Thornaby, in Cleveland.'

'Thomas Fleck? I expected to greet Francis Fleck, he is also from Cleveland.'

'My father, sir. He died, the winter gone - and my mother soon after.'

The merchant closed his eyes for long moments. When he spoke again his voice had thickened. 'Oh! I'm truly sorry. I admired your father; I've known few men so upright. We enjoyed each other's

31

conversation. He often spoke of the grace of your mother.'

'Thank you.' Tom's voice shook.

The dealer took his hand. 'And how do you live, now that he is gone?'

'I look after some beasts for the lord of the manor. I've been given my father's work, sir.'

'You need not address me as sir - already I can see your father in you. I am Isaac Coronel, the friend of your father. This is my daughter Rachel. Come, both of you, sit at the table.'

Tom tried to concentrate on his breathing as he absorbed the scene. Rachel moved like a breeze rippling through barley, he thought, as she walked from the shadows towards the table. The firelight gleamed on jet-black hair, dressed in two plaits that framed a long face before falling across the swell of her breasts. Her green dress gave a faint hiss and he smelt roses as she sat down. Her lips curved upwards at the corners before they opened.

'I am happy to meet you, Thomas Fleck. I also have fond memories of your father. On his last visit, he spoke of you and your sister. I am sorry, I forget her name.'

'My sister is Hilda.' He stammered a little and felt an oaf.

'Is she well?' Rachel asked.

'She's sick, but our neighbour is a healer, and I do what I can . . .' Tom's words dried up.

Isaac shuffled in his chair. 'We should have wine to celebrate a new beginning. Rachel - let us sample that bottle of Portuguese.'

Tom sat motionless, entranced as she poured the wine into glass goblets. He marvelled at how it glowed in the candlelight. It shimmered with the same rose-hip red as the silk scarf that lay around Rachel's slender throat.

'Welcome to the wine of our country. Her bishops make us exiles, but her wines still find their way to us and bring some relief.' Isaac sighed. 'A sin when good citizens must become wanderers because priests cannot bear them near.'

'Why do they feel like that?' asked Tom.

'They have decided that the Jewish people must stand condemned - your priests will have told you why.'

Tom shook his head. 'I've not taken much notice of the priest; he's never bothered himself with us. He mostly tends to those in the big house.'

Isaac nodded. 'I understand. For us - we have become unwanted in the land where we lived for a thousand years. We can no longer rest beside our fathers - and that is a sin. Enough! Let us find cheer.'

Tom remembered his father's advice for anxious times: just breathe evenly and feel the rise and fall of the belly. His muscles relaxed as the wine filled him with new sensations. It had none of the vinegary edge of his sister's fermented apples and brambles.

Isaac kept the conversation going as they drank and discovered the background to Tom's visit. Rachel was straight backed, listening and watching. She showed few signs of a maid's meekness. He was conscious of sharing the air she breathed and wondered at his growing calmness. Warmed with the glow of wine, he grew confident enough to steal glances across the table and admire the woman's graceful movements, her curved neck, and her skin - the colour of moorland honey.

The merchant gave a slight cough and, spreading his hands, asked, 'Now, young man, are you going to show me what you have brought from Cleveland today?'

Tom fumbled as he untied the leather bag from his belt. He drew out a coil of braided wire rope and, skin prickling, placed it before the Jew. It gleamed with a dull golden light.

Isaac's eyes widened. 'Ah yes! It is as though your father had come. Something rare from the northern hills of long ago.' He took it up and unrolled it on the table. It formed a straight, slender rope of woven gold about ten inches long.

'David's temple!' he breathed out. 'This once adorned chieftains! Look here and here,' he whispered. With a trembling finger he pointed at the ends of the rope. 'See these delicate dragon heads? Such workmanship! You bring an object more rare than anything your father ever offered. How did it make its way to you?'

'It belonged to my father. He found it just before he died - I helped him. We dug it out of a mound on the moor top. Dad still struggled with the hurt inside him from the accident. He shouldn't have gone up there. Maybe he sensed he hadn't long and wanted to make another search of that mound. We once found a brooch inside it and he reckoned we should dig there again. He died a few days after we got back off the hill.'

Isaac's smile faded. 'I see. He was determined to make one final provision for his family. Such love makes this circlet even more precious. *Levavi oculos meos in montes unde veniet auxilium meum.*'

Tom's brow furrowed.

Rachel fluttered her hands. 'Father displays his Latin again. In English it says, "I will look unto the hills from whence cometh my help." It is a psalm.'

Tom's eyes lit up with recognition. 'Dad used to say something like that!'

In one swift movement, Isaac formed the rope of gold into a circle and, with a flourish, draped it around Rachel's neck. 'Behold! My daughter becomes a Brigantian princess! Witness how the ancient craftsman's love lives again.'

Rachel's fingers moved around her throat, stroking the torque. 'This is strange - it is as though I have become someone else.'

The golden collar had the slenderness of Rachel's fingers. Tom wondered at how it gleamed on her skin as the candlelight flickered. His gaze drifted lower to linger on her breasts, but her arms covered them quickly as she took off the torque to lay it on the table.

'Father, it's late; you need rest, tomorrow you have other visitors.'

'Yes, daughter, you are right - as always. Let us get to business. Rachel, the balance please.'

Isaac arranged a set of brass scales on the table and made adjustments. He laid the torque in one pan, then loaded tiny lead weights into the other until the scales achieved balance. Tom gaped as the nimble fingers flicked beads along the wires of a counting frame. Isaac called out his reckonings in rapid Portuguese. Rachel, dipping a quill, made notes on paper which she handed to her father.

The dealer leaned back in his chair and stroked his short beard. 'I can offer you eighteen sovereigns for this.' He searched Tom's eyes.

Tom's head swam. Did he trust this foreigner? But even if the Jew should cheat him, he would never again hold so much in his hand - never in all his life. He gathered his wits. 'Master Coronel, sir, I'm a cowman with no learning. My father trusted you and so shall I.'

Isaac clasped Tom's hand. 'Of course what you trade here is worth more elsewhere, for I am a merchant and need my margin; also the next man must have his. Nevertheless, your words do me honour.'

Rachel slipped away from the table and returned with a small chest. She opened it with care so that the raised lid concealed the interior. She counted out eighteen gold coins and spread them out before Tom. He stared open-mouthed at the lustrous pattern they made. Her hands returned to her lap, her gaze to the tabletop.

After a moment, she glanced at him from beneath drooping lids then took back two sovereigns saying, 'It is best if you carried some smaller coins, perhaps.'

Her fingers returned to the chest and counted out a sequence of coins. 'These three angels make one sovereign. These ten testoons make half a sovereign and these groats and pennies will make up the rest. That is better for you.' She sat back again.

While Isaac wrapped the golden torque in green velvet, Tom announced - in an uncertain voice, 'I have another thing.'

'Yet more! Such an evening we have in the Swan.' Isaac sat up. Thomas placed the ring on the table.

'Hmm, this is not so old,' Isaac murmured, turning it over in the candle glow. 'It is a seal ring; it bears the symbol of a rose surmounted by a crown. I've seen this device somewhere before. Let me think - I cannot recall - it is certain this belongs to a man of high office. I am troubled. Before we continue you must tell me how you came by it.'

Under the open gaze of the Jews, Tom related the events in the marsh.

With a sigh, Isaac leaned back in his chair and drummed the table with his fingers.

'Ah! I have it!' He straightened and banged the table with his fist. The wine goblets bounced. 'This ring belongs to the York Herald.' He sat back again, breathing deep. 'Take it back; I cannot deal in this. It would be a serious crime to sell it onwards and even more criminal to melt it down. England banished her Jews long ago; we few merchants dwell in this land under sufferance. We must not do anything that gives offence. I cannot deal in this item.'

'Then I'll fling it into the Tees,' Tom said - a little too loudly.

Isaac's eyes widened. 'No, not that! Such a wasted opportunity. I counsel you to think with care. The ring bearer is the King's Herald. He will lament the loss of the seal ring - it is important to him - he will show generosity on its return.'

Tom's mind calmed. 'You give good advice, Isaac. I'll follow it. Night's here and the carter will worry, so I'd best get on my way.' Tom pushed back his chair.

'Take care. Remember there are rough men in town. Do not risk all that coin in one place. Rachel, could you spare one of your pouches?'

Rachel reached inside her silk wrap and drew out a soft leather pouch on a cord. She lifted it over her head, took out its few contents, then placed the pouch around Tom's neck.

'Carry the valuable pieces in the pouch and keep it around your neck, out of sight within your jerkin.' Her cheeks dimpled like Mary's as she smiled. 'Other coin you can hide inside your stockings. A few small coins in your belt pouch will satisfy any cutpurse.'

'To spend time with the son of Francis is true wealth. I wish you well, Thomas. May we meet again in prosperity and boon.' Isaac closed his cool fingers around Tom's warm hand.

Rachel took him to the door and, meeting his eyes, said in a soft voice, 'Good night, Thomas Fleck. May your life be happy.'

He knew a sense of loss as she disappeared from sight behind the closing door. Meg's eyes flicked open from her doze in the passageway. The little dog yawned and wagged her tail. Tom hid the coins about his body as he thought best and stepped onto the staircase.

5

The Return

The room downstairs still heaved with shepherds and drovers. By the window, a group of men shouted and cursed at dice clattering across a table while two lurchers snarled at each other beneath. The door to the street was wide open and a swaying man with a bloodied face supported himself against the frame. Above the din the fiddler played on, ignored, save for a weedy man who aped every movement of his bow arm. Tom stepped quickly through the beer-soaked sawdust. He tried to squeeze through the doorway at the same time as the innkeeper ejected a troublemaker.

'Take your turn! Take your turn!' The innkeeper yelled. 'Oh it's you. Tha took long enough!' He threw the man into the darkness and leaned against the door frame, breathing heavily. 'Did you get a good price?'

Ignoring the question, Tom pushed past into the cool night. The innkeeper bellowed a curse after him; Tom shrugged and walked on. The moon was lost somewhere in cloud, so he picked his way, by the light of windows, towards the coal merchant's house. Coming abreast of the last sheep pen he heard the creak of leather-clad feet and spun around. Two men faced him, swinging cudgels. They moved to either side and slapped the heavy sticks into their palms. Meg bared her teeth and snarled.

'Right! Hand it over and you'll not get hurt.'

As Tom braced himself to run, a blow glanced off his head knocking him to the ground. Someone straddled his back. Fingers groped for the purse that hung from his belt. He caught the stench of sour breath.

'Ow! You little bastard!'

The robber rolled off to lash out at Meg. Her teeth left his ankle as she yelped. Tom leapt to his feet, but the second man kicked his legs away. He clambered up once more as a cudgel swept in. Catching it in his hand, he held on and gave his assailant a hard kick to the shins with his clog. The first man struck three more times, on his shoulders and on his biceps, and he fell. He lay dazed in the rutted mud, conscious only of Meg's barks. Then new sounds - a series of swishes, soft thuds and grunts, then a man's yelp followed by running feet.

There was a cough and a spit. 'They'll not be back. I thowt I'd better find out where you'd got to. Are ye harmed much?'

Above him loomed Jack Swales, the carter, resting the weight of his heaving frame on a six-foot staff.

The women made a great fuss of his injuries. The carter's wife demanded that Tom strip to the waist. While she bathed the blood from his head, her daughter rubbed butter into his bruises. The girl's face was pink as she held her breath while massaging his shoulder and the muscles of his upper arm.

He met her shy eyes. 'You've a healing touch, Janet. I feel as though I'm in the house of the good elves.'

At last she exhaled, her breath falling like a feather across his chest.

Her mother broke the spell. 'You'll either leave us without butter, Janet, or rub the poor lad away. I don't know which will come first.'

They ushered him into a bed-space beneath the thatch and urged him to rest. Once alone, he checked the hiding places around his body and found all the coins still in place. Both he and the dog fell unconscious as soon as they stretched out.

A cock crowed in the yard, although it seemed a mile away. Hours passed while he lay on his back in a half-dream watching his imagination play with images: the glowing torque around Rachel's neck, Isaac's fingers flicking beads on the counting frame, the blur of falling cudgels, and Janet's innocent smile.

The carter thrust his head through the crawl-way to the bed space. 'Thowt you'd like to know the sun's well up. There's a bite to eat on the table.'

'I'll be down soon to do some work.' Tom mumbled.

The family refused his penny for the late breakfast. He had wanted to wield an axe for an hour and leave them with a pile of firewood, but they said he would have aches enough to cope with and should 'get off home'.

'Be sure to remember me to Agnes Humble,' the carter's wife said as they walked to the gate to wave him off. 'And be sure to come and see us whenever you're this way again.'

Janet reached for his hand when she thought no one could see. He felt a tremor from the touch of her cool fingers and saw her eyes trying to form a question for which he had no answer.

The way home began as a stiff trudge - his head throbbed and the bruises hurt. Five miles clear of the town he entered meadowland. The trills of invisible larks and the '*pee-wit*' cries of tumbling plovers fell from a cloudless sky. They lifted his spirits so that he strode forward despite the aches. He risked shortcuts across fields and through woods. He saved miles by climbing walls and jumping becks, always aiming for the point by Osmotherley where the moor ended and the hills pitched onto the ploughing lands.

The sun dipped as he left the cover of a rook-filled wood where he once built childish camps. Perched on its ridge a mile away the byre glowed in the low sun. Plunging through a hedge he rejoined the track.

'Let's have thee; chuck chuck chuck.' Mary Humble flitted around the byre, shooing stragglers into the henhouse. After fastening the door against the fox, she faced the west. Shadows climbed the slope as the sun lowered onto the fells. The air chilled. A line of rooks headed home to their roost; beyond them, bands of cloud shaded into pink.

'Like a maiden's blush,' she whispered, recalling his touch.

Mary shaded her eyes. As the hollow-way sank into gloom there was a movement between the elms. It took a man's shape. A dog trotted in front. They were home!

Mary called through the byre door, 'He's coming! He's coming!' She was waving as Agnes and Hilda emerged. 'Look! Just leaving the trees! I'll go and meet him.' She skipped down the slope to wait for Tom at the spring.

As he trudged up the slope the colour of the byre's walls changed from old straw to rose. Mary ran towards him, her apron flapping like a gull's wing.

'I could hardly see for the sun in my eyes, but I knew it was you!' She gave him a shy kiss on the lips. 'Oh! Look at your face.' She stroked his cheek. 'The skin's broken all down one side. What's happened?'

'Don't fret - it's nowt but a bit o' bark knocked off.'

She touched his damaged cheek with her lips before tugging him towards the byre. Meg was dancing about the legs of Agnes and Hilda.

He nodded his gratitude to Agnes before giving his sister a gentle hug. 'How are you faring, Hilda?'

'While the trouble's taken my strength, I am mending. They've shoved broth down me whenever they had an excuse. Come inside, you look worn out.'

He sank onto a sheepskin and stretched out, all vigour gone. Mary knelt and pulled off his clogs.

She stroked his feet. 'They'll be sore.'

'They're not too bad. I did forty-odd miles in them alder clogs and they've held up well. They could use new uppers; I've got the leather.'

Agnes hobbled over. 'Stop fussing about his feet, can't you see he's taken a bash on the head and it needs bathing; get some warm water and a lump of lamb's wool. Let's have that shirt off your back, young'un.'

Now Agnes fussed about him, tut tutting as she examined the side of his head and his bruises. 'Who did this to you?'

'Some robbers had a try at me. They got nowt. Jack Swales saw to that.'

'Jack Swales? You mean Carter Swales who wed Ellen Dent?'

'Aye, that's him. He's a sturdy man; fetches coal out of Durham. I stayed with them overnight. Ellen says to be remembered to you . . . Ow!'

Mary stopped bathing his scalp. 'Oh, sorry, did that hurt? There, it's done - I'll just dry it a bit. Ooh! You're skin's greasy - it smells of butter!'

'I know. Young Janet Swales rubbed it all over me last night.'

'Did she now? All over? And is she pretty - this Janet Swales?'

'Bonny enough - like an elf.'

'And did you like the elf rubbing you all over with butter?'

'Leave him alone, Mary. Clear out of the way while I spread balm on that bash.' Agnes produced a tiny pot.

'How's Ellen Dent keeping these days? She grew up around here only to move away when she wed Carter. Has she any family?'

'They're all thriving on her baking - best I've had. They've a daughter called Janet who's handy round the house, sews and is very good with butter rubs. They've two sons who've moved up to

Hartlepool; they're carpenters; Jack says they've gone for the boat building.'

'There, we'll not lay too much on; you need to let the air get to it. You'll have to keep it clean and not lay on that side for a bit. You're lucky they didn't take the lug off, Tom Fleck.'

'And we're lucky to have good neighbours.' Tom replied.

Agnes gave a wheezing chuckle. 'It works both ways. Let's hope the tramp to town was for the best; you can tell me about it sometime. Tonight, I need my own bed. Mary and me will have to get on home while there's a moon.

6

The Manor

Sir Edmond Warren, his broad face set in a frown, leaned back into a carved chair. On the table lay a document. It had arrived two days earlier and needed action - it bore the seal of King Henry the Eighth. He unrolled it and read it once again.

'God's blood!' he muttered. 'Where will I find enough fit men? Sixteen mounted! Christ knows where I'll find them.' He chewed on a few strands of his greying moustache that had crept between his lips.

Hearing a creak on the staircase, he stopped talking to himself and allowed the parchment to roll up.

Ralph Warren knelt to peep through the knothole of the stout door, as he had done in childhood. He straightened up and knocked.

'Enter.'

He ambled across the floor of the panelled room making the broad oak boards creak and give a little under his weight. He stopped at the table and breathed in the faint odour of decay from the tapestries that hung between clusters of halberds on all the walls except one. On that wall hung the painting of a woman in a green gown; he sensed her eyes on him.

'You wanted to see me, Father?'

'Yes, stand there. I need to talk to you both. Where's your brother?'

'Mark is out with his hawks, sir - clearing the pigeons from the kale.'

'I see; as usual following pleasure on the excuse it's work. At least he keeps himself hard. I discern you are getting no thinner - haven't I told you to keep out of the kitchens?'

Ralph shifted his weight a little. 'Yes, Father. I'm eating less, yet somehow, I remain heavy.'

'You take after your maternal grandmother then, she'd a backside on her like the stern of a Dutch galliot.'

Without thinking, the young man smirked.

'You can wipe that daft expression off your face, boy! My body is solid muscle.' Sir Edmond Warren glowered at his son. 'Straighten up and set your shoulders back! You've a stoop on you like a round-shouldered auld biddy. Can you draw a longbow to the full extent yet?'

'Last Sunday I almost did. Unfortunately the bowstring slipped and tore some skin off my thumb.' He held out his left hand.

'Tcha! Pity it wasn't your quill hand.'

Ralph stiffened and, for a moment, a defiant glare passed across his eyes.

His father had not noticed, instead he pushed back his chair and moved to the mullioned window to gaze out across the walled garden. Ralph heard him mutter something about the first real sun for weeks, and go on to grumble about the incompetence of a gardener who struggled to tie the branches of a cordon pear against a wall.

Ralph stole a glance at the pale features of his mother. The eyes in the painting appeared sad today. He thought of their times together, watching skeins of geese pass southwards, like a wavering script written across the white October clouds; then of winter evenings reading poetry by the fireside. He ached for her.

His daydream broke apart at the sound of his father's booming voice. Squinting, he struggled to discern the knight's expression against the glare from the window.

'Listen to me now: since the king took the army to France, the Scots have stirred. They're raiding and worse - war is likely. That rabble never miss an opportunity; they've an alliance with that French popinjay Louis - we can expect trouble. Surrey has charge of defence; he's ordered a muster against the Scots. They shall be taught a lesson.'

'A lesson about what, exactly?'

Sir Edmond glared and reddened. 'What is it that you read all day? Do you know anything at all that matters? Thieving is their livelihood and they're riding out again. It's their habit to lift the cattle of Northumberland whenever they think we're weak. Next thing they'll drove them down to York in the hope we're fools enough to buy them back.'

'And how would we be affected by such an event?'

His father's eyes bulged. 'Affected! What do you mean, affected?'

'Sir, when have we ever lost cattle to the Scots? Does it concern us? We are a hundred miles south of the border.'

'Good God, boy, why are you so feckless? This could lead to a collision of kingdoms. As lord of the manor I have a duty - an obligation.' The white scar on the knight's heavy forehead turned pink.

'I beg your pardon, sir.'

'Enough! In my absence you will take charge here.'

'Me? I've no experience at managing lands. Mark is twenty-four and I'm but eighteen, he's much better qualified.'

'Mark comes with me, he rides well and is handy with weapons; he'll help lead my contingent. You will stop reading books all day and apply yourself.'

Ralph brightened when a clatter of hooves on cobbles burst up from the yard. 'That will be Mark.'

'Then go and fetch him.'

Ralph scurried from the room, puzzled by something he had seen in his father's eyes.

Sir Edmond eased open the window so that he could look down on the meeting of his sons. Mark stood upright and relaxed while Ralph performed his usual gesticulations. Mark's confident voice resonated off the stone walls of the yard while Ralph's thinner tones faded beneath the squabbles of the rookery. The knight bit on a thumbnail, frowned and returned to his chair.

Floorboards creaked and the brothers entered the room. Their father stopped drumming his fingers on the table.

'Well, Mark, no doubt Ralph has told you what's afoot? That I am to raise the wapentake?'

'Yes, sir.'

'You are to take word to my tenants and workers. I want them at muster in two days - this Sunday, after church and on the common. The yeomen are to turn out with mounts, arms and gear for a month in the field. The labourers will get weapons from my armoury. Men will bring what rations they can. We will train on the march. Are you hot for this?'

'Yes, Father, and the sooner the better.'

'Good! Now hear me - this is no roe-deer chase. What we hunt is clever and half-savage. We must match them in cunning and strength or they'll have the entrails out of us. Mark, you will take my orders among the tenants and labourers between here and the bank of the Tees. Ralph will call at the farms south of this house and I'll take care of Thornaby village. I want no one overlooked. You will hear cartloads of excuses but you will judge each man's fitness and rule accordingly. Every man and boy from sixteen to sixty must turn out if they are not bedridden, lame or daft.'

He handed them papers. 'So there's no mistake, those are my orders on the care of the various parts of the estate whilst I'm away. The old men or the wives are in charge while the militia is out. Now, both of you get mounted and report back here by middle day tomorrow. On your way out, send me the blacksmith.'

'Regard it as done, sir. Come on, Ralph.' Mark Warren strode with purpose from the room. Ralph gave a small cough and followed him out.

After his sons had gone, Edmond Warren stood in front of the painting. He regarded it for a long minute. 'These two boys - one like me and one like you.' His voice grew husky. 'They need you. I need you, Alice. I'm lonely. Sometimes it's too much to bear.'

His fingers reached out and touched the figure's cheek. He stroked the ripples of the artist's brush strokes and the beginnings of slight cracks in the surface of the paint.

'Not like your skin, my love,' he whispered.

Beneath the painting stood an oak chest. He knelt on the floor and lifted the iron-bound lid. Inside lay rolls of parchment and a few books. His broad, short-fingered hand reached into the chest and drew out an embroidered pouch. From it he pulled a long scarf the colour of emeralds. He held it to his nose and breathed in, then brushed the cool silk across his forehead and eyes. He picked up one of the books and moved his fingertips across its leather binding. On the first page he read, 'For Alice, my cherished daughter. Marmaduke Weastall 1483'.

Hearing a deep cough and a knock, Edmond slipped the scarf inside his tunic, replaced the other objects and closed the lid of the chest before opening the door. A tall, muscular man wearing a cracked and singed leather jerkin and trousers took a pace back. The tough skin of his whiskered face showed a sprinkling of blue pits, the marks of embedded fragments of metal.

'You wanted to see me, sir?'

'Good morning, Rob. Come in. We need to check the armoury.'

Rob Gibson stooped his great head to ease through the doorway. He stopped in the middle of the room, wiping his hands on the sides of his trousers. 'I'm a bit on the mucky side.'

'Never mind that, sit at the table and take a cup of mead.'

Both men eased their large bodies into chairs. Edmond Warren reached to one side, pulled open a wall cupboard and took out a stone jar and two pewter beakers. He poured the golden fluid and handed a beaker to the blacksmith. 'I get it sent up from Rievaulx. Long life!'

Both men drank and wiped their moustaches. The lord of the manor surveyed his blacksmith. This craftsman had the blend of steady eye and firm jaw that he admired in a man.

'Matters are coming to a head, Rob - you and I could stand shoulder to shoulder in the field again afore long. Just like the old days, except it's the Scots this time. What do you reckon to that?'

The blacksmith placed his callused hands on his thighs and leaned backwards. 'Well, I thowt I'd seen the last of it at Bosworth - it's nigh on thirty years since then. I saw enough blood-soaked grass that day to be going on wi' - and English blood at that. To my mind yon day made no sense - and the wrong side won.'

'It was a mess, Rob - a fight among countrymen. This time it's different. It's the Border and likely invasion. We needs be on our mettle. How's the marksmanship? You still the best in these parts?'

'By a whisker. One boy, Tom Fleck, has grown a man's strength and runs me close.'

'Fleck? What's a labourer doing with a war bow? I don't like the sound of that.'

The blacksmith shifted in his seat. 'It was his dad's. Francis and his own father, Ossy Fleck, made grand bowmen - though they never fussed on about it. Francis taught his lad well. Tom's got his dad's strong back and long arms.' He avoided his master's eyes. 'I mind the Flecks were yeoman once - with their own hide of land.'

'Ah yes! The Flecks. A knotty business that.' Edmond Warren tugged at his full beard and thought of the book he had held a few minutes earlier. He cleared his throat. 'Enough of what's past! We'll check the armoury and see what work there is for you.' He opened a drawer in the table and took out a heavy iron key.

In their separate chambers the brothers prepared themselves for a night away from home. Mark trimmed his short beard, washed himself all over in a tub of hot water, inspected his genitals, rubbed rose-water across his chest and under his arms; finally he eased into a clean shirt and fresh small-clothes.

In the next bedroom, Ralph Warren wrapped up a pair of beeswax candles and a tinderbox. He had no intention of writing by the light of the disgusting tallow stumps that farmers burned. In an afterthought, he pulled on a clean shirt and stockings. He picked up the little book in which he penned his poetic thoughts, wrapped it in oilcloth and placed it in a small wooden box with his inkbottle and quill.

Each young man hoped his last call of the day would be at some comfortable house. Ralph had in mind the matter of his supper and a soft bed, whereas Mark considered which house might yield up a pliable woman.

Ralph slept in a clean bed at Church House, undisturbed except for a brief rattling of the door latch. He had made sure that he arrived at his friend's - the curate of Acklam - in time for supper. Trained in Rome, the chubby young priest had become a scholar of Latin verse and considered his parish beyond the edge of the civilised world. Father Jeffrey's eyes danced with joy when he learned that Ralph would stay the night. Over a sumptuous supper, prepared by his housekeeper, he declared the depth of his friendship for his visitor. They spent the rest of the evening discussing Orfeo and Euridice by candlelight. Father Jeffrey had fondled Ralph's fair curls as he described how Orfeo had braved the Underworld because of his love for the spirit of Euridice. By bedtime, Ralph's face had flushed with the effects of wine and the attentions of the priest, yet he had the presence of mind to slide the bolt of his chamber door.

Mark had a restless night of wind and rain. After restless hours in a musty bed, beneath a dripping thatch, listening to the squabbles of rodents and the bellowing of a cow in need of the bull, his mood remained foul. He had stayed at a farm that he knew had easy daughters, but both of them streamed with colds and had coughed and hacked their way through supper. One of them - the buxom one - nevertheless rolled her eyes at him between her sniffles. The mother encouraged the wench in such a blatant manner that she had appeared at his bedside at some godforsaken hour. Today, his chest rattled as he coughed. Perhaps he had caught the creature's fever.

A shaft of sunlight fell across the track. He squinted upwards and saw the cloud mass overhead had torn apart. As he rode his horse into the patch of watery sunshine his spirits lifted a little. Perhaps the morning was turning fine after all. His two black hounds slavered and panted as they quartered the ground for game.

He raised his linen-clad thighs out of the saddle, thrust a hand inside his cloak and scratched his crotch a few times; something was taking breakfast at his expense. He cursed aloud, 'God's wind! Filthy peasants! And these bloody whins are full of spite today.' He spurred his mount through a thicket of gorse and onto the top of the low banks south of the marsh. The hounds squealed as prickle-laden branches sprang back into their faces.

At the top of the hillock, he paused. Below him squatted an old cow byre that held one of his father's milking herds - husbanded by a labourer. He knew the female of the place and brought to mind her willowy body.

7

Muster Call

Morning came and they had the byre to themselves. Hilda found enough strength to make breakfast for her brother who had spent much of the night with a calving. Tom was outside, washing his hands clean of the birth waters. She leaned into the yard to call him for food. He stood with legs apart, hands dripping at his sides, staring towards Whinny Bank. She followed his gaze until her heart sank. A rider had paused among the whins and, outlined against the sky, was watching the byre. The horseman moved.

'Tom, he's coming here! Promise me you won't cross him.'

'Let's see what he wants first. Never worry yourself; I did some thinking last night and I'll not make any wrong moves.'

'Then come and get a bit of breakfast before he gets here, you'll be calmer with hot food inside.'

They continued spooning porridge as the thud of hooves drew closer. A saddle creaked - boots hit the ground - a fist banged on the door.

'Fleck! Are you in?'

Meg growled. She raised a ridge of wiry hair along her neck and shoulders. Tom calmed her, then eased open the door and silently stood to one side.

Mark Warren stooped beneath the lintel and undid his cape to shake off the rain onto the newly swept floor. He glanced at Hilda before turning to Tom.

'I've instructions for you from my father. You will attend muster on the common, after church tomorrow, with rations and whatever gear you can find. You will go north with the militia for up to a month. We know about the longbow you keep, so you will bring that and any arrows you have - you can get more from the armoury. There is pay at the usual rate and you might profit from what gear you take off the Scots.'

Mark Warren looked him over. Tom stared back with sullen eyes, thinking, I'm just a penned ox under the gaze of a dealer. He watched

Warren's expression and tried to decipher the man's thoughts: well-muscled where it matters; deep chest; labourer's shoulders; the long arms and sturdy legs of a bowman.

'You look fit enough.'

Tom glared at him. 'And who will look after the beasts if I'm not here? Hilda is too sick.'

Mark Warren frowned at the brazen look, but then broke eye contact to glance at the new calf tottering among the straw as the mother's tongue licked the thin body. Scowling, he faced Tom again. 'Will Fisher is coming, he's an old cowman but still able. He moves in here this morning. Make sure he knows the state of the herd before you leave. We will see you tomorrow, straight after middle-day, on the common, for muster.' He threw his cape over his shoulders and, as he ducked through the doorway, banged his head on the wooden lintel. 'Pox it,' he growled, and stamped away, leaving the door wide open.

Hilda stared after him. 'That bastard! There - I've sworn. But it's true! His eyes glittered like a greedy pig's when he saw me.'

'You cuss him as much as you want. Get it out of your system. Then you and I need to talk before Will Fisher turns up. Let's finish our breakfast first.'

'I'm not staying here with that Will Fisher!' Her voice shook. 'I don't trust him, he knocks his wife about and - he's a mucky devil, he hides and spies on women whenever he can.'

They ate in silence until a soft knock sounded on the door, followed by Agnes's cracked voice.

'Can we come in?'

'We rushed up here when we saw him crest Whinny Bank. What did he want?' Mary asked.

'He wants Tom for the militia tomorrow - he has to go north and carry his bow against the Scotchmen.' Hilda wiped away a tear. 'And that Will Fisher is to live here instead. He's moving in this morning.'

'That may be so, lass,' Agnes snapped. 'I'll not see you bide under the same roof as him. You'll stay with us, there's room and we'll be glad. And you, young Fleck, will make sure to come home in one piece.'

Tom took a pace back and glared at them all. 'They're not getting me in the militia - not the Warren's militia anyway, I've had enough of them ordering me about. I'll not go to the muster tomorrow; I'll cross the Tees instead.'

'Shush!' Mary broke in. 'There's someone outside.'

Tom stole a glimpse through the doorway. 'It's Fisher; he's gone into the bull shed. Right, Hilda, get your things and go with Agnes and Mary. I'll see to him and hand this place over.'

Outside, Tom sauntered up to the grizzled man. 'Now then, Will. I'm told I've to show you around.'

Will Fisher gave a sideways look. 'Aye, I'll see to this auld muck heap till you get back - if you get back, that is.'

'What do you mean, if I get back?' Irritated, he leaned towards the scrawny body. Even at eighteen, he carried more muscle than did the older man.

Will backed away. 'I only meant you'd better watch out in the Borders, I've heard them Scotchmen are savage beggars. What about showing me these kine?'

Tom spent an hour pointing out each of the bullocks, the stud bull, the calves, and the half-dozen milkers, detailing their different personalities and condition. He took Fisher onto Whinny Bank to see the six young heifers that grazed there. Will grumbled at the thorns that clutched at the tattered garment hanging from the top half of his thin body. 'These blasted whins are ripping me kersey to bits,' he moaned. 'You should take a billhook to this lot and knock them down, or else get them burned off and let this scabby grass see daylight.'

Tom stopped and scowled. 'Well, it's your job now - after you've seen to the beasts, mucked out the byre, cleared the drains, fixed the gaps in the hedges, done the milking - you can come up here, if you still feel like it, and clear them away. Me, I like the whins thick. They shelter the stock from the blast when the wind's off the sea - and the singing birds nest in them. Listen to that . . .'

They stood still. The sun burned onto their heads. The yellow whin blossom poured its delicate vanilla scent into the breeze. From all directions, across the rough grazing, rose up the husky warbling of linnets and the drawn-out trills of yellowhammers.

Will Fisher sniffed. 'I'll trap a few of them. The ladies like to keep bonny birds in cages; I could do with a few pence extra.'

Tom frowned, bit back a remark, then strode down to the byre to gather up his gear.

The women had gone. Behind the byre he threw grain onto the ground to attract the hens, ushered them into the henhouse and stuffed them, squawking, into two baskets. Inside the byre he leaned against the door-frame, breathing deep as he considered his actions. The calves stared in silence through the bars of their pen. One last time he scanned the rear wall with its hiding place, his imagination slipping back twelve years to watch his father's brown hands reach up to draw out the loose stone.

His mother sat on a stool next to the fireplace where she worked the drop spindle. His childish form sat on a log facing her, with arms held out and hands apart. The grey sheep wool, looped across his fingers, made his arms ache and he kept letting them droop so that his elbows could rest on his knees. His mother smiled at him with her calm blue eyes and wide mouth.

'Are you tired, my little distaff? Never mind, we'll soon be done and when it's all on the spindle you can go out to play.'

He tilted his hands, helping the fluffy wool to snake across to his mother's raised arm. Her deft fingers twisted the wool into a yarn and allowed the whirling spindle to wind it home. His arms still ached even though most of the yarn had wound onto the spindle where it hung like a spinning goose egg. At last the end of the skein arrived, flew out of his hands and set him free.

Tom wiped an eye with his sleeve. A painful lump came to his throat as he backed away to stoop under the lintel and out into daylight. With his travelling pack and longbow across his back and a basket of hens suspended from each end of a quarterstaff that rested across his shoulders, he strode out for Agnes Humble's cottage half a mile away. Meg trotted a few yards in front with her tail hung low; she kept turning her head to look back at him. In her jaws she carried her most favoured bone.

Agnes' cottage crouched beneath blackened straw thatch. The simple structure had rounded ends; without corners, it resembled the blunt outline of a boat. Living memory knew nothing of its history or who pulled its rough stones from the ground when men first cleared the land. Tom touched the unusual carved stones that formed the low doorway and wondered at the ring markings; he had puzzled over similar shapes on the moor. An ancient rowan tree stood guard to one side, its task was to keep away evil; he stroked the gnarled trunk for luck, then ducked into the cottage.

Inside, on a creaking table, Hilda chopped onions while Mary cut a skinned rabbit into small pieces. An iron pot of barley stock simmered on a hook over the fire. Agnes lay on a straw mattress by the hearth, her wrinkled face drawn. Her eyes sparkled like forget-me-nots when he appeared. 'That's a rare load you're carrying, young Fleck, are you off somewhere?'

'I've fetched you eight hens. They're all in lay, except for one hot broody; can you manage them?'

'We rightly can, now the family's grown. Shut them in the hen house for now and they can run out with the flock tomorrow. Keep the broody in her basket though; I'll set a couple of goose eggs under her after we've had summat to eat.'

Still carrying his load, Tom picked his way through beds of herbs until he reached the back of the cottage. At the bottom of a long vegetable plot he passed the goat pen. The nanny and her kid stopped chewing on a pile of cut willow branches; their slotted bronze eyes watched him open up the hen-run. Once he had made the poultry comfortable, he sat behind the henhouse, out of sight, and opened his pack. Gathering his coins together from their various hiding places, he counted them out on the top of a flat stone: he still had eighteen sovereigns' worth. He split the coins into two parts. One part he tipped into a leather pouch and the other he divided and concealed about himself. Some of the sovereigns and two gold angels slipped easily into the little bag Rachel had given him to hang around his neck. Putting his nose to its opening he breathed in a faint hint of roses. Eyes unfocussed in thought, he tightened the drawstring and dropped the bag inside his shirt.

He joined the women at the table. Through tendrils of steam from the ladled-out broth, he peered across the table into Mary's wide eyes. Her voice trembled. 'What are you going to do?'

'I'm crossing into Durham to find a man who lost a gold ring in the mire. I found it, you see, and I should take it to him soon. I'll go early.'

'What about the mustering?' Mary said.

'I've told thee! I'm not joining the Warren's militia; they're not having me at their beck and call any more. So I can't stay here. I'm sorry.'

'When will you come back?' Hilda murmured.

'I'll be back for you - when times settle. I've got a bit of money now, so I'll try to set up somewhere in Durham. I'll breed heavy cattle and drive them south to market. I've met the drovers from the Tyne and we got on well. They're strong, free men and I aim to join them.'

Agnes tapped her wooden bowl with her spoon. 'Now then! It'll take money to do all that. Will you have enough?'

'Enough for a small start. First though, I'll find drover's work and save hard. I want you to take this for looking after Hilda.' He passed her some coins.

'Had away with ye, lad; I don't look for wages. Anyway - if you reckon to buy kine, you'll need every penny.' She pushed the coins back to him.

He touched Mary's hand. 'You've got a good grandmother. You can look after these coins for me and I want you to use them if times get hard. And, Hilda, this is to pay your way till I come back for you.' He passed her a leather pouch.

She closed her hands around it. 'Oh, Tom! I keep thinking it's all a bad dream. I don't like you fleeing alone - I'm coming with you!'

'You can't. I need to move fast and you're not fit. I'd best be gone soon after cockcrow. It's low tide around first light and I must reach the ford by slack water if I'm not to wade up to my chest. With all that rain last week the river's in spate.'

Mary got up and, lifting the lid of a wooden kist, pulled out a garment.

'Try this on, Tom. I've knitted it for you.'

He pulled the kersey over his head. It had enough fullness for his arms to swing with ease. 'This is grand. I can feel the heat in it already. It's a fine colour too.' He examined the wool; it had the uneven, reddish tan of a woodland floor in autumn. 'I can be invisible in this whenever there's need.'

'I spun the thread myself. It's dyed with tormentil. It's got a hood to keep the wind out of your ears; pull it up, let's see how it looks.'

'Canny! This'll keep the chill off. It's light on the shoulders too. If I'm not careful the fairies will have this off me. Thank you, Mary.' He leaned across the table and gave her a quick kiss on the lips. Her cheeks coloured up like sweetbriars.

Agnes Humble watched the two youngsters, her eyes growing distant and her whiskery mouth ever more pinched.

Tom worked outside for the rest of the day, mending fences and clearing drains around the cottage. The women had arms coated in flour as they baked for his journey. That evening they sat around the fireplace talking things over. Agnes gave him the names of families she knew across the river; she had relatives in Durham City and others in Hartlepool. Even though years had passed since she heard news, she urged him to call on them should he come close. They took to their beds only when an owl hoot sounded from the roof ridge.

He woke, fully clothed, before the embers of the fire. A strange silvering filled the cracks of the cottage door. Outside, a full moon bathed the land flat. From the hen-hut a cock crowed once; over the still fields came a faint challenge in response. He pulled on his clogs then built up the fire beneath a pot of porridge. Meg wolfed down a bowl of yesterday's broth.

Tom stirred the pot and the room filled with the smell of simmering oatmeal. He flinched as arms wrapped around him from behind. It could only be Mary. He twisted around and held her close.

'Please come back soon, Tom. Don't forget me.' The whites of her eyes showed pink, and beneath the shawl her softness yielded. He breathed in the scents of her forehead and cheek. Her warmth crept through his breeks as she pressed her thigh against his own and he fought to control his senses, even at that bleak hour.

Hilda, muffled inside a sheepskin, shambled into the room yawning. She took in the scene and hurried outside into the moonlight. Agnes's regular snores in the back room faltered and stopped, she muttered in her sleep then coughed a few times. A plaintive call came from her bed-place, 'Is the whole house awake? It's still black outside. Badger's not gone home yet.'

They clung to each other in the firelight, whispering until they heard Hilda's return. Mary flicked her tongue between his lips then stepped back.

Wrapped in a shawl Agnes shuffled, stiff-jointed, into the room. 'I can smell that porridge starting to set on.'

Mary unhooked the black pot. She filled a bowl, stirred in a knob of butter and covered it with goat's milk. With rapid movements Tom spooned down the porridge in the hope it would calm his stomach. After wiping his soft moustache, ignoring the women's fuss and worry, he made ready for his dash to the river. He set his jaw firm and, handing the longbow to Agnes for safekeeping, shouldered his pack and picked up his staff. With Meg at his heels he ducked beneath the door lintel and out into the cool air. The women followed in silence for a few yards, then huddled together in the mild light to watch him go.

8

The Ford

The first rays of morning touched the dark Tees as Tom reached the riverbank. The state of the water caused a frown; a stiff wind off the sea had delayed low tide. He jumped from the bank onto the mud. The exposed strip of riverbed was narrow; it would be an hour before the ford was safe. He glanced around for a place to hide and chose the undercut bank where a waterlogged tree had stranded. Resting his back against one of the bleached limbs, he relaxed to watch the flow subside.

Meg's ears lifted as a salmon jumped and fell back with a splash. The spreading ripples broke up as another salmon flung itself into the air. The water heaved and a pair of nostrils surfaced, followed by a black head and two soft eyes. Jaws gripped the body of a struggling fish, its silver and red flanks flashing for life. The seal submerged. Just a trail of bubbles swept downstream.

The river smoothed again, except where it swirled around tangles of sunken driftwood. Eddies reflected the dawn sky and began to sparkle. A projecting fragment of branch framed the view of the water. A scrap of bark still clung to the gaunt limb. Odd, he thought, how the bark brought to mind his father's weather-beaten face. Staring past it, towards the shimmering current, images streamed through his imagination; the river was like the flow of memory. His eyelids drooped to filter violet light onto his retinas as the sun climbed higher.

He grimaced as he swallowed against the hard lump that built in his throat. Five months now, he mused; Dad, why do good folk have to die? He cradled his head in his hands and let out a sob. Meg peered into his face, whined then licked the tears from his fingers.

He ran a palm along the bitch's head and felt her shivers of pleasure. They both watched the flow, following the spins of twigs and leaves caught in vortexes. He narrowed his eyes again. The patterns on the water drifted to the edge of his sight as he moved into a trance. Against the blurred glints he had a vision of his tall father loping through heather with a lurcher at his side. Francis Fleck's broad-shouldered frame, wiry and strong, carried the spade and mattock as though they were twigs.

'Dad! Wait for me,' the voice came from somewhere within.

His father stopped for him, laughed and, with callused fingers, tousled his hair.

He heard new things on that first day in the hills. 'Run for twenty paces, then walk for twenty, that's the best way to eat up miles.' Like this, they walked and trotted across the rough ground.

'Dad! Rags is chasing a hare!'

They stopped to watch the hare streak across stony ground and through patches of knee-deep ling. The black lurcher bounded in a wild, zigzag pursuit over the purple glow of the moor. Here and there a grouse catapulted upwards crying out, *'Kok kok . . . kok kok kok.'* The chase ended with a squelch when the hare swerved to skirt a patch of green bog and the dog's long legs failed to stop. Rags crawled out with mud plastered across his curly coat, the white blaze on his chest smothered. He hung his head and tucked in his tail for a moment, then galloped around them both, barking and rolling his eyes. Dad called out, 'Whisht, ye daft beggar, come here!' The lurcher slunk to his master's heel and lowered his tail. Rags managed to run down another hare before dusk.

They spent that night among tumbled boulders at the foot of a crag where a patch of bilberry made a soft bed. They lay under an old blanket with the lurcher between them for warmth and drifted off to sleep. About midnight Tom woke up feeling chilled. The cloud had moved away and the air had a face-pinching bite. The moon had set. He could scarce make out his father's shape in the starlight. Francis Fleck lay on his back with his hands behind his head and a faint glint in his eyes. Tom followed his father's gaze upwards. The sky soared; from horizon to horizon stretched a roof of stars.

Tom whispered, 'What are you looking at, Dad?'

'I'm watching the flashes of light, son. Stars keep shooting down like fiery arrows. Look, there's one, and another. They're all in the same bit of sky.'

'What makes them fly like that?'

'I don't rightly know, son. It's beyond me.'

'I suppose somebody will know. Isn't it summat to do with Heaven and suchlike?' Tom asked.

'Well, your grandmother Skerry had her own ideas. She reckoned those falling stars were bits of burning slag tossed at us by the old gods who get fed up of being ignored; red-hot bits from out of their forges.'

'That's a good story - I like that.'

'It is - though she'd sense never to tell it in front of the priest. And that's not all; can you make out that pale band running across the sky?'

'Where it's all powdered with stars? That's the Milk Road.'

'So it is - well said! Your gran used to call it, "The Road of the White Cow". She went on about how the souls of the dead travelled along it, on their last journey.'

'Is that true?'

'Maybe it is, maybe it isn't - who knows? She was a strange old body, my mother; she'd East Riding blood, you know, and they're a queer lot down by Holderness.'

'Why's that?'

'Oh, I don't know, son - it's just an auld saying. Folk thought her a bit elvish, yet still a canny soul. She reckoned her own granny had a big name as a wise woman - perhaps that's who planted the ideas in her head.'

'Wise woman? A sort of witch?'

'Some folk said so - but not me. She never used her skills for curse weaving. We seek out the wise women when we get ill or need a bit of advice. Now your gran's not here, Agnes Humble is the best of that kind outside Billesdale.'

Tom thought about wise women.

'Anyway, take a good look at the White Cow's Road. Mark where it is and, if you wake up in about an hour, you'll see it's moved - it turns slow and always from east to west. Now, let's get some rest.'

Tom snuggled deeper beneath the blanket, close up to the warm lurcher who uttered soft woofing noises in his sleep as his paws twitched. He breathed in the smell of dog and drifted into dreams of a white road. Along it, old women ushered giant white cows that walked with care, hindquarters swaying and nursing full udders.

At daybreak they began digging into a low mound. Francis Fleck took the mattock in both hands and chopped through the ling. Then he set to with the spade and dug into the peat until he reached a layer of stones. He now worked slower, cutting into tough clay until he had uncovered a small chamber. Except for traces of ash and bits of broken pot, it lay empty. He said in his soft voice, 'Someone's dug here before us, and a long time ago.'

On that day, they carried home just the hare as reward for their effort.

Tom remembered other trips: he grew older and strong enough to help with the digging. Sometimes, when they cut into a mound not dug before, they found spearheads, black jet and amber beads, and shining things that Dad reckoned were jewels. All of these small finds they brought home. Father took extra care not to disturb the clay vessels.

'We mustn't break these auld pots, folk's burnt bones are inside. They might even be our own kin,' he would say in a hushed voice.

Tom had thought about that. On one of the digging trips he asked, 'Do these bones mean we once lived up here, on top of these hills?'

His father scratched at his brown beard, with its glints of copper among a sprinkling of grey. 'Well yes - in a way. Though folk do drift around, you know, and get all mixed up. Our family has a tale that the first Fleck in these parts was a Scotchman who washed up on the sands at Redcar. He got off a wrecked ship and hand-fasted with a local lass.'

'A Scotchman!'

'So the story goes. He belonged Galloway where those shaggy black kine hail from. I know nowt else - it's just another of those auld tales. There again - look at our Hilda's red hair.'

'There's red bits in your beard, Dad.'

'Aye, so there is.'

One Sunday morning, on his fourteenth birthday, they rested on a crag top and looked down onto Swainby village where they could see tiny figures filing into church.

His father growled, 'There they go, creeping into church to praise God and thank him for the rotten harvest we had this year, thank him for the rain and wind he sent to smash down the barley. If he's anywhere about, it's not down there with them psalm-singers - he's up here in the hills.'

Tom glanced at his father, then at the sky. He shivered. We might be struck down - with Dad saying that. Francis Fleck saw the twinge of fear.

'I will seek succour in the hills, from where comes my help.' He gave Tom a reassuring wink. 'That's what the psalm says - or summat like that. I've a friend who belongs London - he can say it in Latin. We'll take a look in yon little mound and see if it's true?'

That day they found a golden brooch among some broken pots. His father reckoned it would help to keep their stomachs from rumbling when the snowflakes were flying. On the way down, the father looked back at the hill and said, 'Something tells me that mound's got more to yield up - I've a feeling about it.'

Francis Fleck arrived home from Swaledale, flat on a cart in winter. Leaving his wife and son in charge of the cattle, he had gone in search of wages in the lead mines. During a November storm, the workings flooded, props went soft and the roof collapsed. He lay trapped for a week among the bodies of other miners. When rescuers brought him out, he could not stand.

He had spent a month in bed. Agnes Humble treated him with poultices and herbal draughts until he recovered strength enough to work with the herd. He watched his urine every day, hoping for signs that the blood might grow less.

In December, Francis confided in his son, 'I'm going back to that mound where we found the gold brooch four years since, I reckon it holds more. Will you come?' Tom argued that his father had not enough strength, but his mouth was set into a hard line.

They waited for a day of drizzling low cloud when they could dig the mound in secret. Clear weather would paint them, like standing stones, against the skyline. Francis sat on a rock in the clinging mist and, grey-faced, stared at the burial mound. His eyes closed and his face softened. Not for the first time Tom watched his father fall into a trance.

'What were you doing, Dad?' he sometimes asked.

'Letting my head go quiet. That way you can get to know the way of things better.'

'How's that? If you've stopped thinking?'

'It's the heart, Tom. That's what folk should witness; the heart knows things that the head never sees. When the head stops its babbling and its chattering you might listen carefully, for there's another voice that speaks very quiet. That voice is who you really are; it bides between belly and throat.'

Tom rested in the heather and watched in fascinated silence. He tried to stretch out his mind to share a little of his father's thoughts. There was something about a space - a closed space. In the background was a whispering that brought a shudder.

Francis Fleck got up and moved around the grave. At the eastern side of the hummock he knelt to examine the ground, gave a grunt, then parted the ling.

'We'll dig here. Let's work fast before we lose the light. We'll take care to do it the proper way. Stand up, son.' He faced the east and called out in a chant, 'All things that guard this spot, we beg you let us enter. We are your kin and need to take from here only because we have hardship.' He swung around to face south and chanted again; then to the west, and finally, to the north.

The dog growled and her hackles lifted. Tom had a rush of goose pimples and twisted his head in the direction of the dog's stare. Out of the corner of his eye he caught a quick movement, and another. His father looked up. 'What's the matter, son?'

'I think we're watched. I saw shapes scurrying about.'

'Aye, it's likely you did. You'll have to get used to that - you're one of us. Sharp as quivering hares are the Flecks. Like hares, we are in tune with the rocks and the trees. We've eyes and ears for things that other folk miss.'

Thud! The mattock bit into the short, wind-blasted vegetation. His father worked for a few minutes then straightened up, wiped his brow on his forearm and rubbed his left side. His face had grown pale.

'Tom, you take over for a bit. I'm not so good.'

He took the mattock from his father. 'Have a rest, Dad. Sit on that rock there. I'll cut the trench.'

'Good lad. You're looking for a table-stone. Go canny now.'

He swung the mattock and built up a rhythm with the heavy iron blade. It struck with a dull thud and soon he had severed the tough roots of bilberry and ling and got into the peat. Swing - thud - slice - pull. He saw his father give a satisfied nod as he relaxed to watch him work. Once through the peat, the mattock cut into grey earth. After a few more swings his rhythm faltered as the blade hit stones. The clay held the rocks in an ancient grip. He laid the mattock to one side and pulled out the stones by hand. After an hour, the cutting was waist deep. His father stopped him, knelt in the heather and stared into the trench.

'There it is!' He pointed at the end of the trench. 'See the big slab stood on end? We need to clear round it and lift it away.'

The next half-hour made him sweat until he had pulled the slab onto its side. Behind it, they found traces of a small chamber three feet into the clay. Other diggers, who had broken into the main chamber to the left, had missed the smaller space that lay off to one side - a little vault that had collapsed long ago.

The golden torque rested among decayed cloth wrapped inside rotted leather. Everything lay squashed together beneath a flat slab that once served as capstone to the burial place. His father wiped the dirt away in silence until a yellow gleam appeared. He gave a low whistle through his teeth, slipped the object into his bag and whispered in reverence, 'We thank you - we thank you.' Grunting, he pulled himself up. 'Right. That will do for today - let's get off home.'

Two weeks later his father lay dead.

Meg's wet nose dabbed his cheek. Tom rubbed his face, blinked, and saw that the river level had fallen. The dog's brown eyes were staring fixedly into his own. He reached towards her, then froze as hooves thudded somewhere to the rear. Above him, on the bank top, the flag irises rustled and hissed. Seconds later an otter landed on the mud a yard away - for an instant it fixed him with a look of terror. Tom caught a glimpse of blood on its face before it bounded into the river and sped off downstream. He heard the panting of dogs and the snapping of twigs. Two slavering black hounds plunged down the bank and hurled themselves into the water to follow the otter. Moments later a black stallion jumped from the bank top, hitting the mud a few feet away. The horse stumbled but its rider, gasping a curse, heaved on the reins and held his balance.

'Pox it! Where's my otter?' Mark Warren yelled at the river. He saw Tom sheltering beneath the bank, and scowled.

'What are you up to, Fleck? Poaching again?' he yelled.

'I mind my own business.' Tom got to his feet.

'Don't take that tone with me!' Warren raised his riding whip. Tom's grip on his ashwood staff tightened. Holding it with both hands across his body, he took up a defensive stance with his right foot forward.

'So the muckman wants to fight, does he?' Warren snarled and spurred his horse forwards, lashing out with the whip. Tom stepped to the side and fended off the blow with his staff and, without intention, caught the rider's hand as he rode past.

Warren wheeled his horse and sucked on his bleeding knuckles.

After spitting out blood he shouted, 'That will cost you. I'll ride you into the mud.' He spurred forward again.

Tom nestled one end of the six-foot quarterstaff beneath his armpit and held it like a lance. With the horse a few strides away he stepped aside. The end of the staff caught the rider in his belly with a force that threw him out of the saddle. Tom staggered backwards under the weight of the impact. The horse dragged Warren for ten yards before he could free his right foot from the stirrup. He struggled to his feet, his fine hunting coat and the back of his head plastered with mud. The horse was a hundred yards away and still running.

Warren reached for the scabbard at his waist and drew out a short-sword. This time he kept a cold silence and advanced with the blade levelled. Tom backed away until he found his boots submerged in river water. Meg leaned against his right leg, teeth bared and snarling. Warren stepped closer, slashing the air with the sword. Tom shielded his body with the staff and retreated deeper into the river. Meg launched herself at Warren's calves as the sword swung down. She fell away with a yelp.

Tom backed further into the river until it pulled at his hips. Losing his footing in the soft bottom, he staggered. Warren swung his sword. The knight's son stood four inches taller and, for a moment, Tom's heart quailed at the sight. He parried; the sword bit a lump out of the staff then skidded along its surface and onto the fingers of his left hand. Gasping, he fixed on Warren's eyes, trying to read his next move.

The man sensed victory. 'You're about to get your first bath. You need it! You stink like your sister!'

The first blow from the quarterstaff thudded onto Warren's wrist and the sword flew into the river. The staff swept around again and the second blow smashed into the right upper arm crushing the muscle. Warren's genitals took the full force of the third blow as the end of the staff thrust forward. He collapsed into the water with his mouth open and face twisted.

Tom leapt on him. The man wriggled like a conger eel. He held Warren under water until he saw bubbles erupt from the clenched mouth. He grabbed the man's collar and heaved him up, yelling into the dripping ear, 'I'm free of you! Think on this day before you curse another labourer!'

'I'll kill you for this, you fatherless turd,' Warren spluttered, even though the cowman still gripped him.

Tom stiffened, released his hold, took a pace back and raised the staff above his head ready to smash it across the man's skull. Mark Warren locked onto Tom's eyes and flinched when he saw the fury in them.

'No, don't! I'm sorry. Please! I'll give you gold.'

Tom lowered his staff. 'Keep your gold. It's shit. Now get off home.'

Mark Warren staggered out of the river, squelched through the mud and clawed his way up the bank. Tom followed and watched from the bank top as the man limped away clutching his right arm.

After fifty yards, Warren raised a fist and shouted, 'Just know that I'll kill you for this, Fleck!'

Tom turned away to look for Meg. He discovered her cowering beside his pack in the shelter of the stranded tree, her face matted with blood. Hands trembling, he picked her up and carried her to the river. In washing away the blood he saw the mangled state of her right ear. Partly severed, half of it still hung by a thread of skin. She squealed as, with a decisive slice of his knife, he cut it free. On the bank, he found moss to staunch the blood and cover the wound. From his spare shirt he ripped off a strip of linen and bound the shivering head.

'There now, lass - though you look a bit daft, it'll soon heal. Thanks for helping me out.'

He straightened up at the sound of a voice calling him. 'Tom, wait.' Mary Humble ran along the bank, her yellow curls bouncing on her shoulders. She held his longbow.

'I saw you fighting with Mark Warren.' Her eyes widened. 'You're bleeding!'

Tom raised his left hand. He had forgotten about the sword wound. Now he winced at the pain and the sight of blood pouring along his fingers.

'Let me see that,' Mary exclaimed. 'Oh! It's your first finger - it looks nasty. Can you move it?'

Tom flexed the finger a few times. 'Aye, it works fine enough. By Hell it stings.'

'Wash it in the river. I might have to stitch it up.'

Blood streamed away from his hand like a veil in the river water. Mary rummaged in a bag and brought out a threaded needle.

'Right, give it here. Ah! It's not that bad - it's not down to the bone. I'll make two stitches: that should fettle it. I'll try to make a proper job of it like Gran taught me.'

After stitching together the severed flesh, she produced a tiny pot of ointment and smeared it into the wound. 'The yarrow in this will help the blood to clot.'

Tom examined her work. 'That's neat - and you've kind fingers. Agnes taught you well. Thanks. Why have you brought the bow?'

She handed it over together with a bag of arrows. 'You rushed off in such a hurry we hadn't time to think straight. There's needle and thread in this bag and your bowstrings as well. There are some other things from Agnes, potions to drink in case you get sick, balm for wounds and cloth to bind them. Agnes reckons you need to carry your bow if you're going to the North. And see - she's right! All you've got is that staff and you've been in a fight already.'

'Yes, I'll take it. And thank her for me, please. Will you have a look at Meg's lug?'

They unwound the bloody strip of shirt from the dog's head.

Mary tut-tutted as she examined the remains of the ear. 'Well even though you've done all right, I'll coat the wound with balm to stop it going bad. There now, that's better. Yarrow, honey and a few other things - Gran swears by her mix. We'll wrap it up with clean cloth, as well as your finger, and it'll be right.' Meg's drooping tail gave a few limp wags.

Tom took Mary's hand and led her to his seat on the stranded tree. They discussed his fight with Mark Warren and Tom voiced his anxiety that the Warrens might take revenge by punishing Hilda.

'I don't think you need worry about that, Tom. Folk reckon he's off with the militia tomorrow and we'll not see him again for weeks - that's supposing he's in a fit state to travel, after you clouted him with that staff.'

Tom got up. 'Look at the water! The tide is on the turn - I need to cross now.'

They hugged and kissed. She handed him a lock of hair tied with a ribbon and stroked his cheek. 'Goodbye, my sweetheart - keep this with you. Please come back safe.'

9

Runaway

With the longbow slung over his shoulder and Meg under one arm, Tom felt his way across the ford. The peaty water swirled around the top of his thighs as he probed for sunken flagstones with the quarterstaff. From the Durham bank he waved to Mary, then took a broad way that cut through salt-flats. He sensed her raising a hand from time to time as she watched him recede. He turned to give one last wave, and strode on.

The spongy track meandered for a mile between channels deep in ooze. Redshank rose up along the margins with piping cries. Floating on the tide a pair of swans hissed at him. Close by, two men laboured to spread fowling nets. They stared as he hurried away to firmer ground.

Despite living close to its edge, he had never crossed the Tees. His family's roots were to the south - in the dales that cut through the moors. This was a flat land with small fields enclosed by thorn hedges, broken up by bits of scrubby common. Crowds of black bullocks closed in on him; at his yells they stamped away with snorts and rolling eyes.

Except for a thin spinney of ash, the land lay naked. He stopped to look back southwards where the Cleveland Hills swept from east to west until they ended in cliffs by Osmotherley; then came Northallerton Gap, that level stretch of ploughing land he knew so well. Further west ran the blue outline of the high fells where his father was crushed. From those Swaledale diggings, yet more rounded fells marched northwards along the western horizon until they faded grey - 'all the way to Scotland', the drovers had said. Before him was open sky and, off to the right, not ten miles away, would be the sea.

After an hour, the empty drove road merged with a broad village street. He strode across wheel ruts, cowpats and trails of sheep droppings, aware that eyes watched from dark cottages. A pack of curs, scavenging a midden, left off to rush forward, howling. Meg took shelter around his ankles until he drove the dogs off with sweeps of the staff.

Ahead, a ragged-looking girl struggled to drive a skittish cow and calf along the street. He trotted up to her and helped to get the animals onto a patch of common land.

'Thanks for helping with the beasts. Where do you belong?' Her voice was thin.

'South of the river.' He noticed her bare feet and the sores on her legs and thought: she looks a bit of a wreckling. 'Is this Stockton?' He sat under the hedge and opened his pack. 'I'm going to have a bite, would you like to share?'

'Ooh! I would! I've not had breakfast. And yes, this is Stockton.' She sat opposite him and pulled her grubby shawl tighter around her shoulders as though to hide her threadbare frock. They both bit into chunks of egg pie, chewed and stole glances at each other. 'You and that dog look like you've been in the wars. Where are you both gannin so early of a Sunday, all swollen-faced and bandaged up?'

Nearby a blackbird burst into song. 'Hark at that merle,' Tom tried to steer their talk.

'My lugs are a sharp as yours.' She wrinkled her small nose at him. 'So, stranger - what are you doing coming through Stockton at this hour? Is it a secret?' She choked on a piece of crust and coughed. He listened to her chest wheeze and rattle, and waited for the spasm to pass. She wiped her eyes with the back of her hands. 'I've not a strong chest.'

'I'm seeking two gentlemen who ride black geldings and are with foot soldiers. Did they pass through here?'

'Oh, those two - they were dressed in money. Aye, but this pie - somebody's a good cook. I saw them late on Wednesday, headed for Norton in the dark. They could be anywhere by now if they'd kept on. But our smith got called to Norton to nail new shoes on their hosses - Norton's farrier is badly this week. He said they'd stay a night or two at the big house. I know nowt else. What's your name?' Her eyes glowed beneath long lashes.

'John Smith.' He glanced away.

'Well, John Smith,' she smirked, 'I'm Henry Tudor. Thanks for the food. I must away now. I've jobs to do. I'll see you again?'

'You might well do. Will you take this penny as a gift, Henry Tudor? Your picture's on it.'

They both laughed. Tom yielded to the urge to give her a hug. She gave off the smell of cattle and milk, like himself.

'I'll treasure it. Thank you kindly. Now, as king, I shall have to knight thee. Kneel, John Smith.'

He bent on his right knee before her and she tapped him on both shoulders with her cattle stick. 'Arise, Sir John of Pie!' They jumped up giggling. To Meg's barks, they held hands and spun around in a dance until the girl began to cough.

She wiped her eyes. 'I'd best be off.'

They touched hands, lingering for a few moments before turning away. After a hundred yards, Tom stopped to look back. She stood watching him. She gave one wave then slipped behind a cottage.

A pair of willows fluttered in the breeze by the edge of the duck pond on Norton green; Tom cast off his load and flopped down beneath the tallest. With his back against the trunk, he half-closed his eyes to watch the front of a plain little church and listen to the sounds that drifted through the open door. After a few notes from a warbling instrument, a high voice commanded it to cease. The voice droned on, in a language not English.

Meg nudged his arm. Her eyes peered from beneath the bandage to give him a pleading look. He set the last of the pie in front of her nose and chuckled to see her swallow it in two gulps. 'You're a tough one, Meg - even though you look daft.'

His skin prickled as he sensed someone's gaze touch him. Beyond a scatter of tethered goats, a watcher was crouched beneath a yew. The figure got up and slowly approached.

The boy's voice had not completely broken. 'I'm sorry to trouble a body I've not met. You look to be travelling and I wondered where you're bound.'

Tom weighed up the slender build, smooth chin and clear eyes, then the faded green kersey, baggy breeches and stockings full of rents. 'Aye, I'm travelling. Who wants to know?'

The boy squatted on his heels in front of Tom and took Meg's offered paw. 'Well, I'm travelling too. I wondered if I could join thee - there's some rough men about.'

'What makes you think we're headed the same way?' Tom asked. 'And for all I know you could be one of those rough men yourself.'

'No, I'm not! I'm Peter Tindall from Whitby. I was raised by good folk.'

'Well that's a blessing. You're a long way from home, Peter Tindall from Whitby. How many years have you?'

'Fourteen, but I'm strong enough.'

'Strong enough for what?' Tom noted the callused hands. 'I see you're no stranger to hard work.'

'I'm a seaman,' Peter blurted out. He glanced over his shoulder and lowered his voice, 'I've jumped ship, you see. There were more kicks than I could bear.'

Peter poured out his story. His father was a hand on a wool ship. The cog had sailed a year ago for Flanders; she did not return. Peter's mother and his small sisters now struggled as a charge on the parish poor box. She had pleaded with a Whitby shipmaster to give her son a place in his crew. After climbing masts for six months on the cold Baltic trade, he could take no more of the mate's bullying.

Two days earlier, the ship ran into Hartlepool before a gale. After they anchored in the tidal harbour, the mate rowed ashore. He returned filled with beer and angry after coming off worst in a fight. Once aboard, he set to and beat Peter with a rope's end. The boy jumped over the side and swam for the shore where he fled through the salt marshes and sand dunes. Pausing on high ground at Hart village, he looked down on Hartlepool Slake spread out below and watched his cog settle onto mud as the tide ebbed. The gale had cleared the air and, to the south, the headlands of Yorkshire reared up, like the prows of black ships, all the way to Whitby. Unable to face his mother's door without wages, he had set out to look for work.

Tom listened, impressed. From his perch on the moor top, he knew the sea only as a shining, and sometimes foggy, mystery. Meg licked the lad's hand as he stroked her and told his story. She's taken to him, Tom thought, perhaps he'll be all right to have along.

'I don't mind if you stick with us for a bit.' Tom fixed on Peter's steady grey eyes. 'You seem a useful lad. We'd best see how we get on though. I'm Tom Fleck from Thornaby way.' He held out his hand.

Peter straightened his back, took the offered hand and shook it. 'I'm pleased to meet thee, Tom Fleck,' he said, this time in a voice pitched a bit deeper.

They finished off Tom's oatcakes while watching worshippers drift out of the church. The priest waited by the doorway making a fuss of the well-dressed while ignoring the labourers. An old man kept tugging at his sleeve. Eventually, just the two of them stood at the entrance. Tom strained to hear their words.

'My grandson's baptism is in that book, I saw it writ down. Somebody's ripped the page out and I want it put back.'

The priest backed away, wrinkling his nose. 'I know nothing about that. The deed was done before I took charge of this parish.'

'There wasn't a book before you came. The bishop ordered that book kept only a few years back - while you were here - and you know it!'

'I keep telling you this is not a church matter. I have no interest in your ancestry. My sole concern is your fitness for the world to come. About your grandson's lineage, you must speak to the heralds. Now is a good time - they are travelling in this County Palatine.'

'Horse-shit, priest! Pure steaming, claggy horse-shit! You ripped that page out. I'll be talking to the bishop.' The old man limped out of the churchyard, grumbling.

Tom approached him with care. 'Excuse me, sir. I'm looking for two gentlemen on black horses, they are with some soldiers. Would they be the heralds?'

'Heralds! Everyone wants to see the bloody heralds! What do you want wi' them? They're nowt but a set of bloodsuckers, the whole crowd. They come here, eat, sup and bed, then pay nowt, and strip five pound off any man who wants his family arms set down.'

'Thank you, sir. Can you tell me where to find them?'

The old man shouted, spittle shooting out of his mouth, 'They were up there, in Norton Manor - you can see it, ower in them trees. Then they cleared off north on Friday. Idle, grasping pirates!' Muttering to himself, he scuffed slowly down the lane.

Tom wiped a hand across his brow. 'I'm going to find them, Peter. Do you want to come? We could face a few miles.'

'Yes, I'll come - a bit of the way at least - till I get work.'

After a hundred yards, the village ended at a high bank that stretched along one side of the road. A clogged ditch fronted the bank; the once impressive earthwork had decayed into an overgrown slope of spear thistles. A wall of dressed stone stood further back. A few paces beyond, an arched gateway pierced the wall. Its keystone carried a carved shield with a central cross and a lion in each corner. Beneath the arch, two great gates stood open. Through the entrance they could see a big house with eight stone-framed windows. The windows shone with many small panes held together by lead strip. Smoke rose up from one of three brick chimneys.

'Look at them oak gates, Tom. There's a lot of fine timber in there.'

'There is, there is.' Tom's voice fell to a whisper. The gates reminded him of looking through another archway closer to home.

With his father, he'd passed the gates of Thornaby Manor many times. They might stop to gaze through the bars at the flower gardens. His father would grunt and pull him away. One time, three years ago, a fine lady moved about in the rose garden; she carried a basket and picked blossoms near to the gates. Seeing them, she waved and smiled before bending to cut another rose.

'Come on,' his father said, 'let's get to the barley.'

'She was friendly to us, Dad.'

'She can't ignore us, not when she shares your blood.' They trudged on, towards the barley field, scythes over their shoulders.

'She's Lady Alice isn't she? Sir Edmond's wife. How's she got my blood?'

'Through Marmaduke Weastall - that woman's sire, he was cousin to your mam. By rights, Lady Alice is your second cousin.'

He gaped. 'So we're her kin? I'd heard we owned a bit of land once,' Tom said, 'Mam told me.'

'That's right. Your mam's family ploughed a few acres the Weastalls gave them. The manor took them away - said they'd no right to the fields.' His father coughed and spat.

Peter nudged him from his musing. 'Here's a rider.' A horseman clattered along the gravel track from the house.

'If you're looking for work, you can clear off - we've no need of labourers,' he shouted as he rode past, turning his horse towards the village.

They made finger gestures at the rider's back, and set off walking.

Peter asked, 'Who are the men you're seeking - and why?'

Tom chose his words with care. 'One of them might be a herald. He dropped a ring on Wednesday and I found it in the mud. If I take it to him he might give a reward.'

'What's a herald, then?'

'A herald? From what old Agnes told me last night - she's a wise woman where I live - the heralds come up from London sometimes, to visit the big houses. They stay a few days here and there and all the gentlemen in the district have to visit and get their names set down in a book.'

'Why's that?' Peter asked.

'That stone shield over the gate back there is a coat of arms. Only rich men have them. The one at Thornaby Manor has a chequer-board on it. When the rich man dies the arms pass to his son, and then to his son and so on.

'That might have summat to do with that daft auld man shouting outside the church,' Peter said.

'It could well have. Agnes says the heralds keep a check on men to make sure they don't use arms falsely. There could be twisted dealings going on around here. The heralds are supposed to keep it all in order and they make a charge for doing it.'

'Can I see the ring you found?'

'Best not. I've got it well hidden.'

The road veered left. After two miles of walking in bright sun, a raft of rain cloud slid in from the southwest. The track began to bounce with hailstones and turned white in seconds, so they ran, stooped and laughing, to the shelter of a huge oak. They leaned against the trunk to listen to the hiss of hail in the leaves overhead. A plump woman soon joined them. She put down her basket and flopped onto a dry spot, out of breath. Straight away, they got the whiff of warm food. 'Oh, I'd not expected this when I set out,' she said. 'Where are you two gannin? That's a queer looking dog - has it got a headache?'

'We're looking for work,' Peter said.

'Well there won't be much in these parts until the hirings. Mind you, I hear they're calling out the militia - that might free up some places.'

'Who's calling it out round here?' Tom asked.

'Herdwick Hall - the big house at Sedgefield. Sir Hugh Blakiston has the manor now. I doubt if he's going though, I hear he's not too well. He's had his ups and downs with them at the top, though he seems well in favour today. The heralds are staying with him and are calling in rich folk to have their records checked.'

She had interesting gossip so they let her talk on. They learnt that Herdwick Hall stood ten miles further up the road.

'Have you any food to spare, mistress? We can pay for it.' Tom nodded at her basket.

'Well now, it's Sunday and I know I shouldn't do selling.' She dropped her voice to a whisper, 'I do have a couple of mutton pies. They're big ones mind, fresh baked and full of goodness. I'd want a farthing each for them. I could throw in a bit of fatty bacon for an extra farthing.' She pulled back a covering cloth. Tom had to push Meg away; her nose crept forward again and lingered at the basket, a long strand of saliva drooling from her mouth.

'That's fine, mistress.' Tom counted out three farthings from his belt pouch and took the food. He gave the lump of bacon to Meg who slunk away to chew on it.

'Ee! You must love that dog. Why has it got its head wrapped up? Has it been down a badger hole and come off the worse for it?' She gave a gurgling chuckle. 'Mind you, that fat it's bolting down will soon fetch a shine to its coat. Well, sky's faired-up, I'd best get to my next call. Good day to you both.'

Tom broke a pie in half and shared it. Savoury vapours floated into their noses as they munched. Peter stopped chewing to wipe gravy off his chin. 'I'm eating thy meat. I'd feel better if you took this farthing in payment.'

'How much have you got, altogether?

'Two farthings - they'd not paid us for a month on that ship.'

'You keep a tight hold on them for now; I've enough to keep us going. You'll soon find wages.'

10

Sedgefield

By late afternoon, the slippery track had led them to Sedgefield, a thriving settlement of ancient houses that lined either side of a broad village green. A drove road cut through the daisy-sprinkled grass. Outside the church, a crowd of yeomen practised archery. Drawing back six-foot bows they attempted to shoot arrows into a dummy made of old clothes packed with straw. The two travellers perched on a stone mounting-block to watch.

Peter laughed. 'They don't seem too clever, they've managed one strike so far and that's in its foot.'

A bulky man in red doublet and hat stood apart from the crowd of farmers. He strode forward and raised his voice, 'I expected better! You've not kept up your practice. From that distance, each of you should bed three arrows in a man whilst he reloads his crossbow. That dummy should look like a hedgehog.'

A yeoman protested. 'We've land to till and drains to dig; we can't be playing at arrows all day.' Muttering came from the rest.

'All right! For the next few minutes I'll pay a farthing for each arrow in the chest of that dummy.'

The farmers pushed forward, jostling to take a shot.

'Don't be such oafs, one at time. Soldier! Keep them in a proper line!'

After a dozen men had loosed arrows, the dummy had one shaft in its thigh and two in its shoulder. The big man spat.

'Suppose he'd been a Scotsman! He'd have shoved his spear into you by now, even with those clothyards in him.'

Tom strung his bow and joined the queue of archers. Men stared at him with curiosity as he stepped up to the mark. After laying his arrow-sack open at his belt, he stared for a moment at the target. His face muscles relaxed as he nocked an arrow and drew back the yew bow. Without pause, he loosed off three arrows in quick succession. The crowd murmured in appreciation when the first arrow clipped the dummy's head, then cheered to see the second and third arrows thud side by side into its chest.

The gentleman approached. 'Fine archery! To hold steady that big bow with your hand in bandage is admirable. Where did you learn to shoot like that?'

'My father - he reckoned not to worry over much about aim. He said to just keep breathing while leaning into the bow stave.'

'Is that all?'

'No - he said you should always let the mind's eye see the arrow already in the target and then - loose.'

'Did he now? You can join us in the militia. You could help train this lot.'

'Thank you, sir. Although I've earned two farthings, I'll not be staying.'

The man laughed. 'I will pay them only if you are part of the muster. Now if you join the archers you'll earn five pence a day with an extra farthing for each mile we march. Alnwick is seventy miles. That could be eighteen pence extra you'd earn - just by travelling.'

Peter butted in. 'That's good pay and we need the work.'

'You'll get a smart uniform. It's a red cassock and brown breeches of good cloth. There's a patch to sew onto the cassock, it's white and bears the red cross of Saint George. I'll make sure you get an iron helmet to go with it - and we feed you.' He looked Peter up and down. 'You would fit into the ranks of my billmen.'

Tom touched Peter's shoulder. 'You must do what you think best. It's not for me.'

'Then I'll say farewell, Tom. You were a friend when I needed one. I shan't forget you.' They clasped hands.

The gentleman shook his head. 'A waste; you wandering the roads when you could be doing the king's work.' He narrowed his eyes. 'My voice has weight in these parts; if there's someone on your tail, I'd see you safe from harm.'

Tom considered for a moment before shaking his head. 'A fair offer, but I must make tracks.' He whistled Meg to his side and strode away.

Half an hour later, he arrived at a pair of tall and ornate gates. He peered through the bars to see a cobbled road running through sheep pasture. It ran arrow-straight for two hundred yards until it reached the threshold of a large house with fluted chimneys. A brick cottage, roofed with sandstone slabs, stood guard behind the gate. The door creaked open and a heavy man made his way over to fix Tom with a stare.

'Would this be Herdwick Hall?' Tom asked.

'That's its name, and there's no work.'

'I'm looking for the heralds who might be staying here.'

'And why would a raggy lad in worn-out clogs want to see the king's heralds?'

He met the man's eye. 'One of them lost summat important a few days ago and I found it in the marsh. I've come to give it to its owner.'

'I see. Well, the gentlemen at the Hall are busy. You can give it to me and I'll take it to them after supper.' He opened the gate and held out his palm.

'Thanks. I'll give it to him myself or not at all.'

'You're a cheeky young beggar, that's a fact.' The gatekeeper wiped his nose on his sleeve. 'Wait there while I let Sir Hugh know.'

He closed the gates in Tom's face, calling to a lad who watched from the door of the cottage, 'Jack! Look after these gates for a bit and don't let him in.' He set off at a rocking amble towards the house.

Ten minutes later the gatekeeper returned, wheezing behind a fast-pacing man-at-arms. Tom's stomach knotted as he saw the green and white uniform bear down on him; it was the giant from the marsh. The soldier halted with a stamping of feet, leaned on his tall bill-axe and gave a fierce look. 'Right, let him in.'

Once through the gate the soldier grabbed him, ran rough hands over his body and demanded, 'Name?'

'Thomas Fleck.'

'Fleck, eh? I see you've a bow - I'll take care of yon bag of arrows. Is there a dagger inside this jerkin?' He ran his hands under Tom's kersey. 'And what's in this pack?' He gave it a hard squeeze.

'Hey, not so rough!' Tom shouted. 'I've got a mutton pie in there.'

The soldier grunted. 'Concealed mutton pie, eh? And this dog looks a wild beast. Gatekeeper - we've got a dangerous man here, trying to gain entry with concealed pastry and a mad dog. Come on then, let's get you up to the house. Be sure to stick right next to me.

On the walk up to the house, he steeled himself. A door opened in the brick front and two men in red doublets and black hose appeared at the top of the flight of steps. He recognised the riders in the marsh.

The fat man's voice was sharp and high-pitched. 'I'm Thomas Tonge, York Herald. If you have something of mine, hand it over.'

Tom reached into one of the leather pockets Mary had sewn inside his jerkin. He took out the gold ring and, without a word, mounted the steps.

Tonge's eyes lit up as he recognised the Rose of York surmounted by a crown. 'This ring bears the seal of my office - how came you by it?'

'I heard of men searching the marsh near where I live for summat valuable that was lost. My dog, Meg here, has a good nose. I took her to the spot they'd raked about in; she sniffed it out in no time.'

'And you brought it across the river to me?'

'Yes, I could see it was special.'

'It is well that you did. I expect you're hoping for a reward.' He handed Tom a few coins from his pocket. 'There you are; be sure to buy a bone for that dog.'

Tom stared at the coins - they added up to two pence. Gulping, he averted his eyes and muttered, 'Thank you, sir.' He descended the steps.

The lean man broke his silence. 'Wait there!' He tugged at a foreign -looking, short beard and raised a finger. 'Young man, I like your honesty. What's your name? Do you have any skills?'

'Thomas Fleck, sir. Just a cowman, but a useful sort of archer, and I can run long distances.'

'Can you indeed? Well, I'm John Young, Norroy King of Arms. One of my men is ill and not able to travel, hence I can offer you his place in my service. Are you interested?'

'What is the work?'

'You would be helping with the packhorses. Later, if you prove reliable, you could also be a messenger. You would be paid four pence a day, with food and shelter provided.'

Tom's thoughts flashed at speed. This could be what he needed until he had a clearer sight of the future. Also, the job had travelling, there would be new things to see and he would be free of the Warrens.

'I'd like to work for you, sir - if my dog can stay by me.'

'Splendid. Welcome to my service, Thomas Fleck. You also, Black Meg of the Bandage - we will have work for you each time something is lost. Thank you, Sergeant Arkwright - please take the recruits to their quarters and see that they have what they need.'

On the way to the stables Tom asked, 'What do the heralds' names mean?'

'Well - Norroy means he's top herald north of the Trent River.

Norroy is out of the French, Nord Roi - the North King. His task is to record all men who bear coats of arms in the north, to make sure there's no cheating. There are very few gentlemen that can match his learning.'

'And York Herald?'

'He works for Norroy - looks after things this side of the fells. He rides out with Norroy when he makes his inspections around here - they're called Visitations.'

He took Tom into the stables. Four men sat on boxes and threw dice onto a stone slab. Another four snored amid a pile of straw.

'This is our new pony-man. The Norroy seems taken with him, so be sure to treat him right.'

'Any chance we'll get fed today, Sarge?' a sing-song voice grumbled.

'In about an hour. I've spoken to the kitchens; we'll have roast pork, turnip and kale, with beer to flush it through. You've no need to look hard done by.'

'We'll have to wolf it down quick afore the rats in 'ere have it off us.' The muttering came from somewhere in the straw.

'If you don't care for the comforts you're having on this trip, soldier, I can always get you posted to Calais where you can eat your dinner to the tune of French cannon lobbing lumps of iron into your gravy.'

'Sorry, Sarge. Only joking. I'm havin' a grand time - honest.' The soldier scrambled out of the straw and stood to attention in a haphazard manner. He had an ear missing and a squint in one eye. His hairy hands made an effort to shape his black beard. The sergeant gave a disdainful glower.

'Bold Riley, in which particular ditch were you born?'

'No ditch, sir. Born in a cave in Antrim, so I was.'

The sergeant pointed to Meg. 'This bandaged hound is also on the strength. She will make an end to your excuses for losing gear - 'cos she's good at finding things.'

'Hey, Sarge! Can she find us some women?'

'You'll find my boot up your breeks, Jones.' He stiffened his back and bellowed, 'All of you! Get yourselves smartened up ready for inspection before supper. Jump to it! Outside and in a line the lot of you!' Tom took a pace back, amazed; he had never heard such noise from a throat - it would have turned a charging bull.

Soldiers rolled out of the straw, brushing their jerkins and breeches with their hands and fastening buttons as they hurried into the yard where they formed a line. The sergeant paced along the rank, facing straight ahead while looking at them out of the corners of his eyes.

'Jones! Your knees are through those breeches - get them mended. Hardcastle, get your hair and beard trimmed and tidied up - you look like a rat peeping out of a pile of old rope. Bentley! That face hasn't seen water for a week - get washed, you dirty beggar. We march out early tomorrow. See to it that your kit is in order. Get the rust off those helmets. I want you clean and smart. Do it now! Dismiss!'

He raised a finger. 'Now, Fleck - even though you aren't a soldier, you're in my charge; you will be tidy at all times as well as obedient and respectful. Come and meet the other drovers.'

Tom followed him into another stable. Two men squatted on the ground among a pile of broken harness with awls and twine in their hands. The sergeant nodded to a wiry little man wearing a grey beard.

'This is Ben Wilson; he's the head drover and you do as he says. Ben, Tom Fleck here takes over from the man who's gone sick. You'll need to show him the ropes. Make sure he's got the right gear for the job. We take the road two hours after sunrise.' The sergeant spun on his heels and marched out.

Ben glanced over Tom's build. 'You look a useful body, what are you like with hosses?'

'All right. I've always done farm work.'

'We've got both Fells and Dales - have you worked them?'

'Never, but I hear they're quiet.'

'They are that; they're tough and they've a wise head. If a man treats them fair, they'll not fail him.'

Tom glanced at the sinewy younger man; he looked a couple of years older than himself.

'That's my son Rob, we always work together. We're from York - where do you belong?'

'Thornaby in Cleveland.' Tom relaxed.

Rob got up to shake hands.

11

Pack Ponies

'Up! You brace of snoring badgers. Up you get!' With pokes of his staff into the straw, Ben roused his drivers before dawn. Coughing and spluttering, the two young men plunged their faces a few times into a horse trough then carried nosebags of oats to the paddock. In the first gleam of morning, late owls still called from the vague shapes of towering elms. After a night of stars, the grass glistened with dew.

Six grey Fell ponies and two black riding horses jostled at the paddock gate and whinnied through plumes of condensing breath. The men fitted the bags onto the hungry heads. While the animals chewed on their rations, the drivers gave a routine check to thirty-two hooves. A hint of pink touched the eastern sky as a song thrush began its first repetitions of the day; moments later a blackbird joined in, and then others. The deep voice of the sergeant, calling out orders, silenced the dawn chorus.

When the drovers returned to the yard, a side-door in the main house creaked open. A cauldron of steaming porridge emerged from the kitchens in the arms of a buxom girl.

Rob ran across the yard and tickled her waist. She flew into giggles. 'Rob Wilson! You stop that, else I'll tip your breakfast among the clarts.' He took the great pot from her and she immediately stuck wriggling fingers into his armpits.

'Now you stop it, Annie, else I give you a seeing to,' Rob stuttered as he twisted about.

'Ooh! Like the other night, you mean?'

Ben shouted from the stable, 'That's enough of your daft blather. Fetch our oats!'

Two hours later the loaded ponies waited, roped in a single line. The heralds sat astride geldings at the head with soldiers on foot at either side. Ben took the lead pony, Rob guarded the third in line and Tom took up the rear with Meg at his heels, a soldier by his side. He grinned and winked at the gatekeeper who gawped as they filed onto the road.

After a mile of open sheep land the cavalcade joined a straight green-road heading north through a rolling country of cattle and grain fields. Under hawthorn hedges, bumblebees clambered among hummocks of clover and straggles of vetches, their droning becoming louder as the sun climbed.

The soldier marching at Tom's side had not spoken except for the odd grunt and grumble. Hoping for a change in the man's mood, he ventured, 'The road's good, we might be doing three miles an hour - what do you reckon?'

'Maybe we are, maybe we aren't,' the soldier mumbled. He coughed and spat.

Tom tried to make conversation. 'The cold bit me last night. Did you sleep all right?'

'Solid. Look here, lad, I've a throbbing head. Too much ale last night. Don't feel up to blathering. Right?'

'Right - sorry.'

The file of ponies bunched together as the leaders of the column stopped without warning - a leather fastener had snapped on the York Herald's saddle. From the doorway of a solitary cottage with bulging walls, an old woman appeared, leaning on a stick. A skinny brown dog rushed out from under her trailing skirts and barked at the soldiers. The woman followed the animal and struck it a blow with her stick, shouting, 'Whist! Howld thy gob!' The dog slunk away, growling low.

The saddle repair took half an hour. Laughter broke out; the sun had begun to warm the soldiers' spirits and two young girls had emerged from the cottage to flirt with the men. In the meantime the old woman had set up a brisk trade selling hot milk and new cakes to the travellers.

'Canny cakes, missus. They're sweet and you've a light hand.' Tom said.

'Aye! I make them with honey from me son's bees. They'll put strength in thee.'

Tom pointed to the herb garden. 'Have you owt for a man's bad head?'

'If ye means bad wi' the beer, a bit of crushed feverfew rubbed under the nose will help lift it.' She bent to pull leaves from a low plant covered in daisy flowers. 'Here, try this. Chew a bit of it, then be sure to take water afterwards.'

Tom handed the leaves to the soldier next to him. The morose man rubbed it between his palms and sniffed.

'By heck, mistress, that's powerful. I'll take a bit more. Have you got owt for fleas?'

'I've some little bags of dried tansy and some of fleabane that you can hide inside your clothes. The fleas can't stand those herbs - they'll soon shift themselves. They're eight for a farthing.'

Within a few minutes, the old woman had sold out of flea remedies - even the heralds made a purchase. As the party moved off, the two girls hopped about in the road, giggling and scratching at their armpits.

'How are you feeling now?' Tom asked the soldier.

'Better with that milk inside me.'

'I'm Tom Fleck from Cleveland; where do you belong?'

'Wherever I hang my shirt. I'm Skipton born - Alan Fuller's the name.' He gave a loud belch. 'Now that's better.'

'You a soldier long, Alan?'

'Seven years. Feels like many more though.'

'Have you had to fight?'

'Just the one time - in France.'

'Did you have to kill any Frenchies over there?'

'They had me shifting cannon about most of the time. By heck! You ask a lot of questions. Instead, why not tell me about the sort of lasses you like best?'

'Well, it's not as though I've given it a deal of thought,' Tom said, flicking a cleg fly off a pony's twitching haunch.

'Have you any sisters at home?'

'One - our Hilda.'

'What's she like - your Hilda?'

'Oh she's quiet, thinks a lot, does the milking and makes butter. She's two years older than me - she's twenty.'

'And what's she look like?'

'Well, she's got long hair that's wavy and copper coloured. Oh, and her eyes are green.'

'Green eyes! Copper locks! I'll wager they shine red and gold when the sun catches them?'

'They do. She has a lot of freckles mind - all across her nose and ower her cheeks.'

'By gum! And has Hilda got a young man she's sweet on?'

'No, she's not and I doubt if she wants one just now.' He broke off the conversation to adjust a pony's girth straps.

They continued at the rear of the line of packhorses, both in silence. Alan Fuller's face grew wistful as he thought of a freckled nose, green eyes and waves of red hair glinting in the sun. Tom grew tense as he remembered the women he had abandoned at Agnes's cottage. He slid his hand inside the kersey Mary had knitted and fingered the little pouch that Rachel had hung around his neck. Dark eyes and an oval face filled his mind. He breathed again that elusive rose-scent then smiled to himself - on both sides of the track a twenty-yard stretch of unkempt hedge blazed with eglantine that tumbled through hawthorn in a torrent of pink and white.

Five miles on, their route climbed to follow the contours of a long, low hillside. The track ran high above the valley floor to keep clear of standing water. Tom heard a half-forgotten bugling call and shielded his eyes to scan the bottom lands. Below the slopes shone flooded levels patterned with stretches of reed-mace. Across a dancing ground of short rushes a pair of slate-grey cranes bowed to each other like a couple at a wedding. Beneath their outstretched wings, two hatchlings tottered on new legs. His heart warmed to see them again. The cranes used to return each spring to the marsh near the byre, but he'd watched Mark Warren kill the last female while her mate circled overhead, calling.

Thickets of scrub oak and thorn hung on the valley sides except where craggy outcrops of buff limestone jutted through the trees like the skulls of giants. Gnarled junipers and yews clung to the face of these crags. A cloud of jackdaws whirled above a rock face shouting out staccato protests at the intruders. A bit like Whitestone Cliff, close by Thirsk, Tom mused, remembering a journey there with his father, to collect a bull for the manor.

The track skirted another limestone spur before diving into a side valley. The scene changed to one of spoil heaps of rock and shale. Scores of men toiled with picks and shovels, cutting tunnels straight into the hillside, or digging bell pits down into the earth. Nearby, where a stream, dark with coal washings, ran across the track, the Norroy called a halt. The soldiers eased their feet in the shade of trees, watching black-faced colliers at work.

'Look at that lot,' Rob blurted out, 'they look like Moors!'

'Hush,' his father whispered, 'they won't care for that. Them pit-men enjoy a scrap and I'm feeling too old for such today.'

A few oxcarts waited alongside man-high heaps of coal. Fresh hewn, the lumps gleamed like polished jet. Ponies toiled in circles around capstans that drove pulley wheels. Ropes ran from the pulleys into the ground. Ponies strained forward, ropes hoisted baskets of coal out of pit shafts and boys grappled with them to tip the black lumps onto heaps. Tom leaned over the edge of a pit to see, thirty feet below, men stripped to the waist swinging picks and shovels by candlelight. He grimaced at the reminder of his father's burial. He turned away, only to see a familiar figure by a loaded oxcart.

'Mister Swales!'

The broad back swung round. 'Why! Tom Fleck! It's queer seeing you in these parts. I'm back for another load at these new pits. They're drawing out hard coal, the sort that burns extra hot. Never mind that, though - what's brought you here?'

Voice just above a whisper, Tom explained his problem; then, 'I'm worried, even though it's only two days. You see, I've left my sister Hilda sheltering with Agnes Humble. Old Agnes knows your wife.'

'Agnes the healer? She does - my Ellen hails from your parts.'

'We are bound for to cross the Tyne, then north to a town called Alnwick. I've not heard of it until today. I wish I could get word to our Hilda.'

'No bother. I'll make sure she gets to know of your doings.'

'Tell her I'm fit and earning good wages. Say that I'll be back for her before the frosts come.'

'I will, lad; somehow I will. There's folk I know that trade Thornaby way. Hey up, it looks like your masters are making ready to go. Go canny up north; get back home before the snowflakes fly, and good luck.'

At noon, they reached Coxhoe, a hamlet of low cottages clustered around an alehouse. The heralds called a halt and stared up at the inn's crumbling chimney and mouldy thatch as the sergeant ducked through the low door into the kitchen.

He emerged, wiping his beard, and spoke with the heralds before calling the men together. 'Right! We've one hour of rest. You'll have meat and drink soon. Put the animals onto the grass behind the building.

'What we having, Sarge?'

'Mutton broth for a change,' the sergeant replied.

'Now there's a treat,' came a slow Welsh voice. Other voices broke in with baaing noises.

The sergeant laughed. 'Never mind; the ale's got bite and body, I've already tried it out for you, and rich smells are floating from the kitchen.'

The drovers each led two ponies onto the pasture. A soldier followed with the herald's black geldings.

'Let's get the packs off and peg them out to graze; let them ease their backs while there's a chance.' Ben gave a quiet grunt. 'Aye, you'll soon learn what we do, Tom. A man should always see to his horse afore himself - ' A rumble of thunder stopped his speech.

All eyes turned to the south and Rob groaned. 'We'll need to get a move on, look at those thunderheads; they're half an hour away and won't miss us.' Unnoticed, columns of cloud had risen to tremendous heights; at their summits, black masses spread outwards like anvils.

In the alehouse, seated on benches around plank tables, the men concentrated on eating. With much slurping they spooned thick broth, lumpy with barley and greasy with mutton, from wooden bowls. Fingers stroked along drooping moustaches and picked trapped morsels from corners of hairy mouths and gaps in irregular teeth. They burped, swigged ale and breathed in the vapours of fried onions. Outside, in the street, a group of ragged children with runny noses crowded around the doorway and stared in, wide-eyed, at the soldiers. Some of the girls carried smaller siblings wrapped in shawls upon their backs.

Although the air hung motionless around the hamlet, the rumbles of thunder grew louder and the light in the doorway dimmed. A sudden gust lifted the tattered skirts of the children. The rain began with a scattering of large drops that exploded in the dust around their bare feet. A brief flash threw the street into a sharp, colourless relief. For an instant, all movement froze. An ear-splitting boom followed in the space of a breath. The deluge dropped upon the street like a falling tree. Urchins shrieked and fled as the wind arrived.

Ben jumped up. 'This is bad! We'd better get them hosses and packs into safety. Come on, Tom.'

The two drovers plunged into the deluge, bent under the hammer of the rain; by the time they got to the horses, they were drenched. The watchkeeper, Rob, had already moved the packs under cover and now struggled to lead the scared geldings into the stables. The ponies seemed not to care, but steamed quietly and tugged at racks of hay. Ben and Rob Wilson, with hoods pulled up, ran to the alehouse leaving Tom to guard the packs.

A mess of old straw and last year's hay filled the rear end of the stable; Tom lay down in it to ease his tired body. Meg shook the rain off her coat and lay beside him. He closed his eyes and listened to the storm. After some time the thunder no longer crashed overhead, the deafening booms had become dull rumbles moving away to the north. There was a sneeze behind him. He sat bolt upright. Goose pimples shivered across his skin.

'Who's there?' The cobwebs and timbers soaked up his words. Apart from the drip of storm water, there was silence. Meg's hair bristled into a ridge along her back and her teeth bared white as her lips curled. She growled. Tom stood up to look into the gloom at the end of the stable.

'Who's there?'

Close by, a hay fork leaned against the wall. He grabbed it.

'Show yourself or I'll stick these tines into you!'

Hands trembling more than he cared for, he gingerly poked the heap of straw with the hayfork. Meg dived into it sniffing and growling. A shaggy head appeared in front of him, followed by two others closer to the back wall. Matted hair surrounded wild faces: strong, lined and hard looking. All had full beards and moustaches. One of the beards shone with the colour of red copper, like his sister's locks.

'Who are you?' Tom shouted.

'Only drovers like yoursel'.' The man with the red beard spoke in accents rich with a well rolled 'r'.

'You're Scotchmen!' Tom backed away towards the door.

'Aye, some might have it so. But it would be truer to call us Borderers - it's just that we come from the north bank o' the Tweed. There's no need to tell the sodgers about us, we're only trying to reach our kin. We'll pay you in English silver if you let us bide without bother.'

The three climbed out of the straw and shuffled towards him.

'Stay back,' shouted Tom, on the edge of panic.

'Whisht, man, we mean no harm. We're plain working men, same as you.' The red-haired Scotsman lowered his arm to Meg. 'A bonny wee dog.' She sniffed the thick fingers and gave a slow wag of her tail as the rough hand fondled her neck. He straightened up and took coins from his pouch.

'Here, tak these and let's say nae more about it.'

Tom stared into the Scotsman's blue eyes. A clear and direct look came back. He relaxed a little.

'You've no need to part with your money - it's no doubt hard earned.'

'You can be sure it is. Will we clasp hands, man? I'm John Elliot from Coldstream and these are ma brothers, Andrew and James.' He held out a massive hand towards Tom.

Tom gulped, the gooseflesh rose, but he took the hand.

'I'm Thomas Fleck from Cleveland.'

The man's grip tightened. 'Fleck, ye say? That's a good Galloway name. Och! It's good to meet you, Thomas. I can tell by your palm that you ken hard work like oursel's.'

'Why are you hiding?'

'There's trouble on the border again and we're in the wrong spot. If the sodgers catch us, I doubt if our bairns will see us for a good long spell.'

A beam of sunlight flared through the stable door and voices rose up from the road. They could hear Sergeant Arkwright giving orders. 'In your places! Comfortable beds in Durham Castle tonight if we're sharp about it!'

'Quick! Get back in the straw. We're leaving,' Tom said.

He rushed to the door in time to see the other drovers, accompanied by two soldiers, making their way towards him.

'The storm's passed. We need to get a move on,' Ben Wilson called out.

The soldiers hurried away with the riding horses as the grey ponies stood waiting for their burdens.

After the pack animals left, Tom closed the stable door while calling out to the straw pile, 'May all go well for thee.'

'What's that?' Rob shouted over his shoulder.

'Nowt! Just talking to the dog. Come on, Meg. Let's away.'

Tom gaped as the party breasted a last low ridge and the broad drainage of a watercourse the width of the Tees spread out below. The river glittered in the sunlight whenever meanders appeared out of the shrouds of woodland that lined the steep sides of the valley. Beyond the woods were patchworks of crop fields and broad pastures sprinkled with cattle and sheep. Farms and hamlets dotted the scene.

John Young raised an arm and reined his horse. 'There she is! Fair Durham City, in the embrace of the River Wear. Her cathedral church guards the bones of Saint Cuthbert and the Venerable Bede; pilgrims travel long roads to pray at the shrines. Kind fortune brings us here, we should approach with reverence. Best behaviour everyone!' He flicked the reins and moved on.

Ahead, on a broad hill protected on three sides by a loop of the river that cut deep into the landscape, stood the mass of buildings that made up the city. On a cliff top, at the head of the loop, soared the three towers of the great church and, next to it, squatted the Castle keep. Half-timbered, white-walled houses of two and three floors clustered around this mass of stone. Some leaned against each other like old men in need of support, others stood alone at the end of long gardens. A spider's web of streets radiated out from a central marketplace and cut through the whole district. Northwards, a mass of poorer dwellings appeared to jostle around a network of ginnels and yards. Tom had never seen such a town.

They entered the city across a stone river bridge and up a steep curving road lined with crowded houses and clattering workshops. A side lane opened into a broad, level space in front of the vast church. A monastery sprawled opposite and the curtain walls of the castle rose up along the right-hand side with the fearsome bastion of the keep at their rear. Tom stared upwards, astonished at the delicate stonework of the cathedral windows and their lattices of coloured glass that glowed in the slanted sunlight.

'Look at yon crowd, Tom.' Alan gave him a nudge. 'Them's the pilgrims come to pray and that lot in black are Benedictine shavelings.'

Tom's ponies were looking wild-eyed at rows of stalls selling food and trinkets to groups of pilgrims. They shied as a line of black-robed monks filed through the evening shadows and across the open space towards the church.

The heralds' column marched, footsore, through a gate in the curtain wall and into the castle forecourt. A captain greeted the gentlemen and escorted them to a house built against the ramparts of the castle. The soldiers and drovers led their animals around the central keep towards a line of low buildings that served as barracks and stables.

The sergeant addressed them: 'We've had a long day, brave lads;

make yoursel's easy. I'm away to see about supper. After we've fed, you can head into town if you want. But have a care, Durham City is wild at night - don't get drunk or get into brawls. We're here for about a week so I want your best behaviour - remember who you are, we must protect the heralds' dignity and reputation.'

'Do we get an advance on our wages, Sarge?'

'No, Dobson, you don't! The army pays out once a month. Next payday is Friday. Today is Monday!'

'I've no coin, Sarge.'

'That's because you fritter it away playing Evans at dice. This dice rolling will stop. I want two men to guard the baggage at all times; you two, Dobson and Evans, will keep the first watch.'

'Bloody hell, Dobson, now see what you've done,' groaned Evans.

'Settle yourselves, there shouldn't be a problem. In the army, if a man wins at dice, then those that lost can always ask him for a loan and he's bound to give it.' The sergeant fixed them with a glare, nodded, then marched away to the kitchens.

12

Durham

Two days later Tom decided to change his shirt. Its reek of Tees river water had caused Ben to wrinkle his nose. In pulling the patched linen over his head, Tom knew that his father's old garment stood in need of a wash. He peered at his bare chest - the bruises from the attack by street robbers in Northallerton had faded to yellow.

He gave a wistful sigh at the sight of the little pouch Rachel Coronel had placed around his neck. Now alone in the stable, he opened the bag and held it to his nose. It took his mind back to Northallerton, to that scented chamber in the Swan. He fancied he could see her again by candlelight around a table that held three goblets of red wine. He half-closed his eyes and, through the lashes, imagined her face framed by hair the colour of fresh-broken coal. Only now did he realise that the eyes that kept appearing in his dreams belonged to the Portuguese woman. He emptied the pouch into his palm. The two gold angels it held for safekeeping fell out - and something else, a tiny silver star with six points. One point carried a minute loop of silver through which a cord might pass. He turned it over and wondered at the skill that could fashion such delicacy. His palm shut fast when Ben stamped into the stable.

'I'm away to the market to barter for oats and get a bit of harness leather. You can give me a hand.'

'Right, I'm just about to heave a clean shirt ower me head.' He replaced the contents of the pouch, returned it to his neck and pulled on the shirt. Sensing action, Meg got up from her doze in the straw, yawning; the bandage had gone and, beneath the crust of dried blood, her wound healed fast.

In the street, a group of women surrounded them; linking arms to bar the way, they offered *soldiers' comforts* for pennies. The head drover pushed his way through, calling to Tom to follow. The women shouted after them with cries of, 'Any chance of a rub down off an auld hoss driver?'

Once in the crowded market they relaxed enough to exchange

banter with the stallholders.

'Fresh pork pies? Wi' runny herb gravy. Do you good! They'll lift your sneck!' A baker shouted.

'Just had porridge - anyway, me sneck's fine,' Ben called back.

'It'll drop again after the beer and then what'll she think?'

'She's eighty mile south - so no matter. We're off north.'

'You'll freeze up there! Have a pie - it'll keep your ribs clagged together.'

'I'm seeking oats at the minute.'

'Aren't we all?' The parting shot was lost among sudden yells from a row of meat vendors.

'Get that shite-hawk!' the cry rose up. Dogs of many colours ran around, barking. The red kite flapped aloft with a lump of stolen meat as a butcher's dog leaped and snapped its jaws shut inches from the bird's talons.

Ben grabbed Tom's elbow. 'Come away - this is Bedlam. Let's find the grain merchants.'

Leaving the head drover to bargain with the sellers of horse feed, Tom wandered off to watch a line of street performers at work. They spread beneath the walls of an inn, juggling with hoops and balls. A drum beat reverberated off the walls of the close-packed houses. He froze when his eyes met those of a hairy monster that reared up on two legs. A cage of iron muzzled its slavering jaws; the eyes had the dull glaze of a sick ewe. A leather-clad man jerked at the creature's neck from the end of a rope and poked its ribs with a stick, shouting, 'Hairy bear! Let's see thee dance! Dance to the drum!' The weary beast grunted, coughed and sat down to jeers from the crowd.

There was an odd pressure on Tom's head; he glanced upwards to a high window. It framed Rachel's face. She smiled and beckoned. He plunged through the open doorway into a beamed and panelled room. A stout, apron-wrapped man stopped serving ale and moved to block the way.

'Tom Fleck. I've come to see Mister Coronel. I'm well known to him.'

The man looked him up and down. 'Upstairs, turn left, left again and first door you see.'

Rachel stood at the entrance to a chamber, smiling in a halo of sunlight that came from a window behind her. Her glossy hair hung loose around her face.

'Thomas! Such a surprise! Come and greet Father.'

Isaac Coronel rose from his chair to grasp Tom's hand.

'Many welcomes to Francis Fleck's son. I had not expected to see you again so soon, Thomas. Come, be seated, have wine. Tell me what brings you to Durham?'

They exchanged news. He learned they were travelling to Alnwick Castle.

'That's in Northumberland!' Tom exclaimed. 'Bad men are riding the hills.'

'Yes, I am concerned. Even so, there is work for me in Alnwick. Lord Percy instructs that he wishes to speak business. He is an important man in this kingdom, I must attend him. I have hired good Lincoln guards to protect us.'

Tom gazed at Rachel for a long moment. When he turned back to Isaac, he knew the man watched him. His cheeks grew hot with embarrassment.

'Will you remain a driver of horses for others, Thomas?' Isaac asked. 'Perhaps, one day you will have your own string and become a trader.'

'Farming is what I know, Isaac. I could breed good pack-hosses and sell them to the traders - although it's kine I best understand.'

'And where would you farm?'

'The country I've travelled between the Tees and this town has the heaviest bulls I've ever seen. It is not too wet and the meadows sing.'

'And the meadows sing? How much would a singing farm cost in this district?'

'I don't know. I'll never be other than a tenant - unless I dig up a lot more gold.' Tom laughed at the thought of it.

'Gold is of no use unless it is set to work - at a proper rate of interest of course. Even so, a lender must consider security. A property bought at the correct market value becomes its own security - that is a mortgage. Perhaps I could help.'

Tom's mind reeled. 'I don't know about such things. I know naught about borrowing gold. My grandfather had land given to him - then taken away. My father lived as a labourer, like I do.'

Tom remembered the drover in the market below, drained his glass and moved to the window. He saw the top of Ben's head turning this way and that as he waited among the stalls.

'I'm sorry. I'm on duty, I must go.'

He remembered the pouch and lifted it from around his neck.

'Rachel, I've something belonging to you.' He emptied the contents into his palm and picked out the tiny star. 'It's a beautiful thing.'

Her eyes lit up. 'Oh! My Star of David. I thought it lost. This is precious. My grandmother wore it; she said it had great age. You kept it around your neck all this time?'

'Yes, even though I didn't know it.'

She met his eyes. 'It has protected you thus far - perhaps you should keep it.'

'No, Rachel, I'm glad enough to know you carry it.'

He said goodbye to Isaac. Rachel accompanied him to the top of the stairs. As they parted, she leaned forward and pressed her lips to his cheek. The warmth of her skin so close stopped the churning of his thought.

'I hope we will see you again, Thomas.'

On light feet, he descended the stairs with his face flushed.

In the marketplace, Ben squatted by a pile of leather. He glared. 'Where the heck have you been? I thought you'd deserted. Come on, we need to get this lot back to the stables and start work on it.'

'Sorry! I lost all track of time. I met some folk I knew.'

They carried the leather towards the quiet of the stables but found the castle yard crowded with armed men. They saw little sign of uniform. Each man wore whatever suited his usual trade: blacksmiths stood in leather-fronted smocks, farm workers coarse woollens and leather jerkins. Against the wall, looking lost, a group of tailors huddled together in linen doublets and breeches. A dozen men, wearing the clothes of shopkeepers, sat on a bench in the sun with shoulders drooping. Most others leaned against the walls or stretched out on the cobbled ground. At the far end of the yard, a group of well-dressed men talked earnestly. A broad man, with his back to Tom, faced a younger man whose arm rested in a sling. Tom stiffened when he recognised Mark Warren and his father, Edmond Warren, lord of the manor of Thornaby.

He slung the bundle of leather onto his shoulder to hide his face before striding across the yard and into the stable. Ben followed at a slower pace and dumped his leather onto a bench. 'Is summat bothering you? You shot in here quick when you saw that lot.'

'Aye, there is. That man with the bad arm. I gave it to him with a quarterstaff. If he finds me here, I've got trouble.'

Rob Wilson stopped brushing one of the black geldings to sit with them on the straw. 'The one with the badly arm stormed in here trying to order me about. He's full of himself - I don't like him. He upset the sergeant straight away. Sarge told him to bugger off. He told Sarge he'd report him. That bay stallion at back belongs to him. Told me I had to groom it. I said I didn't work for him and he should get one of his own to do it. He called me a bloody-minded serf.'

'I see,' said Ben, looking at Tom. 'Looks like we've a problem. I'll talk with one or two out there to see how long this lot's staying.' He sauntered out of the stable.

They rushed to a window to watch his progress. Half way across the yard, he met the red-faced sergeant striding back from the crowd of militia. Ben stopped and engaged him in quiet conversation. The exchange ended as Ben laid a hand on the sergeant's arm and said something that brought a laugh. Both men strode smiling to their quarters. Ben stooped through the door and settled onto a straw bale.

They could hear Sergeant Arkwright in the next stable talking to his soldiers.

'I want you men to take care around that lot of militia that arrived today. They're not trained soldiers - treat them accordingly. You are superior to them and I want you to hold your dignity. They've an officer who you might have heard me speaking a bit plain to. Well that officer isn't a properly trained soldier either. He's already crossed me and I can see he'll get a bad time off his men if he doesn't shed that cocky attitude. You're to keep out of his way; I don't want you getting into a tangle with him.'

'We could straighten him out for you if he's up the town tonight, Sarge.'

'It's good of you, Bentley, to offer your services. I'll deal with him in my own way. Best keep your working parts for when I need you, should we have a run-in with reivers further north.'

An Irish voice chimed in: 'One of them let slip they're going up to Berwick. Will we tramp with them part of the way, Sarge?'

'Riley, I'm glad to tell you we will not. They march out in the morning and we stay another four days. I hope you men are enjoying your holidays.'

'They are, Sarge! Goodness, they are! Since what you said the other day they're all after borrowing coin off me.'

'Glad to hear it, Evans. It's Friday tomorrow - payday - then you'll have it back.'

~ ~ ~

On the other side of the timber wall Ben wrinkled his eyes at Tom. 'So you hit the cocky gentleman with a quarterstaff, eh? Why do that?'

Tom told him about Mark Warren's treatment of his sister and of the fight at the ford.

'Seems it'll be best if you made yourself scarce until the militia clear out tomorrow. He could storm in here at any time,' Ben said.

'Thanks, I'll head into town and find a bed somewhere, if that's all right with you.'

'Do you have enough pence? I can lend you some - it's payday tomorrow.'

'I've enough, thanks. I'd better get off. Look after my things while I'm gone.'

He peered through the doorway. Perched on a box, Edmond Warren, arms akimbo, addressed his militia lined up in the yard. Tom pulled the hood of his kersey over his head and, with Meg at his heels, strode out of the castle.

He hurried to the marketplace. Now trade had slackened, the stallholders called out offers of bargains as he passed. Ignoring them, he hurried to the inn. The hanging sign showed a picture of a nobleman in black armour, along with words he could not read. He paused beneath the sign to straighten his hair and pull a few burdock heads from Meg's coat before going through the important-looking door. They passed through a room heavy with the smells of ale and food, filled with talk and the clatter of drinking and eating. He found the innkeeper in the kitchen giving orders to a plump woman.

'How much is it for a room tonight?' Tom asked.

The innkeeper's gaze ran over his frayed clothes. 'You can bed out the back and share with the others. You'll not want to pay for your own chamber.'

'Yes I do! I want my own and my dog stays by me.'

'Is that so? Well, although we're busy, there's one still empty.' He continued with a doubtful tone, 'Will you be wanting dinner and breakfast served in your room?'

'Er . . . yes. What's the cost?'

'If you're having all that, it adds up to nine pence for the room and food - this is Durham's best inn, you know. Ale and wine is extra. I hope that dog's well trained, you'll have to cover any damage.' Then in a firmer voice, 'And you'll have to pay in advance.'

'That's fine. Can I see the room?'

'Follow me, it's upstairs.'

The innkeeper's heavy feet brought no complaint from the oak treads and risers of the new staircase. He led the way past the door of the room where Tom had met Rachel and Isaac an hour earlier, then along a passage to a door at the end. Tom glanced around the room and thought it splendid, the equal of Isaac's. Handing the man two groats and a penny, he swallowed hard. 'This will do fine.'

'The chamber is fitted out for two guests, that's why it's a bit extra. You'll find everything you need in here. There's that pail of water, a dish for washing, a little ball of good grey-soap and a towel. If there's a chill, you'll find more blankets in that chest. Let me know what time you want your dinner; it's beef and leek pie tonight. Oh, and what name shall I set down?'

'John Smith.'

'Very good, John Smith. If there's anything you need, shout down the stairs for Betty.' He shuffled from room.

Tom tried the wide bed. Meg stopped exploring the skirting boards with her nose and jumped up beside him. He pushed her onto the floor.

'Get your black feet off my gentleman's bed - there's a bit of rush mat under the window for the likes of you.'

He rolled off the bed himself and took time to marvel at the comforts in the room. Two padded chairs stood either side of a square table. Beneath the window, a new-looking blanket-chest of carved elm made an extra seat. A cupboard stood in one corner; on opening the door the scent of new oak spilled around him. The cupboard would have to stay empty; he had not enough clothes to hang on the six iron hooks. He grasped the woollen kersey Mary Humble had knitted for him and, pulling it over his head, hung it on one of the hooks. Standing back to admire its rich tan dye he wondered what Mary would think if she could see it hanging there. It's a fine kersey, he thought, the colour of autumn. That reminds me, I'll need to get home before the sleet comes. It came to him that he had no home. All that lay in the past, he could not go back to the byre.

He had never stayed in a room with a glass window. This one had a thick tapestry curtain hanging at its side, embroidered with climbing plants. They reminded him of the woodbine in the hedges around the byre. Among the stems perched green and yellow birds of a sort he had never seen in the woods.

He tapped the glass with a fingernail. It had little bubbles buried inside it; he had seen ice like that. Beyond the window, row upon row of roofs ran downhill until they petered out among the fields. In the distance lay the river, spanned by a bridge. Oxcarts lumbered across in both directions; they would halt then lurch forward as each took its turn to move onto the narrow bridge, some going into the city, others leaving for the south.

A light knock sounded on the door. Tom lifted the sneck and opened it far enough to see Rachel. He opened the door wide and she rustled into his room.

'I heard you speaking with the innkeeper, Thomas. My chamber is next door.' Her eyes twinkled. 'Why have you taken a room at the inn?'

He flushed. 'It's only for one night.'

She listened to him speak of his anxiety now that the Warrens had arrived at the Castle. Twice she passed a hand across her right temple.

'I can understand. It seems Mark Warren is arrogant and a bully and you have humbled him. He will want his revenge - it is wise of you to show caution. Your life interests me, Thomas. Let us sit at this table; I would like to hear more.' Her words came in lilting English laced with soft nasal sounds. She stroked her temple again and knitted her brow.

'Do you have a headache?'

'Yes, sometimes a pain begins behind my eyes and moves around this ear.' She ran a fingertip around the top of her right ear. 'If I breathe in the vapour of the feverfew herb, it helps a little.'

'My family has a way of easing headaches with the hands. I could try it.' He stammered a little.

'Please.'

He moved around to stand behind her. Placing his hands on either side of her head, he stood in silence. She uttered a slight gasp.

He murmured, 'Close your eyes and let all the chatter and troubles in your head sink downwards into your middle and just feel yourself breathing.'

Spreading his fingers so that the tips surrounded her crown he pressed onto her scalp and mentally counted to ten. Releasing the pressure, he laid his palms on her temples and massaged. He withdrew and looked at her.

She blinked before her face relaxed. 'You have hands of fire. I felt their heat pour into me and now the stabs have faded. And I have not even asked why your finger is bandaged.' Her eyes took on a new shine. 'May we touch our palms together - like this?' She took his hands and placed them against her own.' After some moments with her eyes closed, she blushed and withdrew from the contact. 'I'm sorry - I'm foolish, I feel like a little girl. Now tell me about your life.' Her voice wavered.

'Oh, you've already heard about me; when I came to Northallerton and the wine freed my tongue, you heard a lot.'

She laughed. 'I remember that well, you came in smelling of the country and lifted our spirits. Father and I often speak about that evening.'

Tom looked away and muttered: 'I suppose I did smell of oxen.' He faced her again and his eyes flashed. 'Today I smell of horse! That's my life. I know who I am. I don't belong here.'

She stretched out a hand and touched his cheek. 'I don't belong here either; I yearn for Lisbon, where I lived a happy child amongst my own kind. They are scattered now, spread out, wanderers, all fists raised against them. There is no home, no friends, everything lost.' She blinked tears from her eyes.

He reached across the table and clasped her hands. 'I wish I could heal that loss.'

She stood up, took her hands away and moved towards the door. He followed her. 'Stay awhile, we're both lonely.'

She moved close to him. Her tears had stopped. She leaned forward and breathed him in. 'Ah - you do smell of stables. I had a little riding pony once, that I loved. I like it that you smell of horses.' She pushed her face into his hair, breathed in again and offered him her mouth.

His hands ran across the angles of her shoulder blades and down to her waist. She pressed herself against him for a moment then slipped out of his arms, saying, 'Father will think I am stolen away. Please join us tonight in his chamber for dinner at six-of-the-clock; it will delight him to talk with you again. Thank you for the laying of hands.' After straightening her dress, she departed.

Tom flopped onto the bed. He needed to close his eyes. Meg jumped up and lay down beside him to lick his face. He wrapped his arm around her rib cage and drew her close to his chest. He tried to hold Rachel in his thoughts but they wandered until Mary Humble's face floated before him, smiling. Behind her hovered the brown, wrinkled face of old Agnes, her blue eyes sparkling. While Mary's lips moved, her words stayed muffled and distant. His sister's face replaced the others - she took the form of a little girl peeping into his cradle. His father and mother stood with Hilda and peered down at him with twinkling eyes and happy faces. He grunted with contentment and pulled Meg closer.

13

New Clothes

He woke with a start and jumped out of bed. The angle of a sunbeam that slanted across the room told him he had slept for at least three hours and that the day grew close to evening. He splashed his face with water, pulled his kersey over his head and dashed downstairs with Meg at his heels. Drawing up the hood to cover his face he scanned the marketplace and headed for a clothes stall that stood opposite the inn door.

'Do you have a shirt to fit me?'

The man looked him over. 'I surely do. There's that handsome one in grey linen hanging up. The cost is four pence, but it'll last you for years. It's local made but that soft you'd think it were cambric.' He assessed Tom again. 'I see your breeks are getting on the thin side. If you don't mind my advice, I can do you a strong summer pair of brown ones for another groat and, to make a proper job of it, I'll throw in a pair of stockings cheap for another groat. That's you stood up in new clothes for just twelve pence.'

'I'll take them.' Tom gave the man a silver testoon. 'What time is it?'

The man passed him the clothes. 'It's coming round to six of the clock, I reckon. Can I interest you in a hat? I've some that will impress the lasses; folk are wearing this new style in London, I'm told.'

'No, thanks, these will do me for now.'

'I stock a few herbs to keep the clothes sweet and the moths away.'

Tom considered that and shook his head. He ran his tongue around his teeth. 'Herbs? What about herbs for a sweet mouth?'

'I've nothing of that sort.'

'Thanks,' he said, spinning around. 'Howway, Meg.' She padded behind him, back into the inn.

They had to wait at the foot of the stairs for a serving girl to pass with a pail of water. 'Could you do summat for me, canny lass?'

'Depends if my mother would mind, canny lad.'

'A mixture from the kitchen - a beaker of vinegar, a little spoon of salt and a good spoon of honey?'

She pursed her lips. 'Someone's a lucky girl!'

Minutes later, beaker in hand and a farthing poorer, Tom mounted the stairs to his room where he stripped off his stable clothes and poured water into the bowl. With soap ball and cloth, he washed all of his body to get rid of the sweat and dust of the last few days. Then, plunging his head into the bowl, he washed his hair. Enough clean water remained to rinse away most of the suds. In a small mirror of polished brass, nailed to the cupboard door, he checked his beard. Soaped and rinsed, the gold and red glints shone once more in the brown moustache and around the point of his chin. His beard was thickening up.

He thrilled as his body slipped into the new shirt and breeches, followed by stockings no one else had worn. He scrubbed his clogs in the soapy water, dried them and slipped his feet inside. In the light of the window, he admired the fit of his garments and thought them the neatest he would ever wear. A sniff under the arms picked up the smell of strong soap with hardly a whiff of the stables. Next, he poured some of the salt mixture into his mouth and swilled it around before rubbing his teeth with a corner of the towel until his mouth was sweet.

'How do I look, Meg?' The dog was stretched, head on her paws, across his pile of old clothes watching him; she gave a couple of slow flicks with her tail.

A light knock sounded on the door. Rachel stood outside. 'We are having dinner soon, please come - Father asks for you.'

Tom followed her to Isaac's room breathing in the sweetness that trailed in her wake.

'Welcome, Thomas.' Isaac stood to greet his guest. 'Rachel has told me the reason for your stay at this inn of the Black Prince. Come and sit at table with us.' Isaac's gaze dropped to Tom's bandaged finger. 'I meant to ask you about that when you visited this morning.'

'I usually keep it wrapped until the stitches do their work, though it gets wet when I wash.'

Rachel lifted his arm. 'That wrapping must be changed, I will do it now.' She took his hand to unwind the bandage. 'Ah good, it looks clean; you can pull out those stitches in one week's time, all it needs is a light wrapping to keep the dirt from it; I will do that.'

She ushered him to a seat and took his hand. Her sleeve brushed his arm as he watched the flow of her fingers. She fixed a piece of white linen to the wound and secured it with cord. Her black hair gleamed with lustres; tonight she wore it plaited into a long braid that dressed over one shoulder.

'There, it's done. I will give you more cloth so that you can change the dressing yourself each evening.'

The food arrived and Isaac poured red wine. The serving girl placed knives and spoons on the table and withdrew. Rachel produced three utensils with bone handles and two silver prongs.

'What are those?' Tom asked.

'These are Italian forks; they are still new in England.'

Tom picked one up and balanced it on a finger. 'Well, even though they're tiny they remind me of the pitchfork I use to stack hay. The tines on these are skilfully made, they're a wonder.'

Isaac picked up his own fork. 'Let us see how well they work on this pie. Although it is not kosher, hunger is king.'

Accustomed to holding a heavy spoon or a workmanlike knife, Tom's hard fingers fumbled with the cutlery. Even so, he knew a growing ease with these gracious people. He followed their table manners and watched how they took their food. They chewed with their mouths closed and held off speech until they had swallowed.

When they had finished, Isaac pushed back his chair and beamed at him. Tom returned his smile, saying, 'What did you mean when you said the pie isn't kosher?'

Isaac grew serious. 'Jews are expected to hold to ancient laws. The Book of Leviticus tells us what food is proper, or kosher to eat. The beef in this pie is allowed, even though it has not been prepared by Jewish hands. Today we stray from our kind and must eat where we can; it is a foolish person who would starve for the sake of rules. Are you a religious man, Thomas?'

'I don't know,' Tom replied.

'Then, do you worship a god in his heaven?'

'I don't bother with church talk; I reckon a man can find more sense and more peace among the roots of a tree.'

'The roots of a tree,' Isaac echoed, 'now where have I heard that before? Would you worship that tree?'

'Yes - if I thought it would help. I think I've done that already. I watched my father die without him wanting the priest. I did what I could. Towards the finish, I wrapped my arms around an oak, and willed an end to his suffering. I shouldn't blather on like this - I've had ower much wine.'

'We are not far apart; I too find comfort among the trees. Listen, Thomas - your father is not dead, he lives on in you; such has become clear to me since I have come to know you.' Isaac reached across the table and took hold of Tom's hands. 'I wish more men had such nobility of heart.'

The three of them talked until the night drew in. They lit candles and continued until Isaac showed signs of fatigue. Rachel made a sign and Tom rose to bid them goodnight.

He lay on his back beneath the feather-filled quilt, watching the shadows dance on the walls as a breeze from the window played with the flame of the solitary candle. This is the softest bed I'll ever know, he mused. His body relaxed ready for sleep with a surge of rare contentment. Then the thought of Rachel sleeping in the next room brought cravings to his mind. While he wondered if he loved her, he accepted that nothing could ever come of it. They were differently bred - he, a farm labourer without learning, and she as far from his state as the noble raven from the common rook. His eyelids drooped as his mind drifted away into a memory of boyhood and his parents. They drifted through bluebells beneath bare ash trees. High above their heads a colony of rooks squabbled in eerie silence over the ownership of twigs.

He heard the latch lift and a slight creak as the door opened. He waited for Meg to bark but she lay motionless with head on paws and ears cocked. The candle had almost burnt down. It sputtered as Rachel appeared by his bedside and dropped her robe to the floor. She stood naked in the candlelight as it died. Her wide, dark eyes gazed into his, then, without speaking, she lifted the bedcover and slid in beside him.

14

Messenger

Tom stretched out his limbs and slowly rebuilt, piece by piece, the memory of last night. It dawned on him that if he lived a hundred years it would never happen again - she had gone and the bed was cool.

His chamber reverberated with the cold clangs of church bells that obliterated the cries of vendors in the street below. Beyond the window, with its six panes of bevelled glass, fragments of white cloud floated by. They reminded him of the ships that passed the mouth of the Tees, and of his father pointing out from the moor top the sails of the swan-like carracks. He yawned and threw off the bedding. Ears filled with the clamour of bells, he pushed his feet to the bottom of the bed and luxuriated in a gentleman's chamber for one last time.

Meg poked his bare shoulder with a cold nose and licked his elbow. He grunted and, pulling the bedcover back around his cooling skin, rolled over to imagine Rachel still pressed against his chest. For half an hour more he lay on the bed, sometimes staring at the ceiling, going over the last night in his mind - how she had kissed his bruises. This would not do, he decided, and sat up. As he swung out his legs the scent of Rachel's body floated up from beneath the covers. With a sense of reverence, he peeled back the sheets, and bent over the mattress to fill his nose and lungs, before committing to memory the slight impression of her body.

Meg scratched at the floor and whimpered. 'Yes, I know all about it,' he said. 'We both need to get outside.'

After dressing, he paused to listen at the door of Rachel's chamber before creeping downstairs and out into the marketplace. With hood pulled up in the sunlight, he hurried along the cobbled street until the great rose window of St Cuthbert's cathedral blazed above. Except for a boy sweeping the cobbles, the castle yard lay empty and without a sign of the Warren's militia. The few windows in the bluff walls of the keep seemed dead, so he sauntered across to the stables.

Ben grinned. 'Not to fret - they cleared out at daybreak. By heck! New clothes! Has there been a fire? Did you find a bed without bugs?'

'Didn't get a bite.'

Ben grinned. 'You must have snuggled in with a toothsome bed-warmer, to sleep so long.'

Tom blushed as his hand went to the mark on his neck. 'Is there any chance of summat to eat?'

'Breakfast you mean? It's nigh on time for middle-day feed and it's as well you're back, the sergeant's asking for thee.'

Sergeant Arkwright pushed open the stable door. 'Ah, there you are, Fleck. We've promoted you to herald's runner - just for today. You will take messages to two farms about a mile beyond the north gate - they're close together. The letters come from the Norroy, so make sure you put them into the proper hands. He wants to see the two gentlemen here tomorrow morning.'

'Letters? I've no reading. How can I tell them apart?'

'Easy, this one's for John Eden. Take note of the chevron on his shield. He's at Cauld Knuckles - that's a farm by the big oak beyond Framwellgate Bridge. Just ask your way. This, with the wheat sheaves, is for William Bewley, close by at High Carr. Can you remember all that?'

'Aye, Sarge. Don't the soldiers usually take the messages?'

'I want them for weapons practice today. Soon as you've had a feed get yourself off with these, and keep them out of the muck. You'll need to remember to show respect to the gentlemen. I'm glad to see you're dressed tidy today - that's good.' The sergeant nodded and strode out.

Ben cautioned, 'Be sure not to fail him. He trusts you more than his own men - the way they are just now. He'll reckon that if he sends a couple of them with the letters they'd not get past the first alehouse.'

'Then I'll get straight off with these messages.' He pocketed a wedge of cheese while Meg caught the lump of bacon fat he tossed towards her.

With the letters wrapped in linen and safe inside a shoulder bag, Tom rushed from the castle. Impulsively, he set aside his mission and hurried straight to the inn where he took the stairs two at a time. The chambers were empty. A girl on her knees - scrubbing the floor - squinted up. 'The mistress and her father set off half an hour ago; said

105

they would go by the north road.'

He threaded his way through the narrow lanes at a jog trot with Meg running in front. They skirted piles of rotting refuse and ran down streets lined with buildings that leaned like drunks. Meg cleared the path ahead of clusters of crows and kites that squabbled among the waste. Breaking free of the stinking ginnels, they crossed the Framwellgate Bridge over the River Wear. By a barley field, they halted to fill their lungs with sweet air blown off the hills.

Before them, bounded by hedges, stretched the old Roman road. Leaping across streamlets that shared its bed, they broke into a loping run and kept it up for a mile. On top of a rise, Tom blinked to see riders ahead. A quick wipe with his sleeve cleared the sweat from his eyes. Four horses moved at a cautious walk, picking their way through a network of wheel ruts where the road passed through a farmyard. Rachel and her father took up the rear with their hired guards riding in front.

'Master Coronel!' he yelled.

Rachel smiled down at Tom when he reached the horses. 'Did you run all the way from the town just to speak with us or are you fleeing the castle?'

'I'm running with messages for the herald today. By lucky chance, the gentlemen live on this road, so I can be here to say goodbye. Can I walk alongside?'

Her father nodded. 'Of course. But we must reach Newcastle before dark and there are twenty miles before us. The road is dry here, Rachel, why not dismount and lead your horse? You can walk with Thomas a little way. We will wait for you by those elms at the top of the next rise.' He leaned from the saddle and took Tom's hand. 'Until we meet again, son of Francis, go well with you.' Isaac spurred his horse forward to catch up with the guards who waited twenty yards away.

Tom held the reins as Rachel slid from her grey mare. She rearranged her green cloak and took his other hand. 'Last night will stay with me for life, Thomas. Your hands had a magic I will never forget.'

'I don't know what to say.' He gulped. 'I don't want to bide apart from you - there's a yawning ache inside when I think my eyes will never meet yours again.'

Her fingers tightened on his. 'Hush. That is beautiful, but it cannot be - not for a Christian and a Jew. We must accept who we are - the world will not have it otherwise. All we can hold to are our heart's memories.'

Tom swallowed, as his hope died. 'Where will you go after Alnwick?'

'Back to London, where I expect I will marry a rich man from among our little community. That will be best; there is nothing else for me.'

'Will he be a good man - the man you'll marry?'

'I'll insist that he is honourable. There is one man who is noble of heart - it could be him; he often visits when we are in London. He is Portuguese also. I would become mistress of his house and enjoy a life of comfort.'

Her eyes brimmed with tears. 'I'm lonely, Thomas. There are few of us in England; no more than twenty are known to me and only five of them are my age.'

'So few! I don't know how that would feel.'

'There are others, perhaps another fifty; but they are *converso*, they are become legally Christian. The church accepted them but they are watched,' she lowered her voice, 'because some are suspected of Jewish worship behind locked doors.'

Tom's eyes widened. 'You could do that, Rachel! Then I would come to London and ask to marry you. Or better still, I could become a Jew and worship trees in secret.'

In the shelter of an oak that overhung the road, she kissed him. 'You make my heart glad - I feel things that have no words. We would have interesting children - but it is not possible for us.'

Thomas wrapped her in his arms and buried his head in the mass of black hair. 'It can be so for us if we want it enough. Oh, this hair! How can I forget how it brushed across my chest last night?'

She broke free from him and ran long fingers across her eyes. 'I say farewell now.' Her voice wavered. 'Father is waiting. He understands us. Perhaps you and I will meet again. If not in Alnwick, then - somewhere in another life. Something whispers we have already shared our lives - elsewhere and before. Farewell, Thomas. May the Irinim watch over you.' She thrust a foot into the stirrup, swung her thighs into the saddle and rode away without looking back.

The old sense of futility returned. With arms hanging limp, Tom watched the small party disappear beyond the rise. He yelled upwards, into the crown of the tree, 'Is there nowt we can keep? Why take it all away? Why? Blast you to Hell!' As his boot struck the oak, scraps of yellow lichen fell to earth.

Shoulders against the trunk, he let his anger drain. Meg licked one of his drooping hands. He knelt and fondled her neck. Deep in mental apology, he drifted a few times clockwise around the oak before realising he stood at the entrance to Cauld Knuckles Farm. He took a few paces up the trackway and, through blurred eyes, saw a farmhouse with barns and four plain cottages to one side.

A stout man in leather jerkin and breeches rested his great arms on a hurdle that closed off a sheep pen. The man watched two labourers clip the wool from a group of ewes. The sheep lay mute, pinned to the ground, while the shearers straddled their middles, turning them as they clipped and peeled away the fleeces.

'Mister Eden?' Tom's voice was thick.

The man eased his body around. 'I'm John Eden. I've no need of more hands,' he said, in a kind manner.

Tom still ached inside and could not return the smile. With a lump in his throat he mumbled, 'I'm a messenger, sir. This for you.' He handed over the letter that carried the chevron and watched the yeoman's thick fingers crack the red wax seal.

The man snorted as he read the letter. 'Damn! They'll be asking five pounds of me, I reckon. All right, tell the herald I'll attend on him. I need to gan to town anyway. My thanks to you for bringing it.'

High Carr, a two-floored farmhouse, stood in the middle of an orchard further up the road. Tom had to knock at the door several times before a silver-haired woman opened it. On seeing the sealed letter, she asked him in and gave him a chair at a scrubbed white table.

The bent woman sat with him. 'You look washed out, son. Your eyes are red - are you not feeling too canny?' She banged on the stone floor with her walking stick. 'Bella! Fetch some ale.'

'I'm fine, mistress. I work wi' ponies and sometimes the stable dust gets to me.'

The door creaked open and a strong-faced woman brought in a pitcher and two drinking bowls. She gave him a sideways look and poured the ale.

'That'll do, Bella. Thou can get on with the baking. Now, me lad, if you have to work with mouldy bedding, a damp cloth to cover your face and mouth is my advice - otherwise you'll get a bad chest. My husband shan't be long, he knows you're here; he's out the back talking to the cowman. Is that ale doing any good?'

'It's a grand drop, a bit stronger than I get at the castle.'

She chuckled. 'Well, I don't suppose they want you men singing all night next door to the monastery. Mind you, from what I hear, those pear-shaped Benedictines know how to quaff it down.' She called to the servant, 'Bella! That beef bone with a bit still on it - give it to this dog, will you?'

At that moment, William Bewley entered the kitchen, stamping the cow-clap off his clogs onto a rush mat. The gnarled man was as bent as his wife and rocked from side to side as he walked.

'What's all this about?'

Tom handed him the letter. 'The heralds want to see you tomorrow, sir.'

'I've never been made a sir,' he growled, ripping the letter open. 'Ah! They want to see me, do they; want to record me in their book? Well - tell them I've no interest in their blazons of arms today. I've no offspring to hand things on to. It all dies with me and, if we get another biting back-end, that'll not be far off.'

'Might I say you won't be coming to the castle tomorrow, Mister Bewley?' Tom said.

'That you might, lad. Here - I'd better write all that on the back of the letter, I don't want you getting in trouble on my account.' He dipped a quill and scratched a few lines on the parchment with brown ink. 'There, that'll do it. Now, you're not from round here are ye? You sound a bit Cleveland to me. Sit with us and have a bite o' meat.'

Tom stayed for an hour talking with the old couple. The old lady took him as far as the gate onto the road and said, 'My William's a good man, from a fine old family. He's bitter since our two boys went away to France for the king. They went as men-at-arms and they could read too. The French killed them. Now he's nobody to will this farm to - except for a cousin and he won't want him to get his claws on it; they don't get on, haven't spoken for years. He'll not give it to the church either, says they're fat enough as it is. It's not certain yet what he'll do, he's talking about setting up a charity school for poor bairns.'

The road back to the town steamed as the sun sucked up the remnants of last night's rain. Tom kept a slow pace, thinking about Rachel. The yaffle, a green woodpecker, gave out mocking laughs from somewhere below in the wooded banks of the river; the echoing cries brought memories of the ash coppices around Thornaby.

He thought of his sister, Hilda, and wondered how she fared, living with Mary and old Agnes. What would Mary think of him if she knew what he'd done last night? He had forded the river ten days ago, since when Mary had seldom been at the front of his mind, so much had happened in that time. He thought about her: she's pretty, hard-working and kind, and a good friend too. A picture came of the hot June day when they had lain on their backs in the hayfield, side by side and searched for the dot of a skylark that soared and poured its burbling song into the silver-blue sky. It gladdened his heart, but when he thought of Rachel - he had to remember to breathe. Even so, he supposed that the time would come when he would wed Mary and they would set up home together. Such thoughts filled his mind as he re-crossed the bridge to climb the cobbled way into Durham.

15

Rachel Goes North

Rachel stopped her horse as she neared her father and the bodyguards. Shielding her eyes, she scanned the road - it was empty. She caught a brief movement at the corner of a barn. Was that to be her last sight of him? Her eyes moistened as she trotted up to the party.

Isaac spoke gently. 'You have said farewell?'

'Yes, and I grieve for that.'

'You have a bond with Thomas.'

'My heart is sunken now our paths divide. I hope the road he takes is kind.'

'Rachel, nothing is fixed. You may meet again or you may not, who knows?

'I feel such a leap when I hear that, even though there is no future for Thomas and me.' Her voice broke. 'And what is our own future, Father - yours and mine; what do you see?'

He began in a sombre voice. 'In a few years I will be too frail to travel like this. I must find a safe place to dwell - Norwich or London - where there might be contentment and books. I hope you are near me in old age; I hope to see you happy with a good man and grandchildren for me to tease.' He chuckled.

'Father, there are none of our people in Norwich, none since the killings. It is no haven for us.'

'Jews once flourished there, we even recovered our position after the brutality. Our money built the cathedral. Then most took ship - exiled by King John. A few converted and stayed - they prospered. Do you know of the woman, Julian of Norwich, the Christian mystic? She lived a century ago. Now she's almost a saint. It seems she understood Hebrew. From my studies I've concluded that she is in fact the Juliana who converted in Norwich to avoid persecution.'

Rachel's gaze rested on the neck of her horse. Once again, she witnessed Isaac's love of scholarship. 'I am always fascinated when you tell me such things, Father - but today we are illegal. I know we have discussed this often but I still ache for a true home. How long can we stay in England? Where else is there for us? The Low Countries?'

'We can stay so long as it suits King Henry's purpose. He needs merchants; they make wealth for the country and he can borrow from us to finance his army. If we remain obscure, do not excite envy and keep in low numbers, we will survive here. For how long, I do not know.' He sighed. 'Two thousand years since Socrates and the world still barbarous. We lived at peace under the rule of the Moors - they esteemed our taxes. In those days we held up our heads. Now we keep them low - like the ferns beneath these walls.'

Rachel studied his face. 'Would you convert?'

'Perhaps I would, I grow tired of the road.' He lowered his voice. 'I have lived as *converso* before and I would do so again - though my hands would make their signs, they would never have my heart.'

'Thomas does not seem to need a god; he is content with the spirit of the woods, with the moon on her forehead.'

Isaac laughed. 'That boy is deep! If our roads meet again who can tell the outcome?' His voice lowered: 'He will need to keep his opinions to himself or the priests will light a fire around his feet.'

Rachel shuddered.

Three days later, in the afternoon of the ninth of July, they approached the walled town of Alnwick. A pair of brutish-looking gate-towers loomed out of thin mist. On a nearby hillock stood a three-legged gallows.

'Father! On that knoll!'

'I see it. Pull your head-dress across your face.'

Rachel wrapped the side hangers of her wimple across her nose and eyes as they neared the hanging place. Against her will, her gaze veered in that direction. As though her eyes were not her own - they fought to look between the folds of cloth.

Three men hung by the neck, motionless, hands bound, from a triangular gallows frame mounted on three rough-hewn tree trunks. Their bodies, naked except for soiled small clothes, were beginning to swell. A pair of crows swaggered along the cross-members of the gibbet.

'Who are they?' Rachel asked in a faint voice.

A guard rode at her left side in an attempt to shield her view. 'They'll be reivers, mistress - raiders, cattle thieves, hostage takers.

They get short shrift in these parts.'

They neared the rounded arch that pierced the massive, defensive walls, aware that eyes watched from arrow slits. A man-at-arms stood to one side and allowed the donkey train in front to pass through the gate unquestioned. At the approach of Isaac's party, the guard stepped out to bar the way with a spear.

'Names and where from?'

'Isaac Coronel and my daughter Rachel. We travel from London. These two men are my hired guards, the brothers Will and Jack Simpson, good men of Lincoln.'

An officer strode out of the door of the barbican. 'Foreigners?'

'We are Portuguese living in England with the king's approval.'

'Your business here?'

Isaac straightened in the saddle. 'The earl's business. The matter will take perhaps two days. We hope to find chambers in Alnwick.'

'I'll inform the castle of your arrival. Meanwhile, do not stray north of the town; there are reivers about. They covet folk like you for ransom - more profitable than cattle theft.' He shifted a couple of paces to get a better view of Rachel's face, which was still part covered by her wimple. Stroking the neck of her bay mare, he looked Rachel over; she lowered her eyes. The officer stepped back, his eyes still on her. 'The town is restless at night, have a care.'

'I am grateful to you, officer,' Isaac said evenly. 'We will heed your advice. May we enter?'

'Welcome to Hotspur's town. The chambers at the White Horse in Bondgate are best. Luke Patterson keeps a clean hostelry.'

Bondgate Street opened up as it left the confines of the town gate. A mixture of buildings lined the broad space; most had a lower half of dressed stone topped with an upper floor of bulging wattle-and-daub.

The din of Saturday market hit their ears as the four riders threaded between rows of stalls. After the clean air of farmland, they now inhaled a broth of odours: the sweet smell of baking collided with the harshness of roasting meat and the reek of night soil.

Plaintive cries and bleats rose up from geese, hens and goats awaiting their fate in hobbled groups. Squeals of young pigs and the bellows of vendors cut through the drone of conversation.

Outside an alehouse, beneath the crude bull's head, two soldiers attacked each other with fists and boots, surrounded by shouting comrades. From the high plinth of the market cross rang out the clear words of a brown-robed friar. A few old women gathered at his sandal-clad feet, clutched their baskets and gazed up into his earnest young face.

For safety in the press of the market, they dismounted and led their horses by rein. A half-dozen ragged children took the opportunity to pluck at Rachel's skirts and with pleading eyes beg for the means to ease their hunger. Isaac handed a cut farthing each to the two oldest in the group on the understanding that they would guide them to the White Horse. Once hired, the urchins protected them from further harassment and pushed the crowds apart ahead of the travellers.

Rachel had also dipped her fingers into a pocket that held small coins for this purpose. Even at home, in Lisbon, her father would encourage her to carry small money when she visited the streets. From him she learned kindness for beggars.

'A special bracelet for you, young lady,' a voice called from the cobblestones.

Rachel met a pair of grey eyes set in a motherly face. The woman offered a handful of trinkets fashioned from a dense black wood.

'These are carved by my son. He has no sight.'

Rachel handed her reins to a guard and, kneeling beside the woman, took a bracelet. Three delicately carved dragons chased each other's tails around the circumference of the hoop.

'He likes to get a penny each for those,' the woman whispered with reverence.

'This is beautiful, such fine work; your son is an artist.' Rachel reached into her pouch and passed over a silver penny and two farthings. 'It is worth more than a penny; thank him for me, please.'

'Bless you, me honey, I'll tell him what you said.'

As Rachel took the reins of her horse from the guard, she felt the touch of eyes. By the market cross a priest in black and white robes had fixed on her. His lip curled and his eyes narrowed as he held the stare. She trembled and looked away.

Luke Patterson, a square and balding man, greeted the travellers by the entrance to his stables. 'Welcome to the White Horse, sir; she is Alnwick's best inn. Is this your first visit to town?'

'It is the first time north of Durham. You have a fine inn - it appears to be newly built.' Isaac gazed up at the handsome windows and rooflines. 'Your choice of architect does you credit.'

'Thank you, but I'm just the innkeeper. The building, like most of

Alnwick, is the property of the Percy family. My lads will take care of your mounts and show the guards to their quarters - let me carry your bags to your chambers.'

The following morning Isaac rode out to the castle to meet with Henry Percy, Earl of Northumberland. As he and his guards approached the tough, Percy stronghold, Isaac thought over the matter of the Earl's summons. Because of his lavish spending on entertainment, the Fifth Earl was fondly known as 'Henry the Magnificent'. Has he run out of money again? Isaac wondered. The earl has not fully honoured his debts negotiated in London. He sensed the wet in his armpits, a sure sign he grew anxious about the dealings to come.

Armed men stopped him at the gatehouse and ordered his guards to stand to one side. After questioning, they led him through a narrow entrance that pierced the thick curtain wall of the fortress. Once inside the castle's towering keep, Isaac was ushered into a place of vaulted ceilings, panelled walls and manuscripts. A serving man waited in silence by the door. Not invited to take a seat, Isaac placed himself where he could inspect the bookshelves. He sighed as his gaze roamed the collection - sighing for the contentment he would find in such a library.

Heavy footfalls broke his reverie. A large man, aged perhaps forty, with domed forehead, a flattened nose and scarred cheek, strode through the door. He dismissed the servant and said in a loud and irritated voice, 'Isaac Coronel from the south - you wish to see my brother. I must tell you Earl Henry is not here.'

Hiding his confusion Isaac gave a measured reply. 'My employer is Alvaro Jurnet. He instructed me to call on the earl whilst I am in the north. Master Jurnet received a message from the earl saying he wished to discuss a business matter.'

'My brother is with the king. They are destined for Calais in support of the Holy League in its argument with Louis,' the man snapped.

Isaac chose his words with care. 'Then I will inform my master of that fact. Who should I say I spoke with today?'

'You speak with William Percy; I have charge here in my brother's absence and today I'm busy with military matters. Unless you can advance me enough to pay a thousand archers and billmen for forty days I must bid you good day.'

'If they are paid at the rate of sixpence a day for able soldiers you would need one thousand pounds, my lord.'

A flicker of respect passed across Percy's face. 'You sport a quick brain, Coronel. There are captains to pay - it's best to add two hundred pounds. Do you bring that much with you?'

'Alas no. I can send a message by fast rider to London with the details. I will follow at a steadier pace. You should have my master's reply before three weeks are out. It is my duty to ask what security there is to protect a loan of that size.'

'The name of Percy is security enough; your master will know that much. I expect the usual terms. When the sum is ready, have it sent directly to me. Now, if nothing else remains, I must wish you a safe journey.'

A servant escorted Isaac from the castle. Arriving back at their chambers he slumped wearily in a chair to let Rachel pull off his boots. 'Yet again I have sympathy for the wild goose,' he sighed. 'In the morning we go south.'

16

Chaucer

The Visitation stayed nine days at Durham Castle. Each morning, Tom hurried out with letters that summoned the arms-bearing families of the district to meet with the heralds. John Young and Thomas Tonge questioned the visitors, noted details of their living children and checked these against the College of Herald's register of pedigrees. If the holder of a grant of arms had died, the heralds recorded the fact and awarded the arms to the eldest son.

They levied a charge that passed to the Royal Exchequer. Henry's new cannon foundry at Woolwich and his war with France needed funds. In four years on the throne, he had exhausted the treasury his careful father had nurtured.

On a wet Friday morning, the heralds and their escorts departed the city by the north road for the town of Newcastle. Tom took up the rear as usual alongside two loaded ponies. The Skipton soldier, Alan Fuller, marched beside him as a rearguard. A well-built man with great strength and a rich fund of soldiers' tales, he stood a head taller than did the pony driver. Tom had come to like this blunt-spoken, honest guard, but he knew not to talk to him when the morning had a raw edge. He kept silent as they marched through bursts of heavy rain. After an hour Tom asked, 'How are things with you today, Alan?'

'Well enough this morning. I'm having a rest from the beer and I feel all the better for it. Just as well - we've a twenty-mile tramp today.' He eyed another advancing squall. 'There's no sign of a break. It's Saint Swithin's Day - there'll be forty days of this muck and clart. And how are you faring?'

'I've no grumbles. It's good to be shifting again.' Tom hesitated before asking, 'Alan, can you read?'

'Aye, in a steady sort of way. I'm not fast. Why?'

'I want to learn to read. How did you learn?'

'Mother taught me; she came of a family that did well and she'd a proper teacher come to the house. Dad could never read but Mam had books in her kist. She had one about King Arthur and one called *Canterbury Tales*. She gave me some of the *Tales* when I joined the army; it's in my pack. It's only scraps of the book, mind.' He laughed. 'Mam read the thing till it dropped to bits. She gave me a lump of it when I went for a sodger.'

'I'd be glad to see it sometime, if that's all right.'

'Aye, it is. I try to read a bit when we've finished the day; that way I'm not tempted to sit in the alehouse with the others.'

As they neared the coast, the sky cleared. The party bunched to a halt when the Norroy raised an arm.

'There's the castle!' He pointed across the river to a dark tower. 'Those walls will not be scaled nor broken.'

In watery sunshine, they rattled across the Tyne's wooden bridge. The black throat of Newcastle barbican swallowed them, to the clatter of hooves echoing off stone.

As usual, the drovers shared a stable with the horses. The soldiers had billets in a lean-to against the massive castle walls. After supper, Tom went in search of Alan Fuller. He found him at ease on a bench under the walls of the stone keep, reading in late sunlight.

'Is that the book, Alan?'

'Aye. I'm enjoying reading in this spell of warmth now Swithin's feeling kinder. How would it be if I read you a bit?'

Tom sat close. 'That would be grand.'

The soldier began, 'Well, it's by a long-ago man called Chaucer and it's about some folk on a pilgrimage. They're all going to Canterbury and, on the way, they tell each other stories. This is part of *The Merchant's Tale*:

> *Once there was a dwelling in Lombardy*
> *A worthy knight, who was born in Pavia*
> *In which he lived in great prosperity;*
> *And sixty years a wifeless man was he . . .'*

The soldier's deep voice continued, pronouncing the words as though he chewed a tasty piece of meat. After two pages, he stopped and glanced at Tom for a response.

'Those are fine-sounding words, Alan: Lombardy and Pavia - I've

118

never heard of those places.'

'They're in Italy. That's a region beyond the eastern edge of France.'

'Is that near Portugal?'

'No, no, Portugal is south of here, she sits cheek by jowl with Spain.'

'How do you know that?'

'Oh, by asking questions of folk, and listening, like you're doing.'

'I'd like to have the skill of reading. Do you think I could learn? Can you show me how it's done?'

Tom spent much of his spare time with Alan Fuller and the bundle of loose pages. After the first week, he could recognise most of the letters of the alphabet and form the sounds they stood for. After three weeks, he could read, in a clumsy fashion, entire groups of words. He enjoyed pronouncing Lombardy and Pavia. The words rolled off the tongue with a liquid rhythm that reminded him of water flowing over rocks; more than that, they reminded him of Rachel's melodic voice.

Alan would let out a whistle of surprise that once Tom had read a line a few times he could recall it at will. Soon he could sit at Alan's side and recite whole passages of Chaucer's verse from memory. When mucking out the stables or grooming horses he would speak out lines that he had learned the previous evening. One day, he leaned lightly against a pony's neck, humming as he smoothed down her quarters with a handful of hay. The mare's ears twitched as Tom broke off to recite:

> *'This friar boasts that he knows hell,*
> *And God knows that it is little wonder;*
> *Friars and fiends be seldom much asunder.*
>
> *Out of the devil's arse were driven*
> *Twenty thousand friars on a rout,*
> *And throughout hell swarmed all about . . .'*

'By Harry, that's a good one! And true enough!' the sergeant boomed from the doorway. 'You're coming on a treat. Now leave that pony and get yourself cleaned up quick, the Norroy wants thee. Remember to show respect; whilst he might be plain John Young Esquire, he's also the Nord Roi, the North King of Heralds.'

Tom washed his hands and face in a bucket, smoothed his hair, then followed the sergeant to the herald's quarters. John Young sat behind a broad table, writing on sheets of parchment with a goose quill. The sergeant knocked on the open door.

'Ah. Come in, Fleck. Thank you, sergeant.'

Tom stood in front of the table. 'You asked for me, sir.'

'Yes. What do you think of this vast town - and its castle built by Robert Curthose, William the Conqueror's eldest?'

'I've seen naught like it, sir. It's a deal bigger than Durham and a deal muckier.'

'There's good reason for that. Men are making money from the coal trade. You'll have seen all the ships in the river?'

'I have, sir. And I bump into seafarers all along the quays. They're a wild lot - I keep out of their way.' Although Tom wondered what the Norroy had in mind, he felt at ease - the man had friendly wrinkles around the eyes.

John Young tapped the table with a manicured fingernail. 'You do right! I don't want you injured. We are stabled here another week at least and I have work for you other than driving ponies. Newcastle is prospering and merchants grow richer with each ship that noses upriver. They even seek blazons of arms from The College. The short of it is - I have need of a better sort of messenger and think you might be intelligent enough.'

'I've no schooling, sir.'

The Norroy pulled at his silver-grey beard before wagging a finger. 'Never mistake schooling for intelligence, Fleck. Nor fine clothes for wisdom, for that matter. Your honesty impressed me at Herdwick Hall, which is why I hired you. Now, Sergeant Arkwright tells me that you're learning to read. Let me see if you can decipher this.' He pushed a parchment across the table.

Tom's face grew hot as he stared at a coloured drawing of a shield with writing beneath. On the shield two lambs stood above a broad stripe, below the stripe stood another lamb. He saw new words that challenged his tongue.

'William Lambton son of Percival Lambton. Sable a fesse between three lambs argent.' He paused between each word and stumbled at fesse. 'I'm sorry, sir. My reading is snail-slow.'

'Never mind. Try this one.'

John Young pushed another parchment across the table. The shield had an upright cross as the main feature; in each corner, a silver lion stood erect with front claws striking out.

'Priory of Durham. Azure a cross paty, four lions argent.' He stumbled over azure. 'Sorry, sir. Half of these words are fresh ones and I don't know what they mean.'

The Norroy gave a chuckle. 'You've not wrapped your tongue around the French, though it's no matter. That's good reading for a novice. It's a useful talent and I want you to keep on with it. There aren't many readers outside of the churches and monasteries.'

He passed across the table three sheets of fine grey paper. 'Those hold poems and ballads in English with letters well formed. They're copied in the latest manner by means of a speedy contrivance called a printing press; you can keep them for study. Get yourself a blue slate and lump of chalk. Copy the letters out until you form them right. Go steady with it and don't lose heart.'

'Thank you, sir. I'll do that.' Tom moved to leave, but stopped. 'Who is William the Conqueror, sir?

The Norroy laughed. 'Have you Danes and Angles forgotten already? However, five centuries have gone and I suppose the old stories fade away. Sometime I'll tell you about him. Goodnight.' John Young shone a smile before going back to his writing.

Tom returned to the stables with eyes bright and face flushed. That evening he lay on his straw-filled pallet looking up at cobwebs as they billowed in the draughts. Ignoring Meg as she snuffled through layers of straw, hunting rats, he whispered to himself some of the words in the *Merchant's Tale*, pronouncing them with a rhythm. He thought they sounded like the measured cooing of the ringdove: Seneca, sacrament, Mordecai, Theophrastus, prosperity, rapturous. 'I wish Rachel was here - I could say them to her,' he whispered.

Agnes Humble stood, knife in hand, staring, as she often did, towards the single-toothed outline of Roseberry Topping. The hill reared up in isolation as though cast adrift into the Cleveland ploughlands from the dark crags of the moor edge. As a girl she had done some courting on the sheep-cropped turf of that hilltop. Each morning when she looked that way, she remembered him and those bright days. Where has all the time gone? She mused.

Her young man was a dark-haired, restless sort. His hands were restless too, forever roaming over her body. She never gave in to him and, in time, he would give up and lay quiet, chewing on a grass stem, gazing with far-away eyes at the sea. He would point out the sails that drifted along the coast on the sparkling water. 'I'm going away, bonny Agnes' he'd said, 'I've had enough of slogging through clarts after oxen. I'll get work on one of those ships and see a bit of the world. When I've got money enough I'll come back for thee.'

He never came back. No message ever reached his mother either; she died not knowing if he lived. Lives and dreams, all ending in walls of fog.

She shifted her stiff body to the left and stared with unfocussed eyes, northwards into Durham. As she stood, lost in memory, her grand-daughter Mary appeared at her side carrying a bundle of cut willow branches for the goats. She cast aside her load saying, 'Where do you think he is now, Gran?'

'Oh, I don't know, lass; it's sixty years since he went.'

'Not sixty years, Gran! My Tom's been gone but six weeks.'

Agnes gave a sigh and wiped some wet from her cheek; she'd lately developed a touch of watery eye. 'Sorry, honey. I was far away. Your Tom - yes. It'll be best if you get friendly with another lad and not set your heart on Tom Fleck.'

'Oh, Gran! Don't say that. I love him. Tom bides in my heart and always will.'

'Go and feed the goats, Mary, then come inside. There's summat I need to tell thee afore I get much older.'

17

Northumbrians

The Visitation of Heralds to Newcastle took a month to complete. Whenever vessels from the Thames or the Low Countries floated upriver on the tide, the heralds would be alert for information. They were anxious over the state of relations between James IV of Scotland and Henry VIII of England. Even though James had married Henry's sister, Margaret Tudor, Henry viewed his brother-in-law's alliance with France as a naked dirk at his back.

One day, a breeze off the sea brought a cog into the Tyne. The ship had news of Henry's entry into his territory of Calais on the thirtieth of June. From there he planned to invade the French kingdom. If James IV were to come to France's aid, he would need to attack England soon.

The heralds' little cavalcade cleared the gates of Newcastle on the tenth of August and struck north for the Percy castle at Alnwick. In each village on the route, the gossip told of a Scots army mustering at Edinburgh. The sound of hammers on iron spilled from blacksmiths' forges; in the fields, archers fired volleys at marks and men with spears galloped their ponies at targets.

They found Alnwick's marketplace and inns buzzing with talk of raiders in the valley of the Till. The Scottish Warden of the March, Lord Home led the raid. Knowing England's best was camped in France, he had crossed the Tweed with five thousand horsemen to ransack the English countryside, to burn, loot and sweep up livestock without fear of challenge.

On the first evening in Alnwick, after stabling their animals at the castle, the pony men ventured into town in search of entertainment. The White Horse faced the marketplace; its big rooms, fireplaces, hearty food and clean drink made it a popular ale house. This night it heaved with soldiers and militiamen swallowing beer and throwing dice. The drivers found a table close to the door and settled down with their jugs and mugs. Meg stretched herself among their feet.

'That was a long pull up from Newcastle, I'm fair worn out.' Ben wiped the froth from his moustache with the back of his hand.

'Aye, I found it hard-going as well, Dad; we've gone soft with that month in town.' Rob took a drink. 'I'm not complaining, mind - it's been easy money this far.'

'So it has - but I'm fretting about the big raid, they've been within eighteen miles of here. If they're that close they could be under the walls by morning.'

'The town's packed out with soldiers, surely the Scotch wouldn't dare come any nearer,' Rob said.

A soldier at the next table had overheard. He called across. 'It's reckoned there's thousands of the buggers on scrubby ponies and hefting lances. But they'll not come here - not now they're loaded up with plunder - they'll gan away home. The point is: can we take hold of them afore they get back ower the Tweed?'

They lowered their mugs. The speaker had a big face part-covered with a short, black beard showing grey. Above his moustaches hung a large broken nose, skewed to one side.

'Will the soldiers in Alnwick get after them?' Ben asked.

'We'll be riding out with Billy Bulmer soon. He's gathering up men. Some of us'll stay to guard the town in case they run back this way.'

Ben took a drink. 'The king's in France with the army, what's to stop more of them pouring over the border while he's overseas?'

'Auld Surrey's on his way from Pontefract, he's sent the call out and he'll march here afore long. You three look fit enough. I expect you'll be wi' us when we move out.'

'We're not soldiers,' Rob blurted out.

'That's right - we're pack-horse men working for the heralds,' Tom said.

'That's as maybe.' The man spat into the fireplace, it hit the iron grate and hung there, sizzling. 'So, you're hoss drivers; the army will need your sort for the baggage train while the rest of us get on with men's work.'

The three friends fell silent and sipped at their ale. The soldier glowered at them for a moment then pulled himself erect and weaved out of the inn.

Next morning they were taking their ease on logs, spooning porridge, when Sergeant Arkwright squeezed his great head through the stable window. 'There's a special parade straight after breakfast. Be tidy and in your best gear.'

'What's it for, Sarge? We've hardly got settled,' Ben asked.

The sergeant tapped his nose. 'It's on the orders of the Norroy. You'll have to wait and see - but it's a fair-sized turnout.'

Hundreds of men milled around in the field beneath Alnwick Castle's curtain wall. Crag-faced hillmen, with shields on their backs, waited on ponies, lances secured vertically to saddles. Yeomen with longbows stood by the necks of farm horses. Straggling groups of labourers and shepherds drifted in on foot, empty-handed. The drovers were following the sergeant and his men onto the temporary parade ground when a voice called out.

'Tom!'

In the front row of a block of foot soldiers, the boyish face of Peter Tindall beamed from beneath a round iron helmet. His light frame wore a padded red tunic and leaned on a six-foot pole fitted at one end with a newly ground bill-hook. The weapon's nine-inch curved blade was similar to the hedge-laying tool Tom used at home, but this shaft terminated in a spear point and sported a lethal-looking spike at one side.

Tom halted. 'Goodness! Peter of Whitby! Good to see thee again. You still haven't found a proper job, then?'

'This pays better than most. It's grand to set eyes on thee, Thomas o' Thornaby; I've often brought you two to mind since our roads split at Sedgefield. I'm glad to see you've still got Meg along.' He scratched behind the dog's good ear.

The sergeant gave a bellow. 'Hey! Fleck! Get over here with the rest of us, you can have your blather some other time'.

'I'll see you later and we'll take some beer,' Tom shouted as he hurried away.

The sergeant formed his soldiers into a small block of four by two with the three drovers standing in a group to one side. 'Right, men, important officers are inspecting. Keep in lines and hold yourself like soldiers. Ben Wilson will make sure his two don't shame us.'

To the orders of marshals, the men on foot shuffled, grumbling, into gangs of twenty according to their weapons. Behind them, grim-faced horsemen stood in undulating lines holding the reins of their mounts. Except for the occasional whinny of a pony, the field began to fall silent.

~ ~ ~

Tom turned his head with the others as hooves clattered from the direction of the keep. Five men on tall horses emerged from the castle gate and rode onto a patch of higher ground where they took position to face the crowd.

His eyes widened as the central rider edged the great horse a few steps forward and called out in a voice powered by a deep chest, 'Men of the North! I am William Bulmer, knight of Brancepeth in the County Palatine of Durham. I represent your king until the Earl of Surrey gets here. The Scottish king whets his dagger once more and is mustering in Edinburgh. Our army is gathering from Yorkshire, Cheshire, Lancashire, Cumberland, Westmorland and Durham. It is marching towards Northumberland by way of the North Road and through the dales of the western fells, drawing in men as it comes. We will see a great gathering of our forces. When the earl arrives he will become your commander and mine.'

A murmuring began that built into a rumble of loud voices.

Sir William raised his hand and silence returned. 'While the treaty breaker, King Jimmy, plots in Edinburgh, his underlings cannot wait. As some of us know to our cost and grief, the Scottish Warden of the East March, Lord Home, has invaded this realm with a crowd of thieves. They are torching farms and villages along the valley of the Till. They murder fellow Englishmen; they despoil our women; they terrify our children. Because he and his band of ragged cowards dare not venture to the gates of this stronghold, I propose to ride out, hunt him down and roast his arse. Are you with me?'

A great shout of, 'Aye! Aye!' rose up from hundreds of throats. The commander lifted his arms and the shouts died away.

'All archers will take ten paces forward. Now!'

The weight of men carried Tom forward. The knight looked them over and gave a nod.

'Billmen and all others on foot, with or without arms, will take twenty paces towards me. Now!' Perhaps a hundred men crowded forward.

'All mounted men will trot past and take up position in blocks of fifty at the rear of the archers.'

The prickers, on snorting, thick-set ponies, rode past with nine-foot lances held upright, round wooden shields on their backs, and broadswords and axes at their sides. Tom noted the bizarre assortment of iron helmets, many of antique design, which covered the rugged Northumbrian heads. Long jackets of quilted linen or thick leather protected their upper bodies. The jackets carried improvised armour of sewn-on squares of iron and bone. Lengths of old chain protected vulnerable parts of the body. A few sported breastplates of steel. All wore thigh-length riding boots. He estimated eight hundred horsemen and wondered at some of the hard faces; they would terrify a boar.

Bulmer bellowed across the field, 'Northumbrians! Hold your places and I'll ride with my captains among you. We shall speak with you so that we know each other.'

The commander rode along the front of the blocks of men. He paused to converse with each group. Halting before Sergeant Atkinson's little band, he looked down. 'I'm told you men are professional soldiers in the heralds' guard. It will be good to stand in the field with you.' He scanned the drovers and noticed Tom. 'Perhaps we've met before - not long ago, I fancy?'

'Yes, sir,' Tom answered. 'On the village green at Sedgefield.'

'Ah! You're the archer who declined my offer! Well, I'm heartened to know we have a bowman of quality among us. There is a need for accurate marksmen. I'll see to it that you join a company set aside for special work.' He smiled and moved to the next group.

Tom muttered to Ben, 'I'm no soldier. I'm on a drover's hiring.'

Ben sighed. 'Not any more. It looks like we've no say in the matter. It's a turvy old morning.'

18

The Ill Raid

Half an hour later, the commander and his captains returned to the raised area and faced the men.

William Bulmer called out to them, 'I am heartened by what I've seen. A pity the Lord Home is not here, for he would suffer a loosening of the bowels.' He waited for the laughter to die away. 'It being a fine day, I want you to rest on the grass until food comes. Two hours from now - we march out. Men short of gear will file past those stacks of helmets and other tackle. Those without weapons will each take a pole-bill. Archers must collect arrows to make up a store of two sheaves of twenty-four. One sheaf of the new hardened points that can punch through armour, the other sheaf of long-shot bodkins. I want all archers mounted and to carry side-hangers. Those of you with gear in the barracks will fetch it now.'

The sergeant faced his small group. 'That's us, lads. Back to barracks and get your gear. You drovers better make the ponies ready.'

'Do the heralds know about this?' Ben challenged.

'They do, it was all talked through last night. We're all on full pay with a bit extra and I'll see to it that you come to no harm. And you, Tom, had best fetch that big bow you've been lugging about; it looks like you'll need it.'

The drovers were fitting harness to the ponies when the Norroy Herald entered the stables. 'We are delayed here. In view of the problems to the north, we have no choice but to place our escort under Sir William's command. You pony-men will standby here - he has enough pack animals. Later, when the earl arrives with the army, York Herald and I are to serve as negotiators in any dealings with the Scots - it is then we may need our ponies.'

Tom trembled. 'But, sir - he's said I must join the archers. That's not my work. You hired me as your pack-horse driver.'

'He wants you for an archer? And why's that, I wonder?'

The sergeant stood at the entrance. 'It's because he witnessed a display of marksmanship Tom laid on for the yeomen of Sedgefield, sir. It seems our pony-man has other talents.'

'In that case it's to your credit. While you are with the militia, take good care - I want you back here fit and whole.' He leaned forwards and, in a loud whisper added, 'You are in good hands, the hands of one of your own; the Bulmers are true Englishmen. They did not wade ashore with William the Bastard.' He touched his nose, winked and withdrew.

Sergeant Arkwright frowned. 'The Norroy knows a lot - that's his trade - but best keep that learning to yourself. Don't go telling such tales in front of a Percy.' He slapped Tom on the back. 'Well then, you'd best find your unit. You archers are to ride - so get hold of a strong hoss. And don't forget to pick up a bowman's hanger.'

'A what?'

'A side hanger. It's a short, single-edged sword. Keep it sheathed to your belt. It'll come in handy if t'other lot get a bit close.'

Ben and his son stood in slack-jawed silence. Tom stared at them wide eyed. 'Bloody hell! I didn't see this coming when I took the job - it's a far cry from cleaning tackle. Anyway, who'll care for Meg now I'm off with that lot?'

Rob spoke up. 'I'll look after her; I'll keep her on a bit of rope while you're gone, so she doesn't follow - and I'll make sure she's fed.'

'Thanks, friend. If owt happens to me, I know you'll be kind to her. I'd best get to the paddock for a mount before they get picked over.'

At mid-day on the eleventh of August, Tom rode out of Alnwick. Despite the mild breeze, he shivered and his stomach growled. He had no need to steer his mount in the press of a thousand rough ponies, and even rougher men, which choked the battered way to the village of Wooler. Strings of pack ponies, guarded by billmen on foot, trudged at the rear; somewhere among them were the sergeant and his little band of regular soldiers. He should be with them, they had become his friends - almost his family; instead, he was borne along by a mass of wild-looking strangers. A few arrow-shots distant, mounted spearmen were filtering through the scrub along low ridges to either side of the track; nobody seems bothered about them, so they must be ours, he mused.

At Eglingham village, they met the first refugees. From his saddle, Tom looked down onto the open palms of children begging for food.

Their parents squatted around a fire at the roadside.

'Have you any bread for us?' a little girl pleaded.

A man reached into his saddle pack, pulled out half a loaf and dropped it into the child's hands. 'There you are, hinney, share it out.' The girl squealed her thanks and ran with it to her parents.

The man growled, 'There'll be worse further up the road.'

'We don't see any of this where I'm from,' Tom said. 'But the auld ones say that Scotchmen forded the Tees once, a couple of hundred years back - I don't know.'

'Well there's too much of it up here. You'll not be seeing many villages. They're not worth the building - only to burn down, time and again. The rich folk have stone towers to get inside when there's reivers on the trod. Life's hard here - the raids aren't always from over the Border.'

After a few miles, the column slowed, slowly compressed, then halted while scouts gave news of the raiders. Tom dismounted and joined others. They stamped about and slapped their thighs to revive numb backsides as garbled rumour and opinion passed along the ranks. There were five thousand raiders up ahead. They'd fired a seventh village. The culprits were strung out and streaming home with masses of lifted stock. The thieves would pass to the north of Wooler from the west in two days. Billy Bulmer was swinging our eleven hundred to the east. We'd be making camp at Chillingham - then we'd move into the Till valley to block the track to the border. We're sorely outnumbered. Does Billy know what he's about?

At Chillingham, Tom lined up with others, to practise at targets. While shooting in volleys he became aware of eyes. Away to the right, William Bulmer sat on the great black horse watching the bowmen's efforts with close attention.

In late afternoon, once the August day had cooled, they broke camp and marched to Milfield. They made camp upwind of the smouldering wreck of the village. Survivors garbed in sacks straggled out and came among the campfires, begging.

Tom was in a gang gathering scraps of timber for the camp cooks; he was ripping out a blackened doorframe when the commander rode into the ruins. The fuel gatherers stopped to watch. Tom drifted closer. He saw the knight's nose wrinkle at the stench-fouled breeze, saw him wince at the wails and sobs of women keening over bodies.

The commander peered inside the cotts where, under layers of burnt thatch, lay the charred remains of families not yet gathered up. Close by, in the burial ground of the tiny church, survivors laboured among old graves - cutting new slots into the clay.

William Bulmer shouted across the wall of the churchyard, 'Who burnt this place?'

Men and women limped across, many without boots. 'Reivers came in the night, swooped on us like hawks. They beat us about the head and murdered folk. They took all we had.' The women pulled back their shawls to show their bruised faces.

'Who were they? Give me names.'

An old man coughed and spat. 'I ken them. They were Kerrs out of Teviotdale. Afore they burned us out they wanted to know the spots where the Herons and Selbys bided.'

'And then?'

'They shut them in their cottages and set fires. They're all dead. One lass nigh to birthing.'

The commander growled to a captain, 'This sickens me! Why such savagery?'

'It's the Borders, Sir William; these are marginal lands. English reivers wrought havoc across the Tweed not two weeks since. This is revenge. There are blood feuds here that last generations. The Kerrs have seized their chance to settle old scores.'

Sir William called to the hunched figures in the churchyard, 'Those men still fit can work for me as scouts - they'll be paid. You will come to the camp and be fed, equipped and horsed -' He broke off at the sound of hooves as thirty riders entered the village from the north -east. Ravelled hair - red, blonde and grey - hung below the rims of iron helmets. Coats of quilted leather bulged around dented breastplates. Eight-foot lances stood upright and ready - socketed close to the right knee. Grim eyes scanned the husk of the blackened village.

The captain spoke. 'These men are Herons and Selbys from east of here, Sir William. This is a village of their kin.'

'Who did this?' a blue-jowled rider shouted.

The old man answered, 'About fifty on them came swaggering' in - mostly Kerrs. It was auld Baldy Kerr who fired the cotts with folk inside. He's chopped his way through here afore. He brought his mob again: one had a bad scar across his nose and another was without front teeth. I didn't get a look at the rest - the night was black.

131

'They'll pay,' the rider said in a cold voice. He leaned toward William Bulmer. 'Ye have our service for two days only. If ye ride out wi' me to the sou'-west I'll show ye a spot where a trap might be set.'

A scrawny cockerel shrieked into the darkness. Tom opened one eye and grimaced, thinking, that bird is wondering what's happened to the other champions - not knowing they're stewing in reivers' broth-pots. He grunted to himself. 'I'm in a broth-pot as well - this is never what I looked for.' He rolled from beneath the damp blanket and stamped his feet in the dew; everyone had to turn out at cockcrow and he was ravenous.

Later, with his belly filled with sour rye porridge he jostled unwillingly in a throng of two hundred others with heavy quivers and bowstaves on their backs - trudging behind a mass of mounted spearmen. In the early gloom he got a wave from Sergeant Arkwright, left with the billmen to guard the archers' ponies.

The grey dawn-light showed an easy route, winding through scrub, and well-drained where it ran across the old river gravels of the Milfield Plain. It took them to the top of a fold in the ground, onto a low ridge that overlooked the usual reivers' route from Humbleton Hill as it headed northwards to the very end of England at the bank of the Tweed. In thin mist, they gathered where the broad track passed through a shallow dell bordered by thickets of broom and hawthorn.

The bowmen formed into two main groups and spread out, concealed in units of twenty, half an arrow-shot back from either side of the track. A captain of archers by the name of Edward Jackson had charge of Tom's section. The man ordered them to crouch down amid the clumps of broom. Before he obeyed, Tom had a final look around - they were on their own, just twenty of them at the northern end of string of archer groups, like the last bead on a string. He'd assumed the horsemen would be their protection, but they were barely visible - an arrow-shot away - among thickets of hawthorn and elder.

'Want a bit of hard cheese, young'un?'

Tom met the eyes of the man next to him. They were a washed-out blue and sunken below bushy eyebrows. The grey-whiskered jaw was slowly chewing.

'That's handsome of you.' Tom took the lump of yellow cheese - it made a good mouthful.

'That'll settle your belly. Hast' done owt like this afore?'

'I've not,' Tom said, through a full mouth.

'Ah well, there has to come a first time in all things. Tha'll be a fair shot though, being at this end; only the best here; and we've the best of captains. Here comes the man.'

The broom rustled as Captain Jackson pushed through the bushes, stooped and with head down. He looked around the little group of archers. 'Fleck! Make ready your tackle - same as your fellows.' He faced the rest, 'They're on their way - don't string bows until you hear them. Make no noise and stay low to the ground. No sleeping, either - I want you all alert.'

Tom was dry-mouthed and merely nodded before reaching into his belt sack for his father's gear. He slipped a sleeve of scuffed leather around the forearm that held the bow stave - it would protect the muscle from the lash of the bowstring. Around the two drawing fingers of his right hand, he fitted yellowed tubes of cow-horn, grooved to take the string.

Two hours passed without a sound from the army except for the occasional stamp of a hoof somewhere to the rear. Tom lay on his back watching the circling of buzzards set against the drift of grey cloud. They know something, he thought. He met the eyes of the fellow next to him. The man gave a grunt and nodded. 'Hark,' came a whisper through the broom. 'They're coming.'

Tom heard a faint murmur; it grew over the next few minutes into the rumbling of a mass of horse hooves mixed with the lowing of cattle and the bleating of sheep. Around him, archers slipped covers from their bows and took bowstrings from beneath their hats. As the din grew louder, Tom strung his longbow then peered through the dripping broom.

A long, irregular column headed towards them led by a dense group of mounted men, perhaps five hundred, riding five abreast. A banner fluttered at the front. Behind, other bands of riders herded roped groups of horses. Further to the rear trotted ragged bunches of cattle followed by tight flocks of sheep with men and dogs following. Lines of loaded pack ponies trailed in the rear, guarded by horsemen. The convoy covered a mile of track.

The captain of Tom's company crept among them, whispering urgently, 'I want you to concentrate your fire on the men and horses around that banner. That's Lord Home's device - a lion rampant with popinjays in the corners. The Scottish Lord of the East March is among that lot of prickers and we want him. Use bodkins at this range.'

A horn sounded twice. Two hundred archers broke cover and gave a great shout. Tom, without thinking, joined in the war cry. His fear vanished as the yelling numbed his mind. The bellowing faltered and stopped at the shouts of captains.

'Nock!'

Tom lined up a bodkin arrow so that the bowstring sat in the notch at the end of the shaft.

'Draw!'

He leaned into the bowstave, pushing it out while drawing on the string with two fingers.

'Mark!'

He aimed for Lord Home's standard-bearer, imagining the arrow already in its target.

'Loose!'

The cord thrummed and flight feathers brushed his thumb as the bodkin launched. The bowstring was still singing as he nocked his next arrow. There was no time to watch the flight of the first. He let fly his second shaft to see the Scots stand up in their stirrups and look around as the first squall of arrows hissed down to thud among them. They tumbled from their mounts in scores. Horses reared up or collapsed to their knees with arrows in their muscles; others galloped madly away in fright, their riders helpless.

The slopes around Tom bristled with leather-clad men as the Northumbrians leaned into their longbows and drew back bowstrings to release a third volley of arrows. Six seconds later they released a fourth. Their first sheaves were spent in two and a half minutes. A storm of five thousand arrows had swept down onto the confused raiders. They reached for their second quivers.

He readied his own reserve arrow-sack then paused to look around. The Scots seemed in panic. In the chaos of the arrow fall some of the vanguard had spurred their mounts straight ahead, towards the north and escape. Others were wheeling about and fleeing the way they had come, straight into herds of livestock. Arrows from companies on Tom's left pursued the raiders, but hundreds missed their targets and showered among the cattle. He saw beasts, roaring with pain and fear, stampeding forwards along the track where they ploughed into the mass of retreating horsemen, trampling the bodies of fallen men and knocking down the unhorsed. Tom shivered at the suffering.

'Fleck! Wake up!' Edward Jackson bawled at him through the swish of arrows.

Tom wiped his wet eyes and stiffened again as he looked back at his own company's target.

Some of the leaders had gathered into small groups and, yelling war cries, were charging the archers. A man nearby shouted, 'Look-out! They mean to ride us down!' Twenty of them, with lances couched, plunged through the broom towards Tom's group. The captain called out, 'They've got breastplates! Shoot the horses!'

In the first volley six horses stumbled and fell, others reared and threw their riders onto the slope where they rolled away.

Tom had aimed at the chest of a horse. He wavered as he tried to steel himself to put an arrow into the innocent animal. Instead, he raised his bow and loosed at the rider. The man warded off the arrow with a deft parry of his round shield and fixed him with a fierce glare. Tom put the next arrow into the Scotsman's upper right arm. The rider dropped his lance and, white faced, wheeled away back down the slope.

As the Scots closed in, the captain yelled again, 'Broadheads now!' Tom had already nocked another arrow - his last bodkin point - when he saw a lance approaching. He locked with the rider's eyes and understood he was the man's target. He had only enough time to half bend the bow before he loosed the arrow at a range of ten paces. Even so, it sprang from the bow with power enough for the slender warhead to pass into and halfway through the man's neck. The horse plunged onwards through the broom, dragging its rider by one stirrup -trapped foot.

A speared archer lay close by, writhing on his side and coughing up blood. The riders careered among the panicking bowmen. Among the confused tangle of broom bushes, the lances could only become stabbing spears; the raiders drew swords. Tom retreated further into the broom with other archers, ready to spin around and shoot again. A broken-nosed rider plunged his black horse through the scrub and got among them. He slashed at a middle-aged man on Tom's left. The sword cut into the side of the man's head and he crumpled. The rider wheeled and aimed his mount at Tom, who sidestepped enough to feel the draught as the sword swished past his ear. Now ten paces away, the Scot raised his blade to slash at the captain when Tom released a barbed heavyweight. It whipped through the air and struck the rider in his armpit. The man yelped and the sword spun away into the scrub. The reiver's shoulders slumped. He glared hatred as he spurred his mount and fled, straight into the path of Northumbrian horsemen as they emerged from cover. He screeched as two lances lifted him from the saddle.

Tom moved aside as the Northumbrians trotted between the groups of archers. Hundreds of them lined up and couched their lances. At the blast of a horn, they dug in spurs and, with whooping yells, charged down the slope. He waited among the hard-breathing archers, watching the last of the snorting cattle flee as lances converged on the Scots from both sides. The shock of the charge broke the last resistance and those raiders not crumpled on the ground, fled for their lives. The Northumbrians wheeled around and galloped along the margins of the horse herds and swirling knots of sheep to attack the stock drivers. He turned away.

Out of sight, Tom knelt in the bushes and vomited. He had begun to shake with sobs when a hand touched his shoulder.

'It's all done, soldier, you'll get over it,' Edward Jackson said. 'You're a top marksman. I have to thank you for putting one into that pricker - he almost had me. By rights, you should have his sword. Here, it's a good one.' He stuck the point of a broadsword into the earth beside Tom. 'That was a rough patch for our section, there's two dead and another fading. Even so, we did well to stand that charge.'

Tom got to his feet and faced along the track to where dead raiders and dying horses lay strewn. His stomach heaved. 'What do I want with a sword?' he said. 'You keep it.'

19

Retribution

Boots confiscated, four hundred prisoners shuffled along, roped together in pale-faced groups. They limped in stockings knitted by wives and mothers. Scattered along the track lay five hundred dead raiders. William Bulmer rode through the battlefield with his attendants. They searched among the dead but found no sign of the Scots commander. His standard, embroidered with collared, green parrots, lay trampled into the mud. Lord Home had escaped.

Sir William, with the hoof-trodden banner of the Scots Lord of the March draped over the rump of his horse, rode along the lines of captives. Each time he saw a man wearing expensive trappings he would order a marshal to pull him out of the crowd.

'Who are you?' he demanded. Some replies were arrogant with pride, others mumbled and hangdog.

'That one!' The commander pointed to a man in a breastplate. 'I know him.'

The man shook off the hands that tried to drag him forward. 'Lay off me, you pignuts!' He dragged his ropes forward to stare up at Sir William. 'So you ken my family name do you?'

'That I do, Sir George Home. And I know that your proud brother has fled without you. What have you got to say?'

The captive glared. 'You hear me now, Bulmer! 'Twas an ill raid for us this day - the next shall be no paltry trod! You'll not stand what's to come!'

Stripped of gear, the dead enemy lay half-naked in random heaps ready for burial in pits. Two oxcarts, loaded with the few English slain, creaked towards the churchyard in the burnt village of Milfield. Behind the carts trudged ropes of bare-footed Scots. At day's end, the militia camp was crowded with cartloads of plunder and heaps of pony packs.

Villagers and men from outlying farms soon appeared. They surrounded the raiders, hurling stones and clods of earth into their faces. The captives replied variously with pleadings, curses and gobs of spit.

William Bulmer appeared from his tent. 'Stop this now!' he shouted.

The crowd hung back, silent until a woman screamed, 'That's them! That's the bastards!' She pointed a shaking hand at three men tied together. 'Look! It's him! Auld man Baldy Kerr and his crooked, murdering sons. And them two over yon! They came with them. And him with the scar as well. They're the ones who burned our neighbours alive. Fired that lass - with her bairn just ready to come.'

'Can anyone else recognise the killers here?' William Bulmer waited.

Villagers stepped forward and pointed fingers, spat, and slapped. Prisoners flinched as women screamed into their faces. But the old Kerr chief yelled back in defiance, 'A pox on ye and all yer ilk!'

'I've heard enough. Pull them to one side. A gallows tree stands outside the village. We need an experienced hangman. He will have his fee.' William Bulmer waited.

'I can do it.' Then another voice. 'And me, I've done a few.'

'You're both hired.' He scanned the crowd. 'Sergeant Arkwright, are you here?'

'Yes, sir.' The sergeant waited in the background with the survivors of his small unit around him.

'Be so good as to supervise the process and ensure it's done properly. Put your men on guard whilst the job is done. Hang all fifteen. Do it now.'

'I'm worth a big ransom,' the old Kerr shouted, his voice cracking.

'Indeed you are - but there'll be no trade on this occasion. Right. Get on with it!' William Bulmer strode back to his tent with his chief captains.

In the commander's tent, during supper, they heard the yells of villagers, 'Good riddance! You'll all gan tae Hell on the three-legged mare! May the devil roast your arses!'

Sir William set down his tankard and looked around the table. 'An ungovernable territory and I fear it will continue so until the robber tribes on both sides are brought to heel. What should be done with the captives, think you?

One of the captains spoke. 'Many of the prickers - the spearmen who rode with us today - are border raiders themselves, sir. They regard the captives as their own property and expect to hold them for ransom. It is the custom here. Likewise they will demand the prisoners' mounts.'

'We shall soon be asking again for these wild men's loyalties, therefore I will uphold that arrangement. It's a pity though - most of those geldings are valuable. Also, I wish not to have the burden of surplus prisoners. Lord Home's brother is treasure enough and remains with us - he'll be locked up in Alnwick Castle - Lord Home will wish to bargain at some point. Now, what to do with all the goods and chattel we've recovered?'

Another captain added his voice. 'I understand that much of it actually belongs to men who rode with us, sir. They are already sharing out the livestock according to earmarks and brands. Other yeomen and cottagers will arrive tomorrow looking for their property. News runs like quicksilver in these parts.'

'Hmm. Then anything not claimed by noon tomorrow will remain here under guard. Most of it is from this part of the Till valley anyway. I've no wish for delay as a makeshift magistrate. Tell the local chiefs that I expect their people to behave honestly and claim no more than their own. Whilst our part is done here, we should all mark this: there's a greater task for us before summer's end.'

Crowds of cheering townspeople lined the streets to greet the force as it marched into Alnwick to the beat of drums. When the vanguard neared the marketplace, a group of aldermen rushed forward to surround the commander. He raised an arm to halt the advance. Alnwick's aldermen had panicked at the prospect of their town overwhelmed by triumphant militia.

The front of the column stopped in obedience while hundreds in the rear slipped away, climbed walls or jumped their horses over fences. Hobbled ponies choked the market-place as militiamen abandoned them for the alehouses. Officers shouted orders to the remains of the column and sent hundreds of tired riders and plodding foot soldiers straight into barracks at the castle. On the way, dozens spat on the ground at the aldermen's feet.

At the castle stables an overjoyed Meg rushed up to Tom, jumping around his legs and barking with delight. The heralds appeared and questioned him for an account of the skirmish, but a grim-faced Sergeant Arkwright broke in:

'Welsh Jones is dead, sir. And Bentley's fading. He lost a deal of blood before we plugged the hole. He needs the physician. Can you have my soldier looked at right away?'

The York Herald scowled at the interruption. But the Norroy met the sergeant's eyes. 'Of course, Sergeant. The physician is here and working hard; I will go to him. Put Bentley on his pallet while I fetch help.'

Tom placed a hand on the sergeant's arm and felt the haggard man relax for the first time that day. A band of fleeing raiders had carried out a vengeful attack on the baggage camp. They galloped out of the mist with lances couched. Jones and Bentley were sentries and their warning blasts by signal horn had alerted the camp. Borderers' lances had run through them both. The raiders then plunged into the camp, lunging and stabbing. At the last moment, they had swung away from the gathering lines of bills.

The sergeant had left Jones at Wooler church for burial and brought Bentley to the castle on one of a line of oxcarts filled with wounded. He lay in a fever, with a shoulder pierced through from front to back. Though the sergeant had often berated these two men for their untidy habits and called them, 'a disgrace'. Now, Tom saw how the strong man's face betrayed his grief.

20

Fire

Hilda Fleck glanced over her shoulder. 'Here's that Ralph Warren again; I reckon he's a fancy for you, Mary.'

'That's not so, Hilda. I've caught the way he gawps at thee when he thinks no one's looking. Mind though, he is a bonny man; he has kind eyes and a gentle tongue, though he's not lean like our Tom.'

They giggled beneath their loads of deadwood and edged off the track as the lord of the manor's youngest son picked his way through the previous night's puddles.

'Good morning, fair maids. I note you are exercising your right of estovers in our woods. I hope those twigs make good fuel.'

Hilda glanced sideways at him. 'Thank you, sir. We have ash branches today, they're best for the bread oven.' He has a gentle face, she thought - not cruel like his brother.

'You are baking? I delight in the smell of new bread when I pass your door; it makes my mouth water. Let me help with the fuel, I'll gather another load and carry it back with you. Please wait.' He plunged into the wood and returned a few minutes later with an armful of branches. 'Will these do?'

Mary pulled at a branch that had beads of orange fungi along its length. It snapped and fell to the ground where it broke into pieces. 'There's no use in carrying that one. It's only light 'cos all the heart's been sucked out by them orange buttons.'

'Ah, I see. Then half of what I have is useless.' He threw his load to the ground and picked out the few sound lumps of deadwood. 'There are still some that will burn. Please, good Mary, let me carry your load and you take my few twigs.' He picked up her firewood, heaved it across his shoulders and strode away along the woodland path, whistling a tune. The women shared out their loads and followed.

'That proves it, Mary. He's an eye for you.'

Mary blushed. 'No it doesn't! All that is just to fox us; he's too shy to offer to carry thine.'

'Whatever he's after, he does go by our gate more than he used to.

141

Since his Dad and brother went off and left him in charge, he's got a bit more about him. Shush - he's stopped,' Hilda whispered.

Ralph Warren had cast aside the firewood to stare along the ride at a column of black smoke. 'Drop everything,' he yelled, 'there's a fire!'

They set off running. Mary sprinted ahead and covered the quarter-mile to the cottage first. She ran through the gate shouting, 'It's the thatch! We need haste - the wind's catching it!'

Hilda gasped at the flames leaping around the chimney stack. Mary reappeared, dragging a ladder from behind the cottage; after leaning it against the wall, she dashed through the door. Moments later, she emerged with a knife and shoved it at Ralph.

'Cut the ropes that bind down the thatch!' She yelled. 'We must get it off. Start at the chimney end. Hilda, fetch the fork and rake. We have to stop the timbers taking fire.' She sprang to the ladder and climbed into the smoke. Ralph hacked at the ropes that held down the layers of barley-straw. The bindings sprang free as the rocks that weighted them thudded to the ground. Behind the cottage, the two milking goats set up a bleating.

Mary straddled the ridge of the thatch with her skirts rucked up. Hilda tossed up the hayfork and clambered onto the roof with the rake. Pressed close together, as though on the back of an ox, the girls fought to free the tight-packed straw, hurling it to the ground in showers of sparks.

'It's got too much of a hold. It's falling into the kitchen. Hilda, you go inside and fetch out as many things as you can. I'll dig out a firebreak to stop it spreading. Master Ralph! Fill those buckets at the beck - and be sharp about it!'

He gave her one astonished glance before running to the beck.

They toiled and coughed for half an hour. As he hefted another bucket of water to her, Ralph saw that Mary's braids had unwound and her wheaten hair become stuck to her cheeks with sweat. He stood at the top of the ladder and watched her body swing as she flung the water along the length of a roof spar. When she handed him the empty bucket he searched her face for signs of panic; her eyes held his with the boldness of a goshawk.

'You must leave it, Mary. The wool of your kirtle is starting to singe. Come off there, I'll take your place.' He took the full bucket that Hilda offered and climbed onto the top of the wall. Taking aim, he hurled the water into the centre of a mass of straw as it glowed in a gust of wind. 'Mary, get below and fetch water. I'll cast off more thatch.'

Her eyes blazed at him as she threw the bucket to the earth and followed it down the ladder. She staggered from the beck with another two slopping buckets, passing Hilda bent under the weight of bedding, clothes and a cauldron.

Hilda shouted, 'Most of what's good is saved. We'll have to leave the bed frames. I'll get the pots and the jug and that'll be all.'

Mary dropped the buckets, her shoulders drooping. 'Oh, Hilda! Gran's cottage! And her in the ground not three weeks.' She clung to Hilda and wept as another section of burning laths collapsed into their bedchamber.

Ralph jumped off the roof onto a pile of black thatch. He hawked and spat. 'It's over. All that was alight is off the roof. The main timbers are safe, so we can look inside.'

The cottage had a kitchen and two bedchambers. Except for one chamber, the entire cottage lay open to the sky. Ralph pointed at the wall above the fireplace. 'That's what caused it - see the gap between the stones at the top? There's sparks floating out of it where the thatch bedded against the chimney.'

'It's the oven. I'd built the fire up before we went out. 'I thought it safe but it must have blazed a bit too much,' Mary said in a voice full of misery. 'Gran forever warned me. It's my doing.'

Ralph laid a gentle hand on her shoulder and pointed. 'No, Mary. It's not your fault. None could know of that hole in the chimney - it lay beneath thatch. You mustn't blame yourself.'

Hilda wiped smoke tears from her eyes and squinted through a doorway. 'Your Gran's bed-space still has most of its thatch. We could live in here till the roof gets mended.'

Ralph sat on the flagstones of the floor and leaned his aching back against the wall. He blinked his streaming eyes and looked at the roof. 'All the skilled men are with the militia; the work cannot start until they return. It could be two months before you have a new thatch. In the meantime you can stay in one of the manor's barns.'

'I'll never go near that place!' Hilda shouted. 'Never!'

Ralph shifted with embarrassment. 'Because of my brother's ways? Yes - I'm sorry. But you cannot stay in this ruin.'

'Then I'll go north to find Tom, my own brother!' she blurted out.

'And so will I!' Mary's eyes shone.

Ralph raised a hand in alarm. 'It's too dangerous for you in these times, and who knows where he is?'

Hilda drew herself erect and stuck out her chin. 'We've had a message that he's gone to Alnwick. I've some savings; we'll buy a riding hoss.'

'There are none. All are out with the militia.'

Mary butted in, 'You still have mares at the big house - we've seen them. Let us hire two; you can take our goats and hens as rent.'

Ralph winced. 'I can see my father's face when he gets home and discovers hens and nanny goats in his stables instead of his grey palfreys. Come back to the hall with me and have some food - perhaps there is a solution. There's no one at home now who you need fear.'

Hilda's words tumbled out, 'Suppose your father comes home tonight?'

He laughed again. 'Then we will all have to flee together. But I know he's headed for the Percy stronghold and will be weeks in the Borders. In the meantime, I'll send a cart for your things. Come to the house now. We all look like blackamoors. Let us wash, eat and rest. Tomorrow, you can decide.'

Mary laid an arm over Hilda's shoulders. 'We should welcome his kindness. Let's see to the hens and goats afore we go.'

The housekeeper, a curvaceous widow of thirty-five, opened the great door as the three sooted figures approached. 'Master Ralph, sir! What's happened?'

'A fire, Bess. The Humbles' thatch has gone. The girls will stay here tonight so they can recover. Where shall we lodge them?' He coughed twice and spat into a flowerpot. 'Excuse me, it is the smoke.'

'Best if they stay with the servant girls. There's a spare bed - if they can squeeze in together.' Her eyes narrowed as she looked Hilda up and down. 'Are you feeling any better, Hilda - after your bad patch?'

'I am, Mistress Hutton, thank you. My strength's back - though, just now I need to wash.' She tried to rub grit from her eyes.

'Those eyes are red raw - and yours too, Mary. Come with me, I've a pan of water just boiled.' Bess Hutton shone a smile at her employer's son.' And I'll send a bowl and jug up to your room, sir; you look a bit charred.'

'After these ladies have washed we will share food together. Something hot and nourishing please, Bess.'

The woman stiffened, but Ralph was too entranced by the girls to notice.

Ralph hummed to himself as he washed, stripped to the waist. The world is sometimes interesting, he mused. These girls are vivid creatures - I could write verse about them. Which of them is closest to perfection? If I could take one to my heart, which would she be? Hilda, the red maid, intelligent and deep, perhaps passionate - and with talons? Or Mary, the wheaten maid who glows with vigour, good sense and courage?

A soft knock sounded on his door. 'Master Ralph, sir. I bring your clean clothes.'

He threw a towel over his shoulders and pulled open the door. 'Thank you, Bess.'

With her eyes on the flawless skin of his hair-free chest, she handed him the clean shirt, breeches, stockings and small clothes. She took a pace back. 'Sir, I don't think the Master, your father, would be pleased if the cottagers took their food in the hall.'

'Yes, I'm sure you are right, housekeeper. However, he has placed me in charge and it is what I wish. What delight is for supper?' He fixed her with what he considered a stare of command. She lowered her eyes.

'Baked flounders, just in from Coatham, sir, and cook has raised a fine pie of raspberries to be served hot with cream.'

'Thank you, Bess. It will be a suffering to have to wait. Might we also have a jug of your famed bramble wine?'

'Of course, sir. The two-year-old is ready to pour.'

'We are fortunate to have you in this house, Bess. Are our guests at their ease?'

'Yes, Master Ralph. I've found them clean kirtles to wear. Their smoky old clothes are in the washtub.' Her dark eyes twinkled at him, he thought - even with a hint of coquetry.

He flushed a little and took the clothes from her hands. 'Thank you. I'll get ready.' He backed away and closed the door with his foot. He chuckled to himself as pictures formed in his mind - that ample woman is missing her visits to Father's bed and whatever it is she does for my brother Mark.

At supper, Ralph Warren watched the girls from beneath lowered lids. They ate timidly with the knives and spoons. Sometimes they glanced in his direction to note how he took the bones from his fish. Hilda remained subdued and kept her eyes on her trencher. Mary fumbled with the food as she stared at the tapestries and paintings that hung against the walls.

She pointed with her knife. 'Who is that gentleman in the picture?'

'That is Marmaduke Weastall. I never knew him, though he was my grandfather - my mother's father. Mother often praised his kindness; she loved him.'

'Er - perhaps you take after him, Master Ralph,' she faltered.

'I may have his love of books.' He smiled. 'Please call me Ralph, this evening.'

She blushed and lowered her eyes. 'I wish I could read a book.'

'And I wish I practised as a teacher of books, Mary. I'd like to live as a real scholar - in a library.'

Hilda moved the drape of her white wimple from her face and spoke for the first time. 'Would you have to leave the manor to be a scholar?'

'Yes, I would go to York or Durham to study and find my own students, or even as far away as Cambridge. But,' he sighed, 'it would depend on Father's wishes for me.'

They finished the baked flounders in silence.

Ralph rubbed his hands together. 'Now we can start on the fruit pie. You can see how much I like my food. Too much, perhaps.'

'This wine is making my cheeks hot.' Mary laughed.

'Pray, have some more.' He reached across the broad table and filled her goblet. 'And please take off those wimples if you are hot; I don't know how you can bear them, they must muffle you.'

Mary pulled at her headband so that it freed the square of white cloth that covered her head and cheeks. Her pale, golden locks, dressed into two braids, fell onto her shoulders. Hilda hesitated until, with a slight snort, pulled off her own wimple so that two copper-coloured braids sprang out and fell across her chest. Ralph gazed at the girls until he realised they were embarrassed.

'Now, Hilda, tell me how you plan to find your brother. It may become a tale of adventure, a saga, and I could write it into a fine story that would make a book.'

'We've been told he has work driving pack-hosses for two gentlemen. They're heralds who are travelling to Alnwick on the North Road. They stop at places like Newcastle on the way, so I think we're bound to find him if we follow that road.'

'And what will you do when you find him - if he is hired to the heralds? He may be bound to them.'

Mary interrupted, 'We've talked about that and decided we'll seek out my grandmother's kin in Durham town. Gran said we might one day be cast out of the cottage and that her family are good folk and would help us.'

'Durham is on the Great North Road, likewise Newcastle and Alnwick. What if I rode with you, at least as far as Durham?'

'You have the manor in your care,' Hilda said.

Ralph poured himself more wine. 'I've hardly anything to do; Father's bailiff manages everything. Meanwhile, I'm listless and idle away my days. I've a mind to call on the scholars of Durham Priory and examine their library. I've visited before and they know me. What do you say?' He pushed back his chair. 'Please excuse me; there is something that needs my attention.'

They waited until he had left the room before looking at each other with wide eyes.

Mary whispered rapidly, 'What do you think, Hilda? Do you think he could help us find Tom? How would we do it alone? We've not been beyond Osmotherley.'

'He knows the road and we would be safe, for he's a gentle man.' Hilda shivered. 'Not like his brother. But I've seen the way Ralph Warren looks at you and I worry.'

'You needn't. He's a harmless lad, Hilda. A bit feckless, perhaps. I could even come to fancy him. Shall we trust him to guide us?'

'Yes. What else is there to do? Shush - he's coming back.'

'Wonderful! Tomorrow then! We shall set forth like Parcival on his quest, and Tom shall be the grail.' Ralph poured himself more wine and opened the book he had carried into the room. 'Let me read you travellers' tales of one hundred and fifty years ago. They are by Geoffrey Chaucer - a fine poet. This is part of the tale of the *Wife of Bath*.

> *And as I may drink ever wine and ale,*
> *I will tell truth of husbands that I've had,*
> *For three of them were good and two were bad.*
> *The three were good men and were rich and old.*
> *Not easily could they the promise hold*
> *Whereby they had been bound to cherish me.*

You know well what I mean by that, pardie!
So help me God, I laugh now when I think
How pitifully by night I made them work;
And by my faith I set by it no store.
They'd given me their gold, and treasure more...'

Mary interrupted with a giggle and Hilda made a choking sound as she sipped her wine. He ploughed onwards - by the end of the evening, in his enthusiasm for the journey, Ralph had promised to lend them riding mares.

Moths were fluttering on the swirled window glass before the girls squeezed into one bed in a corner of the female servants' quarters. They fell exhausted into sleep, snuggled together. Mary with her arms wrapped around Hilda, breathing in the smell of freshly washed tresses that brushed against her cheeks.

Ralph slid beneath his bed covers with a contented sigh. He had never enjoyed an evening in this house so much as tonight. Replete with good food and cheeks glowing from the effects of wine, he had a new confidence. He moved his enclosed candle closer and opened his dead mother's volume of Chaucer again. After a few stanzas, he realised they meant nothing to him at that hour. All he had in his mind was a picture of two girls. He wished they could be either his sisters or his lovers. He could not decide, although his body's stirrings gave the lie. He blew out the candle and lay on his back to allow his hand to rest where it felt inclined.

An owl hooted somewhere close by in the elms, followed by another at a distance. As he lay listening to them and luxuriating in the unusual pleasure of aching muscles, his eyelids became heavy and he drifted into a dream of damsels with their hair let down.

Perhaps his own soft groans woke him or the lips around his penis or the loose curls that brushed across his stomach - perhaps all three lifted him back into consciousness. He stiffened, then relaxed and reached down to fondle the locks of hair, wondering with delight what their colour might be. His thighs tightened, but the mouth parted from him and a warm, soft body slid upwards. It whispered, 'Not yet, Master Ralph, not yet. We must make it last.' Fingers stroked across his nipples, followed by the licking of a tongue.

Ralph grunted as his nerves thrilled. He ran his fingers through the tresses, persuaded them towards him and whispered, 'Mistress

148

Elizabeth Hutton, this is new. I had no idea skin could yield such pleasure.'

She took his hand and led it over her body. 'Then please explore me further, Master Ralph,' she breathed into his ear.

21

Court Martial

Northumbrians from scattered hamlets rode into the castle each evening; William Bulmer was intent on moulding these shepherds and farmers into a unified division.

His protests ignored, Tom practised with the hanger sword until he could turn away any spear thrust. He drilled with the archers. Each morning, he squeezed into the midst of a crowd of broad-shouldered men. They shot in volleys and increased the rate of release until their sinews burned. Their captains lined them up in an effort to standardise their gear. Bowstaves were to be rubbed with wax, resin and tallow; all bowstrings to be waterproofed.

Thousands of clothyard arrows, from the fletchers of Kent, were unshipped at Newcastle and carted to Alnwick. The new shafts, twenty-seven inches long, carried a four-inch, socketed warhead. He thought them more finely balanced than any arrow he had held. He practised with a new version of the broadhead, furnished with flanges and a tip of hardened steel, intended to pierce armour.

Half the new arrows were Kentish bodkins. They had no barbs but were long, slender and light. Designed for launching in masses to create chaos among crowded infantry and horsemen, they had a long history; all Europe feared them. Like all Bulmer's archers, Tom had to pull the great-bow to its maximum and find a range of two hundred and fifty yards with the bodkin.

At night, Tom's muscles ached as he lay on his pallet. Ben Wilson and his son watched from their own straw beds as he got up to stretch and rub his shoulder. Ben joined him. 'You've got bowman's strain with all that practice. Take off that shirt and I'll give them muscles a work over with some horse ointment - it's loaded wi' comfrey.'

Tom lay belly down on a bench to let the pony driver's hard fingers work at his muscles and rotate his joints. 'I've never used the bow so much as they're asking of us now. By heck though, I can feel the bones glow under that rubbing.'

'This handling and kneading works for strains on a hoss. It should do well enough for a gristly kine-herd like you, Tom Fleck.'

'I'll take the insult just so long as you keep going, pack-hoss plod.'

After drill, the force had freedom to leave barracks. He used this time to call into Alnwick, asking for news of Isaac and Rachel who should have arrived in town a month ago. As he walked the streets he sensed echoes of them; was it just his yearning imagination? Even though he could hardly expect to meet them again, they dogged his thoughts. He learned they had stayed in Alnwick for two days. One morning they had ridden out through the southern gate with two armed men.

His wistful dreams of Rachel came with guilt. He had to remind himself of the women who hoped for news - of his sister living in the shelter of Agnes Humble and her granddaughter Mary - Mary who waited by the Tees. Since the fight, other images moved through his sleep that caused him to cry out and wake in a sweat.

Three days after the ambush he shared a table in an alehouse with Peter Tindall; Meg lay asleep at their feet. Peter swallowed his beer and said, 'You haven't talked about that fight with the raiders, Tom - I got stuck on camp guard while it happened. I heard we lost sixty. Were ye feared?'

'Aye, when I heard them coming my hands set to shaking. I could hardly unwrap the bow stave and I'd trouble getting it strung.'

'Did you put any clothyards into them?'

'I did - and was sick afterwards.'

'Sick? You mean - threw up?'

'Aye, afterwards. But once the fight got under way, a hush came to my head and I shot arrow after arrow at them. Then a rider tried to fix me with a lance - I put one through him just in time.' Tom's voice shook and he wiped his eyes. 'I'm having some bad dreams, Peter. A man with an arrow in his throat, spitting blood, and terrified kine staggering about bristling with shafts.'

Peter gave a low whistle and filled Tom's tankard. 'Here, sup some more beer.' His speech was slurred. 'I had a bit of a fright as well, nearly pissed mesel' when they rushed the camp. We stood shoulder to shoulder, with our bills held out, to take the charge. I thowt my end had come. But they veered off a few hoss-lengths from us. I can't say I've dreamt about it though. Maybe I have - I don't remember.'

'I'm not made for this soldiering, Peter. I'm thinking I'll clear out of here and get off home,' Tom whispered.

151

'Don't do that.' Peter shot an anxious glance around the room - the alehouse had filled with soldiers. 'Two of our lot ran off. They've brought them back and it could be they'll hang.'

'Maybe you're right; I've run away before - perhaps I need to see this bad patch through. I'd a deal of contentment with the heralds - easy work and learning to read - then this happens.' Tom took a deep drink of beer.

A kick opened the door and four well-dressed men stamped in from the street. The alehouse keeper bustled up to them. 'Good evening, sirs. Welcome to the Bull. I'll clear you a table.'

The newcomers scowled across the sea of heads and back at the innkeeper. 'We want meat and drink,' one barked.

'And we want it served by your most toothsome wench,' another called out.

Tom whipped around at the last speaker and his heart sank.

The innkeeper rested his podgy hands on their table. 'I want you lads to move to another bench. That one where the sergeant's sat will do. I need this'n for these gentlemen.'

Peter, who had drunk his fill, glared at the innkeeper. 'We've sat here all night and we're not shifting.'

'Either you move, lad, or I'll chuck you into the street.' The bulky innkeeper took hold of Peter's jerkin and tugged. He let go and backed away when the lightweight youth raised a fist.

'It's no matter, Peter.' Tom stood up. 'We'll clear out to another spot - come on.' He took hold of his friend's arm and eased him to his feet.

The two friends shuffled off the bench as the innkeeper ushered his new guests to the table and started gathering up the used pots. The four new customers moved to take their seats when one of them stiffened.' I know you,' he shouted in Tom's face. 'You're Fleck, the waster who fled the muster and broke his hiring bond with the manor.'

'And I know you well enough,' Tom shot back. He threw a defiant look straight into Mark Warren's eyes. 'I'll not muck out your byres again. You can do them yourself.'

'Brass-faced young bastard!' Mark yelled and slapped Tom across the cheek with the back of his hand. Tom backed away towards the door. Hackles raised, Meg stood between them, growling.

'And here's the poxy little cur that bit me.' He lashed out with his foot and caught the dog in its chest.

Tom's fist landed full on the smirking mouth. His biceps were flexed to deliver another punch when a pair of muscular arms grabbed him from behind, pulled him to the door and out into the street. Sergeant Arkwright held him against a window mullion. 'Now then, Fleck! I want you to calm down quick. That man's a captain. You've assaulted an officer. Let's not make it any worse.'

He pushed Tom further along the wall of the alehouse and faced the four men who had followed them through the door. Bracing his shoulders, he addressed Warren: 'I saw what happened, sir. You are an officer and you struck one of my men without due cause, and that's not right. I respectfully suggest the matter ends here.'

By this time other soldiers had crowded into the street and gathered around, looking angry.

'Who the hell do you think you are, clouting my marrer across the face like that?' Alan Fuller had size; after a drink he stood even more straight-backed. He strode forward and pushed his face within inches of Mark Warren's.

'You have the breath of a dog's bowel,' said the lord of the manor's son through bruised lips. His hand dropped to the hilt of the dagger in his belt.

Alan raised his huge fist. The sergeant grabbed his arm and bellowed, 'Right, that's enough from you, Fuller. Any more and I'll put a stop on your pay.'

Tom's voice wavered. 'Thanks for sticking by me, lads. I want you all to come to the Oak so I can buy you a drink and a lump of pie. How's that?'

'Aye!' Riley shouted. 'Let's get out of this shit pit and get some proper ale and fodder.'

'And Tom's buying for once!' shouted another.

Arms grabbed Tom from both sides to half-march and half-carry him across the street.

The Oak Inn heaved with militia. The soldiers squeezed around a table and set-to with determination to fill themselves with food and drink. Meg stretched out beneath to chew on scraps of discarded hard crust. Alan Fuller entertained them with stories of France and the peculiarities of French women. Peter wanted to know in what manner they differed from English women.

'For a start off, you don't find many freckles on them,' Alan boomed in a beery voice. 'I'm greatly taken with freckles, as you know. And red hair weakens me legs.'

Hardcastle belched. 'Forget the freckles, man. Tell us what they're like in bed. Are they the same as women over here - or different?'

'Well, apart from the fact that you can't tell what they're on about half the time, they do have one or two special French tricks.' Alan took a drink and said nothing further. The gathering fell silent as men stared into their ale pots and considered the matter. Alan closed his eyes and gave a soft sigh.

'Go on, man. What sort of tricks?' Riley's tone was urgent.

The sergeant laughed and banged the table with his fist. 'That's what you'll find out after this lot's done, when we'll likely get our marching orders for France.'

'I'm not going to France - I need to get off home.' Tom drained his mug and slammed it onto the table.

'You'll not take ship,' the sergeant said. 'Don't worry about that. You're short term. Once this is over you can clear off or you can stay with the heralds - it's up to you. The Norroy thinks you're a useful sort and he'll likely find you work for a good spell yet - if you want it, that is. How's the book reading coming on?'

'It's a lot of thinking - makes my head go queer sometimes. The first letter of a stretch of writing often has all sorts of tricky work hanging off it and it's hard to make out - but Alan helps.'

'He's doing all right, Sarge,' Alan said. 'He'll be after more books soon. He's through the one the Norroy gave him. He's about read all the ink off since he got it given at Newcastle.'

Evans laughed and spat on the floor. 'Why are you bothering with that reading stuff? I can't see what good it'll do thee - unless you're thinking of joining the friars.' The table went quiet except for one man choking on his ale.

Tom broke the silence. 'It's reading that frees a man. I'm sick of scratting about as a poor bloody labourer, taking the kicks and saying nowt.' He raised his voice. 'My grandfather lost his land to the family of that pig who slapped my face. They took his few little fields off him - said they belonged to the manor. The Weastalls gave those fields to my granddad for my mother's benefit. Then when auld Marmaduke, the last of the Weastalls, died, the Warrens took the land off us - said we had no title. They've been pushing us about for years and I'm taking it no more.' His voice fell to a quiet shake. 'Him I punched tonight - is a dirty horn-master - my sister nearly died because of him.'

The table fell into another hush. The sergeant drained his tankard,

154

set it down and cleared his throat. 'I think you'll do all right, Tom. Just keep up with the learning. Meanwhile, keep a rein on that temper and take care who it is you go thumping. Now, I think we've all had enough this night. Let's shift ourselves to the barracks.'

~ ~ ~

On the way back, Peter drew close. 'I've heard of the Weastalls, they used to farm and dig iron up Eskdale. Why did they give land to your folk?'

'Mam said one of our women had their blood, but she'd been sired the wrong side of the blanket. The Weastall acres came with her as a gift when she wed. That's all I know about it.'

Next morning, Tom stood with others practising at the butts when Captain Jackson took him aside. 'What have you been up to, Fleck? I have to march you to the Castle - come on.'

'I had an argument in the Bull, sir. I clouted Mark Warren.' Tom's pulse raced as he followed the tall captain of archers into the courtyard. 'Am I in for trouble?'

'It depends on their mood. Make sure you keep a soldier's straight back, show them respect and give your answers in a courteous manner. I'll speak up for you.'

He followed Edward Jackson through a massive stone doorway, along a gloomy passage and into a ground floor room. Bare oak panels lined the walls and heavy beams supported the floor above. Along one side of a table were seated a group of men. Even though silhouetted against a mullioned window, he knew them all. John Young, the Norroy Herald, was central, with the York Herald on his right. Sir Edmond Warren and his son, Mark, lounged on the Norroy's left. Sergeant Arkwright stood to one side.

John Young snapped his fingers and pointed. 'Soldier, you will stand before me to hear the charge.'

Tom took a position one pace back from the centre of the table and Captain Jackson moved to stand with the sergeant.

'Archer Fleck - I'm told that last night you struck an officer, Captain Mark Warren. This is a serious matter - have you aught to say?'

'He slapped me across the face - called me a bastard and kicked my dog, sir,' Tom said, his voice wavering.

Edmond Warren snorted. 'And you think that sufficient reason to strike an officer, do you, churl?'

'You should hang for this,' Mark Warren shouted, through swollen lips.

John Young glowered along the table. 'Sir Edmond, gentlemen, let me remind you that I'm in charge of this proceeding. We have a busy day. I want this done with speed and fairness.' He fixed Tom with a grim look. 'You admit to striking Captain Warren?'

'Yes, sir, and I've said why. Even though he's a captain he has no right slapping me around the face like that.' He braced his shoulders. 'Labouring men have their pride; I'm no French peasant to be knocked about by any gentleman who gets out of temper.'

'You've a damned nerve!' shouted Edmond Warren. 'And that's not all! I summoned you to attend my mustering. Instead you saw fit to flee the parish and leap the Tees like a coward.'

'And on his way to the river he attacked me with a quarterstaff - then tried to drown me,' Mark Warren blurted out.

'You raped my sister,' yelled Tom, thrusting a finger at Warren. 'Your brat died inside her - she stood close to death herself.'

The Norroy slapped the table hard with his palm. 'Silence! I will not have shouting! I detect a history behind this matter. I now wish to hear from the man's own captain regarding his character and conduct as a soldier. Captain Jackson, would you have anything to tell?' The Norroy leaned back in his chair.

'Yes, sir, I would. This man is the most gifted archer I've worked with. His shooting is a delight. In fact, he put a shaft through the throat of a charging pricker about to ride us down. His next arrow went neatly into the sword arm of another who was about to cleave off my head. I owe archer Fleck my life.'

'Well said, Captain!' In his high voice, Thomas Tonge, the York Herald, spoke for the first time. 'I can vouch for his character. He found my lost seal ring and did wade the Tees to return it. Fleck is honest and upright.' He shot a triumphant glare along the table at Edmond Warren. 'You learn the true reason for what you call his leaping of the Tees!'

In a corner, behind Tom, a chair moved and a firm voice broke in. 'I have heard enough. On this occasion - bearing in mind that we will soon have fresh quarry for archers - I want the man fined one week's pay and sent back to his training with the stern warning that I will stand no more assaults on my officers. Captain Jackson! Take him back to the butts!'

Tom swung round to see Sir William Bulmer seated in an armchair and, as he was marched from the room, saw the knight's eyebrows lift and his eyes twinkle.

On their way to the shooting-field, Captain Jackson took hold of his elbow.

'You know, Tom, you've a sharp head on you. You could get promotion if you kept out of trouble. Would you fancy that?'

'I've no craving to be a soldier, sir. I'd rather breed heavy cattle for my living.'

'I understand that. Well, I'm glad to have you in my section, anyway. But promise me you'll keep clear of Captain Warren in future. And if he gets at you, keep your mouth tight shut and your hands by your sides. Will you do that for me?'

'Yes, sir. For you I will. And thanks for speaking up for me back there.'

They moved off the road as a party of riders approached. Four wore padded linen jerkins, round helmets and carried spears; they guarded two others who wore gentlemen's cloaks and hats. Tom stared at one of them and shouted, 'Isaac!'

Isaac Coronel lifted in his stirrups. 'Thomas! How wonderful! We stay at the White Horse - come to us.' The party rode on through the gate and towards the castle doors.

Edward Jackson glanced at Tom. 'Life is seldom dull. You are full of surprises, bowman Fleck.'

22

Apoplexy

The morning of August 17th dawned typical of that wet summer. Cattle stood under dripping trees throughout the north. Isaac waited with his companion in the same room he had admired five weeks earlier. Their gaze wandered along rows of great, leather-bound books and across the paintings of proud men. William Percy stamped into the room, his forced smile puckering the blue scar tissue on his cheek.

'Ah, Master Coronel. I'd come to think we'd not see you again.' He indicated a group of armchairs. 'Be seated and tell me the news from London - and who this gentleman might be.'

Isaac's companion answered for himself. Like Isaac, he was sallow, dark-eyed and slender. From the similarity of their narrow noses and high foreheads, a watcher might think they shared blood.

'I am Alvaro Jurnet, Master Coronel's employer. The talk in London is of King Henry's arrival in Calais with an army and a train of great cannon; among them are the guns His Majesty has named, "The Twelve Apostles".'

Percy laughed. 'To deliver their preaching through new gates rent in French walls. I wish I were there - but in Edinburgh the blasted Scots are gathering; they'll soon be at our throats like ravening Turks. Do you bring the means of paying militia?'

'The sum you require is at hand. First, we need to discuss surety.'

'Surety!' Percy bellowed. 'The Earl of Northumberland is my brother - Hotspur is my ancestor! Surety is not an issue!' He snorted before speaking at length about his noble lineage. Alvaro Jurnet listened, nodding respectfully until he had finished.

'Sir, I understand perfectly, and the entire world knows and applauds the honour of your family. However, in these uncertain times even His Majesty provides security when he requires finance. Can I suggest the title deeds to one of your smaller manors?'

'I thought it would come to this,' Percy growled, then shouted out, 'Hopper!'

A thin, aged man shuffled through the door to hand a collection of scrolls to his master.

'These are deeds to my lands at Shilbottle; they should cover it. I'll continue to draw rents throughout the loan. What rate of usury do you seek?' His eyes narrowed. 'There is a law against usury, is there not?'

Alvaro's expression held its agreeable cast. 'It is not encouraged. But we may quietly conduct our business, for the king is anxious that his realm's financial needs are not hindered. The rate is the usual ten per cent each year.'

'What? I'll not pay more than eight!'

'That would be two per cent less than is usual in London. Alas, I cannot go lower than nine; the loan arises from several powerful purses and I am answerable to them all.' Alvaro lowered his eyes.

'Then nine will have to do. I tell you, Jurnet, usury makes me shudder; but needs must rule when the devil drives. You'll be repaid within the year. Now, what else must be done?'

'I will return tomorrow morning with a covenant drawn up and a witness, together with the twelve hundred pounds you require.'

William Percy, with a sour expression on his face, pushed back his chair and gestured towards the door. 'Tomorrow morning, then. Good day to you both.'

Once the great front door had closed on the Jews he blurted out, 'Bloodsucking scriveners! Damned inkhorns! They must be as rich as Croesus!'

The two men rode side by side, deep in conversation as they entered the town. Alvaro kept looking at Isaac. 'Your speech is slurred, old friend, is something amiss?'

Isaac passed a hand across his face. 'I feel strange,' he muttered, as he slumped across the neck of his horse.

Alvaro drew alongside and reached out to give support. 'Help me,' he called out.

Two of the guards dismounted and heaved Isaac from his saddle to lay him in the shelter of a cottage wall.

Alvaro bent over his friend, saying, 'Isaac, what troubles you?' When no answer came from the drooping lips, he spoke urgently to the guards: 'We must carry Mister Coronel back to the inn. There is a physician in this town - find him quickly and bring him to the White Horse. Tell him I suspect apoplexy and he must hurry.'

Fifteen minutes later Isaac lay on his bed still unconscious. Rachel had propped up his shoulders and head with pillows. She loosened her father's clothes, cooled his face and neck with vinegar while Alvaro bathed the feet in warm water. Half an hour later a plump man, carrying a leather bag, puffed his way into the room accompanied by a guard.

'Let go of my arm, you ox. Leave me with my patient.' The physician mopped his brow and stood by the bed.

'You think it apoplexy, do you? Well if it is, then you do all the right things. Stand aside and let me examine him.'

The physician lifted Isaac's drooped eyelids, peered into the eyes and then tested the pulse at the wrist. Muttering to himself, he stroked his fingers over the unconscious man's neck and along the arteries, then touched the temples. Finally, he pointed to the drooping lip. 'It would indeed appear to be an attack of apoplexy.' From his bag, he drew a roll of fabric and passed it to Rachel. 'Do you know the craft of poulticing, young woman?'

'Yes. Shall I send for mustard?'

'I have the proper mixture with me. He needs hot poultices of flour, mustard and bran bandaged to the soles of the feet. Take them to the kitchens and have them prepared. While you are there, send up a servant with more hot water. And you, sir,' turning to Alvaro, 'keep bathing his feet - that's the thing to do.'

When Rachel returned with the bowl of steaming poultices, Isaac's breathing had become quiet. His shirtfront lay open and six leeches nestled among the dense grey hair of his chest - other clusters drew blood from the base of his slender neck. Taking her father's hand, she held it as the physician applied the poultices.

'Oh, Father! You are looking at me!' She leaned forward and peered into his face. Isaac stared back with a blank expression and tried to speak. His slack lips gave out a faint mumble.

The physician interrupted. 'Do not make him talk yet; he needs perfect rest for two or three weeks. I'll purge him and that is disturbance enough.' He forced open Isaac's mouth, poured a dark fluid inside, then stroked the gullet until it contracted in a swallow.

Alvaro leaned forward. 'Although I do not know your name, sir, I note you conduct your trade in a convincing manner.'

'I am John Rawlings. I studied under the best physician of York. I was examined there by the bishop. You can rest assured I am neither

160

quack nor wart charmer.'

'We are fortunate you are here,' Rachel broke in. 'I hope you will attend us constantly.'

That evening Tom unrolled the clothes he had bought from the market stall in Durham, the same clothes he had worn when he last visited Isaac and his daughter. Pulling on the grey shirt, he thought of the chamber at the inn of the knight in black armour. Alan Fuller had since explained its name, 'The Black Prince': a soldier's hero from the old days. Now that Alan had taught him hundreds of words, perhaps he might read the sign for himself.

A square of polished brass stood in one of the window alcoves of the barracks; he held the metal before his face. Wiping away a cobweb, he tried again. Even though the brass had scuffs and green speckles, he could satisfy himself he was tidy. Four years had gone since the last of the spots that once cursed him had faded. He had two scar pits on his cheek to remind him of their passing; he knew of others that his beard now covered. The beard had begun to spread further up his cheeks and fill out; it now curled and showed streaks of red among the brown.

He thought of Rachel again and how she had come to his room as the candle sputtered. How she had dropped her robe and stood naked by his bed before sliding in beside him.

Meg whined from the floor where she lay on her side, looking up at him. Her tail flicked. He grabbed the dog and wrestled her in an effort to take his mind off his rush of emotion. He stopped when she growled in play and took hold of his shirt.

'All right, lass. That's enough. I'm off into town and you can come. You might get a treat - who knows?'

He looked down at the scattering of hayseeds and dog hairs stuck to the front of his kersey and breeches. 'Now look, Meg! I'm not fit to go calling on gentlefolk.' He set about dabbing off the hayseeds with a licked finger. He gave up - it would take forever. He grabbed a handful of hay and rubbed himself down as he would groom a pony. 'There now! Right - let's be away.'

Even though mid-August had come, the days stayed cold and wet. Tom strode through drizzle towards Alnwick. In Bondgate, the Wednesday market still traded. Vendors called out their chants over the heads of the gossiping crowds.

'First of the year's herring, fresh landed at Seahouses - still shivering! Come buy! Tyne salmon, Coquet trout. Come buy! Mutton pasties, full o' meat - get them while they're hot! Come buy!'

Children threw sticks at squabbling dogs and soldiers haggled over bargains among the clothes. Tom found a friend crouched on dry flagstones beneath the awnings of a cobbler's stall. Alan Fuller waited in stockinged feet watching, with a critical eye, the cobbler stitch his boots.

Alan greeted him. 'How do, brother? I'm glad to see you swanning about the streets without a care. Come and sit by me for a spell. When this snail of a cordwainer's done fixing me boots, we'll go for some beer.'

'I'd like that, Alan, but I'm meeting somebody who stays at the White Hoss.'

'Oh aye? And who might that be? I see you're all primped up and decked out in your Durham gear. She must be a pretty one.'

Tom blushed.

Alan continued. 'Ah, I'm sorry, lad. It's no matter of mine. But I tell you: I got the bellyache when they dragged you off. You've had a proper court-martial, you know, and I feared for thee.'

'If it wasn't for the heralds and the captain, I'd be in deep clag. But Willy Bulmer was sat quiet in the corner and, after listening for a bit, he put a stop on it.' Tom went on to relate more detail.

After listening to the end, Alan whistled through his teeth. 'By Gum! That's fair. Fairer than the likes of us usually has off a court. They don't care for us clouting their officers. They like to make an example of a man; that way they put the frights up the rest of us. Billy Bulmer needs bowmen at the minute and you're among the best; that's what got you off. Mind you, the Warrens won't forget. You'll need to give them a wide berth from now on.'

'I know,' said Tom.

'Has this lass got freckles?'

'No, she's too dark for them, her locks are jet black.'

'Would she be that fancy, foreign-looking maid I saw going into the Hoss just now?' Alan's eyes widened.

'Er, yes, that was likely her. I'm going to see her father.'

'Of course you are, Tom, of course you are - though it would do no harm to buy her a bunch of roses off that stall yonder.' He shouted across to the stallholder, 'How much for them red roses?'

'They're scarce damasks, fresh from the castle garden. They've the

162

scent of musk, so they're three stems a farthing.'

'What's musk, Alan?'

'It's a fetching scent that rich French ladies - and some of their girly menfolk - dab about themselves.'

At the stall, Tom saw the colour of the blooms was closer to the pink of the eglantine. When he touched the petals, Rachel's cool skin came to mind. 'Can I have six, please?'

'Of course you can, hinney,' she said, picking out a mixture of part-blown and part-opened buds. Each stem carried three or four double blossoms packed with petals. 'I'll wrap the stems in damp moss to keep them fresh. Get them in water soon. There you are now; she's bound to like these. Tell her to mind the thorns.' The woman's eyes lit up. 'The proper name for them is the spice rose; some reckon the spice of love.'

He paid and, feeling self-conscious, carried the flowers away to rejoin Alan beneath the awning. The air around the two men grew fragrant.

'Phew, this heavy air brings out their scent,' Alan said. 'Best get them to her before they wilt; there's no call to squat in the clarts with me.'

'And be polite,' Alan called out as Tom slipped away, holding the roses in his arms like he used to carry a new lamb.

Alvaro Jurnet opened the door. He stared at the flowers in Tom's arms before whispering, 'What do you want?'

With a rustle of satin, Rachel appeared at Alvaro's side and gasped in astonishment. She slipped out of the room and closed the door.

'Tom,' she whispered. She took his arm and led him out of earshot of the chamber. 'I have willed it and willed it, and you have come,' she murmured, laying her head on his chest, 'when I need you most.'

He placed the roses on a window-ledge and stroked her lustrous hair. 'Rachel, what's wrong?'

She stood back, then reached out and touched his cheek. 'Thank you for the flowers, Thomas; father loves roses. It is wonderful that you're here. But my father has taken a sickness; he is paralysed with apoplexy and must be kept quiet. The physician is with him. I must be at his bedside. Please come again, tomorrow - please!'

He saw how she trembled and that her face was drawn. 'I'll come after midday. I hope he'll soon heal.'

~ ~ ~

Alan still crouched beside the cobbler's stall. 'Hey up! That was a quick trip. Did you get chucked out?'

'Her dad's poorly. She's up to her elbows and I'd get in the way.'

'Oh, a shame that. Are you ready for some beer now?'

'Not now, Alan. My head's too full. I need a quiet walk.'

On the way back to barracks Tom lingered by the river. His thoughts rushed down aimless alleyways. He leaned against an alder to watch a white-bibbed dipper as it bounced on a rock in the middle of the current. The thoughts slowed enough to bring quiet spaces where there was just a knowing of the heart. In a blur of wings the bird flew low upstream.

He tossed pebbles one by one into the rain-pitted water. Meg lay beside him and, seeming to understand his mood, watched the splashes without stirring. A pebble fell among a writhing mass of baby eels, parting them. He laid aside his handful of stones to watch the swirling ball of elvers fragment into wriggling black legions that struggled through the shallows on their journey upriver. 'Look at them, Meg. All the way from the wild sea. Heading to quiet pools amid the crags. Nowt will stop them getting where they're bound.'

He returned to the inn late in the following afternoon. Rachel answered his knock and slipped outside to whisper, 'Father has fallen unconscious again, despite the doctor's bleeding. I fear he might never wake.'

'I wish auld Agnes Humble, my neighbour, was here; though she had no leeches and mostly used herbs. I'm sad I know nowt of her craft.'

'Thomas - your hands - I've been thinking of that day in Durham when you took away my headache. Perhaps your hands will help Father.'

'He's got a sore sickness, Rachel, and I've not seen apoplexy before. I've lifted my sister's headaches, but those were commonplace things.'

She took his hands and stroked the palms. 'I don't know what to do.' She gave him an imploring look. 'The physician is not here. Please - you must try. If you are gentle, it can do no harm. He loves you as a son, and will know your touch.' She opened the door and drew him into the chamber.

She led him to the bed where a white-faced Isaac lay on his back, his breathing shallow. 'See - he does not wake, and his feet are so cold. Please try.'

Tom sat on a stool by the bed and placed his palms onto Isaac's temples. He held them there and concentrated his mind, then moved them gradually across the narrow cranium. His hands settled on either side of Isaac's head. They lay without pressure while he took his thought into his heart. He held it there with his mind quiet and a feeling of love in his heart. Long minutes passed and ended with a slight gasp from Rachel. 'His eyes have opened!'

He leaned close to Isaac's face. The eyes gazed back with a glimmer of recognition. The twisted lips tried to shape speech.

'Hello, Isaac. You've had a bit of a sleep and now you are awake. Best not to try to talk just yet, though. I'll give your feet a massage now, to get the blood flowing and warm them up a bit.'

Slipping his hands beneath the bedcovers, he took hold of both icy feet and gave them the same slow massage that once helped his father recover from the mine collapse. As Tom's hands worked, Isaac gave out low, appreciative grunts.

'That will do for now, Isaac. We don't want to make you weary.' Tom got up. 'I'll stop and let you rest. Later on, we could try a bit more.'

Rachel followed him onto the landing and eased herself against him. 'Thank you, thank you,' she whispered. 'I knew your hands would help him; there is something in their touch, I've felt it myself. I ache for you, to hug you as close as moss hugs the rock.' She breathed out against his neck.

He bent to kiss her mouth. 'That's all I would ever wish, to be draped by your moss. But we mustn't linger here; we should sit by his bedside. Let's go back in.'

Isaac lay asleep, breathing easily. They sat holding hands, watching the noble features.

The days that followed were filled with training until the commander was satisfied his archers had reached their maximum rate of volleys. After a week, he had them manoeuvring in companies across rough ground and practising defence with shortswords against foot soldiers and mounted spearmen.

Whenever he had free time, Tom walked into Alnwick to massage Isaac's body. Each day brought an improvement. On the fifth, he could sit up in bed and make slow speech.

'Rachel tells me that you are reading,' Isaac said.

'Yes, though I'm slow and I've nowt but the poems the Norroy gave.'

Isaac gave a chuckle and raised a hand. 'Nowt but poems? Some consider poetry the highest art of all. Can you speak lines from memory?'

'I can bring back scraps, like the dream of *Piers the Ploughman*. It goes like this:

After sharp showers the sun shines brightest;
No weather is warmer than after wet clouds;
Nor any love dearer - or more loving, our friends;
Than after woe, when Love and Peace are masters.
There was never war in this world, or wickedness so keen,
That Love, if he liked, could not make them laughter,
And Peace, through patience, put an end to perils.'

Isaac exclaimed, 'Ah! That wonderful old verse by William Langland! Do you have other poets?'

Tom pursed his lips, thought for a moment, then recited:

'He made a round table on their behalf,
That none of them should sit above,
But all should sit as one,
The King himself in state royal,
Dame Gwenevere our Queen withal,
Seemly of body and bone.

'That is all I have. The Norroy said it's a scrap of something longer.'

Isaac lifted his head off the pillow and murmured, 'I might have the next few lines:

It fell again at Christmas
All came to that place,
To that noble one,
With helm on head and blade bright,
All that was a knight;
None would stay at home.'

Rachel came into the chamber. 'Father, you will tire yourself.'

'Thomas has spoken a fragment of *Sir Gawain and the Green Knight* and I had the rest. We enjoy ourselves. Remember the parchments I bought from that old yeoman in Stafford marketplace? Among them are the verses that tell of Sir Gawain and King Arthur. I will copy them out for Thomas; the effort will be good for me. You can cease to fuss, Daughter. To live again is a delight. Now let me try to recall more of the Green Knight.'

'Not now, Isaac. I must be getting back to the practice butts.'

'Then, my son, I'll have it for you next time.'

Tom was sitting by Isaac's bed telling him about the military exercises when Alvaro entered the room and took in the scene.

'Isaac, it gladdens me that there's a man in Alnwick you can trust. Our dealings here are done; tomorrow I start my journey to London. I've instructed the doctor to attend until you are fit enough to travel. I want you working with me again in London, my old friend and companion. In the meantime, Rachel will send messages so that I can know of your progress.'

'I'll join you soon, Alvaro.' Isaac said, through lips that still drooped at one corner

Jurnet took his hand. 'I don't want to hear of you rushing southwards until you are strong enough. I must now prepare for the morning; we depart at dawn. I bid you farewell, dear friend, only for now. In the time of long nights we will sit together by the fire when al-Dabaran's lamp hangs in the sky.' He bent over Isaac, kissed him on both cheeks and then, in silence, departed the chamber. Rachel left the room at the same time. Tom and Isaac listened to the footsteps descend the wooden stairs.

Isaac leaned forward. 'Thomas, hear me. I could die suddenly, no one knows with apoplexy; it can strike again without warning.' He gathered Tom's hands together and held them. 'Today you are a soldier, but your duty will end soon. The Scots shall go home and the militia be paid off; commanders do not pay needless wages. In this world, what I care about most is Rachel. You are her friend and mine. I need to know if you will protect her, should I die here.'

Tom met the searching eyes. 'Isaac, I'll do that gladly. Rachel will be safe. But you've a good doctor and will be astride a horse soon.'

Isaac sighed and lay back on the pillow. 'You are a fine man, son of Francis Fleck - and with your father's ways. Please show caution -

I hear the Scots are gathering.'

'Never worry about me, Isaac. Whenever the enemy get too close, we archers always shelter behind the billmen.

Immersed in thought on his walk back to barracks, Tom paused in the twilight at a stretch of gravel below the bank of the river. Here, where the Aln altered course to flow around a buttress of fern-hung rock, the channel bent like an elbow. Close by lay a patch of hazel shade where he liked to sit in reflection. A block of stone, half-buried in last year's leaves, offered a dished, moss-covered surface that seemed fashioned to take a man's buttocks. He had told himself that it might even be an ancient throne for the crowning of bards. New ways of saying things came to mind as he sat there.

He threw heavy pebbles at a half-submerged, stranded branch. Meg dived into the water at each splash. She scrabbled around, putting her head underwater until she thought she had found the special stone that carried a faint taste of her master. Tom watched as she emerged and marvelled at how thin she appeared when wet. She would drop each stone egg at his feet and back away, shake the water from her rough, black coat before prancing and barking until he threw it again.

'Whisht, lass! Don't be daft. That's enough.' She calmed and lay panting. Together they watched the swirls of bubbles glide by. He followed the progress of twigs and leaves and pondered where they came from and where they headed. Perhaps they were doomed to be captured by some dark bank - to languish and rot. Where did this sweet stream go? Into wild, cold Scotland? Isaac's urgent words still rang in his head. How could he promise to protect Rachel when the army might march him north any day?

He spied a stretch of fine sand under the opposite bank. Across it wandered a line of scuffed prints that ended in a flourish of disturbance where an otter had landed a fish. He thought of another otter that almost leapt on top of him as it fled from Mark Warren's hounds. Why would any man crave to kill an otter?

He remembered the milk cows he cared for in the sway-backed old byre, now in the keeping of the weasel-minded Will Fisher. More rowan and birch leaves drifted past; then a scatter of petals appeared and softened to a yellow blur as his focus loosened. Everything flowed onwards; where did it all go? Where would he end his time? His thoughts wavered like a bemused moth fluttering between lamps.

This won't do, he thought, and got to his feet; clambered up the bank and continued along the short road to the Castle. He paused to lean on a gate and admire a crowd of cattle. Nearby, three black calves trotted in circles, kicking their legs in the air. They would stop to put curious noses to the ground, start back, then gingerly move forward again. He saw the reason when a mole broke free of a tussock under the nose of a calf and rushed towards the gate. It stopped near to him, sensed his presence and dived for cover among a patch of tall docks.

The calves noticed him, stared for a moment, then galloped off, each to find its mother. They glowed with the joy and vigour of new life and brought back memories of simpler times. He surveyed the grass with interest. It had good body, plenty of bottom and gleamed a rich green. This ground stayed sweet - it had drainage. All over the pasture, white clover showed breaking flower. He recalled his father's words, 'It's poor land that won't grow a decent dock.'

'This is what I want, Meg,' he whispered. 'Good grazing and strong kine: the sort that make good doers and can stand out when the ground is iron-hard. I could breed a fine herd out of beasts like these. Mary would like them as well; she'd make a good stockman's wife.' Then he thought of Rachel and her smooth, slender hands. He remembered her cool fingers on his body. There came a stirring in his groin. He gave a low grunt, leaned into the gate and laid his head upon his arms.

23

Farewell

The next morning, on the 22nd of August, a party of men rode through the gate of Alnwick Castle. They brought warnings of a massive Scottish army that had crossed the Tweed at Coldstream the previous day. The force had begun a march over English lands in the direction of Norham castle.

It took four days for news of the invasion to reach the earl, at his campaign base. He had waited for three weeks, one hundred miles to the south. The aged Thomas Howard was not idle; supported by a walking stick he had pored over maps and made his plans. The whole of the territory was waiting for his orders. He now dispatched fast riders across northern England to raise the towns, wapentakes and shires. At the head of five hundred armed East-Anglians from his own estates, he hurried out of Pontefract castle. He would break the march at the cathedral of Durham where he would collect a thing of great power.

As he travelled the North Road he was joined by the banners of a vigorous old man, 'little' Sir Marmaduke Constable of Flamborough, by militia from Holderness, Whitby, York and the rest of the wapentakes of the Ridings and Durham. Hundreds more came down from high dales in the Western Fells. On the 3rd of September, an army of fifteen thousand arrived on the outskirts of Alnwick. Others were coming from west of the great fells.

He declined to enter the huddled town. Instead, he moved a few miles to the northwest, near to the village of Bolton, where extensive flat ground could make an encampment. This, he declared, would be his final muster point.

That same afternoon, at the Alnwick barracks, Edward Jackson addressed his archers. 'Tomorrow, at mid-day bell, we head for Bolton. Except for the castle guard, we all march out. You must spend the rest of your time here making good your gear for three weeks without shelter.'

Tom approached the captain. 'Sir, I've a friend in town who is ill. I help him with massage. He's expecting me.'

'Yes, I know of your visits to the sick Jew. You can go to him. I trust you to be ready for duty and not stint on the care of your gear.'

Tom met the officer's intelligent eyes, thanked him and set off for town.

From her father's chamber window, Rachel watched Tom stride through the marketplace. She admired how his long arms swung with ease from broad shoulders - archer's arms. He has a body that knows hard work, she thought, and such a thick crop of hair on that head. She noted how it flashed with coppery glints in the sun. The pace of her heart increased. Do I want to live my life beside him? she mused. Even though he is a humble cowherd, a labourer without learning, I have this voice in my breast saying this is the man. She started at a sound from Isaac's bed.

Tom paused at the soft call of a woman's voice. He looked with unfocussed eyes at the vendor's tray of trinkets. Strangely, his mind was filled with sudden images of Rachel, of her legs and arms entangled with his own. Then Mary Humble's sweet face overlaid the vision: she stood on the south bank of the Tees - waiting. His stomach knotted. He shook his head and blinked hard. My mind is no better than a swollen beck!

The stallholder's voice broke through once more. 'Here's a lovely bracelet for your sweetheart.'

'Er - sorry, I was far away. What did you say?'

'A bracelet, me bonny - for your favourite girl. This one's pretty - only a penny. My son carves them - it's all he can do now he's blinded.'

The craftsman had fashioned the bracelet from a dense, black wood. Tom tapped it with a thumbnail and knew it to be bog oak. Three tiny dragons pursued each other around the rim. Each dragon had its jaws clamped to the tail of the one in front.

He met the woman's steady grey eyes. 'I'll take it. Your son's clever with his hands - his fingers see a lot better than most eyes. Here's a silver penny and two farthings. It's worth the extra.'

'Bless you, me honey. He has his bad days. Despite that, when he's at his whittling he's as cheerful as a linnet. There you are then - may it keep you both safe.'

171

Tom dropped the bracelet into his pouch and, squeezing between stalls, made for the door of the inn. He took the stairs two at a time, keen to speak with those who lifted his mind to a state beyond the squalor of the street. He found Rachel holding her father's head and bathing his face with vinegar water.

'Tom! Another attack! Moments ago. He's slipping away. Help me!'

Tom rushed downstairs and sent a serving girl to bring the physician. She returned soon afterwards with a priest.

'I'm sorry, mistress,' she said to Rachel. 'The physic man is gone to Bolton to attend the soldiers. Father Adam is here.'

The priest stepped into the room and without a word approached Isaac's comatose body. He bent his head and listened to the sick man's shallow breathing.

Tom stopped massaging Isaac's feet and watched.

'Can you help my father?' Rachel asked the priest.

'I fear only God can help this man. I understand he is a Jew. If we can get him to speak, and if he is willing, I can make him a Christian and give him the Last Rites of the Holy Catholic Church.'

'Thank you, sir; nevertheless, I know it would not be my father's wish. Please leave us now.'

Father Adam stared at her. 'Jews are forbidden to live in England. They are banished. Our magistrate must be made aware of your presence in his district.'

Rachel stood erect. 'The magistrate's monarch knows of it! My father assists King Henry with finance. He is here to fund the militia William Percy of Alnwick Castle raises to defend this town against the Scots. Would you have us driven out - knowing that?'

The priest scowled. 'So be it. Do not expect me to bury him in the sacred ground of my church - the accusers of Christ must go outside the walls.' His robes hissed as he swept from the room.

Tom's heart swelled for Rachel as, in a faint voice, she murmured, 'My father would not wish to sleep in your churchyard.'

Over the next hour, Isaac became paler. Rachel and Tom sat on either side of the bed, each of them holding one of Isaac's hands. Tom remembered the times he had knelt by a rough straw bed, in the sleeping-space at one end of the cow-byre, listening to a parent's breathing as it waned.

'Father is leaving us,' Rachel whispered. Tom nodded and moved around the bed to sit close by her and lay his arm across her shoulders.

The angular, noble head breathed out a final sigh and its sixty years of consciousness faded. Rachel lowered her brow onto the still chest and, after a wail that wrenched Tom's heart, gave way to silent weeping.

Time passed and she dried her tears on her father's shirt sleeve, kissed his cooling cheek and stood up. 'There are things to do. Please help me.'

The innkeeper offered a hidden glade in a patch of woodland he owned. The sun dipped behind the trees as Tom and Alan Fuller dug the grave through the loam into stiff, yellow clay. Half in shadow, Rachel sat on a log among stands of foxgloves and watched.

'Tomorrow is Sunday; we must bury him then - before the town wakes.'

'Not three days?' Alan asked.

'No - not for us.' she answered. 'Not for us.'

At first light, on a dry day of still air, Rachel, Tom, the innkeeper and a serving girl moved off behind the coffin on its horse-drawn cart. Isaac's hired Lincoln guards, Will and Jack Simpson, walked ten paces in front with straight backs. Alan Fuller and Peter Tindall kept station on either side. Following at a discreet distance, a woman from the marketplace led her tall, sightless son by the hand.

Rachel wore a simple, long-sleeved, black satin dress belted at the waist and overlaid by a sleeveless kirtle of black velvet. From a plain, caul hat of white linen that covered her hair, folds of gauze hung pleated across her shoulders. Tom stole a concerned glance at her features and thought: she moves like a swan in the drift of a river. In this way Rachel walked, her oval face uncovered, with her gaze fixed on the coffin. Seven times, on the way to the burial place, she had the cart halted; at each stop, she chanted verses in Hebrew:

*'El malei rahamim
shokhem ba-m'romim . . .'*

At the graveside, Rachel had the coffin opened. Isaac's body lay wrapped in a sheet of white linen with a single sash tied about his waist. She knelt by the coffin and uncovered his face.

173

'I should not unwrap him - but I must. See, Thomas, how Father's mouth has become straight again.'

She put her hands to her neck and lifted off a delicate chain hung with a silver star. Raising her father's head, she placed the Star of David around his neck and kissed his lips. 'I lay your body here, my father who I love. May you find the true Temple and know peace among your people. . .' Her voice choked as she covered his face with the shroud for the last time.

She took a pace back and, with her knuckles white, ripped her black garments in three places on her right side, from the neck to the heart.

Tom put his arm around her as Alan Fuller replaced the lid. She gently shrugged him off and stood erect at the graveside. As the four men handled the ropes that lowered the coffin into the ground, her voice throbbed, first in Hebrew then in English,

'God filled with mercy,
bring proper rest beneath the wings
of your Shehinah,
to the soul of Isaac Coronel.
May you who are the source of mercy
shelter him beneath your wings eternally
so that he may rest in peace.
Amen.'

The others called out, 'Amen.' Alan Fuller picked up the spade and took a shovelful of earth but Rachel stopped him.

'No - I must do this.'

She took the spade from Alan and shovelled broken yellow clay mixed with dark woodland loam onto the coffin until it disappeared from view. She drove the spade into the pile of earth.

'Please, Alan; now close up the grave.'

Alan nodded to her with respect and set about shovelling.

After standing around the closed grave, each in private thought, the mourners straggled out of the wood in silence. Tom and Rachel were alone in the glade.

Her speech had thickened. 'I will have a marker stone made for him with the Star of David carved above his name. I will search for flowers to plant in the earth that covers him. It is a quiet place and he is safe here. . .' Her voice died in a whisper as she saw the tears on

174

Tom's face and his lips struggle to move.

'I remember his words when I parted from you both after our first meeting at Northallerton: "May we meet again in prosperity and boon." It's as though I've lost my father all over again,' he said and wiped the heel of his palm across his eyes.

She took his hand. 'Then you are the brother I never had. You are much more than that. Father said to me, during his last days, that you and I must rejoice in each other - for the dark will come soon enough.'

'The dark? What did he mean?'

'That life is brief and, though the days seem long when we are young, the dark treads our way. We meet and we part.'

'Only for a while, though. We found each other this time.' He held both her hands and gazed into her eyes. 'I want to help you with the stone, Rachel, but they've bound me as a soldier and we march out today for the mustering. It's said we'll be gone for no more than a month because after that it'll be coming to the time of bad weather.'

'I must go away also, Thomas. I cannot stay here, it is not safe. I will return to London.'

Tom touched her shoulder. 'I wish you could wait until I come back.'

'I'll wait a while in Alnwick for you. For how long, I don't know. This is a wild town; it troubles me - I fear the priest. But yes, I will try to wait. I must see you again, even for one last time. Please stand back from danger when you go with the soldiers. Keep from harm; you are precious; there is no one else left that I love.'

She kissed his hand and moved close to him. He embraced her and whispered into her mass of hair, 'I will keep safe. Give me some time - at least four weeks. Before October is old, you must go south while the days are not short. If I'm late, leave a message with the innkeeper so I'll know where you've gone. Now that I've found you once more, wherever you go I'll seek you.'

24

The March North

At noon, the fields and barns around Alnwick disgorged two thousand men onto the western drove road. They set out to march towards the muster six miles away. A marshal held back the heralds' small band until a column of twelve hundred sailors and marine soldiers had passed through the town. The Lord Admiral of England and his ships' captains led the force, drawn from the fleet at Newcastle.

'Will you look at that lot?' Riley shouted to his fellow soldiers.

The sergeant leaned over him. 'Yes, Riley, you take a good look. They've got discipline and have the manner of soldiers. I want you to take note and carry yourselves as they do.'

The Norroy interrupted, 'That's right. They're the crew that made an end of Admiral Andrew Barton, the Scots king's favourite, and sent his fleet running for home.'

The York Herald joined in. 'Aye, and just remember, Barton got skewered by a Yorkshireman - a bowman from Malton by the name of Hustler. Best in the North, they say; better even than our Tom Fleck.'

'Stand by! Here's the tail end of the ships' brigade. We'll move out behind it. The gentlemen at the front.' Sergeant Arkwright stamped his boots, happy to be on the move again and working his men.

Once the pack ponies had settled into the pace of march, Rob Wilson ran up to his father. 'Dad! There's more folk here than bides in York. We were took on to drive ponies for them heralds - a quiet walk to the Tyne Valley they said; so why are we mixed up in all of this?' He pulled at his father's sleeve. 'Did you ask the Norroy to pay us off?'

'I did, son. He made it plain - in time of war, the herald's service is king's service. We're stuck with it and so is Norroy.' Ben Wilson hawked and spat. 'Both him and York have to turn out as go-betweens whenever the army's in the field. At least we've nowt to do

176

except mind pack animals. Spare a thought for Tom Fleck.' He coughed again, to clear his throat of stable dust, then wheezed, 'He thowt he was a pony man. Today, he's yoked to a mob of archers. He'll be in the thick of owt that happens.'

The drovers' track to Bolton-in-Glendale was slippery going; convoys of waggons had rutted the hollow way. Tom sat on the pony he had used for the skirmish at Milfield. He patted the mare; she had a white star on her forehead, just like Meg, and was placid enough not to mind the dog trotting along by her hooves. Arriving at Bolton, he rubbed her down with a fistful of hay before staking her out to graze with the archers' herd.

A sky the colour of dull iron hung along the naked hills. Slowly, despite the approach of evening, the scene grew brighter from the west as the sun touched the fells. He looked around. The camp covered more meadow than a dozen labourers could scythe in a week. Black domes dotted the grass - low shelters made from canvas spread over frames of hazel rods. With Meg at his side, he squatted in the doorway of one of the crowded refuges. After sharing his biscuit ration with her, he stared across the sloping ground at the comings and goings around the tents of the chief commanders. Putting a hand on the dog's shoulders, he asked, ' Meg, who do you reckon is in that tent with the red beasts painted on it?'

A man, stretched out on his back nearby, rolled over and got to his knees. 'The big'un yonder, with lions on the side, is tent of the earl. He's having a busy time of it. See the lanky body striding across? That's his son, Tommy Howard the Admiral, and the thickset one with him is his brother, Edmund. Looks like a Howard family moot. Seems they're wagering all they've got on this one.'

'Will they be laying plans?'

'They'll be scheming hard. They'll have to be canny about what stores we've got and how long they'll last - like how long they might keep us int' field.'

Inside his tent, the earl reclined in a padded armchair, with one leg stretched across a stool. He sat up when his sons entered the tent. 'I'm heartened at the sight of you two fellows. You are weary, no doubt?'

'A little, Father; the march from Newcastle was tortuous.'

'Have you brought the cannon?'

'We have falcons and serpentines - and carts of powder and shot.'

177

'And the Hanseatic gunners - are they with you?'

'Twelve master gunners of Danzig are here.'

'Excellent - we will need them. Please be seated and have wine. My calculations say we have rations until the eleventh of September. We must bring Jimmy to battle before that day.'

Thomas Howard sat down. 'He may pull back across the Tweed, Father; if he does so, will we follow him?'

'I'm ordered by the king to keep him out of England; I've no authority to invade Scotland. Should he escape us, we can be certain that once we have gone his raiders will harry the northern shires without hindrance. We must close with him within the week and break him while we can.

Next day the army continued to spread itself across the commons around the village. Bands of men from Cheshire and Lancashire still straggled in, mounted and on foot, after threading their way across England through Wensleydale and the valleys of Tees and Tyne. Companies swallowed them up, and divisions swallowed up companies - all to be sent on manoeuvres across bare hillsides.

That evening a carriage conveyed the earl through his assembled army. A campaign veteran of seventy, he suffered so much from pain in his joints that he avoided horseback. He chose a piece of high ground and, spurning help, climbed onto a cart to address the companies gathered beneath their pennants.

He called out in a strong voice: 'Men of England, I am Thomas Howard, Earl of Surrey, charged by your king to defend his realm. Many of you know me. Many of you are brothers-in-arms from earlier days.'

The front ranks stared up at his broad forehead and long, high-bridged nose.

'Witness our banners!'

He motioned to men guarding a row of flagpoles. They pulled ropes and an ancient cloth of velvet bearing the symbol of St George, a red cross on a white field, fell open. Next, the banner of the Tudors unfurled, a red dragon on green and white. Then the banners of the chief commanders: the quartered red of the Howard lions, the three stags' heads of Stanley, the white scallops of Dacre and the blue-and-yellow chequer board of the Cliffords dropped open, followed by the colours of lesser houses.

'Once again the Scots torch our land.' He pointed to the ancient cloth. 'Once again we gather beneath the sacred flag of St Cuthbert that has never failed to bless us with the strength to defeat them.'

A cheer went up.

He bellowed, 'This turncoat of a Scots king! His third invasion in seventeen years!' He scanned the masses of men and waited for the shouts to die away. 'After his last attack on this land, he not only signed with us the "Treaty of Perpetual Peace", he gained the hand of Margaret, our own king's sister.'

He paused to allow captains time to relay his words to thousands of straining ears.

'This double-dealer, hired by French Louis to stab us should we have an argument with that popinjay. No sooner does our brave King Hal land at Calais than once again we have the Scotch loon in our shires. Once again we must show him it is not profitable to murder, burn and rape into England whenever our backs are turned.'

He ended with a great shout: 'Men of England! Shall we kick them back into their beds of thistles? Back into their sour boglands?' He drew his sword and held it high.

Waves of cheering swelled up from the divisions.

The earl shouted again, 'It will soon be done. We march north at daybreak. Make sure you sleep well. Husband your strength!' Captains helped the old man down from the cart. He shook them off to walk, stiffly erect, back to his carriage.

Tuesday, the sixth of September, opened under broken cloud. Blades of sunshine sliced through to warm the chilled muscles of horses and men. The formation had grown to twenty-two thousand. Latecomers still hurried to join the rear of the column of soldiers, oxcarts and strings of pack ponies that crawled along the drove road towards Wooler. Men marched in lines five abreast with waggons spaced at intervals; they stretched for four miles. Overhead, buzzards circled and watched.

In the press of the advance, Tom lost sight of Sergeant Arkwright and his remaining six soldiers. He checked on Meg; she lay below him in a sling fashioned from an old shawl bought in Alnwick. She lay at her ease suspended from his saddle, riding out the miles behind his left leg, safe from the thousands of hooves. Her head and paws jutted from the sling and her eyes gleamed with interest at the passing landscape. As the section squeezed past a group of foot soldiers trudging behind a ponderous oxcart, she barked at the driver. The broad back of Jack Swales eased round.

'Well, I'm blowed! Hey up, Tom Fleck! Tha's got another new job?'

'And you, Jack. Has the coal trade dried up?'

'No, but this pays better. I'm hired to haul whatever they want shifting. It's cannon-shot and powder on this stretch. And another thing - they've given me ten strapping sodgers as guards and to shove when I'm stuck in clarts.'

'Did my message get to Hilda?'

'She got it, lad. She was all right. A bit o' bad news came through later.' He paused. 'Auld Agnes Humble died in her sleep, back end of July. Your Hilda still bides at the cottage with Agnes's lass. I shouldn't fret about her.'

'What's the hold-up? Keep moving, archers!' The officer had a scowling face.

Tom glanced at Jack, who nodded. 'Best get on. Might see you tonight - all being well.'

That evening, in his tent at Wooler Heugh, Surrey took supper with his chief commanders at a makeshift table. A steward carved lumps off a haunch of roast venison whilst the seated men chewed or slaked their thirst with red wine.

His surviving sons, Thomas and Edmund Howard, flanked the earl. Surrey's other son, Edward, had died in battle with the French fleet five months earlier. Sir Marmaduke Constable, another seventy-year-old, faced him. On the left of that tough warrior, lounged William Percy of Alnwick, his scarred face relaxed. At one end of the table, Lord Stanley casually picked his teeth; at the other end Sir William Bulmer of Brancepeth sat upright and attentive. The rugged frame of Lord Thomas Dacre, a man in his mid-forties and Warden of the West March, dominated the scene.

The English Herald, Rouge Croix, had returned from the Scottish camp with news that the enemy had entrenched on a hill called Flodden Edge. Over supper, they discussed what tactics might lure King James down onto ground more in their favour.

The earl's steward lifted the flap of the door. 'My lord, a Borderer by the name of John Heron has arrived with a large body of horse. He asks to speak with you.'

The earl dropped his lump of meat onto his trencher and wiped his moustaches. 'Heron? Would that be the man otherwise called "The Bastard of Ford"?'

'Yes, my lord, he is known by that name.'

'I'm curious to learn why he risks his neck by coming here. Strip him of weapons and bring him in under close guard.'

A minute later two soldiers escorted a tall, weather-beaten man into the tent. He took off his plain, round helmet and gave a slight bow.

'My lord, I hope I find you in good health. I am John Heron.'

'I'm well enough. Come to the point. Why does an outlaw, the murderer of Sir Robert Ker, seek me out today?'

John Heron straightened up. 'I offer you my strength and understanding of the district ahead. And, my lord, I hope that you will grant pardon for my destruction of that troublesome Scots knight.'

The earl's expression remained impassive before the proud, hard face. 'A pardon, eh? That's a problematic issue. Not long ago our king assured his Scottish brother-in-law that you'd be caught and handed over to his justice for the murder of the keeper of his Middle March. Today, we find different times. What else can you offer me?'

'Ninety seasoned men, mounted and lanced, with good half-armour. My close knowledge of every beck and ford, track and moss-way, to the north of here. In particular the country bounded by the Rivers Till and Tweed, Branxton Hill and Flodden Edge, that district wherein might bide the solution to this difficulty.'

'Be seated and tell me more. Steward! Meat and wine for our guest.'

The following day, in the centre of a sprawling Scottish camp, King James IV took his ease in his tent. Before him sat his French officers and Scottish nobles. Each man held a goblet of red wine and would set it down to fix a dirk into a piece of roast beef. The four-walled tent stood tall and spacious, its red lion panels sodden with the effects of days in low cloud. Inside, woollen rugs covered the tussocks of moor grass. Though the lords and bishops were crowded on benches that rocked under their weight, four French officers, legs crossed, reclined in chairs. An unfinished game of chess stood on a low table at the king's side.

The king spoke in French. He wished to know how well his infantry had adapted to the imported Swiss long-pike. His red-brown hair broke around his wide shoulders in waves as he leaned forward in his chair to hear again the French assurances. The thousands of sixteen to eighteen-foot pikes lay in good hands, the English would not stand against massed ranks of pikemen. The Frenchmen described to him once more how the Swiss pike now determined the outcome of European battles. What he heard confirmed his own opinion. The English infantry bill was no more than eight-foot long, its lethal end little better than a farm labourer's hedge slashing tool - what could it do against phalanxes of trained pikemen? The French officers laughed; but in the shadows around the tent walls, some Scottish jaws were set.

A Scots lord sat up straight. 'My men would rather carry their spears and axes, and fight shoulder-to-shoulder - in their schiltrons, like they've always done and their fathers before them. They find the long-pike a clumsy, cack-handed tool.'

The king contrived a pleasant face. 'My lord Huntly - as you well know our schiltrons have not always brought success and it is two hundred years since we routed them at Stirling Bridge. In Germany, these pikes sweep away all opposition. The English have a great shock in store. We will give them a lesson in modern European warfare. Tell your men to march in echelon formation and handle the new weapon exactly as our French allies have instructed; I insist upon it. Remember - whilst we have the greater force, we are sensible; I want the front ranks fully armoured, they must not fall to archers - this will not be another Falkirk. Also, I want bands of light skirmishers: axes, spears, swords - whatever they prefer - on foot, to screen the flanks. There is no need for cavalry. Before we move, my cannon will carve wide lanes through Howard's divisions. We'll disperse him like a cobweb.

Faint shouts reached their ears. They began as isolated cries that soon rose to a hubbub. 'See what that is,' James told his steward.

Moments later, the man returned. 'Sire, the English are here, their army can be seen moving along the valley bottom.'

James Stewart grunted. 'The auld fox has finally arrived.' He took time to drain his wine goblet before rising. 'Well, I suppose this game of chess can wait.'

He stood erect and the other men in the tent followed suit. They watched him slip a hand inside his cloak to adjust his chain. He understood their interest - they knew why he wore the heavy iron around his waist. He wore it as penance for his complicity in a plot against his own father, James III. The rebellion had led to his father's murder, stabbed in the heart by a man disguised as a priest. Some of these same nobles had hatched that plot.

The king stood in the rain on the top of Flodden Edge and stared fixedly to the southeast. His steward tried to hold a canopy over his head but he brushed it away. 'Enough of that. This is a field of battle; my hat will suffice.' With an open palm he wiped rain from his cheeks and beard.

The squall passed away to the east. Broken cloud, patched with blue, appeared above them. In shafts of sunlight, five hundred feet below and some miles away, he could see a long column of men and waggons moving north along the far bank of the River Till. Somewhere in that column, he thought, trundles a carriage in which a crippled, but cunning, old man is making calculations. They had come to know each other over the years and he mused that the old earl would draw on that knowledge as he bumped along that track. He hid a shudder - then, bracing himself, called out in a carefree voice, 'It's a claggy march for them. This rain is a godsend. Let us pray that they're well wetted, likewise their bowstrings and powder.'

Old Archibald 'Bell the Cat' Douglas, the Earl of Angus, stood nearby. 'See how they vanish behind that high ground, Sire. We have neglected to deploy scouts. We must send out keen-eyed men to learn Surrey's intent. I have a bad feeling about this.'

The long, intelligent face of his king gave a brief smile. 'It is clear to me what he intends, Angus. He is manoeuvring. There is no need to cover the country with scouts: I command the greater strength and will meet him whatever he does.'

'Sire, I would counsel that now is the right time to return to Scotland. We could be across the Tweed by nightfall. I urge withdrawal - we have already done enough here.'

The monarch tilted his head to stare into the earl's rain-spattered and wrinkled features. 'Angus, if you have no belly for this, you may go home. Leave me now!'

Archibald Douglas stiffened as he stared back at his king. Moisture leaked from his faded blue eyes. 'Sire, if such be your wish, I will go. My age renders my body of no service, and my counsel is despised, but I leave two sons and the vassals of Douglas in the field. May the result be glorious and the foreboding of Angus unfounded.' He lowered his grey head, took two steps backward and shuffled away.

The king addressed an aide. 'This is no time for faint hearts. Bring my mount and summon my guard. Call also the Sieur d'Aussi; I will survey the ground with him.'

Horsed and surrounded by spears, he rode out with the Frenchman to the highest point of Flodden Hill. Here he stared across to the east and for a time watched through thin rain the blurred form of Surrey's force vanishing behind a wooded hill. They will camp there tonight, he mused, biting a finger-nail. And what of tomorrow? He looked towards the northeast, then north into his kingdom where the lower mass of Branxton Hill obscured the view. 'Now let us cross the saddle of high ground to that hill. I will assess more of this territory. I will anticipate his movements.'

Dismounting on his return, the king heard argumentative voices filtering through the walls of his tent. He strode through the doorway, out of the sweet air of evening, into an atmosphere of meat, spirits and unwashed bodies. There was instant silence. 'What is this, my lords? Do you hold council of war in my absence?'

Lord Patrick Lindsay got to his feet and the dozen other nobles and bishops scrambled from their benches to join him.

'Sire, we are discussing strategy for the coming battle,' Lindsay said in confident tones, looking around at his fellow commanders for support.

'Aye,' came a few mutters.

'And you did not think to wait my pleasure!' the king shouted. 'Tell me then! Have you reached a decision?' He eased into his chair, stretched out his long legs and glowered at his lords as they took their seats.

'We have not, Sire. There is a view that Surrey intends to invade your realm to wreak havoc and draw us back. Another is that he will cut our supply lines and starve us. It is better to withdraw in good order, while we may.' Lindsay lowered his voice a little. 'But we all agree that if we do meet them, your person must not face hazard.'

'It is not for you to tell me how I must lead my army, Lindsay. The world knows I am not a monarch who shelters in a tent at the rear.'

Lindsay chose his words with care, 'Sire, in the vanguard you would be but a single soldier, but as a commander on his feet, ably directing his forces, you are worth a hundred thousand men.'

The Bishop of The Isles leaned forward. 'That is good counsel, Sire.'

'Aye, aye,' echoed the others.

Lindsay spoke with force. 'It is as if a gentleman set about to dice with a common gambler. You are the Rose Nobill and he a bad English halfpenny. That auld, crooked man, lying in his chariot, is not worth the risk.'

'My lord Lindsay!' the king shouted, colour coming to his face. 'Enough of your presumption lest I have you in irons.' He glared at his other nobles. 'Those who have no belly for this fight, like Angus, can leave me. He that runs will never shame me into doing the same. Those that stay will share my wine as I outline my orders of battle.' He called to an aide, 'Bring me the French officers.' The tent fell silent as servants recharged the goblets. 'Here are new orders: cover the territory with scouts, forthwith. I want the size of Surrey's divisions, his disposition, line of march and every move he makes, reported back to me with accuracy and haste.'

25

Barmoor Wood

Tom relaxed into the motion of the Fell pony and looked her over. She had a thick neck and a big head, and her hill-bred legs, short, sturdy and driven by powerful muscles in the quarters, could trot all day. The rain dripped from the sodden black mane as he leaned forward to whisper into her ear, 'You're a tough one, girl; even in all this clart you stride out as if on parade.' He shared her breath as she nickered softly in reply.

Surrounded by other mounted archers, he had little to do except avoid collisions and steer her through the worst patches of ground. Along her back the colour showed a coppery red where the sun had bleached the black out of it. When she grew her shaggy winter coat those red patches would fall away. He welcomed the relief of simple thoughts after a night of fitful sleep in which his head swarmed with worries about his sister and Mary. At Wooler camp he had sought out Jack Swales, but the coal hauler could not enlarge on the news from home.

Shouts broke out from the front of the column. He stood up in his stirrups and craned his neck. The rain had cleared enough to reveal a treeless ridge to the east, patterned with drifting patches of sunlight. Someone called out, 'Look! Flodden Edge to the left! There's tents up there! It's them!'

A dull roar, followed by a gout of smoke, erupted from the near slope of the ridge. Moments later, something smashed into the broom on the opposite side of the river.

'They're saying hello,' the rider next to Tom growled. 'That were a gradely blast; must be a big'un. Let's pray we're still out of range by supper time.'

An officer trotted past on a riding horse. 'Naught to fret about; they'll not reach us on this track. That sounded like a siege gun; it'll take them half an hour before she can fire again. Christ knows why they've dragged that useless lump of iron up there; it will have needed thirty oxen.' The officer rode further up the column.

Tom turned to the crag-faced man at his side. 'What landed in the broom?'

'Nowt but a gobbet of granite someone spent hours chipping into a round shape. They've flung away the man's work. Still, I suppose it's to let us know they've got dry powder; by the sound of that crack, it's good stuff. I hope ours is well covered; if the damp gets to it we'll be able to piss further.'

Tom scanned the forward slopes of the ridge, noting the steep banks of clay on top of sandstone and pondering on its state after days of rain. He voiced his misgivings: 'Are we expected to climb that slope to get at them? It'll be mucky!'

'Nay, I wouldn't think auld Howard is so daft he'd step into such a naked snare. He'll have summat else in mind. Besides, look at the track we're on, it's taking us north o' that lump, straight as a crow-road. We're going past him.'

They rode on in silence until Tom asked, 'Where do you belong?'

'Macclesfield - in Cheshire. There's a few hundred of us bows with Stanley. All that lot behind are Macclesfield too. And thyself?'

'North Riding, though I'm with Billy Bulmer's crowd from Durham.'

'Oh, maybe you were at Milfield. I hear the Scots took a bit of a clouting.'

'We had them from cover as they dribbled home with their thievings.'

The Cheshire man grunted with interest. 'And how did the shafts fly that day?'

'Thick as hail in the few spots they fell - we had but two hundred bows. A lot sank into the cattle; the beasts went mad, ran off headlong, hundreds of them. The poor beggars scattered the reivers more than our arrows did.'

'Well, they'll need a fair few cai up there to keep that lot in meat. I like what you say; let's pray we catch them as easy this time! So what's your work when you're not soldiering?'

Uncertain of what he had become, Tom had to think. 'I'm a cowman. That's why I don't like hurting stock without good cause.'

'Never mind, there'll be plenty of hairy buggers on two legs you can shoot at.'

Tom had a spasm in his stomach muscles. 'What's your own work?' he asked.

'I've a farm with the best of grass and water; good land for beef and milk. We make a lot of hard cheese that keeps well. There's a decent stretch of plough land, too. I've a dozen or so men and a few lasses working for me.'

'It sounds like heaven,' Tom said.

'Not in the short days, when the grass is clarty and thin. We take only the best stock through the lean months.' He twisted in the saddle. 'You look a useful sort. Come over to Macclesfield, I'll set you on. Ask for Christopher Wells.'

'Thanks; I might need a place. I'll think on it.' Tom looked into the sky and pulled down his hat. 'This looks bad.'

The sun disappeared behind a fist-shaped black cloud that had crept from the south-west. The puddles on the track burst into life as hailstones blasted the column. Men hunched their shoulders and cursed; horses lowered their heads and snorted.

'Listen to the moans,' Farmer Wells shouted above the din of hail. 'It could be a sight worse; it's hardly worth hucking up the shoulders for. This land is too well drained to hold the wet for long; I reckon there's river gravel under these clarts.'

Tom chuckled at the man's indifference to the weather.

A voice yelled nearby, 'Ah, Fleck! Found you! Why aren't you with the rest of my company?' Captain Jackson reined in his chestnut mare alongside Tom and squinted at him through the downpour.

Tom could not hold back a laugh as he tried to make himself heard through the roar of ice. 'It was that last beck, sir! A pair of cockhosses got in a tangle when their waggon threw a wheel. So I gave the carter a hand!'

With a final, rippling curtain, the hailstorm ceased. The track glistened in a covering of white beads. All was silent except for the crunch of hooves on melting ice. Farmer Wells broke the spell. 'That's right, Captain sir - him and me took the weight together, and we'd a job on to fish her tumbled cannon out the beck. By the time we'd done, your bowmen were a mile in front.'

Edward Jackson took off his broad leather hat and shook it. 'I see - well, that's all right. I had cause to worry you'd made plans to slip away. Two of my men vanished at Wooler. I've sent riders back to look for them. I hope for their sakes they've got good reasons.'

'What'll happen if they've run off?' Tom asked.

'The penalty in times like this can be a rope and a tree. We all need to bear that in mind. Are you doing all right?'

'Yes, sir. I'm wet through and famished but coping well enough -

I've known harder times.'

The captain drew his horse alongside Tom's pony. 'I'm glad you're with us. This should soon be done. Afterwards, you and that dog can skip off home and sit around the fire for a bit. You'll have earned it.' He grinned at the bedraggled Meg who had jumped out of her sling and now trotted through the layer of hail. 'I suppose you've been feeding her out of your rations. What will you do with her when we meet the Scots?'

'She'll stick by me, sir. She's as good as gold. Can you say when we're likely to need the bows?'

'The earl's got some plan I'm not privy to and, more to the point, neither is King Jimmy. Hear me: our section is part of the vanguard, so make sure you find your company tonight. We're making camp in a wood by Barmoor Castle. It's not far and it's out of sight of those gunners.' The captain spurred his horse and, calling out, 'Make way!' threaded forward through the column.

Christopher Wells pursed his lips and nodded, 'Yon's a gradely man; I like the sense of him.'

'Aye, he's fair and keeps his eye out for us. His crowd will do anything for him.'

'Ye're lucky then; there's some useless buggers in charge.'

They rode in silence until Tom asked, 'What do you think tomorrow might bring?'

'I've been pondering that since we spied them on that hill. The earl's a fox; he'll not tackle them head-on, not while they're dug in up there. I'd say we're heading for the Tweed at the minute, so Jimmy o' the Hill should be having a bad belly at the thought we'll outflank him and raid his kingdom. If we do that, I suppose we'll make a bit of a nuisance of ourselves by burning his towns; that'll sharp bring him down. We'll just have to keep going and see what the auld man's got in mind.'

Tom rode into the camp at nightfall. He tethered his pony among other mounts and oxen in pastures stripped of their usual livestock. Rows of waggons edged the leeward side of Barmoor Wood.

Amid the bustle of an army making camp for the night, a few dozen local men arrived to complain that the Scots had driven off their animals, robbed their barns of grain and their houses of food. Their bellies were empty, they said, and they fed their families on trapped birds and hedgehogs. The earl's son, Admiral Thomas

Howard, ordered a distribution of rations to those who agreed to act as scouts for the next day.

Tom found his company building shelters. With billhooks, they lopped thick hazel stems. They bent and interwove them with ash poles to form domed frameworks draped with the army's sheets of waxed linen. Ash and hazel made up the woodland and, by the time the army bedded down for the night, the men had harvested the eastern half of Barmoor Wood down to the base of its ancient coppice stools. Tom, unable to find a space in one of the shelters, curled up in the lee of a drystone wall among rows of militiamen. Wrapping himself in the thick cloak he had bought in Alnwick, he drew Meg into it and, sharing her warmth, fell exhausted into a sleep without dreams.

In the small hours, something roused him. He eased onto his back and stared at the star-lit sky, listening to the harsh screeches of owls and the snores of men. His drifting mind felt the weight of thousands of sleepers in the woods and of thousands of others, body next to body, beneath the field walls. The position of the seven stars that formed the ox-plough told him it was two hours after midnight.

Meg crawled out from under the cloak. She walked stiff-legged for a few yards and squatted. By the glimmer of starlight, Tom watched her take a long pee, shake herself, stretch out one hind leg and then the other, scratch at the ground a few times with all four paws before looking over her shoulder at him with enquiring eyes.

She reckons it's time we set off home, he thought. I could slip out of here and cover a few miles before daylight. The army would be well into the march before I was missed. It's no matter - I'm nowt but small fry. He tried to calculate how many days it would take to get home - perhaps four if he kept moving. But then what? His mind cleared a bit more and he could see Rachel waiting for him in Alnwick. As if through a fall of gossamer, she gazed at him with those strange, dark eyes.

Something moved beneath the small of his back, so he rolled out from under the cloak to stand up. He swept his foot across the ground and realised what had woken him. During the night, a molehill had erupted where he slept. It gave another heave when the little digger pressed on with its tunnelling.

Pulling the cloak around his shoulders, he walked out into the middle of the pasture. While emptying his bladder he noticed the dim outlines of sentries, two of them, stood side by side. He strained his eyes until one of the figures took the shape of a standing stone. A cow scratcher! Set there by a good stockman. For a moment, he felt cheered. But it might have age, like those by the burial mounds on the moors back home. Either way, it would be where the cows came to rub themselves. When he got his own beasts he would put up scratching stones, so they could ease their itches.

Tom finished his pee and wiped his hands on the wet grass. He rubbed them dry across the front of his cloak before slipping them inside for warmth. His chilled fingers touched the outlines of the silver coins he had concealed within the padding of his jerkin. He had done that in secret at Alnwick and it gave comfort to feel their hard shapes against his chest.

The other figure moved away from the stone and came towards him. Captain Jackson raised a hand in recognition. 'Did you manage to get some sleep?'

'Aye, sir - a stretch. And yourself?'

'About three hours. It'll have to do though. I'm on watch, checking on the sentries in this part and making sure they get relieved.' He searched the sky. 'The stars are going, there's more rain to come.'

'That's right, sir. It's in the air - you can smell it.'

'You seem to fare well enough, Fleck. You stockmen are hardened to weather and rough sleeping. There's some here from the towns - tailors and bakers and the like - who are suffering a bit. I've heard a good deal of coughing and spitting tonight. But there's not long to go.'

'Are the Scots still up there - on that hill, sir?'

'There's reports of movement. Scouts spotted a crowd of them on low ground by the far side of the river. Jimmy cannot stay up there forever, he'll worry about what we're up to, marching past him like this. Now we're in touch with the garrison at Berwick we'll get supplies, but if yon lot stay up there they'll go hungry.'

'Perhaps they'll all go home.' Tom felt hopeful.

'That's one choice he has, if he's sharp about it. Otherwise we could cut, in one stroke, both his supply line and his escape route across the Tweed at Coldstream. Now Berwick's close, he'll worry that we can sit it out.'

'And if he doesn't pull back?'

'He'll have to come down and meet us. If we keep moving he can only guess where that might be.'

From the river valley came the distant barking of a dog.

'What would you do, sir?'

'If I was in King Jimmy's boots, you mean?' The captain gave a quiet laugh. 'I'd clear off home and look to my kingdom, because it's naked. He's smashed down three English castles; that should be enough if he's only after a bit of glory. I hear he's given to rashness - so who knows what he'll do?'

'I'm scared, sir,' Tom blurted out.

The captain put a hand on his shoulder. 'I'm glad to hear it! That means you won't do aught foolish. Anyway, it's usual to come over queer at this time of night; you'll feel more solid in daylight. I've not forgotten Milfield Plain; you had plenty of nerve on that day, and a cool head. If you'd not, I wouldn't be standing here. Think on that. Now I must get off and finish my rounds. Goodnight, soldier.'

'Goodnight, sir.' Tom watched the tall, long-armed form of the captain of archers merge with the dark.

26

Across the Till

Tom saw the first hint of grey appear in the east. To the beat of muffled drums shadowy figures went along the lines, banging on rough shelters and poking with sticks those sleepers who had not stirred. Twenty-six thousand slowly stood erect, up to their knees in a counterpane of thin mist. Across the grazing came the dreary piping of a whaup calling to its mate. The fields emerged like graveyards rising to the sound of the Last Trump at the end of the world.

Joining the queue at a feeding station, he joined others who stamped and slapped the cramps of the night out of their limbs. He took his ration of two thick oatcakes and a lump of stiff cheese from a yawning camp cook. Soldiers snapped the oaten hard tack into pieces and dipped chunks into their meagre issue of ale. In the half-hour they had to prepare themselves, they sucked and chewed on this breakfast before washing it down with stream water. After sharing his rations with Meg, he pushed into the woods to find some privacy. The hazels had gone - cut by the army; he crouched among the stumps with thousands of others.

Back at the horse lines, men were grumbling about orders to leave their ponies at the camp. All ordinary soldiers had to dismount, except for Lord Dacre's fifteen hundred border lances who would form a light cavalry screen.

'Why can't we ride like them? We'd be that much fitter,' shouted an angry archer.

Tom watched a captain stride over to give a caution. 'Orders, man! Orders from the earl's tent! There'll be a good reason. Now, get on with checking your gear.'

The archer stamped away and joined his comrades sheltering beneath a drystone wall.

'No mounts for us!' he snarled from the corner of his mouth. 'We've to trudge from here. Why's that? I want to know.'

An older man spat. 'It means but one thing, Jack - that we'll tangle with the Scots before the day's done.'

'Aye, and to make sure we stand, they've barred us from riding. We've nae chance of making a run for it should the job turn sour,' another called out.

Jack cleared his throat. 'Then let's hope we get a spot nigh-hand them marines, they look hard-boiled enough.'

It took seven hours of effort, along a rutted track in steady rain, before the vanguard reached Twyzell Bridge. Behind Tom and his fellow archers snaked a column of regimented units interspersed with artillery. Bowmen and billmen added their muscle to that of horse and ox. They cursed and slithered in gangs, manhandling the wheels of ammunition waggons and cannon carts through greasy clay.

Tom waited among the damp thousands; each company standing beneath its own pennants and banners, to take its turn to pass across the narrow stonework of the bridge over the River Till. The press became so great that, even though the river flowed in spate after a fortnight of rain, some units broke away to risk the fords further upstream.

On the far side of Twyzell Bridge their seventy-year-old commander, caped against the rain, stood on a cart to shout encouragement to his footsore men as they cleared the bridge. When Tom's company passed beneath his platform, he called out to them: 'Today you fight like Englishmen. This day you take my part - and that part is the king's part.'

The marchers' backs stiffened. They looked him full in the face. A grey-haired, little man squinted up and shouted, 'Divn't worry tha' sen, auld hinney; the clothyards'll fly well enough th'day - we'll sharp fettle them for ye.' On hearing the man's cheek, laughter broke out.

The earl slapped his thigh, pointed a finger and yelled, 'You'll do! Come and see me afterwards and share a tankard.' He noticed Meg. 'And you'll do as well, little one-lug with her tail up! Those jaws will fettle a few raggy arses for us before long.'

A marshal called out, 'Keep moving and turn south! You're a Durham company so keep behind that red banner up ahead. Be sure to keep your tackle dry.'

Persistent light rain spilled off the brim of Tom's leather hat to find its way down the back of his neck. He slipped a hand beneath the limp headgear to check his packet of wrapped bowstrings. Satisfied they remained dry, he next made sure the longbow and its two quivers of arrows rested secure. He touched his side hanger - the short-sword lay snug in its scabbard. He felt his bowels tremble and, in an instant knew he needed to find somewhere to squat. Captain Jackson marched alongside the column. Tom called out to him, 'Sir! I need a shit.'

'Then see to it! I want you back in line in two minutes.'

Tom hurried to a patch of broom and, trembling, lowered his breeches. Meg took the chance to rest. Her coat steamed and her tongue lolled from her mouth. A few other men crouched nearby; one by one they got to their feet and ran on ahead. Nothing much left Tom except wind. He felt sick and realised he had fright. A man next to him grunted, pulling up his breeches. 'It's the colic. It's what comes of supping scummy beck watter instead of ale.'

Another squatter called out, 'Hey up! What's all that reek yonder?'

Away to the southeast, columns of black smoke billowed into the low cloud. The dark mass hung motionless before drifting north-westward, pushed by the wind. Tom stared at the smoke; it grew thicker. His attention swung towards a column of billmen marching past a few yards away. Rain, mixed with sweat, dripped from their beards, and traces of vapour rose from their rain-blackened shoulders. From his crouched position they towered like leather-padded giants; among them, a slight figure waved a hand. It was the boyish frame of Peter Tindall. Tom waved back; grabbed some grass and cleaned himself. He pulled up his breeches, checked his gear, and jogged up the column until he reached his friend.

Peter gave a weak grin. 'Tha'll feel better for that. Tha looks fair washed out.'

'You're not too rosy-cheeked yourself this afternoon, Peter; though you look brave enough under that iron bonnet.'

A voice boomed behind him, 'Archer! Find yer company and be sharp about it!' A massive, bearded man, wearing Tudor green and white, glared at him.

Tom shook Peter by the hand, met his eyes and told him to take care. He set off running, past the moving mass of shouldered bills, through flattened rushes, until he rejoined the archers.

Once he had caught his breath, Tom stared through the rain across a sea of leather skull caps and iron helmets that stretched out, bobbing, for two hundred yards in front - the distance a bodkin arrow could fly. The smoke in front had thickened and blown across their line of advance. He could no longer make out the high ground they were heading for.

Fifty yards in front, two bulky men carried poles that held aloft an old red banner. Embroidered flowers garlanded its sides, framing in its centre a faded red cross on a white square. Tom tried to concentrate on it. The way the wind played with the banner took his mind off his queasy stomach and helped to hold back the bile that threatened to flood into his mouth. In front of him paced a fair-haired youth with a good quality longbow on his back. The boy's old-fashioned, crested iron helmet kept intruding into Tom's line of sight. A spade-bearded, older man on the lad's left, wearing a helmet inlaid with brass, spoke in reassuring tones:

'With a bit o' luck it'll be all over by tonight, son. Once it is, I doubt if they'll keep us much longer. Stick hard by me; I'll cover you. If we look out for yen an' other, we should be right.'

'I've only shot at targets and that one wild pig; I don't know how it'll be to shoot at men,' the youth said.

'Treat them as if they're boar coming at you with mucky yellow tusks. Howld steady; keep breathing long, slow and even, and you'll do fine.'

'Is it right what they say, Dad? That we've never lost when we've stood under Saint Cuthbert's banner?'

'Right enough, Percy. So it is. That's why the auld earl had Saint Cuddy's cloth fetched out of Durham Cathedral, so he could raise it here.'

The talk dried up. The column marched in silence except for the odd cough and spit. One man broke into song and others took up the refrain, so that it passed along the ranks:

'Mary Lumley's sweet and fair,
combing down her yeller hair.
I'll mak sure she marries me,
pretty Mary Lumley.

Mary Lumley's often there,
when I gan tae Durham Fair.
With her buckles I'll mak free,
pretty Mary Lumley.

Mary Lumley's having a bairn,
for tae dangle on her airm.
On her airm and on her knee,
pretty Mary Lumley.'

'It's not far now. Keep your voices down.' Heads shifted to see Sir William Bulmer's armoured figure astride a heavy horse. He cantered along the line, the broad hooves of his gelding throwing up clods of earth. 'Keep up the pace and keep together. We need to make the top of Branxton Hill before they get wind of what we're about.'

'What's all that smoke up ahead, sir?' someone shouted out.

'They've fired their camp. They're on the move,' the knight yelled over his shoulder.

A group of horsemen trotted past. Among them, the face of the chain-mailed Earl of Surrey winced as his horse covered the lumpy ground.

The man on Tom's left spoke. 'Look at him go; I hope I'm that fit at seventy. Mind you, with his bad joints, he doesn't care for the saddle.'

The horsemen swung away to their left and rode through the sword leaves of flag irises until they joined the vanguard of another division that had forded a mile upstream from the bridge. A mass of Tudor green and white led the column.

The man spoke again. 'That's likely the main lot; the auld man will take charge of it. They look to have waded Heaton Ford - they'll be damp.'

'Who's in charge of us?' Tom asked.

'His son, the Admiral. We're the vanguard. There's green and white here too. Looks like they've sprinkled the marines among us. A bit of stiffening no doubt.' The man wiped rain off his face. 'Heyup! We're swinging right and the earl's lot are off to the left. Seems we're splitting up; I hope they know what they're about. And where's Stanley's rearguard? He's a couple o' thousand archers under him. I've not had sight of them since well afore the bridge.'

On Tom's right, a quarter-mile away, he could see masses of horsemen riding parallel. 'Look over there!'

'That's Dacre's crowd of wild men; the only cavalry we've brought. He must have a couple o' thousand prickers there.'

Half an hour later, a broad stretch of soggy ground separated the vanguard from the main force. Far away to the right, silhouetted on a hillock, a group of horsemen watched their progress. One of them broke away and galloped to the south. There were shouts of: 'Look! Scouts! They've seen us.'

Pushed by a freshening wind, the wall of smoke arrived to swirl around the plodding thousands. Militiamen coughed as they breathed in the stink of burning straw. Out of the smoke hobbled a group of poor-looking men with bundles on their backs, followed by a cluster of shawled mothers clutching babies and trailed by grubby-faced children.

'Where you from?' a captain shouted.

'The village. The Scotch are coming back. It's best we get out of the way. There's still some that'll nae leave.'

Branxton village loomed out of the smoke. First to emerge was a peel tower with smashed door and smoke-blackened arrow slits; after this, a straggle of thatched huts along the bank of a stream. Half of them were flame blackened, their charred frames slumped in disarray. Out of heaps of steaming ash, burnt timbers pointed upwards like curved and beckoning fingers. Tom shuddered at the waste of it: folk had built those huts with nowt but an adze and bits of lashing, now they'd it all to do again, if they'd the strength and if they'd life. Around him men cursed, 'Those cauld bastards!'

A thin lurcher rushed at them, barking. It made a lunge at Meg. The man behind Tom shouted, 'Bugger off,' and kicked it in the ribs. The dog yelped and bolted.

'We can't have our lucky lady mascot beaten up, can we now?' he growled.

A gaunt woman, wrapped in a threadbare shawl, danced out of the gloom. Her eyes searched around, wild and crazed. Tom shivered when the mad stare fixed on him. She swayed across the track. 'Sodgers! Sodgers!' she sang out, 'bonny sodgers, gannin this way. Cummin ower the bog, an' through the broomy bits. Gannin this day - maybe tae gan doon in the clay - this day - this day.' She let out a series of hysterical laughs.

A man ran through the mud towards the woman. 'Betty hinney! Come away now, come away!' His bony arms wrapped around her from behind and pulled her towards the doorway of a hut. As the man pushed the door closed, Tom made contact with his eyes and saw a reflection of his own fear.

A simple stone chapel hugged the ground at the far end of the settlement. As Tom's unit approached, a bent old man got up from the shelter of the graveyard wall and hobbled towards them, leaning on a stick. He took off his woollen cap and held it out in silence, staring at the ground as they passed. Some archers paused to toss him coins. Behind the wall lay a row of new graves.

At the side of the track, next to his chapel, stood a pale young priest. His white linen surplice hung in rain-soaked slabs against a

198

thin body. He held a crucifix in his left hand and blessed them as they trudged past, making the sign of the cross with the fingers of his right. He called out at intervals, 'In nomine Patris, et Filii, et Spiritus Sancti. Amen.' Most of the archers took off their caps and crossed themselves.

27

Flodden

'Form into a column fifty men wide,' a breast-plated marshal shouted above the chanting of the priest. 'Stay to this side of the beck. Follow Cuthbert's banner.'

'Keep up close behind me, lads.' Captain Jackson urged his company of one hundred onwards, their boots wading through an acre of trampled oats.

A few yards to their right the ground fell steeply into the tiny, thorn-clad valley of the Pallinsburn, its waters humped in full spate. Close by, on their left, a regiment of billmen squelched out of the oat field and onto rising ground. Tom felt the slope steepen beneath his feet. Axles squealed somewhere in the smoke ahead. Minutes later the archers were filtering between oxen and gangs of sweating gunners heaving on stuck wheels.

He sensed a shift in the breeze and watched the smoke peel away to reveal the open grassland of a broad, shallow depression straight ahead. Beyond that low ground the slope of a long hill loomed out of the greyness. A roar erupted as more of the sweeping gradient unveiled. Cackling in alarm, a covey of partridge rose up and, with a skirr of wings, abandoned the ground to the armies. Another roaring boom sounded from the top of the emerging hill a mere five hundred yards distant. Under fluttering banners, four great battle groups stretched for a mile along the crest. Weary after a march of ten hours, the English were too late to claim Branxton Hill.

Tom stared in horror as dark humps on the ridge took the form of huge cannon. He shrank backwards a step as his eyes met the cold gaze of a gun barrel. He looked around at his fellows and knew that each of them had frozen like a rabbit transfixed by a stoat.

'Ye seek a target, ye daft loons?' The shout came from a little man in front of him. Tom recognised the archer who had joked with the earl at the bridge. The grizzled man shouted again at the Scottish line, 'Then see if ye can plug this!' He turned his back on the cannon, pulled down his breeks, bent and bared his backside. 'Howway, bloody firedrakes - fill it up!' The laughter died when tongues of flame and gouts of smoke belched along the hilltop.

They flung themselves to the ground. With a rushing sound, the spheres of lead and of granite passed overhead, high above the forward ranks, to fall at a steep angle among trudging soldiers who still crowded the farm track. Others smashed into columns of infantry that had passed to the north of the village and were, at that moment, in the midst of leaping the torrent of the Pallinsburn. Scores of them stopped in bewilderment; others shouted, 'Take cover!' Those already on the high ground ran back down the slope. Captains with drawn swords ran among them, yelling, 'Hold! Hold!'

The man with the brass-inlaid helmet got to his feet and set about stringing his bow; others took their cue from him. Captain Jackson paced up and down. He shouted, 'That's good! Well done, lads! Keep your ground till we get orders. Those big guns are slow to load and bad to aim, they'll not hurt us much.'

A marshal rode up. 'Captain! Pull your men back until they're out of sight of that artillery. A hundred yards to the rear should do it.'

'Jackson archers to me, to me!' The captain yelled as the entire vanguard regrouped further down the slope.

The marshals, bellowing from horseback, rode up and down, struggling to sort the companies into a semblance of battle order. Meg stayed close to Tom's legs in the push and shove of thousands of billmen and archers trying to keep contact with their own kind. Behind them, ammunition and artillery waggons still plodded out of the village, urged on by harassed gunners. Tom caught sight of a familiar broad back as Jack Swales manhandled a wheeled cannon off an artillery cart.

The units assembled into a broad front as the coughing of heavy guns continued. Balls weighing thirty-six pounds fell, at a steep angle, from the sky. Instead of skipping along the ground and knocking men down like skittles, each shot ploughed a short trench into the waterlogged earth with a single, squelching thud. Men craned their necks and looked upwards in the faint hope of dodging the shot. Here and there someone was smashed to the ground.

The Admiral, Thomas Howard, rose out of his saddle in alarm. He grabbed the medallion that hung around his neck and snapped its cord. 'Aide!' he shouted to a horsed man. 'Take this to my father with all speed.' He flung his divine protector, the Agnus Dei, towards the rider, who reached out, caught it and glanced at the image of the Lamb and Flag. 'Tell him, I beseech he come with all haste, for we are not enough to withstand an attack!'

Watching the aide gallop away, an archer groped into the bottom of his arrow sack. 'Seems like a good time to finish me bit of hard cheese.'

The spare figure of the admiral climbed onto a cart to survey his own division and that of his younger brother, Edmond. Whilst making rapid calculations in his head he ran a hand beneath his shining helmet and down to his pointed chin, wiping away rain. He grabbed the arm of his chief marshal. 'Keep everyone out of sight. He must not see our weakness. At present we are but two divisions facing the four that I can see . . . then there is his rearguard. When the earl arrives we will have adjustments to make. I must know where Stanley's division is - send out riders to find them.' He pointed to the northeast. 'And send two companies of billmen to bring up those guns.'

With two marshals beside him and the Lords Ogle and Gascoigne following, the Admiral rode along the contour of the slope, out of sight of the Scots. He reined in alongside Sir William Sydney and the other captains of marines. Summoning his tall, younger brother, Edmond Howard, together with Lord Lumley and Sir William Bulmer, he gave out new battle orders.

Half an hour later Tom leaned on his bow shaft next to 'Brass Helmet' and his son. They stood behind their captain in a block of a hundred archers. With five other blocks, they waited on the right flank of a mass of eight thousand billmen. He closed his eyes and listened to the drone of speech around him. Accents, familiar and unknown, filtered through from voices bred in Northumberland, Durham and Yorkshire. He opened his eyes and looked around. Half an arrow-shot to the right stood another division, perhaps three thousand men from Cheshire and Lancashire with a stiffening of two hundred veteran marines wearing green and white. In loose groups to the rear of those men, he could see bands of horsemen from Tynemouth, Berwick and Bamburgh in dulled breastplates and rusted iron helmets - border raiders who worked for their own gain. In the hundred-yard gap between the two divisions, bands of oxen, yoked to wheeled cannon, steamed quietly. At the rear, carts of powder and shot waited. The drivers leaned against their oxen, stroking the blindfolded heads.

They crouched in this position, out of sight of the Scots, and waited. Every few minutes, heavy cannonballs dropped in twos and threes into their ranks. Other volleys crashed among a body of light horse. The yells of men and the neighing of terrified mounts filled the air until the contingents from Bamburgh and Tynemouth panicked and galloped from the field.

Edward Jackson ran back from a brief meeting with the marshals. His men cried out, 'What's happening, sir?'

'We stand here until Surrey and Stanley arrive.'

A voice, rough and cracked with an edge of fear, asked, 'Where've they got to?'

Another shouted, 'No bother! They plodged across the Till higher up. Look! There's a crowd coming by way of that little brig ower the beck.'

A man next to Tom broke in. 'Them's Surrey's banners. I see nowt of Stanley. It'll be a bugger if we're left on our own, the Scots look thicker than nettles.'

The captain waved his bowstave to get their attention. 'All right, soldiers - the centre's on its way. Stand-to, till I tell you to move. Sky's coming in black. Un-string bows and store them cords under your hats. We'll keep them dry until they're needed.'

Tom slumped down on the soaked ground. No matter, he thought, I'm already drenched with rain and sweat. Meg lay alongside his thigh and fixed him with a wild look. He stroked her head, taking care not to touch the scarred ear.

'Aye, auld lass, we've been in some queer spots, you and me.' She licked his hand. 'This is the queerest spot of all, you'll be thinking. When we get through this patch I reckon we should take a bit of a rest - put our feet up, sit around the fire, eat cakes. Here, have this.' He took out his last hard biscuit and gave it to Meg. She crunched it down then sniffed among the grassroots for crumbs.

The Scottish cannon still belched their deep roars and balls dropped out of the sky further to the rear. They didn't seem to do much damage, Tom thought, except that you never knew where they'd land. Men's faces were twitching. Tom looked to the rear to see more of the mounted prickers drifting away, despite the shouts of the marshals.

~ ~ ~

Five thousand foot soldiers and archers arrived in blocks across the saturated grazing. After leaping the burn they were marshalled into a broad front two hundred yards to the left of the Admiral. A battery of artillery squatted in the gap. Surrey now stood on the field, only Stanley had not come. The Admiral galloped across to greet his father. They spoke briefly then made a hurried redistribution of men.

The Admiral returned to his command behind Cuthbert's banner. He stood up in his stirrups, looked back at his own nine thousand and held aloft his sword. Trumpets sounded. To the beat of drums, all three divisions moved forward on a broad front. Alongside them, teams of blindfolded oxen dragged artillery to the top of the slope.

Once again they stood in full view of King James's army that lined the ridge of Branxton Hill for a mile; the largest army Scotland would ever field.

'This is our day, lads. This is what we came for,' the captain called.

'It's not what I bloody well came for,' Tom muttered. 'Nor you, Meg. You'll be thinking you'd be better off with some other master.' He bent down to fondle her neck, and she responded with a soft whine.

Captain Jackson passed through the ranks. 'That distance is three bowshots. Nothing for us yet. Keep them under your hats. Check your gear and stand by for orders.'

Over the clatter of noise from the batteries, a marshal yelled, 'Get those bloody oxen out of the way!'

Tom watched Jack Swales lead his frightened oxen, their tails swishing, back down the slope to relative safety. On all sides now, men waited in the rain, silent and vulnerable, listening to the distant shouts of enemy marshals. The Scottish pikes grew along the ridge like a forest of winter saplings.

A cheer went up at a sudden blast of noise. Tom knelt among the host of archers' legs to calm Meg's yelps. With a series of deep, rippling coughs, the eighteen English falcons had opened fire, leaping off the ground on their wheels and recoiling backwards into restraining ropes.

Compared to the huge Scottish guns, the lightweight field cannon were simple to manoeuvre, elevate, and load. Today - firing uphill - they might be lethal in the hands of the Admiral's professional German gunners. Their first target was the Scottish artillery.

Once the initial salvoes had found the range, iron balls weighing two pounds whipped through the Scottish batteries. The shot scattered men and smashed into carts. With dull roars, five brass serpentines joined in to lob five-pound iron spheres at the same targets. Tom could discern men on top of the hill dragging away wounded. Others with shovels struggled to pile earth into ramparts. One by one, King James's pride - his cannon - fell silent, leaving only the cries of injured artillerymen.

Coughing amid the acrid stench of gunpowder, the gunners now brought the muzzles to bear onto the massed ranks of pikemen. Once they found their targets, volleys of balls cut narrow lanes through the standing infantry.

'Brass Helmet' looked at Tom. 'They'll not suffer that for long,' he said. 'They'll either pull back out of sight or come at us. If they rush us, stick hard by me and my son. We three will cover each other.' Tom could only nod - his dry tongue was stuck to the roof of his mouth.

Shouting broke out and trumpets sounded from the left wing of the Scots line. The yelling died away to a hush, broken moments later by the beating of a dozen drums. On the western end of Branxton Hill, the Scots division that faced the Lancashire and Cheshire men on Tom's right was in motion. Except for the thud of drums, they moved in silence.

'String bows! String bows! Ready quivers!' Captain Jackson moved among his company.

On every side men worked fast with hardened fingers. Tom fumbled and swore at his trembling hands as he strung the bow. His heart raced and he tasted bile. Meg whined again. He grasped his bowstring and pulled on it a few times. He checked, yet again, the sheaves of arrows at his waist; yes, he could reach them and the flights had kept dry enough - for the moment. He pulled at the bone finger guards on his bowstring hand: might they be too tight? Were the grooves in the right place? He pulled at them with his teeth. Next, he fiddled with the leather sleeve that protected his left arm from the whip of the bowstring. Shit! Bloody hell. Dad, I'm shaking - tak howld! Tak howld! He coughed and spat out phlegm. Men around him knelt on their right knees and made the sign of the cross. Squalls of cold rain continued to thrash the left sides of their faces.

The captain announced in a casual voice, 'The wind's hunting about today, though the gusts are mostly from the left-hand, front quarter; you'll need to bear that in mind. We'll not make two hundred yards in this. Best not to waste shots on empty ground. Listen out for my orders.'

Away to the right the Scots lords, Home and Huntly, descended the hill with nine thousand Border pikes in rigid echelons. Skirting the division's flanks, a thousand highland sword and axe skirmishers led by Gordon chieftains advanced in rough formation behind round wooden shields. The pikes covered the ground in long, staggered blocks, each one a few paces behind and to the side of the block in front. Each block consisted of hundreds of men marching in disciplined silence; they had the effect of a broad, moving arrowhead. Once free of the steep hillside they advanced on Edmond Howard's division across sloping ground, the sort of ground King James's French advisers claimed ideal for the deployment of the Swiss pike.

At two hundred yards, the Cheshire and Lancashire arrows flew in volleys. Many shafts that reached the echelons collided with the mass of vertical pikes and fell, useless, to the ground. The fall of arrows built to a pulsing rain of points that made a few gaps in the ranks. The armoured legions hardly wavered.

At one hundred yards, the front lines of Scots lowered their pikes and the arrows now bounced off helmets and breastplates. Only a few found homes in unprotected parts of men.

Tom's company, waiting for orders, could only watch. In the division to their right, the archers exhausted their quivers on the advancing troops; but they failed to break the advance and, at the last moment, took cover behind the ranks of their own billmen. The eighteen-foot pikes smashed into the triple rows of billmen. Wielding eight-foot bills, the English militia fought to lop off the points of the moving pikes but, outnumbered three to one, their line wavered, then buckled inwards. The front ranks fell like scythed wheat.

Tramping over the fallen, the pikes pressed onwards until the English right wing ruptured and the long spears broke through followed by axe-wielding skirmishers. Hundreds of billmen and archers fled to the rear. Hundreds of others took refuge among beleaguered groups still on the field. Tom saw the banners of the small and great houses of Lancashire and Cheshire fall to the ground in twos and threes amid terrible shrieks.

'By Our Lady!' breathed a man nearby.

The ground trembled. Behind them, Lord Dacre's fifteen hundred mounted Northumbrians were in full charge. In a shower of clods of earth and with banners streaming they galloped to the rescue of the crumbled right wing. Tom's mouth fell open and rain lashed his teeth as he gaped at the mass of horsemen thundering past. Whooping and screaming, 'A Borderer! A Borderer!' their lances swept lower. Through the war cries and the rumble of hooves, Tom heard his captain bawling out orders:

'Stand by! Square your legs! Take an arrow!'

The Scottish division facing them had begun its own march down the hill. At the right of this new echelon another battle group was pounding down the slope towards Surrey's banners. Further right yet, as though awaiting orders, a Highland division of spears and swords stood motionless upon the eastern end of the hilltop. It faced no immediate opponent - Stanley had still not arrived on the field.

The image of seven thousand pikes advancing in silence towards him burned into Tom's brain. His knuckles whitened, so tight was his grip on the bow. Close by, frantic gunners cooled barrels with water-soaked swabs, reloaded, covered their ears and fired. Each reload of cannon took long minutes and failed to break up the echelons of pikes. A hare sprang from the cover of a patch of thistles and darted away from the Scotsmen's feet; it kicked and sped towards the archers before veering off to flee along the front of the English line.

Someone shouted, 'Run for it! Run for it, you lucky bugger!'

They waited. He sweated with tension. His shirt was stuck to his chest by the time the order came.

'Company! Bodkin heads! Target the front block of pikes! Nock! Pull! Mark! Allow for wind! And - loose!'

On all sides bowstrings thrummed.

'Front pikes again! Pull! Windage! And - loose!'

Tom grunted with satisfaction.

'Same again! Pull! Windage! And - loose!'

As Tom worked, he became aware of his father's quiet voice: 'Lean into the bow. That's right, son - gather yourself. Remember to breathe. In your mind you'll see the arrow already in the target, and when you do - let it fly.' Tom felt the pressure of Meg's shivering body as she leaned against his leg.

'Bodkins still! Take front block centre! Where the banner is! Steady! Mark! And - loose!'

207

Tom stood near to the captain aware that the officer was drawing and shooting at the same time as the rest of his men. All this time he had a relaxed bearing. He worked his bow as though at a Sunday archery contest but shouted orders at the same time. Around them, other companies of archers fired off dense volleys to the calls of their own captains. In this way, squalls of arrows fell upon the Scots, but many - tugged by gusts of wind, fell into vacant ground.

'Bodkins! Straight ahead, take the nearest block in front. Shoot at will!'

The Scots closed in. The bodkins clattered off steel, and the archers realised the extent of the armour they faced. Here and there a pikeman collapsed, clutching an arm or a leg or lifting his hands to his face. A trumpet blasted out one coarse note. Immediately, the forest of pikes levelled at the English line. Someone shouted out, 'Christ! It's like a bloody great hedgehog rolling down the hill!'

Captain Jackson's voice became firmer:

'Right, lads! Broadheads now! Nock! Aim for the tender parts! Shoot at will!

'Coulson! Take down the black and yellow standard on the right!'

'Tweddel! See that drummer? Mark him!'

'Harrison! The blue banner, front rank! Bring it down!'

'Horsley! The black chevron flag. He's yours!'

'Fleck! The big one - front rank - helmet wi' two feathers! He's yours!'

Tom worked without a thought. He had fallen into the rhythm of the orders - they had a soothing effect, like a chant. He stayed with the breath, nocked an arrow, leaned into the bow, pulled, marked and loosed. He paused; the Scots had closed the gap and the pikes were now below him. The echelons had reached a shallow depression that ran parallel with most of the English line. He searched for 'Two-feathers' and saw him - a tall man in armour with a red skirt over his metal-clad thighs. The man held aloft a two-handed sword and, lifting his visor, shouted out orders.

As Tom saw the tender place, the man's visor dropped. It made a difficult shot. He sighted for the eye slit, and loosed. It flew straight but glanced off the visor. He loosed again. The pikes had almost closed with the bills. The arrow thudded into the slit. The man dropped his sword and raised his mailed hands to his face as he buckled.

Tom called out to the captain, 'He's down, sir!'

'Well done, Fleck! Archers! Shoot at will but keep sharp for orders! Things are changing.'

Tom nocked another broadhead and scanned for a target, puzzled. The front echelon of pikes now crashed about in disarray. Men in full armour struggled through a stretch of marshy ground that lay either side of a shallow beck. Some, who gained firm ground, stopped and waited for their countrymen to follow. Meanwhile the ranks behind still pressed forward. Hundreds crowded together like trees in a logjam. The relentless march of the awesome Swiss pike had come to a halt on a few yards of waterlogged grazing.

'Archers! Follow me to the right! Give the billmen room!' Edward Jackson moved his company thirty paces to the right. 'Bodkins again! Into the masses at the back, shoot at will!'

Thousands of shafts fell into the Scottish rear. Tom's focus wavered as he saw the unarmoured small folk reel and crumple beneath the shock of successive curtains of arrows. Gaps opened in their ranks and the lines faltered - but they closed up and came on. Away to his left he heard orders barked to the English billmen: 'Listen to me! Chop the point off the pike in front! Then drop him before he pulls his sword! Forward in ranks!'

Captain Jackson bellowed above the shouts and the clang of metal on metal. 'Keep aim on the middle and rear! Leave the front ranks to the bills!'

Tom lost concentration when, with a roar, thousands of billmen charged down the shallow slope to meet the pikes. It flashed through his mind that somewhere among them was the boy, Peter Tindall.

The echelons still struggled to regain formation and advance uphill towards the English line; but they'd lost momentum. Without steady forward motion, the long pike had become no better than a cumbersome prodding tool. Many a pikeman cast his weapon into the rushes and drew his two-handed claymore. The knee-high sword leaves of the flag irises crumpled beneath the weight of boots. Brown water squirted between the spread toes of bare feet. Each man locked onto the eyes of his enemy as they parried and thrust. The hollow filled with grunting violence. Along the course of the insignificant beck, armoured bodies crashed into the mire.

'Stand by! Look to the right! Skirmishers coming! Broadheads for this lot. Shoot at will.' The captain's yell wrenched back Tom's attention.

A section of pikemen, mixed in with skirmishers armed with claymore and shield, had broken away from the confusion of the swampy ground. They headed up the slope toward the archers. Tom got off four broadheads before the captain shouted - this time with alarm in his voice, 'Draw swords! Pull back behind the bills! Keep together!'

Tom struggled to sling his bow over his shoulder and at the same time draw his sword. As he fumbled, he twisted around to see the point of a pike bearing down on him. It caught him full in the chest and he fell backwards. The half-armoured man ran onwards, up the hill, shouting. A second man, bare-footed for grip, in bone-plated leggings and jerkin, stopped by him and raised the vicious, curved blade of a Lochaber axe. Tom rolled away as Meg dived for a naked ankle.

The axe swung at Meg. Tom rolled again, this time to see the man crumple to his knees with an arrow in his throat. Another axe-man, arms and thighs wrapped in iron chain, jumped over Tom, his eyes intent on someone else. More Scotsmen poured up the slope to attack the Admiral's right flank. Tom sat up and called out for Meg. She crawled towards him, whining. Blood matted her side. He drew her towards him as a shadow fell across the pair of them. The cautionary maxim, 'archers get no mercy', sprang into Tom's head, as a tall man raised a stabbing spear and prepared to strike. Meg gave a squealing bark and the man twisted his thrust so that the weapon's point thudded into the ground. He pulled out the spear and stared for a moment - glanced around, then knelt down.

'I know ye and I know this wee dog,' he said, his breath rasping.

Tom looked into a face with a full, red beard. 'Aye, we've met before,' he gasped. 'I'm Tom Fleck and you're the drover, John Elliot.'

'That's right, laddie. You were good to me and ma brothers at Coxhoe a bit since.' He glanced around once more with anxious eyes, but the fighting had moved on. He shook his head. 'A Sassenach wi' a braw Galloway name. Are ye hurt much?'

'I don't know. A pike got me in the chest.'

'Lay still. If things go right for us, I'll come back. If not - well - good luck tae ye.' Elliot stepped away a few yards to return dragging a body. 'Here,' he panted, 'I'll dump this a'top o' ye. Stay still and pretend you're as dead as him. And here . . .' He reached inside his pouch. 'Take this lump o' bog moss, it's mixed wi' stuff that'll clot. Plug it where it bleeds as soon as ye can. Night's coming on, so bide there till it's safe to move.' He draped the body over Tom and hurried away.

28

A Fallen Rose

Hidden by the corpse, Tom lay on his back with Meg pressed against his chest. She gave little eruptions of trembles that travelled through his arm. 'There now, lass - there now,' he whispered. She nuzzled his armpit as his free hand stroked her neck.

A lift of the eyelids showed a leaden sky. He shut them quickly, stiffening at the swish of arrows and the thump of footfalls. Armour creaked, iron clanged and the gasp of tired lungs came and went as the struggle continued around him. He screwed up his eyes as though that might shut out the noise, but the yells of berserk men came as much from the twisted faces that floated through his mind as from his own ears. He groaned and thought: harvest time; we should be at home, beating sheaves on the threshing floor. Here we are, poor bloody labourers, herded together, mangling one another for the sake of a few soft-handed lords.

Two bowshots east of where Tom lay, the King of Scotland realised he had but one chance to save his reputation from disaster. He pulled his pike from the belly of a buckling Englishman and took a few paces back among his bodyguards.

'To your king! To your king!' he bellowed above the grunts of tense throats and the clatter of metal. His men still fought in silence, as the French had advised.

A cloth of gold emblazoned with a black, wing-spreading falcon flapped above him. 'With me! Charge for that carriage! Cut through till we have the auld earl!'

The Earl of Surrey watched from his covered cart with grim satisfaction as the main body of Scots came under attack on three sides. He stiffened - the falcon banner was moving his way; it was clear that James Stewart was intent on reaching him. He leaned out of the cart and addressed his marshals, at first in a calm tone.

'I want five hundred bills in ranks ten deep in front of me, and archers to the sides.' Then he yelled, 'With haste!'

The Scots monarch jabbed at a man in Tudor colours, but the experienced marine brought down his bill with such force that the shaft of the king's pike splintered in his hands. He threw down the weapon and reached for his sword. The bill swung again but faltered. The king's illegitimate son, the young Archbishop of St Andrews, felled the marine with a downward blow of his mace.

With a hundred retainers the king charged deeper into Surrey's bodyguard, chopping down billmen as they pressed forward to block the way. The royal attendants had fought to within fifteen strides of the earl's banner when the Earl of Cassillis collapsed at the king's right side. Earl Morton stepped into the gap. Two sweeping bill strokes to the ankles brought him down in a crash of metal. With a gurgle, the royal standard-bearer dropped to his knees, clutching the arrow in his gullet. The falcon banner fluttered to the mud to be trampled under the boots of cursing English marines.

'To me! To me!' the monarch yelled with his visor raised. 'And charge!'

Leading a wedge of weary men in full armour, he made a last desperate attempt to reach his adversary. With only twenty feet of ground to fight across before he could cut down that old man, an arrow thudded into his lower jaw. At the same time, a bill slashed into his wrist and he dropped his sword. His armoured knees were slowly buckling when the blade of another bill sliced into his royal throat.

On the eastern end of Branxton Hill - to the king's right and rear - the Earls of Lennox and of Argyll were restless. Their orders were to face an expected enemy division - but it had not come. With alarm, they watched the struggles of their king's battle group. Unaware that James lay dying, they ordered their five thousand highlanders to charge down the slope to his aid. They were also unaware that the overdue English left wing, under Lord Stanley, had finally arrived. The Lancashire lord rapidly scanned the field, divided his division into three brigades and set them to climb the western end of the ridge. His archers kicked off their boots so that their toes would better grip the saturated hillside, and ascended. They unleashed an arrow storm into the flank and rear of the highlanders just as those woollen-clad men began their move downhill. A welter of confusion followed. Lennox and Argyll both fell as they attempted to stem the rout.

Tom lay still until the shouting and battering of metal had moved away. His left arm was numb due to the weight of the body that pressed down on him. He wriggled out from under the corpse and slipped his right hand into his jerkin. When the fingers had found the place where he felt most pain, he brought the hand back out - there was no blood. A further grope around the front of the jerkin found a rent in the padded leather. He poked a finger into the hole. It made contact with the hard shapes of coins he had stitched into the quilting for safekeeping. Now he understood why he wasn't bleeding: the tough discs had served as a layer of mail. He gave a quiet grunt. It's a good job King Harry's been corrupting his silver with hard base metal. He tested his chest with a cough, felt a stab and hoped it marked no more than a broken rib.

The corpse gave a faint groan. Rolling over he saw the face of Captain Jackson. A livid weal marked one side of the man's head. He reached across with his right arm. The movement hurt as he shook the officer's shoulder. 'Captain Jackson!' The eyes opened with a flicker of recognition.

With a wrench, Tom sat up and looked around. An arrow-shot away, masses of men hacked at each other. The captain whispered, 'Be careful.' Tom saw blood dripping down the captain's side from a slash in his leather jerkin. He took out the knife that he always kept razor sharp and cut away part of the leather. A short gash flowed with blood. He took a lump of the moss the Scotsman had given him and packed it into the captain's wound, then searched for his hat. It held his spare bowstrings but was nowhere in sight.

He became conscious of weight on his back and straps across his shoulders. The arrow sacks! They held other spare cords. He cut more of the jerkin away to expose his linen shirt. Cutting a square of linen, he folded it twice and placed the pad over the wound. He glanced around again - the closest soldiers struggled in small groups many yards distant. In between were scattered bodies and occasional movement where men were sitting up or beginning to crawl away.

Lifting the captain's shoulders, he reached beneath the shirt and fed a bowstring around the chest to bring the ends together, close by the linen pad.

'Breathe out and hold it like that till I tie this cord.'

Tom fastened the knot and lay down again.

'Thanks for that, Fleck.' The voice was faint.

'You've had a bash on the face, Captain. What did that?'

'A clout from a poll-axe.'

'We'd best keep still and low to the ground, sir, like a pair of couched hares. When it's dark we can sneak away.'

He remembered Meg. She lay on her side, looking at him. Her tail gave a couple of feeble wags. Blood seeped from her coat. Parting the matted hair, he uncovered a gash, and beyond it the gleam of ribs. He took more of the moss and laid it in the wound. A forceful wrench tore a length from the bottom of his shirt. He bound it around Meg's chest, then lay back again and rested a hand on the dog's head. Rain began to lash his face. He opened his mouth wide. Sweet, cold drops fell onto his cracked tongue. He raised his head to let more trickle down the length of his nose and into his mouth.

Low cloud drew in the night before its time. A trumpet sounded to the north and another from the hilltop to the south. Adversaries that could still see each other slowly backed away. The wind had lessened but steady rain still fell. Uncertain who had won the day, few of the wounded risked crying out. Apart from an occasional groan mixed with the whispering of bulrushes, the battlefield lay hushed.

Tom helped the captain to his feet, slung the man's bow across his own back, and linked arms on his good side. They hobbled for a few yards until they heard faint words. 'Father, Father . . .'

He knelt beside an archer. Despite the gloom, he recognised the youth. Here was the slim boy he'd walked behind on the march from Barmoor Wood - the youth with the good bow - whose dad sported brass-work on his helmet.

Tom touched the cold forehead, his fingers came away sticky. 'What's your name?'

'Percival Bell.'

'That's a grand name, Percy. See if you can get on my back. I'll bear thee.' Tom sat down beside him.

'I know him,' the captain whispered. 'He's Henry Bell's youngster. His bow is the best in Hart village - here it is - we'll carry it back.'

'Sir - see if you can get his arms around my neck, but don't force your wound.'

Tom had lost no blood and, though his empty stomach ached, he still had strength. Lifting the youth onto his back, he straightened. Pulling the floppy legs around his waist, he made him secure. They moved off again and, in a few minutes, paused for breath on the crest

of the low ridge from where they had first loosed their arrows. A half
-mile away the points of campfires studded the night like fireflies.

'That's Branxton village. Let's pray they're our men,' the captain
said. They rested every score of paces until they heard a shout.

'Who comes here?' It was a West Riding voice.

'Billy Bulmer's archers. Three of us!' Tom called back.

'Come on then - slowly mind! Let's sithee!'

They limped through a cordon of sentries and along a line of cottages.
Snoring soldiers crammed every low dwelling. Outside, thousands of
men lay wrapped in cloaks or sat, with drooping heads, huddled
against the walls. There would be no roof for the three of them that
night. Instead, they hobbled towards the little church.

In the burial ground a vast yew tree sprawled its limbs. The ground
beneath lay thick with old leaves. It made a dry enough shelter.
Crawling beneath, they dragged Percy into the pungent interior and
lay down. Tom wrapped up the bows in waxed linen, rested a few
minutes, then sat upright. 'I'm going to find water and a bite to eat.
Meg, you keep guard here. Stay!'

Tom jumped over the churchyard wall under clouds fringed with
silver moonlight. He felt muddled - he had left Percival Bell under
the yew without checking his wounds. He swayed, shuddering at a
sudden sourness in his gullet, then sank to his knees in the pale light,
and vomited. During the spasm, something brushed against his face
to give him painful kiss.

He rubbed his cheek, but stopped to listen to a low clucking sound
close by. Staring hard he made out the shape of a squatting hen
among the stinging nettles. Wincing, he inched his hand forwards,
grabbed her neck, and pulled her towards him. The broody lay limp
in his hands, her breast burning hot. A layer of pale eggs marked her
sitting place. Grasping her legs, and putting a hand behind the head,
he stretched her body ready to wring the neck.

Rough hands pushed from behind. They grabbed the bird and
snatched it away. 'Give it 'ere!' growled a phlegmy voice. 'This is a
good bit o' broth.'

The man strode off towards the fires. Tom ran after him and
jumped onto his back. As they hit the ground the hen seized its
chance, struggled free, and flapped away, cackling. Tom stood up and
coughed; he swayed a little and his ribs ached. The other man got to

his feet, squared to attack, but faltered when a voice called out.

'Is that you, Tom Fleck?'

Footfalls squelched through the dark. 'I'm glad to see you're all right. Is yon lump giving bother?' Peter Tindall swished the blade of a bill at ankle height. They both faced the man until he muttered a curse and stamped away. The two friends embraced.

'Has thee owt to eat, Tom?'

'I have now! Come with me.' Tom felt his way back among the nettles and winced. His hand brushed the hairy stems as he gathered up the eggs. He slipped eleven eggs into his arrow sack. 'I hope these are not full of chicks.'

'I've still got four oatcakes,' Peter said. 'Swap a couple for two of them eggs?'

'You're welcome, so long as I can use your helmet to boil them in.'

'Just so long as me head's not in it, you can. I'll ferret out some watter while you find a spot by yon fire.'

The friends slapped hands together to seal their bargain.

An hour later Tom and Peter crawled under the yew tree with a helmet of hot water in which floated handfuls of moss and mashed-up yarrow; their pockets bulged with hot, hard-boiled eggs.

'Rain's stopped, sir. We've got some forage and boiled water. Can you crawl outside? This is my friend, Peter Tindall. He's going to help me with Percy here; we need to get him into the moonlight while it's here.'

They took hold of Percival Bell and slid him out from beneath the yew. Tom ran his fingers over the boy's head. The scalp was hanging loose - he could see a bit of skull. He pulled off his own jerkin and ripped up the remains of his linen shirt.

'Peter, my hands are thick with muck; are yours clean?'

'Aye, I washed them in the beck; they were bloody - from the shaft o' me bill'.

Tom stared at Peter for a moment, remembering the nervous boy who had approached him at Norton two months earlier. 'I want you to bathe his head with that yarrow mix; can you do that?'

'It'll hurt; he'll wriggle.'

'Do it, Peter. I'll hold him.'

Percival Bell lay unconscious. When Peter bathed his wound, he woke up and yelped. Tom lay across the boy's chest to hold him down as Peter washed the wound. He cleaned his fingertips with boiled moss before rolling the torn scalp back into place. While binding up the trembling head with strips of shirt, he noticed blood seeping through the boy's clothes.

'Oh hell! Let's get this jerkin and shirt off, he's bleeding from somewhere else!'

The boy had a hole in his side - a pike wound. They tried to wash it clean.

'We'll have to plug it with moss, dress it, and hope for the best,' Peter muttered.

Captain Edward Jackson lay on the ground, watching. 'It's in God's hands.'

'I doubt it,' Tom snapped. 'I've seen nowt of Him in these parts. He'll be taking things easy in the Pope's palace.'

'That's a wrong thing to say, Fleck,' the captain said in a weak voice.

'My dad always said you could know a body by his deeds. If the Big Man's in charge of things hereabouts He'll have blood up to his holy elbows.'

'Tom! What you do now is a sign that He's here.'

'Maybe so, sir - maybe so. For the minute, I just hope we've got all the muck out of these wounds. Do you think you can manage a boiled egg?'

Red blotches and threads showed in the yolks - signs of the beginning of chicks - they wolfed them down, together with Peter's oatcakes. When they tried to feed Percival Bell, he clamped his jaw shut. The captain whispered, 'We should keep back a couple of eggs in case he gets through the night. I wonder where his father is.'

They dragged the boy back beneath the shelter of the yew and lay down. They fell asleep huddled together - four men and a dog.

29

The Hut

The two friends lifted the weight of sodden yew branches to peer out into a washed dawn, then crawled back through the leaf mould to where Percival Bell lay between the knuckles of tree roots. He still lived, but his face had the colour of whey. Even so, he swallowed one of the eggs and the last scraps of oatcake. Leaving him with the captain, they emerged from their den with one thought: more food. Standing among the marker stones of the churchyard, they yawned and slapped their limbs. Meg stretched her back legs then scratched her bandage a few times.

'You two! Over here and form up with this company!' The command came from a haggard-faced officer on the other side of the drystone wall.

They had bills thrust into their hands. With these spears-cum-axes across their shoulders, Tom and Peter were shoved among a bedraggled column and marched back to the battlefield.

The place of yesterday's struggle lay hushed beneath a pale sky. Bodies dotted the hillside like stumps in cleared woodland. The friends could not know that thousands more lay crumpled in the rushes at the foot of the hill; just a few showed as dark humps in a thin quilt of mist.

A score of figures - villagers and a few soldiers - moved among the fallen. They dragged along sacks, lumpy with bits of salvage. The looters stooped and rose up again, slinking from corpse to corpse. Clusters of grey-backed, hooded crows and a pair of guilty-looking ravens lifted off the ground with hoarse, cursing cries before settling a few yards away. Overhead, two buzzards mewed as they circled and others glided in from the Cheviots to the west. From the wooded banks of the Tweed, kites rose on the first weak thermals of morning and, with the barest of wing beats, drifted towards Branxton Hill.

At the sound of a trumpet the looters straightened, snatched up a few last things and fled with their bundles. One figure remained motionless, thin and upright among the dead. He covered his face with his hands before lifting his arms skywards. The young priest then slumped to his knees beside a body.

The officer shouted, 'Soldiers! Spread out and look for any man of ours still breathing. Take note of his condition and mark the spot. If you find a nobleman alive, report to me immediately. And I want to know about any Scots gentlemen that still breathe. Common Scots will have to wait for their own kind. I'll punish anyone caught robbing bodies. This section takes the right wing.' He divided men into small groups and allotted them areas to search. 'Fan out and go over the ground with a keen eye.' He addressed Tom and Peter and pointed westwards: 'You two, search over there - around that hut.'

Once free of the column the two friends trailed their heavy bills across the grazing, with the bandaged dog at their heels. They stepped over grass slicked with blood. Every few paces a man lay stiff in death. Bows, bills and axes lay where they had fallen. Peter knelt beside a grey-bearded corpse and untied the man's pouch. He pulled out a fist-sized lump of grey cheese and two bannocks. 'You'll not be needing to break fast today, old man. Me and Tom thank thee for this food and hope your sleep brings peace.' He picked up a round shield and laid it across the weather-beaten face.

The simple stone hut stood in the middle of the shallow slope where the English right wing was broken. Two figures moved among bodies scattered around the hut. As the friends approached, the men moved closer together and, with shoulders touching, levelled spears. Tom recognised the red beard of John Elliot. He called out, 'It's not safe for you here!'

Peter shouted in alarm, 'They're Scots!'

'I know. It's all right. You wait there.'

'I won't. Thou's mad - but I'm coming.' He gripped his bill with both hands and took position alongside his friend.

Tom still trailed his bill as they picked their way through a litter of stiffening Cheshire and Lancashire bodies and the occasional green-and-white marine. They stopped a few paces from the Scots. With Elliot was another man whom Tom recalled from Coxhoe. Meg walked forward, stiff-legged. With her spinal hairs bristling, she sniffed John Elliot's leg.

'What are you doing here, John?' Tom asked.

'Looking for Jamie, our brother. We've searched since before first light but cannae find him. I lost him hereabouts. He grows a square-cut beard and wears a jerkin of black leather covered in iron studs.'

'We've orders to search this ground. We'll look out for him. But you're not wise to stay.'

'That's true - we'd best not tarry. Though I'm glad to see you're on your feet again.' John Elliot offered his palm.

Tom stepped forward to be gripped by the huge hand for the second time in two months. 'Friend . . .' he murmured - his voice thickening. 'I'll not forget your kindness.'

'That's fine, laddie. We are men of the plain sort, who can be good to each other when we might. At Coxhoe you showed how true that is.' He turned to his brother, 'Come on, Andrew. Let's away from this drear spot.'

They watched the Elliots wade through a bed of nodding thistles. Peter leaned on his bill. 'Thou took a chance - I'd like to hear about Coxhoe, sometime. For now though, we'd best make a start. A man's trying to move over there - look!'

Beneath the wall of the shepherd hut, three men lay tangled together. An arm lifted out of the heap. They hurried across. A big man lay sprawled, face down, across a slighter body. On rolling the heavy body over, the blank eyes stared back at them like bits of sea-washed glass. Clay matted his black beard.

'He's English,' Peter said in a low voice. 'It's about here the Cheshire men stood. See yon sprig of oak leaves pinned to his jerkin? He's one of them.'

Tom gagged and swallowed hard at the sight of a deep wound in the big man's stomach.

'This lad underneath is still living,' continued Peter, with a lift in his young voice.

They looked down into an angular, boyish face. Tilted to one side, an oversized iron hat still clung to the head. Peter severed the cords that knotted beneath a thin brown beard. A breastplate guarded the narrow chest.

The boy lifted an arm. 'Water.'

'From the shape of that axe he's got by him I'd say he's a Scot,' Tom said. 'Our orders are to leave them be.'

'He's just my age, man! At least I can give him a sup.' Peter untied the goatskin bottle at his side, pulled out its wooden stopper and held the spout to the cracked lips. 'Open up, Scotty and take some o' this.' The boy gulped down a mouthful of the peat-stained water. 'Right, that's all thee can have, there'll be others yet!'

Peter glanced over the slim body until he saw, beneath an armpit, a red patch on the knitted shirt. As they knelt, and as Peter scraped with his fingers at the bloody, clay-smeared wool, a shadow fell across them. The Elliots had come back.

'We couldn't leave - not with our Jamie lost. Let me see this one.'

Tom scanned the vicinity. 'You'd best be sharp; more of our lot are heading this way.'

John Elliot bent down. 'He's young Robby Watt; I ken his daddy. Put the lad on my back; his sisters will tend him this night.'

They hoisted the boy across the shoulders of the borderer. 'Och! He's no weight at all,' he said. He locked eyes with Tom once more and, with a sigh, shook his head. Bent under his burden, the Scotsman trudged away. His brother carried their spears at his side.

The friends checked the third body. Tom groaned, knelt beside the broad chest and touched his fingers to the neck. There was no pulse. Hands trembling, he brushed a fly from the blue lips. Lifting off the man's helmet, he placed it over the strong, lined face. He got to his feet on weakened legs and leaned against the wall. Facing the stones, he buried his head in his arms.

'What's the matter?' Peter put an arm around his shoulders.

'It's Christopher Wells, the farmer.' The wall muffled Tom's words until, wet-faced, he turned around. 'Why is it always the best? We talked most of the way to Barmoor. He's the finest of yeoman. I would have gladly worked for him.' He gave a choked cough and spat. 'Waste! Waste! Look around, man. All these . . .' His voice cracked. 'And the bluebottles have come.'

'That means we'll have to get shifted.' Peter grasped Tom's hand. 'It's too late for these. Come on. We'd best see inside the hut.'

They paced around the rough, drystone walls of the little dwelling until they found an opening. Tom pushed against the crude, plank door, it yielded a few inches then stuck - something held it fast. He pushed with more force until it moved enough for Peter to squeeze inside. After scuffing sounds from within had ceased, the door creaked open.

'It had a body stuck behind it,' Peter called out, 'and there's more in here.'

Tom ducked beneath the lintel, sniffed the urine-tainted air, and waited for his eyes to adjust. 'It's that still in here, just the drone of flies,' he whispered, 'it makes you half-afraid to speak.'

Enough daylight spilled through the door for them to discern men lying around the walls. With the weak light reflecting off armour, they appeared like knights arranged in a dim tomb. Tom bent over a large body. The man's visor had closed. He lifted it and stiffened as he recognised the broad face of Edmond Warren, his former lord. The knight's cheeks were ashen, his lips blue, his wrist without warmth or pulse. The right hand made a fist that lay on his breast. The heavy knuckled fingers clasped the folds of a silk scarf of the palest emerald.

He pulled off the gauntlet of another armoured body stretched alongside that of his old master. The pulse beat well enough. A helmet lay upturned on the earth floor. Beneath an arm that covered the face, the mouth began to babble. He lifted the arm to one side. Feverish eyes blinked open. Hands shot out and gripped his throat. Meg leapt forward to clamp her jaws around one of the wrists as Peter's boot descended on the white face. The hands fell away from Tom's neck and he rolled to the side and got up. Peter had a dagger against the man's throat. 'Try that again and I'll cut thee.'

Rubbing his windpipe, Tom stared into the twisted face of Mark Warren. 'All right, Peter, leave him be. He belongs Cleveland.'

Tom held his water flask to the bruised lips and the man drank in gulps until he choked. Tom took the bottle away and Mark Warren coughed. 'You're Fleck!' He spat out a tooth.

'Have you a wound?' Tom asked.

'My left leg hurts,' came the whisper.

Tom ran his hands along the limb and located a twist in the shin. 'You need a bone-setter.'

'And my belly's sore.'

Tom lifted Warren's mail shirt to reveal a gash at one side of his stomach.

'Have you found my father?' The man gasped as the mail was lifted higher.

'He's right beside you.' Tom met the fevered eyes. 'He'll not leave here - I'm sorry.'

Warren gave a coughing sob of despair. 'Will you help me, Fleck? I'll make it worth your while.'

'I'll do what I can; there'll be nowt to pay. Peter, go tell the officer there's a wounded North Riding gentleman in here. Bring him as sharp as you can.'

'I want more water,' Warren said, more strongly.

'Right. You shall have it - just a mouthful. Swill it round, then spit it out - that's good. You need a few stitches, so we don't want your belly too bloated. Now keep still so I can take a better look.'

Tom unbuckled two leather straps and pulled off the mud-caked breastplate to reveal more of the dull coat of mail. He lifted the bloody metal links away from the stomach wound.

Warren grunted. 'That's grandfather Weastall's mail shirt. Has it done its job?'

'Well enough; nobbut a few links gone.'

Tom poured water over the congealed blood of the wound. Satisfied that the belly cavity was not pierced, he reached into his pouch. It held the little bag of useful things Mary had given him at the ford on the Tees.

He got up from his knees to stand in the doorway. By the weak daylight, he made repeated attempts to thread a bone needle with sheep-gut thread. His eyes had lost their normal acute focus and his hands shook with fatigue. Something fell from the little bag to gleam unnoticed on the mud of the entrance - a lock of yellow hair tied with ribbon. At last, the gut slipped through the eye of the needle and he returned to Mark Warren's side.

'I'm going to close that wound with stitches. You'd best keep still. Are you ready?'

'Yes, yes, Fleck! Get on with it, man!'

Tom shot him a hard look and growled, 'You can get off your high horse, Warren. That high-nosed, shite talk will do nowt to steady my hand. Lay quiet.'

He smeared the wound with a honey and yarrow ointment and did the same with the thread. Plunging the needle into the skin, he drew the thread through the gashed flesh with his right hand while the fingers of the other held the wound closed. Four more stitches finished the job. Mark Warren had grunted but once

'There now - it will have to do. So long as you don't give it strain, it'll hold. Best keep the muck out of it.'

'Thanks, Fleck. You're fair with me - after all that's gone before. How is it you can stitch wounds?' The voice had lost its power.

'From sewing up the throats of your own ewes - after your slavering black hounds got among them. Let's say nowt else about it. Lay quiet till help comes.'

Tom checked the others in the hut. Eight men had crawled inside to shelter with their wounds; now seven were stiffening among dark stains.

An officer ducked through the door. 'Where's the wounded gentleman? Who is he?'

'Over here. It's Mark Warren, eldest son of Sir Edmond Warren of Thornaby Manor. His father is next to him - he's gone.'

'Address me as sir! And his wound?'

'Belly wound, sir. A blade. Didn't go right through - meaning his guts are still all of a piece. I've stitched him. He'll need bearing flat and kept still.' Tom pointed a bloody finger. 'His leg's out of true; he should have the bone-setter.'

The officer bent to view the sewn-up wound. 'Hmm, that's a fair job. All right, I'll take over. You get on with the search outside; and send those two soldiers in here.'

'Wait!' Mark Warren held out his right hand. 'You can come back to the manor, Fleck.'

Tom bent down, gripped the offered hand, gave a grunt and ducked out of the hut.

30

The Abbess

Their shoulders touching, the friends strode away from the hut, stopped and stared across the battlefield. Soldiers in pairs knelt beside bodies. Others bent beneath the weight of wounded men as they carried them up a slight rise towards a line of oxcarts. In level ground, squads dug broad pits.

Tom's eyes misted over. He shivered as the pale shapes of men emerged from the smashed beds of flag irises that lined the margins of the beck. They rippled like faded pictures on an ancient and threadbare tapestry that hung between him and the world of flesh. The images hesitated and wavered, like reflections on a river, then formed up into ragged columns that set off to climb the slopes of Branxton Hill. Others drifted away along the track heading for the village. On all sides figures moved as though lost. One of them stared with blank eyes in his direction and lifted a slow arm in salute. He wore an iron helmet inlaid with brass.

Tom took a few steps towards the image. As it faded, he sank to his knees remembering his father's words on the moor. 'Aye, you did see them, Tom. You'll have to get used to that - you're a Fleck.' But that time he'd seen mere vague shapes. Now, he told himself, these are men. These are men and they're hurting.

Callused fingers tried to prise his own from his eyes. A hand gripped his shoulder. 'Tom! What ails? Thou's gone white.' Arms rocked his body and something licked his face.

Helped by the arms he stood again - swaying. The tapestry had gone.

'That's better, your colour's coming back. You had me worried for a spell. It was like you were having a fit.'

'Not a fit - Peter.' The slow words emerged, 'It might be more true to say I was having a Fleck.'

'Best take a drop o' this; it'll brace the heart.' Peter offered a small flask. 'I took it off a Scotchman. It's fiery, like what they swigged on the ship.'

Tom sniffed the neck and took a sip, then a pull. He coughed and gasped, 'By heck, that's stiffening! I feel a bit more alive.' He met Peter's grey eyes. 'You've been a good friend - but we'll soon be taking different roads.'

'Aye, Tom. We've had rich time. I'll miss thee.'

'Will you go back to Whitby after this? Now that you've a soldier's pay to take home to your mam?'

'I will, and we'll not starve - now I've got this.' Peter tapped the bag at his belt.

'What's in there?'

'Coin. Yeller and silver coin. A lord in full armour give it me for his life - after I'd knocked the mace out of his hands. He'd felled a few around me wi' it.

'A mace you say? A bishop maybe.'

'Aye; he went on his knees afore me - whimpering. Said he was a man of God. But one of them sailors chopped him down - said our orders allowed no quarter that day. I feel bad about it - sick inside.'

Tom took Peter's hand. 'We'll both have a job to clear all this from our dreams. We need homes and honest work.'

'So we do . . .' his friend broke off. 'Over there! Who are all that crowd?' Peter pointed to where a line of cloaked shapes threaded towards them.

'Who knows?' Tom took another drink and, with eyes watering, coughed again. 'They look like nuns.'

The leader walked with care through a mass of hoof prints where Dacre's cavalry had driven off the infantry of Lord Home. She led a column of forty women dressed in the stark black and white robes of Cistercian nuns. Two oxcarts and a small crowd of old men and boys took up the rear. She paused to stoop each time she reached a fallen man.

Coming nearer, she levelled a finger. 'You two men! Where are your officers? I will speak with whoever is in charge here.'

The woman's commanding voice startled Tom. 'There's a captain in this hut, Holy Mother.'

'Reverend Mother is enough; the Christ is not my son.' Imperious eyes fixed on them; the friends lowered their gaze.

'If I must enter that hut, you two braw Christian men will unsheathe your swords and attend upon me.'

Tom met her pale blue eyes, set wide apart under arching brows. She's near fifty and bred like a fine horse, he thought.

'There's nowt to fear, mistress,' Peter blurted out. 'It's all done.' He rubbed a sleeve across his dripping nose.

Three roars blasted the still air. On a nearby hillock, gunners frantically reloaded light cannon. Tom swung around to his left, at the same time as the woman, to see a mass of horsemen disappear behind a low ridge two bowshots away.

'It would seem that all is not yet done,' the nun announced in calm tones.

A shout issued from within the hut and the officer appeared at its doorway. 'What's afoot?'

'Riders, sir - yonder! The cannon scared them off,' Tom answered.

The officer made a swift survey of the battlefield. The loading of wounded onto carts had stopped. To the south, on the summit of Branxton hill, English troops guarded the jumbled remains of the Scottish battery.

He strode across to Tom. 'No doubt they've plans to recover their artillery. Too late though! We look to have secured it. Who are these women?'

The tall nun met his gaze. 'I will answer for myself. I am Abbess Hoppringill of Coldstream. I've brought my people here to help the wounded and to search for the mortal remains of Scotsmen of noble birth. The sacred grounds of my abbey will receive our fallen gentlemen. As a Christian will you provide for our safety whilst we do this?'

The officer narrowed his eyes. 'Only the dead can be removed, Reverend Mother. The rest are prisoners.'

'Have you not achieved enough? Surely the wounded can come to my hospital?'

'No! Any alive must stay with us.'

'I see! Then we are to endure another season of ransoms,' she snapped.

'That is not my affair. I will provide you with guards; they will ensure that you do not remove the body of your monarch - when it is identified.'

'The king is dead?' Her eyes widened. 'The Rose Nobill?'

'We are certain of it. He fell by the wet ground yonder.' The officer pointed eastwards.

With a dozen armed men, Tom and Peter escorted the robed women to the centre of the battlefield. Looking across the long hollow, Tom realised how fortunate he'd been not to stand there.

Peter grasped his arm. 'There's thousands in the rushes, and see: the beck's clogged with them - the watter's red!'

Tom gradually became aware of the litter of corpses. Stripped of armour and outer clothes, their nakedness made the mutilations all the more lurid. The party stopped at the edge of the carnage. He felt faint. Some of the novice nuns wailed and sobbed. One shouted, 'Sweet Christ! It's a charnel ground. They're scattered ower the ground like damsons!'

Abbess Hoppringill, now white-faced, raised her voice. 'Enough of that! Stiffen yourselves! There is work to do. Come with me.'

She stepped over the leather-clad corpses of lesser folk with her eyes fixed on a group of spears driven upright into the mire. Scraps of rich clothing and bits of armour hung from the spear shafts. English soldiers paused in their work of stripping weapons and mail, to watch with curious eyes. The Abbess knelt by a well-built body that stretched out naked except for small clothes - he lay face down.

She summoned the youths in her company. 'Turn him over that I may see.'

Two boys hurried across and rolled the muddied body onto its back.

'Dear God,' she murmured, 'it's George Hepburn, Bishop of the Isles.'

She recited a prayer in Latin and tried to close the dull eyes. To the Scots in her party, struggling to keep her voice even, she gave orders: 'Bear him to the waggon and gently lay him there.' She began to search for other men of quality.

A man lay on his back. His face mangled by a blow from a billhook.

'Oh, Davey!' she cried. 'He's my kin - it's David Hoppringill of Smailholm, the Laird of Galashiels.' She stared at other corpses nearby and wailed. 'And his grown sons around him, all four of them! Dear God!' Her voice choked. 'Scythed down like flowers at hay-time.'

The soldiers waited in silence until she had recovered. With an eye on the Abbess, the English sergeant of the guard quietly told his men: 'Some men have come a long way to die here. Bear these five to the carts and lay them alongside the Bishop with care. Get the mail-shirts off them first, and those gauntlets. Strip all armour. None of this metal shall go to Coldstream.'

Abbess Hoppringill surveyed the heaped cartloads, her face grim. 'The great houses of Scotland are in these waggons.' Her voice cracked. 'We are broken-backed! Their children must govern our country! Take them to the Abbey; lay them together in the coolest part of the cloisters. Send the carts straight back here.'

Oxen were prodded with goads and men put shoulders to the rear of carts. Wheels rolled as the clay released its grip. Tom straightened up to ease his back. A stab of pain around his ribs brought a memory of the pike-man's grim eyes as he closed in.

'Tom Fleck! Is it you?'

The blue-pitted face of Rob Gibson, the Manor's giant blacksmith, looked down on him.

'Rob! I didn't know you were here.'

'Nor me, you, Tom. I thowt you'd run off to dodge a stint with the militia.'

'Well, whatever I did, I've still ended up here, though I'm foxed as to how it's come about.'

'Have you seen owt of the Master? I was at his side last night. We were rushed and I lost sight of both him and his eldest.'

'Mark's wounded and is on his way back to camp by waggon. He might heal, but his father's dead; he's in that stone hut.'

'Oh, Jesus! Take me to him.'

In the gloom of the hut, they looked down on the stiffened body of Sir Edmond Warren. The blacksmith knelt and touched the cold brow. His broad fingers tried to close the eyes. The lids refused to move.

'I'm sorry, old friend.' His voice choked for a few seconds. 'I hope it came quick for thee.' His shoulders straightened. 'We stood back to back at Redmoor and they couldn't touch us. This time we had not our youth. I'll bear thee to Branxton church and find a spot where a knight might sleep.'

With his massive arms, he encircled the body, armour and all, and cradled it. 'I'm away to bury him with the others; all our gentlemen are going into the churchyard.' He struggled through the door into the light.

'And the small folk - what of them?' Tom shouted after him.

'Pits in the field - they're all being bundled in together.'

'Nowt's changed then! Even after yesterday our flesh is still no

230

more than muck to feed grass.'

Rob Gibson glanced back through the door. 'That's the way of it, Tom - that's the way of it; no stone lions at our feet, nor a brass plate to cover us. There'll be nowt apart from green rushes to mark our spot.'

Tom watched the blacksmith toil up the slope with his lord on his back. Words came to him: 'and rushes on our face will lie'.

At the end of that day the decorated floor tiles of Coldstream Abbey were covered by the bodies of nine Earls, fourteen Lords of Parliament, the Provosts of Edinburgh, Glasgow, Perth, and Aberdeen, and three hundred lairds, gentry and knights, together with their sons. Among them, lay Alexander Stuart the bastard son of King James, now stripped of the insignia of Archbishop of St Andrews and Chancellor of Scotland. The body of King James was on its way to Berwick on an English cart.

31

Disbanded

The bleating cries were faint at first. Tom scanned the bright sky until he saw their silhouettes pass like broadhead arrows beneath a white cloud. Necks outstretched, feet tucked beneath their tails, the geese were crossing the coast once more. Two wavering skeins passed overhead. The matriarch at the point fell back to take her rest and another took her place.

He listened: *'I'm here! I'm here! - Are you there? - I'm here! I'm here!'* they called to each other. The sound took hold of his heart as it did each September. The wildfowl are early this year, he thought. They'll bring hard weather from the north. Tomorrow, they'll be on the marsh below the byre and, soon enough, the redwings will land. All is moving; what is it that I need to do? Rachel, I'm on my way . . . wait for me.

Dreary days of rain had ended. Rachel leaned against the parapet of the bridge. It was a delight to press her stomach against the sun-warmed stones and to fill her lungs with pure air. Each night that had passed since the militia marched north she had rested on her bed at the inn and listened to the noises of the town. Each dawn she had risen to vomit a little, before asking for plain food in the privacy of her chamber.

She gazed up at the raw battlements of Alnwick castle, then down into the water. The Aln rushed beneath, swollen and brown; a tangled raft of leaves and twigs divided to swirl past the pointed bows of the stone buttress. She thought over the scraps of news that trickled in of a great battle on a hillside. It had happened three days ago. She urged her thoughts outwards: I caress you in my dreams. I wait for you.

Behind her, crowds pressed into town for market day. Women with bundles on their heads, children driving a flock of honking geese and men leading pack-ponies, waited their turn to cross the narrow hump of the bridge. Osier baskets nudged her hips and the wool of pattering sheep brushed her skirts. She remained oblivious, only sensing him move south, the distance growing less, yard by yard.

'Rachel Coronel!' A voice belled out above the chatter of people. She twisted around to see a grey-bearded man, in wine-red linen doublet and trousers, astride a horse. Alvaro Jurnet gave a whoop of joy, dismounted and, handing the reins to his guard, embraced her. She pressed her face into his tunic and breathed in the faint musk of her own kind.

'Alvaro! Such a surprise!' She wiped away a tear.

He released her and smiled. 'After your message reached me at Pontefract I could not rest for thinking of my friend's only child. I turned back and have come north to bring you home. On the way - calculating usurer that I am - I will conduct a little business at Sunderland where there is much building of ships. Now I know you are safe, tomorrow I go to stay with Sir John of Long Horsley, a few miles away - more business.' He gave an awkward laugh.

'Alvaro, you go everywhere lending money at interest. Do you not worry that it might stir up the old hatred?'

'Sometimes I do,' he whispered; then his voice swelled, 'What other trade have we? It is all Nebuchadnezzar allowed. Before his day we grew vines and tended flocks as people of the soil.' His tone became tender. 'Where does your father rest? I have yet to stand by his grave.'

'He is in the glade of a quiet wood. I go there now - it is not far.'

'We will go together.' The tall Jew offered his arm and Rachel showed the way off the bridge and onto a green track that ran by the river. The mounted guard followed leading Alvaro's horse past a long hedgerow overgrown and jewelled with brambles.

Within the glade, the air hung still. Rachel stopped and touched a finger to her lips. She held Alvaro back to let him listen to the quiet sighs of tall grasses. A squirrel, perched high on a branch of hazel, let out a harsh chatter.

She laughed. 'The little red fairy thinks himself guardian of this place, and so he is.' She took Alvaro's hand and led him to a spot in the centre of the clearing. 'Father is here. Look, I planted eyebright, forget-me-nots and tiny blue speedwells above him; I found them by the hedgerow. And here is a stone carved with his name and some words. And see! Among the flowers, new plants are poking through; already new life is beginning.' Her fingers stroked the tiny first leaves of wild parsley.

Alvaro translated aloud the Hebrew script: 'Though I have gone down with the Sun - the night is brief.' He took Rachel's hand. 'I think Isaac says he will return! Are those his words?'

'They are mine, but I have heard him speak of taking another birth. He knew the book of Zohar.'

Alvaro knelt to stroke the earth between the humble flowers. 'Isaac, my friend, I have come to visit you and take care of your child - this intelligent young woman. My heart is sad that we will not journey together - at least for some time. I will miss your loyal friendship and deep wisdom. May you fare well and know freedom.'

He got to his feet and faced her. 'The things we leave behind are not engraved on stone monuments, they are woven into the lives of others.'

She sighed in appreciation. 'From the Greek?'

'Pericles. But we must make plans. When my business here is finished we can return to London.'

'Alvaro, I cannot leave until I see Thomas again. He is with the army in the north. There was a fierce battle. He lives - my heart knows he comes this way.'

'Ah, that young man, a close friend of yours. He is good, but not of our kind, Rachel. Remember that.'

'I have knelt here and told my father that Thomas Fleck is the man I wish to grow old with. If I bake bread for any man, it is for him. I carry his child.'

'Aaron's beard!' Alvaro sucked air through his teeth. 'Hmm - I see. I will stay a while and hope to speak with him. I can wait a few days in this district. Rachel, soon we must go home. He can travel with us; you will not wish to live in the north.'

'His people will be my people - where he goes, I go also.'

'Ah! If you speak the words of Ruth, what am I to say? I too am of your people. Whatever you decide, Rachel, I will help in the manner I know. You have wealth in London and are your father's heir.'

'If I do not return to London, can you complete my affairs and send me what is my due?'

'Gladly and - if you permit me - I'll advise on how to make it multiply to your benefit.'

To limit the drain on the royal purse, the Earl of Surrey paid off the bulk of the army five days after the battle. He had no orders to invade Scotland, and besides, the campaigning season had closed. The shattered Scots would now have to face the opportunist raids of

English border clans. He had entirely accomplished the king's command. The house of Howard would return to favour. He was content.

Thousands of militia pressed homewards. They carried their pay and whatever scraps of booty they had seized on the battlefield. Lines of oxcarts, escorted by the Lord Admiral's green-and-white marines, trundled the muddy road south. Captain Jackson and a few of his archers formed protection for a dozen waggons of wounded. Sergeant Arkwright and his five surviving soldiers walked their ponies behind the last waggon. Tom stayed close to his friends as they threaded through the ashes of Milfield village.

The sound of heavy horses caused them to stop. A party of mounted men approached from the rear at a trot. Once past, the sergeant growled, 'There goes Billy Percy, off home to Alnwick Castle, looking pleased with himself. It's Sir William now, of course. He was knighted after the fight - him and thirty-odd other gentry. Favours from the auld earl.

An Irish voice grumbled, 'And all we got was a few bits of low-grade silver.'

'We get a soldier's pay for a soldier's work, Riley. Most of the time a soldier can dice away his days on full pay; rarely is he obliged to fight. Anyway, from what I saw you strip off that Scottish lord, you'll have enough to set up that piggery you're always on about.'

'I took him down, Sarge - it's mine by rights.'

'Fair enough, I'll say nowt else. Keep it hid otherwise someone'll have it off thee. And - are you listening, Evans? There'll be no gambling at cards, or dice or owt else before we reach Alnwick. I want no arguments. I'm thankful we all got through with hardly a bit of bark knocked off - not like the skirmish here at Milfield . . .'

'Tom had the worst of it,' Alan Fuller interrupted. 'How's the ribs?'

'Hurts when I laugh.'

Alan and Tom rode together, happy in each other's company once more. 'You won't have done much reading of late, Tom.'

'None. There's been no time to look into books lately. Anyway, I learned enough back there to keep this head brim-full for years to come. I wish I could forget it. Did anyone count the bodies?'

'After a fashion. It's said we buried ower five thousand of theirs and fifteen hundred of our own.' Alan lowered his voice. 'And these waggons get lighter by the mile.'

~ ~ ~

They halted for food among the ruins of Milfield, a village the Scots had rampaged through twice in three weeks. They saw householders still working to salvage half-burned timbers to lash together into shelters for their families. Militiamen were digging graves for those who had not survived the first stage of the return journey.

A sob came from the waggon in front. Tom handed the reins of his pony to Riley and jumped onto the rear of the vehicle. Percival Bell's white face stared at him. Tom rolled over the stern and knelt beside the boy. Around him, a dozen men lay on their backs; others sat against the rails.

'Percy, how are you faring?

'Where's my father?'

Tom took his hand. 'I'm sorry. Your dad did not see the end of it. We buried him in Branxton churchyard. I've kept his bow and mail coat for you, and his helmet - the one with the brass fancy-work. You're going home. Captain Jackson's with us - he knows your granddad. Let's have a look at your bit of a cut.'

Percy's eyes glazed with shock. He tried to rise then slumped back onto his bed of straw. 'Was it clean?'

'I'll tell you once I've seen it.'

'No! Father's dying - was it clean?'

'Aye, Percy. Quick; he'd have known little,' Tom lied. 'Now, let's see.' Once more he unwound the linen strips from Percy's head to inspect the torn scalp. Curls of blond hair lay stuck to the skin under a crust of dried blood. He felt the boy's forehead and said, 'You're a good bit cooler. Another day and you can risk a wash.' He passed his hands around the slender neck and found no swellings. 'Roll over and let's look at that side.' Tom lifted the jerkin and the bloody shirt to check the wound that he had temporarily packed with moss at Branxton. 'That's not too bad, there's a grand-looking scab on it. You're on the mend. We'll get you home right enough.'

Tom moved among the rest of the wounded and wondered how many would survive until Alnwick. By the side of Percival Bell, a grey and wizened man lifted his head. 'Have you a sup of ale, hinney?' the man asked in a cracked voice.

Tom uncorked his flask and held it to the man's lips. 'Try this. It's only Scotchman's ale, though a sight better than the crawling muck we hauled up there.'

'I'll drink any bugger's ale at the minute.' The man gave a cough.

'And auld Howard owes me a quart. If you see owt of him, tell him that Billy Rowntree fettled a good few and that he's waiting for the tankard he was promised.' He lay back in the straw and gasped, 'Here, lad - give us your lug.'

Tom bent over while the old man whispered, 'It were my shot that did for him, thee knaas. Others might claim it, but it were my bonny arrer that found his jaw.'

'Whose jaw, Billy?'

'The Scotch king's! It were my clothyard dropped him, man! I got him from ten paces!' He wheezed and coughed again.

'They should knight you for that.'

'Aye! And that'll be summat to take back to the auld woman. Aye, aye, Bella! Sir William Rowntree at your service. Break out the brandywine and fluff up the bed!'

Tom gave Billy another drink then emptied the rest of the flask down the throat of a flushed-faced man nearby. Leaning over the stern, he called to Riley for the reins of his pony.

'This dog of yours is limping,' shouted the Irishman.

Tom jumped off the waggon and picked her up. 'Oh, Meg! Your paws are red raw. You've done too much padding along rough roads in bare feet.' Passing his hands beneath her belly they pressed against a row of small lumps. 'Well, I'm blowed! You've been walking out with a friend without asking me. I hope you chose well.' He tucked her under his arm and climbed back into the waggon.

'There now, lass. Cuddle up to Percy and keep him warm. Let's have a look under that bandage.' He peeled back the strip of linen and found dried blood and matted hair. He touched her nose - it felt hot and dry. Eager teeth grabbed the lump of cheese he held out. 'All right, even though you're still a tough one, you can ride out the miles from here.'

The sergeant called out, 'We'll make Wooler in two hours. We'll halt at the churchyard there and pay our respects to Jones's grave. We should plant a marker for him.'

'I've fettled one, Sarge.' Evans unlashed from his saddle a lump of oak plank he had salvaged from a torched cottage. 'I've carved it deep, following the letters Alan scratched on it.'

Sergeant Arkwright slapped his thigh. 'David Evans! You've cheered me today. Will you read it out, Alan? As our unit's scribe.'

Alan Fuller read from the whittled surface, 'Merfyn Jones, good soldier, 1513.'

The sergeant gave an appreciative grunt. 'That's a fine piece of work, Davey. Somehow we'll have to get word to the man's kin.'

'He'd never let on where he hailed from, Sarge. Though he let slip he knew his way around Monmouth town. His way of speaking would fix him there.'

'I have his pay from the earl and he's owed some from the Norroy's purse. I'll enquire from the muster roll as to where it should best go.'

~ ~ ~

The drove-way twisted between high banks then dipped into the village of Wooler. Tom rode beside Captain Jackson.

'I suppose I'll have to hand over this mount at Alnwick Castle. She's a bonny mare, and steady. She carries a white star on her forehead, just like Meg. I'm fond of her - I'll buy her if I can.'

'Don't worry about the price. I'll buy her for you.'

'That's good of you, sir. But I do have a bit of coin kept safe.'

The captain replied in measured tones. 'You will make a gift to me, Thomas - if you accept my token of regard. No matter; tell me - what will you do now?'

'I don't know yet, I need to get to Alnwick first.'

'Of course, someone waits for you there.'

Tom frowned. 'Yes - how did you know?'

'Oh, talk among the men about how you're sweet on a maid from foreign parts. After Alnwick, what will you do?'

'I don't know, sir. It might depend on her. Knowing her as I do, I reckon she'll have worked out her plans. What about you, Captain? Where's your home?'

'I've a house and lands at Elwick, on the high ground above Hartlepool. I have parents and children waiting. There are beasts to make ready for year's end. We've a new windmill that has work to do - if the rain's not spoiled the ripening.'

'What manner of kine do you keep?'

'Durhams, the brown and white sort mostly. Father favours the colour and admires the long sweep of the horns. We've had them for generations. They have long feet that don't puddle the pasture. Sometimes they throw white calves with black noses, like those we saw in Northumberland - he gets excited when they come.' Edward Jackson sensed Tom's interest. 'There's a place for you - if you're looking for somewhere. Our cowmen are getting old. There's an empty cottage with three acres up at the Hurworth Burn end - you could have it as your own spot.'

'I hope to keep a few beasts of my own. It's what I've a yen for - living as my own man. I've no wish to work for a manor again. And I must make a home for Hilda, my sister.'

'Ours is a yeoman's farm, Tom. The labourers become like family. Take Hurworth and work with us; later we can find good land to rent that'll get you started. We've lived through a lot together; I value my friends.' He reached out and placed a hand on Tom's shoulder.

'Are there wet bits at Hurworth?' Tom asked.

'Wet bits?'

'Aye, rushy patches where the peewit nests.'

'Ah, the green plover! Yes, every spring they forsake the salt marsh and come home to breed. I admire the sprig of plumes that grow from their crown. That bird keeps the world from utter loneliness.' They continued in silence, Tom absorbing the officer's words.

'Yes,' he said quietly, 'they are free spirits. Thank you, Captain. I'd be light of heart with them bubbling overhead.'

Tom's mind filled with pictures of plovers tumbling and rising in the sunlight, their wings flashing green and bronze above the backs of cattle chewing the cud. The scene triggered a memory of old Agnes and young Mary as they walked towards the byre beneath the same birds. Ten weeks had passed; much had happened and none of it looked for.

32

Reunion

Rachel bent over a fabric stall in Alnwick marketplace. She fingered a length of fine cloth. The stallholder leaned across and whispered, 'It's French - from Cambrai. Hard to come by since King Henry's war started up.'

'Yes, I see the weave is cambric linen. It is strong, yet soft.'

'The best for making into a lady's small clothes, and it's only four testoons for the length of a Flemish ell . . .'

The draper broke off at a man's bellow, 'That's the one! That's the Jew!'

'She's no right here!' yelled a crackling, female throat.

Rachel stiffened. A few yards away, a scrawny man and a woman of squat build swayed towards her. The man shouted again, 'We divn't want Jews in wor toon! Gan back where ye come from!'

She took a pace backwards as they advanced on her. The woman pressed so close that the stench of sour beer hit her nostrils like a fist. She shrank from the glare of yellowed eyes set above a cluster of wens. A black-nailed hand struck her on the breast. 'Banished, ye are! Banished! Banished!' With each yell the voice became more shrill. Rachel's thoughts froze. She stared at the one brown tooth suspended above a frothing tongue.

'Let the lady be!' the stallholder called out.

'Nowt to do with ye! Howld thee gob lest I tip yer stall into the clarts.' The drunken man seized the edge of the stall, its owner spreading out his arms to keep it steady.

Rough hands pushed at Rachel's shoulders. Staggering, she fell across the stall among the rolls of cloth. She regained her footing to see the woman, hands on hips, swaggering and laughing.

'Do not put your hands on me.' Rachel's voice shook. In searching for an escape she met the mocking gaze of the priest. He peered between heads at the rear of the gathering crowd, his eyes narrow.

A fish head thudded onto the bodice of her green kirtle. The squat man hooted and bent down to gather more missiles from a pile of waste. Grunting, he hurled a pig's foot at Rachel; she swayed enough for it to brush her shoulder and strike the bolt of cambric. As he aimed again, a grizzled onlooker hit the drunk on the biceps with a walking stick. 'Leave the lass alone!' the old man shouted before a shove threw him to the ground.

The woman leapt forward, tore the wimple from Rachel's head and seized the black braids that sprang free. Her slender neck yielded to the force that yanked on her braids. Long fingers shot out instinctively to rake the grubby face with pointed nails.

The woman shrieked. 'I'll tear your bloody liver out and make you spit mackerel blood!'

Other hands appeared and other fingers fought to unpick the woman's grip. Young voices cried out, 'Get off her, you ale-sot! Let her be!' In the struggle, breasts and arms rubbed and pressed against her own. She smelt wholesome country bodies as she broke free and stood erect, swaying as nausea stung the back of her nose. Hands patted her shoulder and others closed around her palms. Voices came - voices of a dialect she loved: 'There, there, honey. Never mind. Come away wi' us two.'

Arms linked her own and hurried her from the marketplace, along a short street, beneath an arch and into a graveyard. 'Where are you taking me?' she gasped.

'Into the church till things settle down. Nobody'll touch you in there.'

'No! Not the church - I must not go there. The priest!'

A pair of wide, green eyes gazed at her - they had the depths of a lake. 'Then where should we hide thee?'

'I'll go to my chamber at the White Horse. There is no danger there - the innkeeper is a good man. But please, come too - perhaps you will honour me by sharing a meal.'

The other young woman's face lit up. 'Ooh! That'll be good! I'm fair famished. We've been living on bread and cheap onions - onions that would open a garden gate.'

The three women squeezed along the back of stalls towards the White Horse. Rachel froze when she saw the priest addressing a small crowd by the inn's doorway. Casting around for another route, they rushed through narrow ginnels and small yards until they found a way to the rear of the inn. One of Rachel's escorts banged on the rough back door three times with her fist. It creaked open in the hands of a surprised innkeeper.

'Mistress Coronel, this is not the entrance for you.'

'I'm sorry, Mister Patterson, there is violence in the street outside your front door so we came this way. I have two friends with me; please could we have food and wine in my chamber?'

'Of course. Today there's roast duck in the oven, followed by apple dumplings - served with custard. Is that to your liking?'

Rachel gave her rescuers an enquiring look, saw their arched eyebrows and open mouths, and replied, 'It's perfect, Mister Patterson, thank you. We will go upstairs.'

Rachel's heart rate calmed as she watched the two women gaze around her chamber from the edge of their seats. 'My name is Rachel Coronel and I am deeply grateful that you sprang to my aid. But for your courage I would now have injuries to my body and to my dignity.' She smiled at them and waited.

The freckled woman blinked her green eyes. 'I'm Hilda Fleck.'

Rachel's lips parted and her eyebrows arched. Hilda failed to notice; she had turned to her companion who had seized her hand and blurted out, 'And I'm Mary Humble. We're sisters . . .'

A voice called from behind the door, 'Mistress Coronel! I've brought the wine.'

Rachel opened the door to a serving girl. 'Thank you, Beth. Place it on the table, please.'

'I've brought both wine and ale, mistress.' She glanced at the visitors' faded shawls and grey, travel-stained kirtles. 'The master said your guests might want ale.'

'We will begin with ale, Beth, and keep the wine for the supper.'

'The food is only halfway ready, mistress. It'll take an hour yet. I'll be back to set the table afore it comes.' She gave a little curtsy before rustling from the room.

Rachel looked longingly at Hilda. She knew that dialect and yearned to hear it again. 'If Hilda Fleck is your name, where is your home?'

'We belong Thornaby, mistress. That's in Cleveland - on the south bank of the Tees, a few miles upstream from the sea.'

Rachel's hand shook while pouring the ale. She passed the goblets to her guests and, raising her own, took a sip. 'Please call me Rachel, we surely are friends. Hilda, do you have family still in Cleveland?'

'Nobody close, now. There's a brother who drives pack-hosses . . .'

'He's called Thomas,' Mary interrupted, 'and we've come north to find him.'

A line of oxcarts, laden with wounded and trailed by a column of militia on foot, blocked the track to Alnwick Castle, waiting their turn to enter. Seeing the congestion, Sergeant Arkwright gathered his small party together.

'Right, lads. Soon as we're able, we'll march into the castle in good order and with straight backs. You as well, Tom Fleck - the heralds will want to speak with you.'

'No, Sarge, not yet. I'm straight to the White Horse. Tell the Norroy I'll report to him later.'

'Ah, yes. I understand. Good luck to you.' The sergeant formed up his five soldiers, each holding the tether of a loaded pony, and prepared to march them towards the arched gate in the castle's curtain wall.

Captain Jackson took hold of Tom's arm. 'Give me a hand with Percy. Help me get him onto my mount. I want him bedded in a chamber until he's strong enough to travel home. We'll find him somewhere clean.'

Thousands of militia crowded Alnwick's narrow streets. Hundreds gathered around the doorways of packed taverns, clutching mugs of ale. They spilled into Bondgate to spend their pay and to swallow whatever food they could find. They devoured the stacks of bread and meat, and drained the stew cauldrons. But the ale-brewers and pork-roasters were ready. Children ran frantically with baskets and pails between the marketplace and the little yards that housed the ovens and vats.

'Make way,' Captain Jackson shouted. Tired men shuffled aside from the crowded entrance as Percy was helped into the inn. A flustered Luke Patterson - who had never known such a brisk trading day - looked up from his row of barrels.

'We need beds,' stated the captain.

'There's not much left. I can squeeze you into the stables.'

Tom stepped forward. 'Not the stables, man! We want your best chamber for three!'

Luke Patterson's eyes widened at Tom's fierce expression. 'Yes, well . . . Seeing it's you, Tom Fleck - there is my son's room in the attic. He can share with me. It's but one bed, mind - two men on the floor. It'll be a squeeze . . .'

'We'll have it!' Tom interrupted and took hold of the innkeeper's arm. 'Mistress Coronel - is she still here?'

'She's in her room. The lady has guests at her table.'

Tom's heart sprang like a flushed hare. 'Good! Help the officer get this man to bed.'

He nodded at his captain and, with Meg racing ahead, bounded up the stairs to Rachel's chamber. He stood in the passage-way for a few moments, calmed his breathing, then knocked. The door opened to reveal Rachel with her braids coiled on top of her head. He stared at the oval face and elegant neck, speechless. Meg rushed into the room, barking with excitement.

'Oh, Tom!' She blinked back tears and held out her arms. They kissed, broke apart to gaze at each other and kissed again. 'Do I taste of apple pie?'

'You do, and I'm famished - give me more,' he murmured.

Over Rachel's shoulder, he caught sight of Hilda and Mary. They stood side by side, with expressions of startled delight on their faces. Meg ran in circles about their feet. He gulped and released Rachel. She whispered into his ear, 'You must be ready for new things, my love.' She took his hand and drew him into the room.

Hilda rushed forward so that he tottered backwards in her embrace. 'Thomas! What a day! First we find Rachel and now you appear - as if by elf-magic.' He looked into clear eyes set in a glowing and freckled face, so different to that of the pale sister he had abandoned to the keeping of Agnes Humble. She hopped from one foot to the other. 'Praise the saints! It's been so long and we bring such strange news. You'll be surprised at what you hear. We've talked with Rachel - things should turn out right.' She pulled Tom into the room and stood back.

Dumbfounded, he stared at Mary as she came forward - her cheeks flushed pink. He felt her lips tremble on his own. She half-choked, 'Oh Thomas, my brother, I've found thee.'

He sat on a low stool and stared up at the three women who had overwhelmed his world. Mary's words came in bursts. 'Ralph Warren took us as far as Durham Cathedral. We sat on a cart the rest of the way. We had to find you! First, Gran died, then our thatch took fire . . . we'd no roof . . .' The torrent of words subsided. 'Before she died, Gran gave up her secret. She said thee and me share the same father.

244

Thomas, love - I'm your half-sister . . .'

Tom broke in sharply, 'How can that be?'

Mary wiped her cheeks with the back of her hand and seemed without words. Hilda slipped across to Tom and knelt by his knee. She took his hands. 'Because our dad loved two women - our own mother as well as Mary's. I never knew that. Maybe Mam did - but we'll never know.'

Mary had become calmer. 'When my own mam died, I was little. Gran cared for me all those years and kept the secret. She always said my dad was lost at sea . . .' Her voice faded among tears.

Tom knitted his brow and looked at the floor, struggling to comprehend. Still flushed with confusion, he got up, pulled Mary to her feet and hugged her until her sobs ended. He lifted her chin, kissed her forehead and leaned back to search her face. 'This explains so much, honey. All those things that puzzled me - the things I felt. It's small wonder that we've been close, you and me. All is now plain - why we were such timid sweethearts - we must have sensed the truth.'

'Oh, Tom,' Mary said. 'I've had six weeks to get used to it - for you it's a shock.' She kissed him like a sister - lightly on the lips. 'I'm thrilled to meet your lovely Rachel.'

Hilda broke in, 'Mary, we should look around the market; Rachel has hardly spoken with Tom.' She picked up her shawl.

'Oh yes,' Mary said, with a knowing nod. 'Let's gan out for an hour or so, I need to find a stall that sells stockings.'

Rachel and Tom held each other in silence until she whispered, 'You have survived. You have survived and come back whole. I heard such terrible things had happened on that hill - that many are killed. Carts filled with poor, wounded men, crawled through Alnwick for the last two days. I have looked into many of them. Such wounds I saw, such staring eyes. You were never among them. I asked for news of you, but no one knew your name. Yet, all the time, I felt you living and on the road.' She went limp, breathing deep.

He stroked her cheek. 'The thought of you kept me from harm. It's finished and I hope never to see the likes again. I've come back, as I vowed; I'll keep you safe, as I promised your father. I must hear from your own lips, Rachel - what sits in your mind?'

'Alvaro is here. He tries to persuade me to travel back to London with him. I have said no.' She laid her head on his shoulder and murmured, 'All I wish for is to live with the father of my child.'

'Your child? You mean you carry a bairn?' He stiffened slightly.

'Yes, Thomas!' She laughed. 'Our bairn! Here!' She took his hand, placed it below her navel and moved it around. He will be born in March, so wherever we dwell this winter, the dwelling must be warm and safe.'

He shared her breath. 'Ours! You would live with me? I had not looked that far.' Tom's mind swirled. 'Is it so? You would be my wife?'

She hugged him closer. 'Yes! If you would be my husband. Oh, my love! Are we not like two white cranes that fly, side-by-side, in search of quiet meadows?'

'Rachel - listen: with me you'll not know much comfort; the work never ends, your hands will harden, the wind will burn your cheeks.'

'There are also the hardships of the wanderer and I know them only too well: the longing for a home, the loneliness - and the farewells. There are many ways to live a life, Thomas.' Her dark eyes filled his own. 'I will share yours again - like I have shared it before.'

'You have,' he murmured, 'on clear nights, when I've looked up at the sky - powdered with stars - I've known it.'

'I bring troubles to you this time - I am a Jew. I cannot go to church.'

He lifted her chin. 'Where I come from, only lords and yeomen, and those in between, bother to marry in church. For common folk, like me, it's enough to jump over a broom; my kin have always taken such as being rightly wed. We'll not seek the blessings of a priest.' Holding her shoulders, he met her eyes. 'I'll always cherish you. We'll get ourselves a spot where no one knows us.' He leaned back and passed a hand across his brow. 'I've enough coin to keep us going till spring, though it's best if I find wages soon. I could always stand in line at Michaelmas. Better still, my captain has offered work as his cowman - with a cottage at a place called Hurworth.'

'Don't worry about the winter. We will have enough meat and drink, a good fire and I will sleep alongside you in a soft bed; this bride brings a dowry.' She leaned into him.

'You bring yourself, Rachel - you are riches enough. A man should provide for his family - it's his duty and his pride.'

'I understand that, and have thought much about it. Why stand at the hiring fair, with cap in hand, to sell your labour? You will protect our family, and that will be your duty. You shall breed the finest bulls in the north country and they shall be your pride.' She took his hands and held them to her face. 'There is only you in my life and this child that begins.' She went to the door, slid home the bolt, turned to face him and pulled her kirtle over her head.

33

The Glade

The glade shone with the light of a bright morning as Tom emerged from the cover of the trees with Alan Fuller and Peter Tindall on either side. Each of them, freshly washed and groomed, wore wide-shouldered doublets of madder red and matching flat bonnets that sported a cluster of pied feathers. A few yellow leaves, released early by the birches, floated around them in the light breeze.

At one side of the glade, a cart laden with food and a barrel of beer stood on a scythed patch of grass. The innkeeper, Luke Patterson, and his serving girl, Beth, sliced up bread and beef on the tailboard. To one side, a cluster of beggars and urchins watched with hungry eyes. From the shade of an oak, the scarlet-caped Norroy and his assistant, the York Herald, gave half-bows to Tom and raised their flasks in salute. The market woman who had sold him the bracelet called across and waved. She linked arms with her tall son, his sightless gaze directed at the tree-tops.

By Isaac's grave, a four-walled tent stood, fashioned from poles driven upright into the ground. White linen formed the canopy and sides; the drapes were drawn back and tied to the poles so that all sides of the tent stood open - Abraham's sign that all were welcome. Captain Jackson, waiting at the entrance, beckoned to the newcomers. Alan took Tom's elbow and ushered him towards the tent.

The captain looked at Tom's legs, then beamed at him. 'How's my bowman feeling, this white-stocking day?'

'It's like some sprite has tipped a box of wrens into me belly. Though they're not fluttering so bad as the morning of Flodden, I could do wi' summat strong to settle them.'

Their talk halted at the soft thud of a drum. A fiddle struck up a series of chords followed by the sweet notes of small-pipes. The captain pointed to the musicians entering the glade. 'You'll get no more drink as a single man, your bride comes near.'

~ ~ ~

Sunlight glittered on the Castle's ceremonial halberds as Sergeant

Arkwright led the procession with his soldiers guarding its flanks. Four of his men, in Tudor green-and-white, halted to make an arch of the tall weapons. They held them high for Rachel to pass beneath and enter the glade on the arm of Alvaro.

The emerald velvet of the bride's dress rippled and swung to her supple stride. A veil of white lace kept her face, head and shoulders from view. Below a headdress of flowers, lustrous waves of black hair fell from beneath the veil to hang down her back and curl around her upper sleeves. She moved out of dappled shade into sunlight, the white lace shining in dazzling contrast with the green of the velvet. She held a posy of pale blue, water forget-me-nots. Her attendants, Mary and Hilda, followed two paces behind holding posies of wild yellow flowers in front of their chestnut kirtles. Mary's blonde tresses and Hilda's copper curls, threaded with daisies, flowed across their shoulders.

Keeping rhythm with the music, the bride's party stepped to the centre of the glade. The players allowed their instruments to fade when Rachel broke away to stand by the grave in silence, her whole attention fixed on the marker stone. Tom moved to her side.

Kneeling among the flowers of eyebright, she murmured so that only Tom could hear. 'We have chosen this place, Father, that you might share our joy and sense the quickening of your grandchild.' Rachel laid the forget-me-nots at the foot of the stone. 'I have brought your good friend, Thomas Fleck - this man who loves and admires you and who will be my husband.' After long moments of silence, she took Tom's hand and led him into the tent. They stood alone beneath its canopy.

She faced him:

'May he kiss me with kisses of his mouth -
for his love is sweeter than wine.'

Tom tried to discern her expression through the veil as she went on:

'Sweet are your oils to inhale -
oil of Turaq is your name -
draw me after you, let us run. . .
Dark am I, but lovely,
O daughters of Jerusalem -

like tents of Kedar -
curtains of Salmah.
Pay no mind that I am dark -
the sun has gazed upon me.'

Rachel drew back her veil to reveal, encircling her slender throat, the torque that his father had taken from the burial mound on the hills of Cleveland. His eyes widened when a sunbeam caught the circlet of coiled gold wires. Light like fire flashed from the torque's dragon heads that rested on the intense green of the velvet. He met her smile and struggled to form a reply. He swallowed hard before speaking loud enough to fill the glade:

'You are the first gleam of dawn
that swells the green linnet's breast,
and throbs his heart with joy.

You are the sun at Noon,
that golds the barley, and pulls
the bee to the ling on the moor.

And in the evening, the friend
of my hearth side, and lover
- when the whaup falls silent.'

Murmurs of delight came from the onlookers.

Captain Jackson stepped forward. 'The proper time has arrived. Do you desire the handfasting?'

'We do,' they both spoke together.

'That being true: clasp hands, speak it to one another with your mouths and with your eyes, and declare it before all gathered here.'

Tom lifted her hands, kissed them and said, 'I do wed thee, Rachel Coronel.'

Rachel took a deep breath. 'And I do wed thee, Thomas Fleck.'

'Now drink from the same cup.' The captain handed a goblet of red wine to Tom who took a sip before offering it to Rachel. She sipped once - her eyes locked with his. She drank deeper and handed it back. He stood alone with her, gazing on her wine-damp lips, then drained the goblet in one swallow.

From a pouch, he drew out the black dragon bracelet and slipped it

250

onto her wrist. She gave a soft cry of joy and lifted her arm to show the crowd. From a pocket, she brought out an identical dragon bracelet and slipped it over his hand.

Captain Jackson stepped forward and, with a strip of red linen, bound Tom's right wrist to Rachel's left. 'Witness how the knot is tied!' he called out to the crowd.

Rachel gazed at Tom. 'I am my beloved's and my beloved is mine.'

Tom responded, 'I am my beloved's and my beloved is mine.'

The watchers clapped and cheered.

'Don't move!' Alan Fuller shouted. He strode to a patch of broom, pulled off a dense branch and returned to lay it on the ground before the couple. 'It's not done until you leap the evergreen!'

The laughing couple stepped from beneath the canopy and, hands still bound, jumped together over the broom.

Captain Jackson raised a palm. 'Forever cherish and cleave each to the other. May you prosper and be fruitful while life lasts. You are now joined together and become husband and wife.'

As they embraced, the glade filled with whistles and applause. Hilda and Mary rushed forward to shower the kissing couple with petals. The bracelet seller led her son forward.

His blank eyes searched the space above their heads before he stammered, 'It's not much. I've carved this for the bride. It's to bring fruitfulness.' He blushed, hung his head and held out an egg of polished elm burr.

'Oh! The markings in the grain are like a sunrise and its surface feels so smooth it might be a rosebud. Thank you. I will treasure it.' Rachel stepped forward, hugged him and kissed his cheek.

The fiddler struck up a series of bright chords. Feet tapped as the drummer took up the beat; seconds later the piper's elbow squeezed his instrument into bubbling life. The musicians strolled out from beneath the trees, playing together, and took their positions on top of a small knoll. 'Let's step the round dance!' someone shouted.

All rushed forward to join hands and form a circle around the couple. They danced to the left and danced to the right, stepped into the middle to curtsey and bow before starting the round once more.

At the end of the tune, Mary ran forward and pulled the newlyweds into the circle calling out, 'Play the Swan's Wedding.'

The piper began a slow melody as Tom and Rachel, with arms linked, led the dancers through drifts of seeding grasses, in a long and graceful circuit of the glade. They glided ever inwards until they danced around the tent and the grave of Isaac.

'Food is ready!' The dancers broke up and rushed, laughing, to the cart. Tom picked up a wedge of hard white cheese and a chunk of bread smothered in butter. He was chewing when someone nudged his elbow. John Young, the Norroy Herald, beamed at him.

'Your reply in verse to Rachel's *Song of Solomon* - where did that come from?'

Wiping crumbs from his lips, he swallowed. 'From nowhere, sir. It sprang off the tongue.'

'I think it rose up from a deeper place. I admire the pictures you painted with words in the first turning of three lines. Are you still reading the poets?'

'Yes, sir. I've read what you gave me - over and over again. Also, Rachel has given me a book of verse that belonged to her father.'

'If a poem comes to you, where do you set it down?'

Tom tapped his skull. 'In here. It's like an empty barn; any amount of space for more.'

The Norroy laughed. 'Nevertheless, you should pen them. Please accept this.' He handed Tom a leather-bound book the size of a man's hand. Tom opened it, and stared at the blank pages.

'You must cut a quill and write down your best thoughts before they fly away like the migrating birds of autumn.'

'The migrating birds of autumn? Now there's a canny line for a poem. Thank you, sir - I'll do that.'

'I've been talking with Captain Jackson: he told me of your doings at Flodden Field. You've a staunch champion in him. If you must leave my service - which I regret, for I thought to engage you as a guard - I would urge you to keep the captain in sight. Men who get close should stay close.'

'I'll think on that, sir.' Tom glanced across at Alan Fuller, who sat on the grass talking to Hilda. The soldier appeared spellbound by her freckles. Nearby, Peter leaned on the cart and held the hand of a giggling Mary. Tom went on, 'At the start of this year there were few I called friend; today I am surrounded. You've been good to me too, sir - always kindly.' He blushed. 'And like a father, even.'

The Norroy sighed. 'Ah, young man, my house is filled with maids; a son of my own would not come amiss.'

'What a great day, Tom Fleck!' Thomas Tonge, the York Herald, clutching a lump of pie, elbowed his way through the groups of drinkers.

'York! I was saying how we will miss this useful man.'

'We will! Look how he has come on, in three months. It was a formative day when our archer decided to return my lost ring.' He held up his plump hand to show the seal ring. It gleamed in the sunlight. 'Your scrabbling about in the mire for a scrap of gold has brought you treasure in the form of a bride. Remarkable how events work their way through . . .' He broke off when the shadow of a tall horse fell across them.

'Tom Fleck! Might I invite myself?'

'Master Ralph Warren! You're a long way from home . . .' Tom's speech dried and he broke eye contact.

'Yes - I know my father is killed; one of his party rode long days to tell me.' Ralph dismounted. 'I've been to the Castle to see my brother. Mark is mending well - he showed me the wound that you stitched. The leg must stay in its splint for another month and he'll need a crutch. I come to thank you for tending him.'

'I'm sorry about your father. He lies in the churchyard at Branxton. Your blacksmith, Rob Gibson, has planted a marker stone.'

'I know - I've spoken with him. When the border is quieter, perhaps I will visit the place. Are your sister and Mary here?'

'Yes, Mary is by the cart. I thank you for showing kindness when they were burned out.'

'To help, brought me delight - they are good women. I'll make fast my horse before I go and speak with them.'

'Mary Humble! We meet again,' Ralph called through the crush of guests around the cart.

She turned away from Peter to see the chubby features of Thornaby Manor's second son. 'Oh, Master Ralph! What are you doing here?'

He pushed through the crowd. 'I've come to take my brother home. He won't like it, for it'll be in a cart. Can we walk a little way, Mary? I wish to speak with you . . . if this young man will excuse us.'

'Sorry, Peter - I'll not be long.' Mary touched Peter's hand.

Ralph guided Mary to the quiet edge of the glade. The words tumbled out. 'Mary, my heart beats in my throat. I've known restless nights since we said farewell. I've thought much about you.' He saw her lips part and felt his cheeks grow hot as he struggled on. 'I keep thinking of those few days we spent in Durham City and remembering the joy. I've written something for you.' Hands trembling, he pulled a folded sheet of paper from his pouch and

253

offered it to her.

She opened it and drawing herself upright said, 'I don't have the power of reading. You'll have to tell it to me.' She handed the paper back.

'Oh! I had not thought.' He searched for the right words. 'Mary, it would be my delight to teach you.'

She touched his shoulder. 'It's no matter. What use is reading for someone who hasn't a book?'

Ralph searched for words. He saw how the fine down on her cheeks caught the sun and shimmered as though dusted with gold - how her cheeks formed dimples when her lips spread into a smile. The blue eyes held his own as he fumbled with the paper. He calmed his breathing enough to read:

'Mary's Braids

Reflected in a veil of blue - thy features
on mine eye impressed like no rare damask
but a simple daisy asterism.

That fair Cleveland forehead, bounded
either side by morning-woven braids -
pray hide them 'neath thy wimple -

lest I lose my mind.'

34

Hart

Troops choked the stone bridge across the River Tyne. Weaving between creaking coal-waggons, disbanded companies straggled into Durham. Tom and Rachel, now married for five days, waited beneath the towers of the Newcastle barbican to watch a great press of horses, oxen and men crawl past. Urging their mounts into a gap in the line of carts, they followed Edward Jackson's grey mare onto the bridge.

Tom admired the man's wide shoulders and straight back. 'See how the captain sits, Rachel,' he whispered. 'Nowt's an effort. He never slouches in the saddle nor lets weariness bend his spine; I like that man. Are you still in favour of the cottage he offers?'

'Aye, Thomas. If it is clean, warm and safe, it will do for now.'

'For now?'

'Yes - until Father's property in London is sold and Alvaro sends what is my due, and those of my father's belongings that I treasure. Next year we should have the means to rent more space. Already I carry a bairn. I hope to be fruitful in the bringing forth of many more.' She laughed to see Tom's parted lips. 'I remember the joys of the big Portuguese family, and I long to live in a house filled with small voices.'

'Might I be godfather to one of them?' Percival Bell rode behind with Peter Tindall.

'And I, to another?' Peter shouted.

Tom twisted around. 'Get in line, Peter Tindall - I can see a queue forming. And, Percy, you're sounding more lively with every mile. How's the wound?'

'Well scabbed and itching, so it's mending. I'm ready for my own bed; we should be there by morning.'

At the mention of godparents, Tom had heard a slight gasp from Rachel, and understood. He leaned across and touching her hand, whispered, 'Don't worry, my love, I'll make sure we are not troubled by priests of the Alnwick sort.'

Their horses shrank back at the sight of churning waters below the bridge. The rain-swollen Tyne met and fought with salt water as high tide forced its way upstream. On the southern bank a two-masted ship lay alongside the river quays, her mooring ropes groaning in her struggles to keep a grip of the quayside. A line of blackened men with baskets on their heads risked disaster on the pitching gangway. One by one, they climbed the ramp to tip baskets of coals into the hold.

It was with relief that they reached the other shore and left the maelstrom behind. They dismounted to walk their ponies up the steep road from the river and into the little town of Gateshead. Here, the column tangled in confusion with a line of coal-carts heading for the river-bank.

'You hope for a lively dwelling, Rachel - though not so lively as this black town perhaps. Best is somewhere with less noise and muck. Though the cottage at Hurworth is reckoned a quiet spot, it looks to be crowded already - Hilda and Mary will bide with us.'

She gave him a playful nudge. 'Your sisters may soon dwell elsewhere. At our wedding, Mary went walking with Ralph Warren. I saw how her eyes shone when they crept out of the woods - and Ralph's cheeks were well-coloured.'

'And Hilda?' Tom's eyes widened.

She touched a finger to her lips, then whispered, 'Have you not seen how close Hilda and the captain have become? It is a year since his wife died; his children need a mother.'

Once through the noise and grit of Gateshead they overtook a horse-drawn waggon. Thornaby Manor's blacksmith, Rob Gibson, held the reins. Ralph Warren rode alongside on a tall horse. In the middle of the waggon, his elder brother, Mark, lay cushioned among sheepskins and baggage. He shuffled himself to a sitting position as they drew close.

'Fleck! Strange how we keep meeting.'

'That's so. How's the leg?'

'Still aches - and it'll be forever skewed. At least I still have it.'

As the group made ready to move on, Mark called out, 'Wait, can we not all stop for rest here? There's a level spot between those slag heaps.' He looked up into Tom's face before his gaze drifted to the women - first to Rachel, then to Mary, finally it rested on Hilda.

Hilda shuddered. 'No, Tom. We should keep moving; there's a long way to go.'

Captain Jackson agreed. 'We need to reach Houghton-le-Spring before dark.'

Ralph coughed. 'Perhaps Tom and Mary might stop a short space. They can easily catch you up.'

Tom looked at Mary, who nodded.

'But not too long.' Tom dismounted.

'I will stay with you,' Rachel said, watching Mary and Ralph ride a little way off the road.

'I owe you something, Fleck.'

Tom stared for a moment at the right hand held out by Mark - then took it. 'I have all I need.'

'No - listen,' Mark whispered. 'In the manor house is a chest that holds my father's documents. In that chest are deeds that show title to some ploughing land. By rights, those acres are yours.'

'Plough land? You mean the Weastall fields that my grandfather once worked?'

'Yes - only a few fields, mind; but the mould is deep, and they're yours. You know them well enough; your old byre stands at one end. You can build a cottage there. If you can't bear me near, you can just draw rent from the land. Either way, I wish to restore what is yours. I've learned that we are not so distant. On the road to Flodden, Father revealed that you and I share the blood of the first Marmaduke Weastall.'

'Yes, Dad told me a few years back how your mother and me were second cousins. Why yield up the land now?'

'Father is dead and I live. Flodden Field has sobered me. Though I'm not made like a saint, I have come to know my better parts. Take that parcel of land; it's yours - I've acres aplenty.'

Tom grasped Mark Warren's hand again. 'When my wife and I are settled at Hurworth I'll come to Thornaby for the deeds. I thank you for this honest act.'

'And I'll come with you, brother.' Mary had returned. 'At your wedding Ralph asked me to be his wife, and just now I gave my answer. We'll wed in springtime.'

Mark Warren looked aghast. 'Brother! That is not what our father would have permitted; he would declare it a misalliance. There are well-bred women of the shire who would have brought money, land and blood with them. You must go visiting again.'

Ralph put an arm around Mary's shoulder. 'One circuit was enough! The daughters they pushed at me had the dull wits of oxen, with looks to match. And what might they have brought me? A few acres of cold clay as stiff as their hearts, a box or two of hoarded baubles, and generations of inbreeding; whereas, this lovely Saxon girl has a truly noble heart, and a wit that flashes brighter than any gem.'

Mark spluttered. 'Getting land and heirs is your duty, little brother. It is who shares your marriage bed that matters. You can still have whichever toothsome field wench you fancy.'

Ralph tightened his hold of Mary as she began to shrink away. 'That might be the style of things in some houses; it shall not be such under my roof. You have Thornaby Manor and I wish you well with it. Whilst I love you as my brother, my life is now my own.'

Mark's scowl softened. He clasped Ralph's hand. 'I return your love, brother. Much has been lost. We should hold to one another. I see the change in you - you are grown. Think now - where will you live? Father has willed you money, but the manor and lands are in my keeping.'

'We've decided Durham City is best for us. The Prior made me an offer when I visited; I'll be able to study in his wonderful library and have my own students.'

'And I will learn to read.' Mary raised her chin. 'Ralph will not have cause for shame.'

Ralph gave a delighted laugh and threw his arms around her. 'The eglantine of the hedge-row has no need for shame. Read if you must, but otherwise stay as you are and lift my heart each day.'

Rachel touched Tom's cheek. 'And you also, my love.'

After a night's rest at Houghton, with cousins of the captain, they headed for the village of Hart. The travellers were thoughtful, affected by the sombre mood of Percival Bell who rode alone at the rear. Sometimes the captain would ride with him, speaking in low tones.

The Bells' farm lay at the end of a sunken lane that meandered from the rear of Hart's Saxon church. After half a mile, the smell and clatter of the village workshops faded. In the midday sun, the eroded yellow limestone of the house and its barns glowed through the dark of ash trees. Percy cantered ahead until he reined in his horse at a gate. 'Welcome to my home,' he called to them. 'It'll be a blessing if you come inside and help with my story.'

The seven riders dismounted and walked their horses for the fifty yards to the front of the house. In the garden, a young girl set down her basket of damsons and ran towards them calling out, 'Percy's home! Percy's home!'

He bent to kiss her. 'Aye, little sister - I'm back.'

'Where's Dad? Is he following?'

'Ellen... Where's Mam and Granddad? Are they well?'

'Mam's well and Granddad's coping with his bad legs, as usual.' She looked into his eyes and saw grief. 'Oh. Dad's not with you . . .' Her voice faded.

'I'll tell you about it soon. Where are they?'

'Mam's in the kitchen with the maid; they're making ale. Granddad's out the back, mending summat.'

A lean woman, with silver-streaked hair drooping below her wimple, came to the threshold as they approached. She squinted into the sun and searched the faces as she wiped her hands on her apron. 'Percy! You're safe home!' She came forward, hugged him, then stepped back, looking around. 'Well - where's your dad got to?'

The words came slowly. 'It was a big battle, Mam. We were taking care of each other - but we got rushed. He fell right next to me.'

'Oh no! No! Not my Henry . . .' Her voice tailed away to a whimper. Percy pulled her into his arms. Captain Jackson knelt by the silent Ellen and comforted his neighbour's child, telling her that it was good for the tears to come. The rest of the travellers, each with throats that hurt, looked at the ground.

Percy's mother broke away and ran the heel of her palm across her cheeks. She looked with blurred eyes at her visitors. 'You'll all be famished; come into the house and take some broth.'

The track snaked through thin woodland, skirting soft ground and flooded holes. Below the white trunks of birches, scattered clumps of late flowering ling brightened the ground with shades of purple. Edward Jackson swung round in his saddle. 'We are here! Hurworth Burn is through the birks.'

The cottage blended into a south-facing slope of a shallow dell. On top of a few courses of yellow stone, wattle and daub walls were plastered between oak timbers. Tiny glazed windows peeped out from beneath a thatch. Rocks, suspended on woven osiers, held down the blackened barley straw. From a single low doorway a track, paved with sandstone flags, led to a burn that gurgled over its bed of clay.

Rachel dismounted and knocked at the open door. At the sound of pattering feet, she found herself pulled to one side by Tom as four ewes erupted into the daylight. She shrieked, 'It already has tenants!'

The captain leapt from his horse. 'I'm sorry. They can't have been here long. The wind must have forced the door.'

Rachel ducked inside and stood on the flagged floor. 'I see someone's furniture here: a chest, a bed, and two chairs by the window.' She went into one of the two side rooms. 'Another bed in here, and empty hooks on the walls. Who owns all this?'

'They are the belongings of a family that's taken work with the Cliffords at Hart Manor. The man is a waggonwright and clever with tools. He made all of this and might be glad to sell you these bits and pieces.'

Leaving Meg to sniff at the furniture and in the corners, Tom walked through the three rooms searching for signs of black damp in the walls. He returned to look into the throat of the fireplace and jab his knife into the mortared joints of its stonework. 'The building seems tight enough, Captain. What do you reckon, Rachel?'

She took his hand. 'It will do for now, Thomas. That hearth looks useful, I could cook on there. Let me see the other rooms before we look outside.'

'Outside there's a cow byre at one end, and a cart shed,' Edward Jackson broke in, 'and by them is a garden that's been mucked for generations.'

'A garden? I shall grow roses!' she sang out.

'Not so many that they shade out my leeks,' Tom said, in a feigned, gruff voice.

Rachel gave him a playful punch on the arm. 'There's a broom under that bed. You can start sweeping out the little round gifts the sheep have left us and spread them on your vegetable patch.' Then more seriously, 'Sometime we shall have our own fields, and barns - and byres.'

'Aye, Rachel, and maybe some plovers of our own.'

A brown and white bull left a trail of bruised grass as it lumbered across the frosted pasture towards a motionless windmill. His yard-long horns swept upwards when he raised his great head and, with nostrils flared, scented the air. Stooped under the precious load astride his shoulders, Tom walked behind, admiring the beast's potent and swaying pouch. Together, man and animal climbed the hill until the bull spied his cows and broke into a trot. Tom eased his back into a hollow in the sun-warmed stones of the windmill and watched him go.

A hare streaked through the frost and he sighed to see his grizzled old dog, in game, but futile, pursuit. The animals vanished over a rise and his attention moved eastwards.

Two miles distant, beyond a belt of sand dunes, a yellow-cliffed headland thrust like a finger into a flecked, steel-blue sea. At the furthest point, the tower of a great church stood in silhouette above the huddled cottages of fisher-folk. On a sheltered beach, men launched cobles into the rising water.

The tidal flood of Hartlepool Slake shimmered in the morning light as the sea returned. Tom Fleck knelt on the thawing earth, wrapped an arm around the shoulders of the little boy at his side, and pointed to a two-masted ship that reefed white sails as it entered the haven.

--The End--

Lightning Source UK Ltd.
Milton Keynes UK
UKOW051235090112

185014UK00001B/346/P